The Three Sixes

What They're Saying
about Mark Alan Leslie

The Crossing
"With a genuine flair for compelling, entertaining, and deftly-crafted storytelling, *The Crossing* is very highly recommended ..."
—Midwest Book Review's Small Press Bookwatch

Chasing the Music
"A gripping story told with the maturity of a seasoned wordsmith. I'll put *Chasing the Music* in the class with John Grisham or other secular novelists touted for producing today's best fiction ... Readers can't go wrong with the intricately woven plot, intriguing characters, and crisp writing style."
—Randall Murphree, editor, American Family Association's *AFA Journal*

"One word to describe *Chasing the Music?* ADVENTURE! ... This was *Indiana Jones* wrapped up in *Romancing the Stone* overlaid with *National Treasure*—all my favorite action movies between the covers of one book ... It definitely reads like the best action adventure movie I've ever seen ... I definitely recommend that adrenaline junkies read this book."

—Pam Graber, *BookFun* reviewer

"I was blown away at the many scientific connections and historical ones in *Chasing the Music*. The extensive depth of information was exceptional. Well done!"

—Lynda MacDonald, Heart to Heart Ministry, Nova Scotia, Canada

Fast action and high suspense ... The read [*Chasing the Music*] was exciting, following clues and moving from place to place. I loved it."

—Randy Tramp, freelance writer and author of *Night to Knight*

The Three Sixes

Mark Alan Leslie
with Darek Leslie

Elk Lake
PUBLISHING, INC.
Plymouth, MA

Cover Design: Darek Leslie, Jeff Gifford
Interior Design: Cheryl L. Childers
Editors: Judy Hagey, Deb Haggerty

Published in the United States by Elk Lake Publishing, 35 Dogwood Drive, Plymouth, MA, in association with Les Stobbe Literary Agency.

Library Cataloging Data
Names: Leslie, Mark Alan (Mark Alan Leslie) with Leslie, Darek (Darek Leslie)
The Three Sixes / Mark Alan Leslie with Darek Leslie
414 p. 23cm × 15cm (9 in × 6 in.)
Description: Elk Lake Publishing, Inc. digital eBook edition | Elk Lake Publishing, Inc. Trade paperback edition | Elk Lake Publishing, Inc. 2017.
Identifiers: ISBN-13: 978-1-946638-60-1 (trade) | 978-1-946638-61-8 (POD) | 978-1-946638-62-5 (e-book.)
Key Words: Yale, suspense, Islam, jihad, Max Braxton, Kat Cardova, Israel
LCCN: 2017962278 Fiction

Dedication

Dedicated to those who care about the future
of America and God's place in it.

Acknowledgments

One synonym of acknowledgment is byline. That's appropriate since readers will notice "with Darek Leslie" after my name.

My first and foremost recognition is the contribution to this novel by my son, Darek, a far more creative writer than I. In addition to crafting the assassin Stetson and Stetson's stand inside the Washington Monument, Dax created the "bat cave" with all its technology components and software that comprise Operation Mongoose. Since Dax works closely with Salem State University students, his help with their lingo, repartee, etc., was vital to the reality of the scenes with my Yalies.

I invite readers to check out Darek's thriller, *Splinter*, and his teen mystery, *Cure for a Kill*, both available at www.amazon.com and www.barnesandnoble.com.

Thanks, always, to my wife, Loy, who has more often than she knows talked me off the wall when I was miserable at witnessing the plight of this country under years and years of feckless leadership. Her message always: "Don't worry. God is still on his throne and remains in charge."

To my wonderful publisher, Deb Haggerty, and editor, Judy

Hagey, who notices every little not-quite-right word, uncrossed *t* and undotted *i*: Graci.

Les Stobbe, who has stood behind me and before me for years, stands out as one of the country's most diligent and esteemed agents and will always be on my thank-you list.

Most of all, I thank the Lord for opening doors of opportunity through my books which are really His.

Prologue

Max Braxton slipped a butterscotch drop into his mouth. If he were to die in the next minute, he fancied a sweet taste.

He checked his Luminox watch. In thirty-three seconds, two members of his team would detonate explosions in the munitions building at the northwest end of this sprawling North African camp—one of the world's deadliest terrorist training bases. In forty-two seconds, he would be at the doorway to the bedroom of master terrorist Anwar al Fayed, a private getaway at the opposite end of the camp. Tossing a concussion grenade into the room would take two seconds, entering the room and two double-taps to the man's chest would take just under three seconds. Another three seconds and he'd be back in the hallway, joined by two other members of his five-man team.

Twelve seconds later, the team would rendezvous outside the camp, leaving members of ISIS, al-Qaeda, Hezbollah, Hamas, Muslim Brotherhood, Algeria's Armed Islamic Group, Northern Ireland's IRA, the National Liberation Army in Colombia and terrorists from Uzbekistan, the Philippines, Uganda, Ethiopia,

Tunisia and other countries wondering whose thunderous sword had struck at their midsection.

The entire operation would consume twenty-nine seconds if all went according to plan. Of course, in every man's war, even perfect plans too often end up as starter paper in a barracks woodstove. He'd set a few ablaze himself.

Max prayed no freelancing would be needed on this, his birthday. He removed a photo from a shirt pocket, kissed the image of his mother and hoped time would be swift to heal her heart if this were indeed the day he punched out. He replaced the picture and pressed the memento to his heart with affection.

Darkness still enveloped the compound, even as the rising sun turned the edges of the horizon to a pale yellow. The stillness pounded in his ears. Deafening. The guards keeping watch along the camp's four borders had been forever silenced and trainees were asleep in a half-dozen barracks-type buildings strewn about the property with no logical placement.

Indeed, from what Max and his team had observed as they'd fried lying under the desert floor in their camouflage over the last few days, these trainees were as frenzied as a band of caged, wild gorillas. But they could do one thing: pull a trigger. And they did so with crazed abandon. One lucky squeeze and one of his men could go down. This was his biggest worry. Not Mom. Not whether they got Anwar al Fayed. Not his own safety, but his men's.

Max took three deep breaths and looked again at his Luminox. Four seconds to detonation. He removed a concussion grenade from a hip pocket, gripped the little bomb tightly, counted "two, one." Then, as two explosions lit up the camp like a strobe light, he took off in a sprint to al Fayed's dwelling.

C4 is a wonderful thing. He looked around. Stetson was fifty yards to his left, Tolson forty yards to his right, converging with him on al Fayed. Then a series of blasts from the munitions building crunched the air and rocked the earth beneath his feet. The noise was thunderous, staggering.

At the corner of the dwelling, Max vaulted over a three-foot-high railing, turned left, leaped up two steps and burst through a side door. Four steps down the hall, he turned left and busted a shoulder through al Fayed's bedroom door. The terrorist was standing, about to pull a *jellaba* over his head. His face registered two expressions: shock and alarm.

No need for the concussion grenade. Max stepped forward and double pumped, sending al Fayed to meet his Maker, glad he'd saved two seconds.

But a scream rang through the room. Max swiveled and saw a woman sitting up in al Fayed's bed. Her eyes were wide with terror, one trembling hand covered her mouth. *She is not supposed to be here.*

He turned to leave having lost those two "gained" seconds. Time was up. The clock in his head had counted thirteen seconds since he began his sprint. Twelve left to the rendezvous. But Stetson stood before him, pointing his assault rifle at the woman.

Startled, Max pushed down the barrel of the weapon. "Leave her," he said.

"She's an accomplice to terrorism," Stetson objected, his jaw tight.

"She's an innocent. We're losing time." Max pointed. "Out!"

But Stetson aimed his rifle. "Not until—"

Instinctively, Max grabbed Stetson's right elbow with his right hand. The grip twisted the rifle to the right, pushing Stetson's shoulder forward with his left hand and wrenching Stetson's upper arm backward.

Stetson hollered in pain, struggled to hold on to the rifle with his left hand, and glowered at Max. Max glared back and growled between clenched teeth, "Clock's ticking. She's collateral. Get moving."

The woman continued to scream nonstop like a siren, and men's shouts began to fill the camp outside. Chaos erupted as gunfire rang out. In the turmoil, Max distinguished Arabic, Farsi, German, and English.

Stetson shot a hate-filled glance at the woman. Max pushed him out the door.

Tolson, standing in the hallway, hollered, "Hurry."

The three men rushed out of the building, with Max at the rear. The pungent odor of gunpowder filled his nostrils.

A hailstorm of bullets crackled in the air. As Max hurdled the three-foot railing, he felt a sting in his left shoulder. Flesh wound. No problem.

Slugs puffed around his feet, sending dust into the air and splintering the railing. Then a knife-like stab, this one just above the hip, sent pain screaming along his nerves.

Max squeezed his eyes shut from the agony, but kept his feet moving. A moment later, he opened his eyes. Tolson had come back to help and offered his shoulder. He glanced ahead. Stetson was pulling away in a dead run.

He prayed Phillips and Blais, his men who had set the charges, were safe and en route to their rendezvous spot.

"Come on, Captain," Tolson urged, and they began a weaving dash to dodge bullets. Each right-hand swerve sent a shock wave through Max's body. Good thing, he thought wryly, those guys are better at shooting into the sky than at a moving target.

Bullets continued to strike desert dirt around them but faded farther and farther away. Were the terrorists more compelled to remain in camp than chase the intruders?

The thirteen seconds to the rendezvous had turned into a good twenty. Max and Tolson lunged to the cover of a small clutch of desert trees. Phillips and Blais were already there. Stetson stood waiting, glaring, rubbing his shoulder. His dark eyes pierced Max's, contempt out in the open.

"They're coming." Blais pointed back toward the compound. "Two truckloads full of 'em."

Max peered at his watch. "The copter should have arrived thirty seconds ago. Where the blazes is it?"

He winced as he reached his hand to click on his earphone radio. "Five in the bush, downrange. Boo-coo rats here soon. What's your ETA?"

"Peekaboo!" came the reply.

The batter-batter of helicopter blades split the air, and yards away, an MH-60G Pave Hawk rose above a high dune. The aircraft had been flying low to the dunes below tree height.

The pilot added, "Sorry we're late. Infrared system's kaput, so we couldn't see so well."

With Tolson still giving him leverage on his right side, Max and his team raced toward the bird. Stetson was first aboard, with Blais and Phillips close behind.

Tolson heaved Max the three feet through the Pave Hawk's open door and onto the floor, then followed suit. Stetson noticeably slinked away, a brooding, angry look filling his face.

Just then, two flatbed trucks, engines racing and loaded with terrorists, burst over a dirt mound, aiming straight at them. Gunfire exploded from the truck. The clank of bullets hit the copter. Mixed with the piercing beat of the copter blades, they sounded like handfuls of rocks being thrown full-force at sheet metal.

The Pave Hawk slanted away, leaving the terrorist camp and a dead Anwar al Fayed in the dust.

Max reached for the wound near his hip and recoiled in pain. He pulled away his hand, slimy with blood, then gazed at Stetson. Stetson met his glare with a fierce glower and eyes as frigid as an Ice Age.

Chapter One

Nine Years Later
10:55 a.m. Tuesday, January 21

The air was frosty but stifling high inside the Washington Monument, and Stetson's body ached from lying still for the seventh straight hour. But the thought of taking down the leader of the free world warmed his heart. The apex of his career. The height of any assassin's legacy.

A smile curled his lips as he leaned forward a tad and took a sip of water through the straw of the water pack. The water was already icing over. He envisioned a long, hot shower to soothe his aching muscles. He thought he might be getting too old for this, but he shook the thought from his head. I'm only thirty-seven, he reminded himself. With resolve, he pulled the Barrett 50 rifle up tighter into the crook of his arm. Subsonic ammunition and the silencer would help dull the release, but he knew the real genius was his location, concealed enough to hide the flash.

He concentrated, looking through the scope. Various scenarios played out in his mind. On the stage decorated in red, white, and blue banners, he had only one target. Forget the veep—as much as he despised the little twerp. Forget the chief justice—as much as he hated the justice system. No, this time he wasn't taking any chances.

Not after the incident which landed him in Qincheng Prison.

Stetson glanced to his right and smiled at the red blinking box. One push and his escape would be—what was Momma's expression?—a piece of apple pie. Shifting his leg to the left, he felt the reassurance of his backpack containing plain clothes, radio, and rope.

Drops of perspiration edged down his shaved head, across his brow, and over the scar—one inch above his left eyebrow and a half-inch below the eye. His clothing was a bit too warm for the occasion. January in Washington, DC, was hardly a trip to Cancun, but he always preferred to be too hot than cold. Cold and your fingers go blue. Cold and you shake. Cold and you don't move as quickly. Cold and you miss your target. And he never missed a target on the job. Not once. Well, then again, there was Beijing. He cringed at the thought of the guard at Qincheng who hated him most, who tortured him with ceaseless and relentless pleasure.

He shook away the memory and grunted, then worked his right shoulder in a circle, and cursed the self-righteous black-ops team leader. His faced twisted at the thought of Max Braxton—who had dislocated his shoulder, stopping him from killing al Fayed's mistress. The raghead wasn't worth a dislocated shoulder. But no, Braxton had to get in the way. If only Braxton were on the stage up there too. Talk about making Stetson's day complete. Maybe he'd picture Braxton's face on the president's body.

Shaking his head at the thought, he checked his watch. Almost time, he thought, and he clicked off the safety. A smile creased his sweaty lips.

Then time slowed. Tick-tock became tick——tock. He could see the crowd through blue smoke, his breath transforming into steam in the air before his eyes. America's new president emerged from behind the stands, waving his arms high. Dark scarf, long dark coat, cries of anticipation emerging from the crowd through the winter chill.

Stetson leaned forward, checking the American flag waving in the distance. He pulled an instrument from a front shirt pocket. The wind gauge he'd placed on a street lamp the week before read 5.7 mph north-by-northeast. He adjusted his scope and settled in again.

He had to wait for one final call from his client, but he'd be ready. He aimed between the brows. Deep breath. Deep frosty breath. He aimed again, steady, and feigned squeezing two quick bursts, splitting bullets past the hairline. Even at this distance, Stetson had no doubt of the hit. He coughed out a quiet laugh, turned over onto his side and stared up into the peak of the Washington Monument, closed for renovation. Very soon this presidency will be closed for business, too.

He clucked and smiled. *My biggest payday, plus fame in the shadow world of paid assassins. Might as well enjoy it.*

Chapter Two

11 a.m. Tuesday, January 21

A heavyset guy sporting a goatee, stocking hat, and L.L. Bean parka thunked his bulk onto a seat, dropped a notebook on the tiny writing surface, and elbowed the fellow next to him.

"Think this'll be interesting?" he asked.

The brawny young man beside him craned his neck to look up from a smartphone, finished a tweet with a flourish and nodded. "Hey, Hank. Hope so. It's the one nonelective I can take this semester."

"Yeah, first two years suck. No choices." The big guy patted his shoulder. "No time at all and you'll be rid of the garbage courses and taking nothing but top-drawer stuff you love, Josh. Gaming, cybering. You'll ice this place unless you decide to turn pro first."

Josh nodded, ignoring the pro part. He was a good linebacker, but not pro good. Plus, he was in the wrong school for athletic greatness. Yalies didn't turn pro. They were lucky to beat the Crimsons and Tigers of the world.

The two young men looked around. The Yale University windowless classroom, built with stadium seating, was filling up. The hall was a crazy-unusual mix of people. Freshmen, seniors, what looked like a few grad students, poured through both rear doors and a side door down at the front right.

He and Hank were smack-dab in the middle of the room, all the better to check out the *femme fatales* in the group. Hey, good football players are good football players, even in a small pond, he thought.

"They'd better not have overbooked this class," Hank scowled. "I don't wanna come in here some day and have to stand a whole hour, no matter how good the show."

"Show?"

"Well, you know. Terror. Terrorism. Anti-terrorism. Hostage negotiations. Yeah, this guy's supposed to be one of those black-ops types. War-gamed with the SEALs and Rangers, secret missions inside Turkey and Syria—"

"Where'd you get so much information?"

Hank smiled. "Deep research. Plus, he wrote a book, man. Didn't you know? The book's why I signed up for this course. I'd like to blow up a mosque or two." He rubbed his hands together with the flourish he used when smacking a blocker to the turf. "They've smithereened enough synagogues and churches and embassies around the world. Blew up the World Trade Center. Cut off enough heads. Payback's what's needed."

Josh shrunk back in his seat and whispered, "Better keep those ideas quiet, man. You don't know who's listening."

Hank tilted his head and squinted at his friend. Obviously, he doubted any danger. "Yeah, I guess."

"Hank," Josh said through his teeth, "a class like this? Big brother might be here taking names. Yale is a distant galaxy away from the heart of democracy. We're in PC heaven, man."

Hank shrugged. "Yeah, well, remember what Charlton Heston said at Harvard—"

Josh flashed a questioning look.

"'Political correctness is tyranny with manners,'" Hank quoted. "I was kinda shocked this course was even being offered. Did a double-take to make sure I wasn't hallucinating."

"You know the Army-Navy store back home? Downtown?" Josh asked.

"Yeah."

"I'm sure Homeland Security has the store under surveillance. Doing this classroom is feasible too."

Hank wrinkled his nose. Maybe was the message.

After a moment, Josh chuckled. "Just tugging your chain, big guy. Stay clear of those conspiracy theories."

"Yeah, right." Hank smacked him hard on the arm.

"Ouch."

"You know I love conspiracies, so don't kid about 'em, okay?"

Josh smirked. Over his friend's shoulder, he spotted the Yale quarterback, Tommy Jacobs. Josh waved. He'd rung Jacobs' bell a few times in full-contact practice but the kid gave him a thumbs-up.

Just then, a hand tapped Josh from behind.

"Gonna be cool, huh?"

The silky voice of Jill somebody-or-other, a girl in Josh's Sociology 101 class. The pretty one with the sparkling blue eyes, the gleaming, long blonde hair, and the smile for which he would even consider diving off Killer's Rock at Mattapasset Lake.

Josh sat up straight, widened his shoulders and turned. "Cool?"

"An easy three credits."

"You think?"

The girl cocked her head. "Well, why not?"

"Don't know. Just not sure."

"Well, the course has attracted attention." Jill nodded toward the back of the room. "Check out the back row, third seat from the right."

Josh and Hank both strained to see past the students milling about.

Sitting there was a tall man, bald on top with a pony tail hanging below his shoulders, dressed in a dark blue T-shirt and brown tweed sport coat, sporting an air of superiority like a cheap bow tie. From what Josh had observed, Dean Stewart didn't belong here. At least Stewart himself thought he didn't. Instead, he thought he belonged—well, above everyone here. He was the Dean of Academic Affairs, and all had darn well better hail the dean. Josh had learned his lesson the hard way.

He recalled their one exchange all too well: "My name's not Mr. Stewart. It's Dean Stewart, young man. You'll do well to remember."

Yeah, Stewart was an annoying man, but a fearsome one. And he was—here.

"What's he doing here?" Hank spoke the question on all their minds.

"I hear he was vehement in his opposition to our new visiting instructor," Jill said.

"Why in the world?" Josh asked the question and his forehead wrinkled, but he just wanted to hear her answer.

"Too—extreme, I think. Not amicable to our friends in the Middle East. Not a supporter of our State Department. Has blood on his hands—"

"All the standard stuff we don't accept here," Hank said.

Jill's eyes narrowed as though she didn't understand, perhaps didn't agree with the premise.

Josh looked at his watch. Eleven o'clock. He snapped his fingers. *Darn.* He'd miss the president's inaugural speech. *Well, this had a better chance of being enlightening. Let the games begin.*

Three minutes later, everyone was settled in their seats. The visiting instructor was late. Not just Josh, but others were checking their watches. Not a splendid start to a teacher's tenure. He looked back. No doubt Dean Stewart was seething. Josh took pleasure in the fact and thought he spotted a drop of sweat which dared to meander down the dean's cheek.

With sudden force, one of the back doors slammed shut. A few seconds later, the other closed with a clink. Locked. People turned in their seats to see what was happening, but there was no sign of anyone at either door.

Another ten seconds elapsed, then the front door banged shut, and immediately, all the lights went out. Sudden, can't-see-your-hand-in-front-of-your-face darkness. Before anyone could object— bam-bam-bam! Was the noise from a rifle? A pistol?

The room turned into a kaleidoscope of red, yellow, and green flashes, bright streaks across the ceiling and white flashes reflecting off the walls.

People screamed. Many started to stand, then fell to their knees or stomachs, ducking for cover. These were small seats. There was no room to hide behind or beneath them.

Kaboom! An explosion rocked the room from the left front. The sound was like a subwoofer gone horribly awry. It seemed to shake the floor.

Sprack! Another, this one sharp and high-pitched, cracked the air near the right rear door. Josh, still seated, pushed his head down between his shoulders and turned, craning his neck to see the back of the room. No more than three feet away from the source of the sound, Dean Stewart was holding up his cell phone as a light.

Stewart jumped toward the wall, crushing a female student beneath him. His phone clambered to the ground and even the monitor's feeble brightness was lost.

More screams. Hysterical. Terrorized. Too stunned to breathe.

Rat-a-tat! Rat-a-tat! Semiautomatic gunfire, Josh guessed. He dropped to the floor on his bottom, with his knees to his chin. All the elements of a firefight filled the room—except smoke. *Or is there smoke and I just can't see it?* Josh wondered.

Sta-king! The sound of a bullet ricocheting off a seat somewhere nearby. Several students shrieked.

———◆———

Mayhem. I'm too young to die. Jill believed intelligence and beauty weren't meant to meet death so soon. Then as suddenly as the attack had begun, the lights came on.

Startled, she and everyone else looked around. The death scene was not terrifying at all. Josh and Hank stood up in front of her. No lifeless bodies lay in the aisles, no carnage at all.

The chaos quieted to murmurs of disbelief and wonder. The screams—gone.

Jill looked at her hand. She was still alive.

She spotted a friend, Suzy, from her dorm, and they locked eyes. What did Suzy's eyes reveal? Wonder? Relief? For sure, relief and embarrassment that they'd been fooled.

Indeed, the Yale University classroom was as it had been when she sat down. Except the front door. The entryway was wide open and in the doorway stood a tall—Jill guessed six-foot-two—broad-shouldered man, hands on his hips. A frown furrowed his brow while an amused smile played on his lips.

Jill gasped as she took her first look at the new instructor. Square-jawed, square-faced. Short, curly hair with streaks of gray. *His middle name must be Hunk.*

———◆———

Max Braxton scanned the room, evaluating his students, and, oh, yes—surprise—Dean Stewart in the back, stumbling to stand up and pull a girl to her feet.

Satisfied at the stunned expressions and the students scurrying to get up off the floor and into their seats, Max studied one face here, another there.

"Take your seats, please."

When everyone had complied, his eyes zeroed in on a young woman three rows up on the right-hand side of the room. He pointed at her. "Don't worry, young lady, your pooch's mistress will return to him after classes today. You're in no real danger." He hesitated. "Unless there is, indeed, a terror attack in the future of these four walls."

The girl's brow knit in a question. She wondered how he knew she had a dog.

"And you, young man," Max walked up to a white student sitting front-row, center-seat. "I'd beware the religion you're testing out. May not be the love-and-goodwill fest its literature proclaims."

Max, saddened and amused, watched the student double-check his fingers, his wrists to see what betrayed him as a Muslim-to-be. Nothing, but of course, he couldn't read the disdain engraved on his own face. He stumbled over a response but nothing cognitive escaped his mouth.

Max walked to the left-hand aisle and began a gradual climb up the steps.

Halfway to the back he stopped, looked toward the middle, down the row past two stunning coeds, a couple of kids he'd guess were on the chess team, and a heavyset young fellow wearing a stocking hat.

His eyes stopped at the next fellow. He nodded at him and asked, "Your name?"

"Josh Andrews."

"Josh, consider a future serving your country, not your wallet."

The boy's jaw dropped.

Max turned and continued his leisurely ascent. At the top step, he turned and looked down on the classroom. *Two-fifty, three hundred young people, the future brains of the country. To his right, Dean Stewart. And, well, some who think of themselves as the current brains.*

"People." Max's voice was loud, clear, and urgent. "Are you prepared? Are your friends, classmates, fraternities, sororities, teammates, family? Indeed, is this country prepared?" He hesitated ever so slightly. "Prepared for the next terror attack. Are you on the alert? Are you vigilant? On the watch for anyone among you who could bring an attack to your very own doorstep?"

Max took two steps back down, waiting for an answer, for any hand to be raised. Silence and stillness met his question.

"Were you prepared for an attack on this classroom five minutes ago?"

"No, sir," someone mumbled. Max looked to his left. The response had come from the muscular, good-looking young man to whom he had spoken.

"No," Max confirmed. "There was a lot of fear, scrambling, and shouting—"

"We were scared, Mr. Braxton." A teary-eyed brunette to his right was beside herself. "I was frightened."

Max nodded. "Good."

Descending three more steps so he would be at eye level with the girl, he asked, "Have you heard about the USS *Cole*?"

She shook her head.

"How about PanAm Flight 747 which exploded over Lockerbie, Scotland?"

The girl shook her head again.

"Okay, then, how about the basement-garage bombing of the World Trade Center in New York City—eight years *before* 9/11?"

The girl shook her head.

"Does Sheik Omar Abdel Rahman—the blind sheik—sound familiar?"

Again, a shake of the head.

"What's your name, young lady?"

"Pamela."

"How old are you, Pamela?"

"Twenty-one."

"Aha … and these attacks are not in your history books, eh?"

Pamela shrugged.

Max flashed a knowing look at Dean Stewart, received a scowl, then descended to the front of the room and faced the class.

"Does anyone in this room know anything about the 1998 attacks on United States embassies in Nairobi, Kenya, and Dar es Salaam in Tanzania, when truck bombs exploded and slaughtered two hundred and twenty-four people?"

At first, no hands were raised, then, slowly, one did go up in the back of the room.

Max spotted the arm. "Aha, Dean Stewart. You remember."

Stewart nodded.

Max offered a wry smile. "A man of a certain age remembers."

He ambled to his right.

"Then, let's get closer to events during your own lifetimes. Seeing most of you are in your late teens and early twenties—perhaps a few doctoral folks sprinkled in here and there—who recalls the suicide bombings of three American hotels—the Radisson, Grand Hyatt, and Days Inn—in Amman, Jordan, in 2005?"

Nobody responded except Stewart.

Max walked to the right side of the room and eyed a fellow he guessed to be a graduate student, judging by his haircut and well-ironed shirt and slacks.

"How about the 2008 car bombing and rocket strike on the US embassy in Yemen killing sixteen, including four civilians?"

The man nodded. "Oh, yes, sir. I remember the incident."

Max folded his arms and shook his head sadly.

"Seventeen American sailors were killed in the attack on the USS *Cole* by a group linked to Osama bin Laden or the al-Qaeda terrorist network. October 2000.

"The Lockerbie attack in 1998 killed all two hundred and fifty-nine on board and another eleven on the ground. Passengers included thirty-five Syracuse University students and many US military personnel."

Max looked around and asked, "Anyone here know any Syracuse students?"

Several voices responded positively.

"Anyone here know anyone in New York City?"

"My parents," a male student responded in front of Max.

"You're from New York. Then, you might have known one or two of the close to three thousand people killed in the 9/11 attack on the Twin Towers."

"My folks do."

Max sighed heavily.

"The first World Trade Center attack, in 1993, killed six and injured more than a thousand."

He looked up at the crowd before him.

"Six dead here, two hundred murdered there, three thousand slaughtered over there. More recently, in 2010, Major Nidal Hasan gunned down thirteen at Fort Hood."

"And how about the Boston Marathon bombing in 2013 where three were killed and two hundred and sixty injured?"

Hands shot up into the air all over the hall.

"And who did it?"

"Two college kids," a few people replied.

"Born in Russia," said someone in the middle of the room.

"Born in Russia, living in America." He breathed a heavy sigh. ""Living on welfare on your taxpayer dime. We've had homegrown terror cells detonating bombs in malls, high schools, middle schools, and even elementary schools. Last week, three terrorists were caught trying to destroy Hoover Dam." He scanned the students. "Now, you *have* heard this story, no?"

Heads nodded and voices consented.

"Good because your history books are being sanitized—written to avoid confrontation with scary themes like terror, anti-Semitism, suicide bombers.

"Writers of modern history books apparently don't want to deal with questions like 'Who are these people who hate us?' 'And why?'

"When they do face these questions, they distort the real answers. They make excuses. They call terrorists 'misguided folks.'" Max made quotation marks in the air. "'Jobless' perhaps, or 'upset their houses were foreclosed on,' or 'driven to it.'"

"Yes, driven by those horrible Jews who, inexplicably, want to live in their own homeland in peace, and by this horrid America which supports the despicable Jews. Yes, the Big Satan—America—and the Little Satan—Israel—are forcing these poor urchins to lash out and murder. Murder, mayhem, beheadings but not the terrorists' fault."

Max raised his arms to his shoulders and shrugged. He looked up toward Dean Stewart. The man was stoic.

"Yes, this is what many educators would have you believe. But in this classroom, when I'm teaching, we'll explore the facts, not the fiction, the reality, not the idealism."

Max stepped to the dais at the front of the classroom, held up a brochure for everyone to see. "This is your syllabus. Says this course is Terrorism, Anti-terrorism, and Hostage Negotiations.

"In this class, I won't make excuses—either for the terrorists or their targets, for their religion or its hatred. Terrorists are on every continent and in between."

Max turned to the whiteboard behind him, picked up a marker, and began to write names. "From the Communist Party of the Philippines, the New People's Army (he jotted down CPP/NPA) to the Salafist Group for Call and Combat active in Europe, Africa, and the Middle East, (he wrote GSPC), to the United Self-Defense Forces/Group of Colombia (he added AUC), and Euskadi Ta Askatasuna, a Marxist/Leninist group whose name means Basque Homeland and Freedom, (he wrote ETA), armed men and women are plying their trade of horror to seize control."

Max turned to face the classroom. "But, mind you, ninety-five percent of the terrorism in this world—minus the drug-related type driven by groups like FARC, ELN, and AUC—is sponsored by members of a religion born thirteen hundred years ago, expanded by war and oppression, converting cultures by the sword and holding them captive by fear.

"To not name the religion is to avoid reality, and in a real sense, to slit your own throat. Victory can only come when you first confront your enemy, name the enemy, and then set about to annihilate them. Avoid those steps, and you invite your own death.

"Suicide by stupidity."

Looking about the classroom, Max spotted Dean Stewart—his disgust obvious. The rest of the class displayed mixed responses. Some were upset; they would bow out of the course. Some were on the edge of their seats; they were certain to be aboard for the semester. Some showed signs of anger, not at him but at terrorists. He would have to keep a keen eye on these people.

"Your first textbook is my book, *The Eye of Evil*." He smiled broadly. "One of the benefits of teaching a college course, I've discovered, is you get to peddle your own stuff. So, get started on the book, and I'll see you again in two days, Thursday—at least those of you who aren't so ticked off at me, or so stuck on politically correct rhetoric, that you're going to sign up instead for European History 101."

Scattered laughter met his last remark.

As students poured out of the room, Max looked toward the back. Dean Stewart, the school's European history guru, had slipped out. *No confrontation today. I wonder what grades he'll give me in the faculty coffee room.*

He noticed several small clutches of students loitering along the aisles. A couple shot him killer looks, others mouthed words like "SEALs" and "Ranger." He wished they would esteem policemen and firefighters as well.

Just then the muscular young man he had spoken to—Josh, was it?—stepped in front of him. The overweight kid with the stocking hat stood beside him, and a pretty, blonde girl, who had sat behind the two, looked over the boy's left shoulder.

"Mr. Braxton," the brawny boy said, "you read my mind today. Can we talk?"

"Josh, is it?" Max asked.

The boy nodded.

Max looked at the three of them. "My office is in Rosenkranz Hall at 115 Prospect Street, room 203. Five o'clock?"

"It's a date."

The boy extended his hand. Max shook it.

"I'm Hank Clauson," the heavyset kid interjected, shaking Max's hand. "I'm on the football team with Josh."

"Ah, football. Great sport." Max gauged Hank's grip. Strong for a heavy fellow. "Offensive line?"

"Defensive."

Max nodded, then turned his attention to the girl.

"I'm Jill Thule," she said. She smiled fetchingly but remained where she stood. The look in her eyes was not hard for Max to read. He'd have to put a quick end to the thought stirring in her mind.

"Glad to meet you, Jill. My office is open to you, too. My rule will be if and when I meet with a female student, another adult must be in the room with us."

She flashed an odd, questioning gaze.

———— ◆ ————

A few minutes later, stepping into his Mustang, Max turned on the radio. The president was speaking.

Ah, the new sheriff in town. Max started the car, turned up the volume, and weaved through Yale's Old Campus streets toward Beinecke Library. He wanted to cuss at the one-way morass. But as he listened to the speech, the object of his cursing shifted. He flipped the radio to a music station, any music station.

This is what happens when you elect a man you know nothing about, whose life is a haze from childhood to adulthood, whose family lived abroad in Southeast Asia and the Middle East—except for the short time they were in America when he was a newborn. This is what happens when a man gets elected on a catchy campaign slogan. This is what happens when a nation is asleep at the wheel—and in the ballot booth.

Max turned the car into a small parking lot and hopped out, a briefcase in hand.

———◆———

Stetson closed his eyes and wiped his perspiring forehead with his sleeve. The president was prattling on. He checked his scope again, aiming toward the mike, and pictured the scene for the fourteenth time. This time, he chose the nose. *How many men could shoot from this distance in this breeze and be able to choose the body part he's going to blow away?* He smirked and rolled to his side again for a momentary rest.

Suddenly, his earpiece squawked. *Great. Here's the 'Go.'* He held the earpiece steady in his ear with his right hand.

"Stay sharp. Crying Eagle *may* be postponed."

Postponed? He'd been up here for seven hours. Ever since shuffling into the monument in the dark. There's no way they were going to postpone this. This was POTUS. The big hit.

"What do you mean postponed?" Stetson spat the words into the radio attached to his sleeve.

"Don't strike unless the order is given."

He swore under his breath and flicked the safety on. He was going to get paid with or without the hit, but his baby wanted to be fired. More importantly, he wanted this hit. How many could claim to have taken out the leader of the free world?

Chapter Three

11:55 a.m. Tuesday, January 21

In his private Gulfstream IV cruising at 560 miles per hour over the Atlantic Ocean toward Reagan National Airport in Washington, DC, Avner "Avi" Navon fumed.

First, an important business deal had kept him in London to sign papers, preventing him from being at the Presidential Inauguration. This was the first time he had immersed himself in a presidential campaign. He considered Ridley Jones's election his own personal victory as well.

Second, watching a satellite television on the shelf to his right, he was flabbergasted. Had he heard his good friend, the new president, say what he thought he'd said?

Jones could support no more Jewish emigration to Israel? There should be no more checkpoints at the borders of Arab and Israeli lands? The existing protective fencing between violent Arab territories and the Jewish homeland would have to come down?

Avi had spent several millions of his fortune—besides the enormous amount of time and his own personal and political capital—pushing Ridley's run from obscurity to the presidency. And a substantial amount of his support was based on Ridley's assurances.

Namely, if elected, he would turn the table on his predecessors, and indeed, walk the talk in support of Israel and the nation-state's right to exist.

Now, what he considered impossible had happened. Ridley, a city councilor and the head of a food bank distribution center in Atlanta, had been elected president. The story of the century—of history—and Avi was acknowledged as a major reason for the victory. But what was this? Mere moments after being sworn in as president, Ridley was taking a meat cleaver to his promises?

Avi nudged his assistant. "Sweetheart, are you hearing this?"

Her big brown eyes locked onto his and she reached out a hand to touch his—a touch he knew as one of love, affirmation, and hopeful pacification. Her brow knit and pain filled her pretty face.

"Yes, Papa. I haven't been able to breathe for the last two minutes. I'm astonished."

"What have I done, getting this man elected?"

"What you thought was right." She squeezed his hand.

He squeezed back. "Instead, I seem to have helped put a knife in the back of my own race."

"Maybe it's just posturing, Papa. Maybe he feels he has to say these things, to appear non-dictatorial—"

"Non-dictatorial?" Avi harrumphed. "Poppycock, Lana. I'll non-dictatorial him. Wait 'til I get him alone. I'll skin him alive—president or not."

Avi recalled his youth as a member of the Israel Defense Forces when a close friend was kidnapped and skinned alive by Palestinian terrorists, who broadcast the butchery on Al Jazeera television. He shivered. *Well, maybe skinning alive is going too far.*

He thought for a moment, then asked, "What time, exactly, will Ridley arrive at our inaugural ball?"

Lana pulled an iPod out of her handbag, tapped the screen a couple times, then scrolled down a daily planner.

Looking at her father, she said, "First, he has the Commander-in-Chief's Inaugural Ball for the military, wounded soldiers, and high medals winners at the National Building Museum. Then it's our Home State Ball in the Air and Space Museum. He's supposed to arrive around ten o'clock, then head over to other balls at the Washington Convention Center."

"Get in touch with Zaps and tell him I want Ridley alone as soon as he steps in the door. Five minutes is all I'll need."

Lana had worked long hours on the campaign with Ned Zapper, Jones's chief of staff.

"Shouldn't be a problem," she said.

"Better not be."

Lana could not remember the last time she had seen such a scowl on her father's face—perhaps when he had faced a hostile takeover of one of his companies.

———— ◆ ————

Yale's six-story, brick-and-glass Beinecke Rare Book & Manuscript Library seems to stand on stumpy little "legs" at the building's four corners. To the uninformed eye, the Beinecke is a blasé, even austere and characterless square building with cutouts appearing to be windows but not windows at all. Indeed, the library, set smack-dab in the center of the university grounds, is windowless for a reason. The Beinecke is the largest building in the world reserved exclusively for the preservation of rare books and manuscripts.

The book stacks are surrounded by walls made of a translucent Danby marble, which transmits subdued lighting and provides protection from direct light.

The stacks were unlike any Max had seen anywhere. The three levels below ground and six levels above were all glass-encased, with myriad circular recessed lights in the ceiling along each aisle.

From where he stood, he could look down outside the stacks to the ground floor, where a few people milled about or sat on long sofas conversing. A few minutes before, he had watched as two library staffers unlocked a glass encasement, and wearing special gloves, turned the pages of two Gutenberg Bibles. Every day a page was turned in each Bible—a ceremony of sorts.

The Beinecke is, appropriately, less than a block away from the huge Grove Street Cemetery, for most of its manuscripts are either dead or long dead.

Despite the precautions, and perhaps because some manuscripts had deteriorated a bit before being rescued to the Beinecke, Max could detect a faint stale smell.

He didn't mind. The odor reminded him of his great-aunt's attic, where he'd played with his cousins as a child and where bookcases held stacks of old *Life* magazines, *Reader's Digest Condensed Books*, and the like.

Besides, he was on a mission. He had found the Medieval and Renaissance Manuscripts section and had climbed to the top step of a six-rung moveable ladder. Welcome wonder lit his face, and he pulled an ancient book from its place, stepped back down the ladder and looked around for a study nook.

If he could remove the book from the building, he would pull his jacket tight against the January chill and sit out on the side lawn in the Hewitt Quadrangle between the library and Woodbridge Hall or even rest by a tree on New Haven Green, a short walk to the east.

But the books were too valuable to be loaned out. What Max had found was in the long-dead category, one of the earliest versions of the Prophet Mohammed's auxiliary writing, the *Hadith Qudsi'* (Sacred Hadith). While Muslims believed the *Hadith* contained God's thoughts revealed to Mohammad in a dream or through revelation and expressed in Muhammad's words, they believed the *Hadith Qudsi'*, collected in the late 800s, were the direct words of God.

He whistled in anticipation of his findings. The tune was the Marine Corps hymn, "Halls of Montezuma." The melody may have been taken from Offenbach's comic opera, *Genevieve de Brabant,* but to Max the performance was no comedy. He had close comrades who had died for the country. He'd even held his best friend in his arms when he breathed his last.

As he whistled the tune to the lyrics, "to the shores of Tripoli," Max was struck by the fact that "the shores of Tripoli" referred to the Barbary Coast War. At the turn of the nineteenth century, the American schooner USS *Enterprise* fought against Muslim pirates who had for years terrorized merchant ships around Northern Africa.

The Qur'an, according to Tripoli's ambassador to England, declared all nations which had not acknowledged the prophet were sinners, whom the faithful had the right and duty to plunder and enslave; every Muslim who was slain in this warfare was sure to go to paradise.

Two hundred years later, America was again facing Muslim terrorists filled with hate and the intent to go to paradise as killers of infidels.

No, this was no comedy and when he whistled the hymn, he did so with back erect and pride in his demeanor.

We fight our country's battles in the air, on land and sea;
first to fight for right and freedom and to keep our honor clean.

Great stanzas, like the next:

Our flags unfurled to every breeze from dawn to setting sun;
we have fought in every clime and place where we could take a
gun;
in the snow of far-off Northern lands and in sunny tropic scenes;
you will find us always on the job—the United States Marines.

Well, guns were still in most instances allowed in a fighting man's hands, but the rules of engagement were so severe weapons were often rendered useless.

But such was another story, one spelled out in his book. His immediate concern was finding this early manuscript and the exact Muslim scriptures explaining *jihad* and *takeyya*. He could read and speak modern Arabic, and with original documents to prove his case, though his translation would be slow, he could establish beyond a doubt what he was going to claim in class was indeed provable and true.

Max moved into a study cubicle, gently set down the manuscript and pulled an IRIS scanning pen out of his pocket.

Wearing plastic gloves from the reception desk, he began leafing through the *Hadith Qudsi'*.

A short, low woof broke his concentration, and he looked for the source. Three feet from him stood a handsome, almost regal, black-and-white border collie. The dog barked again, a low-decibel statement. Max cocked his head. The dog cocked his head. Max extended his hand. The dog retreated a step and woofed again, then turned to leave. He took a step, looked back over his shoulder, and woofed a little louder, a bit higher-pitched, adding urgency. Or exaggeration? Border collies, after all, were no-nonsense, used to being in charge.

Max grinned. He lifted the book from the nook and followed the dog, who was moving along at a good clip—purpose in his step. A few yards along, the dog again looked over his shoulder, as if he were making sure Max was tailing along. Max could have sworn he read a smile on his muzzle.

A right turn, a left turn, and they approached a woman seated in a corner nook. The dog turned and sidled up to the woman, his shoulder touching her leg.

Her slender hand held open a book. Max noticed the fingernails were short and not painted. Indeed, this was the hand of a woman who was more focused on her work than on glamour.

He looked her over and caught his breath, then released the air. This was a lady of class, of elegance—a refined woman who didn't need to gussy up to look tantalizing. Green eyes. Short, curly, red hair.

Max tilted his head and took an even longer look. Lanky, athletic, about five foot eight, about thirty-five. Whatever she was selling, he was interested.

At last, she looked up and spotted the *Hadith Qudsi'* in his hands.

Max cocked his head—a silent question.

She cocked hers—a silent response.

He noticed the dog cock his head and suppressed a laugh.

He looked down at the *Hadith Qudsi'*, then back at her.

Her eyes glittered, flirting, "Want some help with your book, sir?"

He nodded.

She stood up, stepped past her dog, and fell into his arms.

"Now *this* is some kind of help," he whispered. He leaned down and drank in her aroma. She smothered her face in his chest and wrapped her arms around him.

They stood motionless for a minute. Every few seconds, the dog yipped. Max put his hands on the woman's shoulders and appraised her at arm's length.

"I accept your offer," he deadpanned.

She raised an eyebrow and smiled.

"I'm Max Braxton." He offered a hand.

She ignored the hand. "I know."

"You do?"

"I read your course curricula with interest."

His smile was crooked, hers sublime.

"Really?" His response was half-questioning, fully curious.

"Fascinating background for a visiting instructor and especially at Yale, of all places." Her voice sounded like a breeze through a pine grove, a familiar wistfulness.

"Some would have me gone before my visit. How about you?"

"I reserve judgment."

He pulled her close again and kissed her—as long and tender a kiss as he could while restraining himself.

Seconds disappeared into—into what? He didn't know. The clock in his head, so exact in military operations, was thrown askew.

After a time, they pulled apart to take a breath.

"I missed you," she said.

"I've been here a week. I thought you'd never get here."

"I just gave my final lecture. In Berlin."

"I know. At Freie Universitaet. I followed your itinerary. Hebrew University in Jerusalem, Cambridge and University of Sheffield in England, University of Edinburgh, Utrecht in the Netherlands, University of Tokyo—"

She tweaked his arm and interjected, "Gave you time to finish your book, though, didn't I? And, I'll say, you did a great job. The hardcover's in bookstores, even at airports around the world."

He shrugged. "But I never want to do this again."

"What? Write a book?"

"Stay apart and out of contact." Max hesitated, daring to say no more. As one of a handful of people commissioned with authority to go far beyond off-the-books in clandestine operations for Uncle Sam, he could get a call any time from the head of the Joint Chiefs of Staff or the chairman of the Subcommittee for National Security for the US House Oversight Committee. He and his comrades could defy laws even these people couldn't—all in the name of freedom.

When that call came, he would not be able to refuse the mission, even in the midst of this six-month sabbatical.

Kat broke into his reflections, saying, "Well, you broke our agreement when you let me know you were teaching here."

"Yeah, but—"

Again, she leaned into his chest. He absorbed the warmth of her body and thought of all she'd been through in the last few months, ever since they had discovered the music of the Psalms in Israel. Ever since they escaped death in Petra and again in Dublin and in Wales. Ever since Katherine Cardova's name had ascended into the neon lights of the world's most famous archaeologists. All that and yet, she was still the same. How he admired this woman.

He took a deep breath. "I want to hear all about your travels. But wait 'til you hear about my first class," he said.

"Just what will I hear?" She looked up at him and raised an eyebrow. He remembered the look. He liked the look. He had longed for the look.

"Oh, I'll let you enjoy the experience of discovery—"

Max heard voices and stepped back from her. Three coeds walked around the corner, spotted them and the dog, then all crowded in on the dog, oohing and aahing and ruffling his ears. He enjoyed the attention, perhaps more so after watching his mistress share hers.

Max turned back to Kat. "Say, you didn't tell me your name."

Playing along, she extended her hand and answered, "Katherine Cardova. My friends call me Kat."

He shook her hand. "Glad to meet you, Kat. You work here?"

She laughed at the masquerade.

"I teach. Anthropology and linguistics." Her voice was mellow and inviting. "My specialty is semiology, the study of sign processes. And, more specifically semantics: the relation between symbols and the things to which they refer, their *denotata*." She chuckled. "But I'm sure you've heard this all before."

Max chuckled back. "Yep. But the second time through can often be the best. Know what I mean?"

She stood on her tiptoes, kissed him on the cheek, and said, "I think I do."

"Join me for lunch?"

"Sorry, not today."

"But, Kat!" The exclamation escaped before he could stop. He was surprised. He looked at the coeds, who were peering at them now. He shrugged with exaggeration, then turned back to Kat.

"I'm sorry," she said, "but I'm meeting with the dean. We've got a lot to catch up on."

"Tonight, then?"

"I'll beat tonight." She glanced at her wrist watch. "Coffee and danish, two o'clock."

Now her smile was singing through the pine grove.

"You're on."

"Me and my buddy, Tuck," she said, pointing behind her. "You remember him."

"I've just heard him over the phone," Max said, recalling when he and Kat were in Israel and she'd telephoned Tuck's caretaker and carried on a conversation of sorts with the border collie.

The coeds had walked away, leaving Tuck to again concentrate on the pair at the desk. Max looked him over. *A stunning dog for a stunning lady.*

"Tuck," Kat said, "meet Max, the man I've been telling you about."

Max kneeled and extended his hand. Tuck met his hand with his paw and they shook.

"Handsome boy," he said.

Tuck smiled. The dog smiled!

"He's better than good-looking," Kat said. "He's my protector, best friend—well, second-best—and he's a bit smarter than some high school graduates I've met."

"He must be—to be allowed up here in the stacks."

"He saved President Hall's granddaughter's life," she said. "The girl was walking out into traffic and Tuck rushed out, grabbed her coat and dragged her to the sidewalk. A car missed her by a foot. Since then, he's had carte blanche anywhere on campus."

"Wow. Impressive," Max said.

"Besides, they know me here." She shrugged.

"Of course, Tuck's invited to come, too," Max said.

Kat smiled, winked, then turned and walked away.

Max spent the next few minutes delving into the Muslim concept called *Al Takeyya*. Here he found ancient, original-document proof of the principle that gives Muslims permission to lie to prevent denigration of Islam, to protect oneself, or to promote the cause of Islam.

"This includes lying under penalty of perjury in testimony before the United States Congress, lying or distorting the truth to the media such as claiming (as it does in Holy Quran: 2, 208) that Islam is a religion of peace, and deceiving fellow Muslims when the one lying has deemed them to be apostates."

Max knew some in his class would quote verses in the Qur'an from the early part of Mohammed's ministry—peaceful texts preaching tolerance toward non-Muslims. But in Islam, newer verses replace older ones—so the day is won by passages filled with prejudice, intolerance, and endorsing violence upon unbelievers.

Surah 9:5 in the Qur'an said the command forcefully: "Fight and kill the disbelievers wherever you find them, take them captive, harass them, lie in wait, and ambush them using every stratagem of war."

Satisfied, Max stood to leave, very much looking forward to two o'clock. Lost time. A commodity that can never be recovered in full, but he was darned well going to do his best.

Avi was out of his seat before the Gulfstream reached its hangar.

He glanced at Lana, who was stuffing papers into her briefcase in a hurry to keep up with him. "The copter's waiting?"

"Yes. But, Papa, you might want to wait for the plane to stop and the steps to arrive before you hop out the door." She pointed to the forward exit door where the company's flight attendant waited with a wide smile planted on her face. The attendant had no idea a cornerstone of Avi Navon's dream—the one he had set in motion to help change the world for the best—had cracked, and this fissure might threaten the infant presidency as well as any peace her boss's beloved Israel might attain.

Avi looked over the three men and two women, from thirty to sixty years old, occupying the G500's luxurious seats. All were in various stages of putting away paper or closing laptop computers.

"Jonas," he said, nodding to a well-dressed young man, "you're with Lana and me. Everyone else is going to the hotel via limo."

"Right, sir." Jonas Mandrell stood up and pulled a satchel over his shoulder.

"Which hotel did you book?" Avi asked.

"The Willard."

"Good. I didn't like our little experiment last week. I'm not hip or chic enough for the Jake, the Frank, or whatever the name."

"George, Papa." Lana shook her head and smiled. "The Hotel George."

"Yeah. That one. So, we're in The Willard—"

"Yes, sir," Jonas said.

"Well, then, what room?"

"You've got the Oval Suite. Lana's in the Executive."

"Swap them."

"Sir?"

Avi turned to his daughter. "Honey, I know you love the Oval parlor, so let's swap rooms. You take the Oval Suite."

Lana grinned.

"Are the rest of our gang all there as well?" Avi asked.

Jonas nodded.

"Good." Avi looked over his staff. "We'll meet in Lana's suite, the Oval, at five o'clock to finalize the Osterman deal." He winked at his daughter and whispered, "The Oval's my favorite, too. I promise this will be your sole sacrifice for solitude."

Avi looked back at Jonas. "We'll call in room service—I'll take the filet—then we can all get ready for the ball."

————◆————

Max and Kat strolled through the Yale campus, taking time now and again to stop under an old oak tree or sit on a bench—Tuck always walking or sitting between them.

Now and again a student or professor would wave to Kat or walk up and congratulate her on finding the music. One student asked her to sign a textbook. Kat carried it all off with aplomb and grace.

Max wanted to know all about her travels, speaking about the music, how Danny Arens was recuperating, and the progress of the Third Temple Faithful in building a synagogue on the Temple Mount.

The cold snap in the air didn't faze them.

Had Kat seen her parents in Nebraska, and how was their landscaping business doing? Had she been invited to speak at her alma mater, Bryn Mawr College, or the University of Chicago where she earned her PhD?

On a bench in a commons area, he asked if her bodyguards had been sufficient.

"Not as 'sufficient' as you," she said, raising an eyebrow. "Of course, they didn't have to resort to medieval weaponry or golf course accessories."

He laughed at the memories. "We SEALs use what's accessible. What impressed me more was your expertise with the crossbow."

"Pure luck."

"I think not."

"As for body guards, I'd rather have had you, of course. But you did needed time to write, to decide if you were going to re-up with the military, teach at the Naval War College or The Citadel, or whatever. And so, what's your future?"

"This semester at Yale and near you," he said. "I loved my time war-gaming with the SEALs and Rangers, so I might re-up and take on a posting at the Naval War College. Then, again, I might go back to Israel as kind of a special-ops consultant. A lot depends on my personal life."

By her expression she noticed the nuance wrapped around the obvious, pausing, then stretching out her hands to him. He took them. Tuck, sitting up between them, looked at the interlocked hands, cocked his head, whined and laid down.

"As I said, Tuck is my protector and best friend. Clearly, you pass muster for him," Kat smiled.

Max pulled her to her feet, and they strolled along hand in hand.

He filled her in on his widowed mother, Clair, and younger sister, Maise, and her husband and two children in Arlington, Texas.

Occasionally, Kat would toss in a phrase or sentence in Hebrew or Arabic. "Just testing you," she said, "making sure you're keeping up your language skills."

He'd prattle on a few sentences to impress her, and she'd shrug passive approval.

"You know," she said, "the kids are going to dig up as much about you as they can—either for good or for evil—"

"Good luck to them. Any yummy tidbits are locked up—at least to civilians."

"Some will be looking to dredge up blackmailable information. Others will be checking you out because they think you're, um," she hesitated and smiled, "'cool.'"

He laughed. "Cool? The coolest thing I do is play the guitar and not very well."

"You'll have to show me, and I'll be the judge," Kat said.

Just then a couple students walked by and Max's eyes widened. He looked at his watch. "Oh, I'm sorry. I have to get to my office. Got a meeting with some students."

"Student meetings already?"

"Can I see you tonight?" he asked.

She turned and presented a look saying, "Go on ..."

"My place. I'll cook."

The expression remained in place, inferring, "Yes, and ..."

"Mandarin."

Her mouth tightened.

"Indian cuisine—and I'll go light on the curry."

"There's a meeting of the History and Archaeology board tonight. We'll have to have dinner Thursday."

Her smile lit his world. "Eight, Thursday?"

"Right."

He scribbled his Orange Street address on a slip of paper and handed the note to her. "Third floor. The apartment with the turrets."

She took the paper. "Eight. Turrets. Right."

"Bring Tuck," Max said, smiling at the dog.

Through the exchange, Tuck watched in apparent amusement. At the mention of his name, he gazed up at Max. Max thought the look approving.

Then Tuck barked twice. Kat looked at the dog, then back at Max. "Seems I'm seeing you tomorrow at the café, again."

Max clucked twice at Tuck. "Thanks, boy."

Chapter Four

6:00 p.m. Tuesday, January 21

Avi Navon stood at the huge oval window for which Lana's suite was named. To his right was Pennsylvania Avenue, to his left Fourteenth Street, both lit by street lamps and a mob of cars' headlights. History had been made here. History had walked down the wide expanse of the avenue before him. Presidents had marched Pennsylvania's length, waving to adoring crowds as they passed. Chiefs of state had been carried to their resting places aboard horse-drawn hearses here, too. No matter our fame, death awaits us all, he thought.

At this moment Avi considered which position, prone or on supine, he would like to see President Ridley Jones at this moment. He was furious. Friend now turncoat.

In the last couple hours he had read and re-read the text of the inaugural address. He remained flabbergasted. Liar seemed stamped on the three pages devoted to the Middle East.

Avi Navon considered himself a man of self-control—prone to neither verbal nor physical attacks. As a soldier in the Israeli Defense Forces, he had seen enough violence before immigrating to this country.

His two older brothers had both died in action—Ehud in the Six Day War in 1967 and Benyamin in the Yom Kippur War in 1973.

When his younger sister died from a missile launched from Gaza in 1982, the only family he had remaining were a handful of cousins, his wife, Ruth, and their two-year-old daughter, Lana. To protect Lana, they moved to America, where Avi had earned his university degree in finance.

But Avi and Ruth had continued to keep extensive ties with his homeland. Avi started an import-export company, importing the many Israeli inventions in technology fields. His fortune allowed him to provide venture capital for several new R&D projects. Semiconductors, computer software, GPS telecommunications, biotechnology and medical instruments—even a remote-controlled, mechanical housefly fitted with a spy cam—his hand was in them all.

And when he befriended a young Atlanta city councilor, getting to know him and his family well, Avi decided to help launch the young man into the national spotlight. First came a successful US Senate race, and three years into his six-year term, a brilliant run to the presidency. Phenomenal. A success of amazing proportions. Here was a man who had assured Avi he would stand at Israel's side, come what may.

Liar!

Avi crumpled the inaugural speech and flung the ball of paper over his shoulder, staring, though not seeing, the heavy traffic below on Pennsylvania Avenue.

This was Max's first visit to his new office. He'd been getting his apartment in shape, putting off the inevitable of being relegated to an eight-by-ten-foot workplace. Once inside, he found the room worse than he had imagined. How many generations of faculty preceded him, Max didn't know, but his new office was well lived-in and well eaten-in too if his nose wasn't fooling him.

The previous resident had boxed up most of her belongings—books and personal stuff—but had left behind piles of student papers, a half-full trash can, a clock-radio from a previous era and a hot-pink National Association of Women coffee mug containing several lipstick-stained cigarette butts adding to the semi-nauseous smell of tobacco smoke. The room's one outside window faced the neighboring brick building.

Perhaps this was the customary room for the newbie visiting lecturer. Perhaps the ambiance, odor and all, was a gift of Dean Stewart and his cronies who had been aghast at their beloved free-thinking university hiring "this murderous anthropoid" as one gentle lady from the zoology department described him.

Just as Max laid his one box of belongings on the scarred wooden desk, he heard feet scuffling through his doorway. He turned to see Josh Andrews.

"Hello, sir," Josh said. "You said we could speak."

"Sure." Max waved the young man into the office.

He lifted a stack of papers off a chair facing his desk, elbowed all the rubbish off his desktop and into an empty box, then pointed to the now-empty chair. "Have a seat."

Josh chuckled. "Yes, sir."

They took their respective chairs, then Josh said, "You said I should consider a future serving my country, not my wallet. Like you were reading my mail."

"Really." Not a surprise.

"How did you know?"

"Your look, your carriage, your confidence. You're not like the other kids your age—even here at sophisticated Yale."

Josh thought this through, nodded his head in slow motion, then looked at Max. "You also pointed out we're not ready for a terrorist attack."

"A-huh." Another neutral acknowledgment of facts.

Josh was waiting for an explanation. Max didn't expound, and at last, the young man gave up, clasped his hands, and folded them. "I've been rethinking my future." He shook his head as if the muscles hurt to do so. "I don't know. I feel this is lost time—these years studying here."

Max nodded. *He's nineteen, twenty. Not the first kid to question his decisions.*

"Josh, I'm not a counselor or faculty adviser—"

"No-no-no." Josh raised his hands in front of him. "I know. I don't want to put you on the spot, Mr. Braxton. But you've got all kinds of experience. I just want your input."

Max thought for a moment, then asked, "By 'lost years,' what do you mean, Josh?"

"I mean, what's my goal? What am I accomplishing? I feel like I'm treading water, nothing else until something important happens in my life. Thank God, I'm on full scholarship, so college isn't costing my Mom and Dad anything."

"Nineteen and you want your life mapped out." Max suggested.

"John Quincy Adams was abroad with a Russian diplomat at the age of thirteen."

"Point taken. But you won't find such a thing happening to thirteen-year-olds in today's world."

"No, but what I mean is, he had a clue."

"The career was forced on him."

Josh hesitated. "But he did have a mission as a teenager. He was abroad with his father. He grabbed at a future."

"Grab at yours."

"But what is mine?"

"I don't have your answer, Josh. But I do know this: Young people every year waste their own time, not to mention the time and talents of university staff, their finances, and the savings of their parents while they search for their calling in this life. I say, 'Search on your own dime.' Get off the stoop and make something happen while you're waiting for whatever directional nudge, or 'still small voice' you're expecting to hear."

"Make my move how?" The look on Josh's face approached anguish.

"What are your grades?"

"Three-point-four, three-point-five GPA."

"So, you can leave and be pretty much assured of being accepted back to Yale when you're ready."

Josh thought for a moment. "I guess."

"You want action?"

"Yeah, but action's not all."

"You love your family?"

"Yes."

"You love your country?"

"Yes."

"You love liberty?"

"Yes."

"You want to protect America's way of life for yours and future generations?"

"Yes."

"Well, there's a start. Perhaps you should think these things through and then decide your next step."

Josh looked out the window and chuckled.

Max followed his eyes and asked, "What?"

Josh smiled and waved a hand at the surroundings. "After all your exploits, this is what you get?"

Max laughed and shook his head, then smiled at his student. "Well, Josh, I'm sure your future is brighter."

"Thank you, sir." Josh rose and extended his hand. "You've given me something to think about."

"Not enough, I'm sure, but a start," Max said. "Listen, come into class Thursday and I'll give you an assignment to stir the juices."

"Really?"

"Really."

--------◆--------

A variety of aromas mingled through the apartment as a pot boiled, a skillet sizzled, and something in the oven stirred the hunger pangs. Max stood at the kitchen counter, dicing a large cucumber. The kitchen opened into the living room, and Max glanced over.

Kat caught his look as she sat on a comfortable couch, her right hand stroking Tuck's fine head while she observed the well-appointed living room and struggled to identify what her host was cooking. He had been so secretive.

"I don't want to be embarrassed if the meal comes out poorly," he'd said. But she doubted his veracity. Either Max Braxton wore humility badly or incapacity itself was uncomfortable in his presence.

She recalled their first encounter—she, pounding on the steering wheel of a car refusing to start in Tiberias,. He, appearing at her window and offering to drive her the ninety minutes to Dragot where her colleague was under gunfire. She, with dread and trepidation, jumping into a stranger's car. He, undaunted, alerting friends in the Israeli police force about the attack, and driving, with skill, at breakneck speeds behind a police escort. She barely breathed through the ordeal. He took command and proved trustworthy and a gentleman at every step.

These last few months had been a thrill, speaking at some of the world's great universities and interviewing for cover stories in *Current Archaeology, The Smithsonian, Biblical Archaeology Review, Christianity Today, Worship Leader,* Israel's *Azure* and a host of major newspapers worldwide, including *The Jerusalem Post, The Guardian,* and the *Sydney Morning Herald.* She'd been the Power Player of the Week on *Fox News Sunday* and was told she was a vote or two away from being named *Time Magazine's* Person of the Year.

She looked again at Max, who was leaning over the stove, and thought of the bullets he'd warded off with a Roman shield in the vault beneath St. Michan's in Dublin. No, Maximus Braxton did not undertake tasks he couldn't handle.

"Ouch." Max winced as a spit of boiling water flew out of the pot and landed on his hand. Well, maybe he *has* overstepped here, Kat thought to herself.

She sipped a glass of Australian Shiraz and meandered to a small built-in bookcase. Tuck followed at her heels.

Beside the bookcase stood an acoustic guitar on a guitar stand.

"You been able to keep up playing?" she asked.

"Thank you for calling my strums 'playing,'" he said. "You've heard me. Playing is an exaggeration. I have a ten-year-old niece who plays better. But I do intend to learn more than the four or five chords I know now."

Kat chuckled and turned to the bookcase. The shelves were full for a man who'd just moved in and might be gone at the end of the school year in late May. Eclectic, she noted as she scanned the titles.

What's this? Kat grabbed a thin leather notebook-sized book with no markings. Opening the volume, she found a copy of a *New Yorker* magazine article entitled "Survival" about John F. Kennedy's heroism when PT-109, the motor torpedo boat he commanded during World War II, was sunk. The article had been reprinted and bound.

———— ◆ ————

"Ten minutes." Max's words startled Kat. He approached her from the kitchen.

Kat turned to see him. "Ten minutes?"

"We have ten minutes before the meal's ready."

"Aha." She hesitated, then held the leather book up toward him. "I've been investigating your psyche."

"I pity you."

"Pity's a strong word."

"Strong's necessary in my case."

"You need analysis, do you?" she asked with a smile.

"Are you qualified?" He returned a smirk.

She didn't reply, but tilted her head and looked up at him.

"You're giving me the look Natalie Wood used with her leading men—like James Dean in *Rebel Without a Cause* and Warren Beatty in *Splendor in the Grass*."

"I don't know what you mean," she said coyly, "but let's see how I do with the analysis."

She turned to the bookcase. "JFK's PT-109 story and *Entebbe: A Defining Moment in the War on Terrorism* about Yoni Netanyahu's Entebbe raid. These tell me you admire the heroic in people. Perhaps this explains your undertaking a lifestyle of danger and heroism."

She hesitated, putting her forefinger and thumb to her chin. "Or perhaps JFK and Netanyahu remind you—of you."

Max laughed and shrugged. "Not in this life."

"I beg to differ." Her hands were on her hips, defying his deflection.

Meanwhile, Tuck sidled over to him and sniffed at his right-hand pants pocket.

"Got a good sniffer, don't you, boy," Max said. He put his hand into the pocket, pulled out a dog treat shaped like a person and held out the snack to Tuck, who scarfed up the offering in one bite.

"You want to win my dog's affections," Kat said with an accusing smile.

"The way to a woman's heart is often through her best friend."

Kat smiled. "You might be right. But we—actually, you—digress."

She turned back to the bookcase.

"*London to Ladysmith via Pretoria*—hmm, a book about Churchill's Boer War experiences, right? And his escape from the Boers after the armored train attack?"

Max nodded agreement. "Another hero—and this one a brilliant man as well," he said.

"And here," she said, pointing to a thick hardbound book. "*The Gulag Archipelago* by Aleksandr Solzhenitsyn, a literary and cultural hero."

She ran her finger down two shelves to Ayn Rand's *Fountainhead* and *Atlas Shrugged*. "Here's where you show your bent toward independence, man standing up for himself, winning and losing on his own terms, buoyed by his personal strengths and battling the interference of others—whether corporations or governments."

"Admiration of heroes and independence," Max said. "You're doing well. Keep going."

47

"Okay, but know this: Ayn Rand hated religion."

"I didn't know. Not good."

Kat nodded agreement, then replaced the PT-109 reprint and pulled Thomas Wolfe's *You Can't Go Home Again* from its place. "If I recall, this takes a fellow in search of his own identity, from New York to Germany to Paris, where he parties with an uninhibited bunch of expatriates." She waggled her finger at Max and shook her head. "Naughty."

Max grimaced.

"But when he returns to America," she continued, "he rediscovers America with sorrow, yet with love and hope. You've held onto this book, so I think Wolfe may reflect your own feelings about the country you've fought for. No?"

"Sometimes," Max admitted, "more than ever since recent elections, seeing my presidents apologize to the world—a world our fighting men and women have saved more than a couple of times and a world our humanitarian organizations have helped in dozens, hundreds of catastrophes."

"Uh-huh." Kat's eyes bore in on his. "Takes me back to heroes, Maximus Braxton, and your disappointment with a nation that fails to appreciate them."

Max stood silent.

"Churchill was at times loved and at times reviled by his colleagues," Kat said. "Solzhenitsyn was loved by many but imprisoned by his own government. JFK was elected president but then assassinated by Lee Harvey Oswald and/or who-knows-who. Yoni Netanyahu? Well, Yoni was killed during an act of heroism."

"But," Max interrupted, "as a direct result of Yoni's operation, the United States military developed extraordinary rescue teams modeled on the Entebbe rescue."

"Still," Kat said, "Yoni died—and he died a hero."

Max shrugged. "You're right. I must love heroes."

"What baffles me," Kat said, "is this one." She pointed to *The Blithedale Romance*. "A communal farm working on anti-capitalist ideals. At least, that's what I remember."

Max nodded. "I found interesting this book tells what happens, even in the mind of the socialist. The commune is destroyed by the self-interested behavior of its members. Bizarre—and telling."

"So—" Kat asked. "Why hold onto the book?"

Max smiled. "It reminds me of a question I'd like answered someday."

"What?"

"A quote from Nathaniel Hawthorne. He wrote a manuscript, but after some sort of harangue with a publisher burned the book."

Kat stepped back. "Really?"

"Yes. He said the book 'deserved a better fate than being published.'"

"That was his explanation?"

"All that I know of."

Kat frowned. "Must have related to his belief in transcendentalism."

Max shook his head. "I can't explain. But if you work out the answer, let me know. Then I can remove the manuscript from my bookcase." He smiled broadly.

"You'll be the first I tell," Kat replied.

A buzzer sounded in the kitchen.

"My entrée," Max declared. "Have a seat, professor." He pulled out the chair for Kat to sit in at the dining table. A snap of her fingers brought Tuck to her side.

She sat down. "Sure I can't help?"

"Just sit there and be beautiful. Your host will take care of the rest."

———— ◆ ————

Max started laying out the meal.

"Israeli salad and haroset," he said, laying down small- and medium-sized serving dishes.

"Ooh, I love Israeli haroset." Kat rubbed her hands.

"Made with walnuts, apples, cinnamon, and sweet wine, but with something they add in Egypt—"

When he didn't expound, Kat asked, "What did they add in Egypt?"

"Wait for it, wait for it," he teased, then answered, "Dates and raisins."

"Aha."

"The salad is cucumbers, tomatoes, and onions garnished with garlic, parsley, and mint, all drizzled with olive oil and lemon juice. And," he said, laying down a flat dish filled with warm pita pockets, "you can stuff the whole works into these if you'd like."

"Oh, my."

Next came a dish of couscous. "I hope you like the chopped celery and ground nutmeg I added," Max said.

Kat's smile broadened. "You bet."

Max stepped back into the kitchen and took a roasting pan out of the oven. He moved the contents, a whole chicken, from the pan into a serving dish, added a herbal garnish and a surround of orange slices, and with a flourish, laid the dish on a hot plate in the center of the table.

"The pièce de résistance," he announced and scrutinized Kat as she surveyed his creation.

"Smells wonderful, looks familiar," she said.

"Israeli Orange Chicken, a recipe from a Sephardic Jewish lady

I know in Tiberias."

"Really? Let's see." Kat smiled as if she possessed particular expertise and reached into the chicken's orifice. Max laughed as she pulled out a whole orange.

"I'm shocked." she declared.

"You're familiar with the dish," Max acknowledged.

"Yes. Orange, honey, onion slices, a few herbs, salt, and pepper—"

"And ginger," Max added.

"If this is anything like I've had before, the taste is genius." Kat remarked.

"Well, let's hope so."

"I feel like I'm back in Israel at a post-dig dinner. After every excavation, we award ourselves with a feast. I'm so impressed. When in the world did you have time to learn to cook like this?"

"Besides Mrs. Herzog and her orange chicken, you mean?" Max smiled. "My Mom, growing up. She said I'd have to cook whether or not I got married, and I should learn the right way, not the microwave way. I can hear her now: 'We may be a microwave society, but I will never consent to its dominion in my house.'"

Kat laughed. "You're an enigma, Colonel Braxton."

"Ha! After such a successful pre-meal psychoanalysis, you're willing to call me enigmatic?"

With a turn at the corner of her lips, she nodded. "Well, mysterious at least."

"Then I've succeeded." Max chuckled and took a seat opposite Kat at the table. "Shall we see if the meal is, in truth, a success, or just looks that way?"

"May we say grace?"

"Of course. Please do."

———— • ◆ • ————

They plowed into the meal as if they hadn't eaten in days.

"Delicious to the nth degree," Kat oohed.

"Thank you."

"A far cry from the hot dogs over the fire on the Israeli National Trail."

He nodded, then said, "That story never appeared in any of the articles I read about you."

Her return look was keen. "What killed me to not include in my interviews was your involvement, Max."

"But I thank you for acceding to my will."

Kat dabbed her napkin on her lips and said, "I want the anonymity to end. I want you by my side, along with my parents, at one special occasion."

"What?"

"Next month, at the Archaeology Festival at Cardiff University, the Royal Archaeological Institute and English Heritage are naming me Archaeologist of the Year. And Danny Arens will be there to receive Rescue Dig of the Year.

Max couldn't help himself. He leaped out of his chair and wrapped his arms around her. *What a girl.*

———— ◆ ————

A half hour later, with Tuck enjoying bits of chicken off a plate on the kitchen floor, Kat sat side-by-side with Max on the couch drinking espresso con panna and nibbling on baklava, which Max admitted was "the one thing I bought. I ran out of time, I'm afraid."

"You're excused." Kat grinned. She sized up the man beside her. Though she'd thought she knew him well through their adventure finding King David's music, there was a lot to him she had not discovered.

Tuck wiggled up close to them, looked at Max and cocked his head as if to thank him for the chicken and ask if he could have a nibble of baklava as well.

Max chuckled and scratched the dog's chin. "You got a hollow leg, boy?"

Tuck seemed to laugh in agreement. Maybe he just liked his chin scratched.

———◆———

Avi Navor stepped out of his limousine and extended his arm toward Lana, who with grace scooted out of her seat and placed her hand on his forearm. The evening had turned cold. Before them was the well-lit Jefferson Drive entrance to the National Air and Space Museum on the Washington Mall. Streetlights glittered along the broad way and revelers, arm-in-arm, some singing, made their way in all directions to parties celebrating the election of their president—the man of transformation.

A block to their left stood the National Museum of the American Indian, and beyond the museum, one of the favorite places in the world of his beloved wife Ruth (God bless her soul): the United States Botanic Garden. To their right, shrouded in darkness, was another of Ruth's favorites: the Mary Livingston Ripley Garden.

This was to be Avi's proudest moment. Indeed, in a way it was. His daughter was stunning. The single pearl hanging from her neck accentuated her beauty. She needed no diamonds, no dazzle hanging from her ears or wrists. Her loveliness shone through her being. Yes, she was the proudest accomplishment of his life and—he thought of his deceased bride—Ruth's as well.

But on the other hand. He looked toward the United States Capitol steps where President Ridley Jones had been sworn into office mere hours before.

Avi glanced at his watch. Just shy of ten o'clock. Fashionably late, but just before the president's expected arrival. He straightened his bowtie—how he hated these blamed things—took a deep breath and turned to smile at Lana.

"Ready?" he asked.

She nodded and flashed the look which had melted him since she was a child.

Avi bent down and spoke through the open door to Stan, his chauffeur. "In forty minutes at this spot," he said and shut the door.

They walked to the front entrance as if he were the father giving away the bride. He winced at the thought as he remembered the death of Lana's fiancé in a terrorist bombing in a Manhattan subway eleven months before.

A tall, jacketed man nodded and acknowledged them by name, holding open the wide door. They stepped inside. A big band somewhere to the left played Georgia-style music with gusto. Despite a trainload of decorations hanging from rafters, a huge faux trellis draped with stunning red, white, and blue flowers and various other decorations attempting to make the place homey, the museum's expansiveness won the battle.

In the center of the floor where happy couples danced, lay a huge carpet emblazoned with the presidential seal.

On the far wall, a mammoth American flag hung at the back of an elevated platform. Smaller American and red-white-and-blue State of Georgia flags stood side-by-side at each end of the dais.

To the right of the reception desk, three ladies stood and waved hellos. Lana left Avi's side to speak to them.

For a moment, Avi regretted not sticking with the original plan to hold the dance in The Willard's Grand Ballroom, which dripped with style and elegance. But then he looked beyond the decorations to the aerial history of a nation he hoped would not dissolve under God's promise to curse any nation which cursed the Jews.

The Spirit of St. Louis, in which Charles Lindberg made the first solo flight across the Atlantic Ocean, hung from the ceiling. To their right, Chuck Yeager's Bell X-1, in which he first broke the sound barrier, dangled in defiance of gravity as did the North American X-15, which would leave Avi's own Gulfstream IV far behind in a cloud of mist.

Avi resisted the impulse to laugh at the thought of his jet racing the X-15. For Avi, this night, meant for dancing, levity, and joy, had turned sour before starting, and he steeled himself for a bad time.

Seeing Avi and Lana arrive, a swarm of people descended, all lighthearted and cheerful. Avi stepped to his right, taking hold of his daughter's hand. He forced smiles, even winked at Lana, but held her right hand close to his side. As popular as she was, he didn't want to lose her into the crowd of revelers. She knew—he was certain she read his mind, always—and remained close.

"Victory." Georgia Attorney General Dana Corey exclaimed.

"Congratulations, Avi. It's your victory as much as anyone's," declared Kazim Carter, the party's state chairman. Carter grabbed Avi's right hand and squeezed it between his two hands.

Atlanta Mayor Shirley Tumlin stood on her toes and kissed his cheek.

Avi deflected their praise with a shake of his head and crooked smile.

All the while, three young men who were active in Georgia's Move On for Jones campaign circled Lana like wolves eyeing a tasty morsel.

Avi turned to Lana. "Gotta go, darling." He pulled her along with him as he stepped away. "We'll speak to you all later," he said and waved.

"Thank you, Papa," Lana said as they got out of earshot. "My abba. My savior." She smiled.

"Honey, take me to where we're to meet Ridley."

They walked past the Early Stage of Flight Room. A male dummy held tight to a sturdy V-shaped rod, soaring on a rare 1894 Lilienthal glider below a large wing *ala* Batman. Then came the 1909 Wright Military Flyer, the world's first military airplane. Then, in the Jet Aviation Room to their left, two jet-age milestones dominated the floor: a German Messerschmitt Me 262, which was the world's first operational jet fighter, and the Lockheed XP-80 Lulu Belle, the prototype for the first full-production, operational US jet fighter.

Four feet off the ground beside the Messerschmitt and Lulu Belle, a McDonnell FH-1 Phantom, the first jet fighter used by the navy and marine corps, seemed to be trying to get airborne.

Avi knew them all well. He had spent hours here, wishing he could put his pilot's license to use flying any one of these marvels.

Finally, they strolled past the America by Air Room to their right. Exceptional men and women. Extraordinary challenges overcome. A history written in dreams, imagination, exhausting work, and sometimes, death.

This display depicted the hard-fought history of a nation deserving to be led by the best the country had to offer. Not by a deceiver.

Lana pointed to a corner room beyond. "There," she said.

Avi's mouth was dry, his throat constricting—familiar pre-battle signals. He remembered his first combat, as an infantryman in the IDF forty years before. His battalion, a couple of whom were non-Israeli religious Jews from the United States, was hunkered down in the grassy high dunes of the Golan Heights, tight to Israel's border with both Lebanon and Syria.

Dry throat? Constriction in the throat? Obvious, a battle lay ahead. Tonight, in Washington his life might not be on the line like against an enemy called Hezbollah, but the lives of many of his countrymen were in danger—and these signs were evidence.

He stepped through a wide entrance into the Simulation Room. The 3D SpaceWalk, the Cosmic Coaster, an F-18 Experience and other interactive "rides"—all were spaced out around the large square area.

Thinking of the Lilienthal glider and scanning this familiar room, Avi grappled with how he must approach the president.

Just then, he heard someone call his name. The voice was familiar, yet strained.

He turned. "Ridley."

Jones flashed a look Avi found curious. *The man wants to be called "Mr. President," Avi thought.*

Jones smiled and nodded at Lana. "You look lovely tonight, Lana." *A nice sentiment but he sounds tense. He'd better be afraid.*

"Thank you, Mr. President," Lana replied.

Secret Service men flanked Jones on either side. His wife, Tamika, was not with him.

"We need to speak alone," Avi said.

"Of course." Jones held up a hand, signaling his security guards to stay in their places, and followed Avi behind the SpaceWalk. *Interesting the ride's Israeli blue, Avi thought.*

Avi turned and looked at Jones in silence. After a few seconds, Jones found the encounter awkward and broke the hush. "I know what you're going to say."

"No, you don't."

"You don't know what I'm facing—" Jones began.

"*You* don't know what you're facing," Avi countered.

"Really, Avi—"

"No." Avi held up his arm as if he were a traffic cop demanding a delinquent driver slam on the brakes. Confidence rose within him. The self-assurance of a billionaire, a man of the world. A warrior.

Avi could read the tinge of dread roiling within Jones. Not mortal panic but the trepidation of a young student called into the principal's office. The exact reaction Avi wanted.

"Ridley, did I not give you a personal guided tour of my homeland?"

"Yes. I remember the time well."

"Well, then, do you remember discovering Eretz Israel is a tiny little plot of land, just one-sixth of one percent of the landmass of the Middle East—about half the size of Lake Michigan?"

Jones nodded.

"And Israel has only two percent of the population of the Middle East. Therefore, the Arabs have far, far more land per person than the Jews?

Jones nodded.

"Did you not observe, first-hand, the Palestinian Authority's and Hamas's incitement to violence in their media and schools, their racist pronouncements calling for a Judenrein Palestinian state?"

Again, Jones nodded.

"Did I not take you on a helicopter flight over the Golan Heights, Ridley?"

Jones twitched like he was wearing a woolen body suit.

"Did I not tell you of the thousands of rockets the Arabs launched from this high perch into the towns along the Sea of Galilee—until we took the Heights?"

Jones nodded.

"Rockets not aimed at soldiers, but at women and children, Ridley?"

Jones sighed deeply.

"Did I not relate the history of Israel giving land—first evacuating South Lebanon in 2000 and, second, Gaza in 2005, dragging people from their homes and livelihoods—only to be rewarded, first, with multiple kidnappings, cross-border attacks and heavy militarization along the border and, second, with unrelenting mortar attacks from Gaza into Jewish neighborhoods?"

Jones nodded, crossing his arms and hunching his shoulders forward. *Defensive and feeling inferior, which he darn well better be.*

"Did I not describe to you the excruciating pain beset upon Jewish people forced from their homes and businesses—businesses which employed many Arabs, by the way—hoping upon hope the terrorists would leave us alone? And what did it accomplish? It gave Hamas a closer target for their unrelenting rocket attacks while using their fellow Arabs as human shields."

"Um-hm. I know this, Avi." Exasperation spilled from the words.

"I don't want to bore you, Ridley. Except this was all lost on you, apparently." Avi's eyes bored into Jones's and the president looked away. "Because I wasn't at your side for the inaugural address, did you think I wouldn't hear your words?"

Jones shook his head.

"Ridley, a simple shake of the head will not suffice." Avi's voice rose.

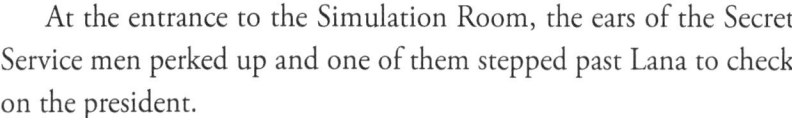

At the entrance to the Simulation Room, the ears of the Secret Service men perked up and one of them stepped past Lana to check on the president.

Lana put her hand on his shoulder. "I wouldn't," she warned.

"POTUS is our responsibility, ma'am," he said.

"I know. But the president and my father are longtime close friends. There is no possibility of violence."

"Nevertheless," the agent said and quick-stepped around the SpaceWalk. Jones spotted him and waved him off. "Leave us be, please," he said.

The agent shrugged. "Yes, sir, Mr. President.

———— ◆ ————

Jones turned back to Avi. "Avi, I have to go. Tamika's waiting. They're all waiting."

"And they can continue to wait."

If Lana had been there she might have noticed the body language, the indicators her father was entering a higher stage of confrontation, the kind she had witnessed time and again in tense boardroom encounters. Ridley had little such knowledge.

"You promised me you would stand by Israel," Avi said. "The word was 'forever.' In fact, you didn't stand with her one day, one hour."

Jones set his jaw. "I've realized as president I must be a realist."

"You don't know realism until a bomb is dropped on your house with you inside." Avi pointed a finger at the man's chest. "I lost three-fourths of my family in the Holocaust, two brothers and a sister in the intifada and so many others I can't count them. I don't intend to sit idly by while that happens again because of American naïveté—your naïveté."

"I'm leaving," Jones said and started to walk away.

Avi grabbed his elbow with his right hand. Jones grimaced. The older man had the grip of a vise.

"You'll leave, but I'll have my say first." Avi ground his teeth in anger. "Let me recount the nails you yourself hammered into the coffin of Israel today. You, you staunch supporter of the only democracy in the Middle East."

Avi held up the index finger of his left hand. "You said there will be no more Jewish emigration to Israel. No more."

He held up his middle finger. "No more checkpoints at the borders of Arab and Israeli lands. Let the bombers in."

He held up his ring finger. "Tear down the protective fencing between violent Arab territories and the Jewish homeland—fencing so obvious in some European countries like Greece, Italy, and Spain. Fencing protecting the Jewish people."

Jones tried to pull away. Avi tightened his grasp.

"I'm just getting started. The worst is yet to come. The unbelievable. The unpardonable." Avi raised his little finger. "While cutting US loans to Israel, you will increase aid to Palestinians."

He raised his thumb. "Israel must approve the Arabs' 'right of return.' You do remember, don't you, Ridley, they left their homes on the Jordanian promise the Arabs would kill all the Jews, driving them into the sea?"

Jones pressed his lips together and shifted his feet.

Avi switched hands, gripping Jones's elbow with his left hand now, and continued his count with the index finger of his right hand. "Israel must withdraw and give up all the land back to pre-1967 borders. Oh, that will help, seeing the Arabs attacked us even when they lived there before."

He raised his middle finger. "Israel must give up East Jerusalem as the Palestinian capital. Right. You do know while Jerusalem is mentioned scores of times in the Jewish holy book, the city is never mentioned, not once, in the Qur'an."

Avi raised his ring finger and snickered. "Oh, yes, this one I thought was comic, although you didn't laugh. Israel must release all Palestinian prisoners except those convicted of terrorist acts. And, for good measure, those murderers left in jail must have computers and cell phones. Computers and cell phones. Are you serious, Ridley? Or crazy?"

Jones shrugged.

"But, finally, the biggest and worst nail of them all, the nail that would remove the last remaining defense since the world has already demanded Israel cannot use forward defense by fighting wars on enemy territory. Israel can have no active defense by militarily disrupting or dismantling its enemies, and the country can use no passive defense such as the blockade to prevent enemy rearmament.

"This final nail—that Israel denuclearize itself. The world does not know if Israel truly does have nuclear weapons, but the simple threat restrains her enemies. Now what?"

Avi loosened his grip, stepped back and looked at his president. "Now what, Ridley?"

Jones shook his head, then aimed a pleading look at him. "Avi, what are we to do when the freedom fighters are at our door? The Mall of the Americas. Hoover Dam—"

"Did I hear you say, 'freedom fighters,' Ridley?" Avi was flabbergasted.

Jones shrugged but did not answer. Instead, he said, "Are we to ignore them? Ignore the carnage, the threat—"

"Ridley, in Israel I lived with the constant threat of mortars, even in my neighborhood, not just on the battlefield." Avi's fury was becoming more difficult to contain. "The answer to your question, Ridley? Do not negotiate with terrorists. You beget more terror because the terrorists—that's Muslim terrorists—see only weakness. The Middle Eastern culture is not American culture, and yet you continue—just as American leaders have done for a century—to operate as though the two were the same. Unbelievable ignorance."

"But we will have more bombs like the Manhattan subway—" Jones pleaded.

Avi held up a hand. Anger seethed at the effrontery of using this example of Muslim terror. "You know I lost my future son-in-law in the Manhattan bombing, Ridley."

"Yes, I know, and you're still blind to the answer." Jones spat out the words.

Avi controlled the urge to slap the man.

"Now you can leave, Ridley. Don't expect me to ever again raise a finger to help your causes."

"But, Avi—"

"But nothing. As a matter of fact, expect me to do everything within my considerable powers to assure your reign is brief and fruitless."

"But, Avi, we've stood for so many of the same things—" Jones protested.

But Avi Navor, his benefactor and mentor, his close friend and longest political supporter, had turned on his heel and walked away.

———— ◆ ————

Ridley Jones looked down at his shiny black shoes, took a deep breath, grabbed his lapels and straightened his disheveled tuxedo. His hands were shaking. His hands never shook. He was never nervous. But in this moment, his hands shook uncontrollably. He felt his heart beating like a drum in his chest. His heart never beat this fast, except now. He took another deep breath and another.

One of his Secret Service protectors stepped into view, but he waved him away. "Give me a minute," he said hoarsely.

He needed time before he felt he could emerge from behind the large SpaceWalk and join the Secret Service agents and then his wife and the hundreds of people celebrating and hailing his ascendancy to the leadership of the free world.

When he and Tanika stepped into the enormous ballroom area of the Air and Space Museum, Avi and Lana Navon were gone.

Chapter Five

A 1956 T-bird replica cruised by the coffee shop, cloth top down. Idiot kid, Max thought of the driver, a boy with his baseball cap twisted askew. *January in Connecticut and the dope has his top down. How does a fellow have the brains to get accepted into Yale but the complete lack of common sense to avoid getting pneumonia?*

"People are funny, aren't they?" Kat's words revealed she was thinking the same thing he was.

"Funny or stupid?" His eyebrow raised, his eyes studying this treasure before him, Max reached for his cup of espresso.

"Funny and stupid. God made all kinds." Kat reached down and stroked Tuck's head, something the dog relished, no doubt. "Even the four-legged kind, eh?"

"He did." A statement. In stone.

"And all kinds attend Yale," she said.

"I'm sure."

"And you'll have all kinds in your class."

"Am I hearing a punch line, or the penultimate statement leading to one?"

Kat's eyes sparkled. She tilted her head, revealing a pearl-studded earlobe. "They're not all spoiled rich kids, Maximus."

Max smiled at the use of his full name. She'd used his name in Petra, in Wales, and now in Connecticut. "Maximus" conjured visions of a Roman centurion, a comparison he liked.

"No?" he quizzed.

"No. The school gives out many scholarships to a wide range of kids—some from, let's say, less favorable neighborhoods. Please don't just consider them all meat for the lions.

Lions. Again, she reads my mind. She's right there with me at the coliseum.

"How do you consider them—those bright kids in your class on semiography?" Max asked.

"Semiology," she corrected. "The study of signs and symbols, like the sculptures in the courtyard outside Beinecke Library—the pyramid represents time; the circle represents the sun; and the cube chance. But, you asked how I consider my students. I think they're thoughtful, intelligent, tending to be liberal like most of us were when we were in college—"

"Little sponges or impervious rock?" Max asked.

"By the time they get to semantics, they're sponges. Early on, in the anthropology classes, for instance, many are there just for the grade, to get the class over with. If they stick with the major to semiology and semantics, they're serious. And, like all of us, they learn better, they desire to know better, when they're interested, when the field of study is one they're eager and curious about." She looked at him with intensity. "You'll find the same to be true in your class—and with far more, um, passion than I do in mine."

"Oh?"

Oh, yeah, Colonel Danger's My Name.

"Colonel Danger's My Name?" Max repeated with a chuckle.

———◆———

Kat was startled. She had thought the words but didn't realize she'd spoken them as well. In her mind, the thought exuded dark humor. She only hoped he wasn't offended.

She smiled enigmatically, then waved her hand as if pointing to a cartoon bubble, "Secretive, black-ops, super-hero Colonel Maximus Braxton." Her green eyes locked onto his, smile lines crinkled ever so slightly, and she added, "The inscrutable always intrigues students."

"And you?"

"Are you asking if the inscrutable intrigues me, too?"

He nodded.

She placed her chin on her fist and made an elaborate display of contemplating an answer. Finally, "Me, too."

"Good."

Just then, a handful of coeds came through the door, spotted Kat, and rushed to gush over her. Kat seemed to know them all and they all adored her. No doubt.

Kat introduced them to Max. Their eyes went wide, they giggled, then collectively guessed they should be on their way and waved bye-bye.

When they'd left, Kat took a moment and buttered a cinnamon-raisin scone which had cooled off in the hour or so they had spent together. She sipped her second cup of green tea and winced as Max downed his second double espresso con panna from a demitasse cup, then swiped the foam from his upper lip with a finger. She had watched John Wayne drain a shot of whiskey the same way in *The Quiet Man.*

The thought somehow gabbed her throat, and she winced.

————— ♦ —————

"I never told you this," Max said, "but espresso, in various forms, is my favorite drink since I swore off hard liquor. Café con leche with steamed milk —sometimes on the side, café Romano—with a twist of lemon, café crème—with an ounce of heavy cream. I'll drink them all. Can't seem to get café Ristretto anywhere in the States, though."

"What's café Ristretto?"

"A very strong shot with only about half the water and double the coffee."

"Very informative." She spoke dryly, but Max spotted a twinkle in her eye. *She's toying with me.*

"How did you become a connoisseur of espresso?" she asked.

Max shrugged. "Here and there. Italy, Austria, Spain, France, Cuba, Latin America, a place or two I can't mention."

————— ♦ —————

I keep discovering there's more to learn about this man. Cuba? What was he doing there?

"I have to admit," Max said, "at one time my favorite was caffé corretto."

"Corretto?" Kat said. "'Corrected' in Italian."

"That's right. the drink is 'corrected' with a shot of brandy or, in my case, cognac. I got acquainted with the drink in a little café in Melbourne, Australia."

"Oh, my. You not only have strong taste buds, but you get around." Kat put a fingertip to her full lips. Her eyes twinkled merrily.

"Hey, *we* got around plenty and in just a few days, remember?" he said. "Petra, Jerusalem, Dublin, Wales, Aitlet—"

"Yes, and I lost count how many times you saved my life."

"And you mine, m'lady." He lifted his cup in a feign toast.

She leaned forward, forgetting the scone, the tea, the people scuffling around them. She didn't notice the coeds, who often sneaked a look at the striking man across from her. Nor did she notice the dark-haired, dark-skinned man with the baseball cap pulled down to his ears and the Yankees jacket who slid through the door, walked in the opposite direction and sidled into a booth, sitting with his back to them. So intent was she on her conversation with Max, she didn't even notice the low growl escaping from Tuck's mouth as he peered at the café's newest customer.

"You know, Max," she said, "I've been researching the symbols associated with certain terrorist groups lately. A curious coincidence, eh?"

He sat back. "I don't believe in coincidence, and I'd love to see what you've found out."

"There's more to discover, but what I've found might help with your class."

"Absolutely."

"Hey, whattaya say we walk a block?" she asked, as lighthearted as she could.

———— ◆ ————

Seconds later they walked out the café door. Tuck, walking alongside his mistress, peered at the back of the man who had slipped into the nearby booth. He seemed to be willing the man to turn around.

———◆———

Max looked over the classroom. He was surprised there weren't fewer students than on Tuesday and guessed attendance had increased. He walked to the whiteboard, popped the top off a blue marker, and began writing:

"You can't say there are good terrorists and there are bad terrorists."

"Good morning, class," he said. "I'd like to share a few of my favorite quotes about terrorism with you. Dennis Miller said, 'If Bill Clinton had only attacked terrorism as much as he attacked George H. W. Bush, we wouldn't be in this problem.'"

The class, settling down, laughed.

"Then there's one from Sam Kinison who said, 'I don't worry about terrorism. I was married for two years.'"

Max smiled as more laughs came from the class. Then he noticed Kat in the back of the room, standing against the wall, shaking her head but smiling.

"More seriously, Bradley Whitford said he heard an Israeli say, 'There's no military solution to terrorism. If there were, Israel would be the safest place in the world.'"

Max paused for a moment, then pointed to the whiteboard. "Let's take a look at this quote. Can anyone tell me who said this?"

"Martin Luther King, Jr.?" a girl up front offered.

"Nope, but good guess," Max replied. "How about you?" he asked, pointing at a young man a few rows back.

"Nelson Mandela?"

"Nope, what about you?" Max asked the girl next to him.

She shook her head. "I don't know, maybe Mahatma Gandhi?"

"No, but all good guesses. All people who spoke about peace. The speaker was Condoleezza Rice, US national security adviser under Bush 43. But we have a dilemma here. How do we separate a terrorist from a freedom fighter?"

"Easy," a student three rows back said with a laugh.

"Really?" Max asked. "What's your name, young man?"

"Brian."

"Okay, Brian, tell me what makes someone a terrorist."

"Well, if you blow up a building or fly into one, like the World Trade Center."

"What if the building were a military complex, full of soldiers?" Max proposed.

"Then it wouldn't be a terrorist act. It would be a military strike," the girl next to the boy offered.

"Good. Now we're getting somewhere. What if there were eighty soldiers, but twenty civilians? Or ninety civilians and ten soldiers? Or a thousand civilians, but one truly lethal dictator, like, let's say, Saddam Hussein? Would a bomb be a terrorist act or a military strike with collateral damage?"

The class was silent, contemplating. Max looked over the room. "That, of course, leads to another interesting question. Must a terrorist act be committed by a nongovernment group, or can the attack also be committed by a government?"

The class was quiet, attentive.

"Does anyone know what FTO stands for?" Max asked.

"Foreign Terrorist Organizations." The words came from the blonde girl, Jill, who had come to his office. Josh was sitting in front of her, his neck twisted around to see her. Jill looked down at Josh briefly, blushed slightly, but continued, "FTOs is a list created by the secretary of state and renewed every two years."

"I can see someone's been doing their reading." Max smiled. "The list is very important and does come out of the office of the secretary of state, but an interagency process creates it. What about you, Hank? Did you do your reading? Name three terrorist groups on the list."

Hank shifted in his seat. "Well, you've got the IRA and the, um, well, the lunch lady in the quad kinda scares me." The class chuckled.

Max joined in. "That's good, Hank. I'll give the FBI a call and have them look into her. It doesn't appear you've even been reading the newspapers, though. Naming three should be a piece of cake. What about you, Josh?"

"I know a few off the top of my head." Josh held up his hand and ticked off his fingers as he listed them, "There's ISIS, al-Qaeda, Hamas, Hezbollah, Islamic Jihad, Abu Nidal—oh, and Hank," he elbowed his friend, "that's the real IRA which is different than the defunct IRA."

"Very good, Josh, but I wouldn't say the IRA is defunct exactly. When we talk about terrorist groups, there are a lot of gray areas,— things get glossed over as splinter groups form."

Max went to the whiteboard again and jotted down a few questions, speaking as he wrote. "I'm going to be giving you overall class assignments. A few of you will be given special tasks, though, throughout the course of the semester. I want you to each pick one of the terrorist groups on the FTO list, which you can find in your reading, and answer the following questions:

"1. Does it matter if the victims are soldiers or civilians?

"2. What if an attack happens during war or peacetime?

"3. What if the act is performed for a good cause, and, if so, how would you define 'good cause'?

"4. Does the threat of attack qualify as terrorism, or does the attack have to take place?

"5. Can governments, or only nongovernment groups, perform acts of terrorism?"

Max stepped away from the board and faced the room. "Put some thought into this. I don't want you brushing the surface. Delve into the group you choose and if you disagree with what the secretary of state has listed as an FTO, don't be shy about expressing your opinions. I like the rebel as long as they put thought and wisdom into their decision."

"How can we disagree with the secretary of state, though?" The question came from the student sitting in front of Hank.

Max turned away and continued writing the questions he had posed on the whiteboard for the students to transcribe for their homework as he answered. "Between you and me and the other couple hundred students in here, who I am sure won't rat me out." Max turned again, smiling. "Government agencies are not always the smartest bunch. Prime example—there was an individual who said, and I quote, 'We plan to eliminate the state of Israel and establish a pure, Palestinian state. We will make life unbearable for Jews by psychological warfare and population explosion. We Palestinians will take over everything, including all of Jerusalem.' This same person won the Nobel Peace Prize in 1994. Yasser Arafat. Now tell me how such a coveted prize could be awarded to a man who said such things?"

"Wait now, the PLO is not on the FTO list anymore," a student in the back interjected.

Max paused. "Yes, thank you for proving my point. As I said, feel free to disagree with the FTO list. Just make sure you back up your findings."

"Can we team up?"

Max looked at the center of the room and noticed Jill had asked the question. "The class can team up in groups of five, except for you. I want you, Josh, Hank and—is your name Jose?" He pointed to a young man sitting in front of Hank who had asked the question. Jose raised his hand and nodded.

"And the girl who pointed out the military strike, what's your name?"

"Ashley," she said, picking up her knapsack.

"I want you five to meet with me down front. The rest of you can be excused, a bit of an early dismissal to get started on your assignment."

The students rose slowly, forming the groups they were going to work with before they left the room. The five Max had chosen grabbed their bags and made their way to the front.

In the back of the classroom, Kat caught Max's eye and waved before turning and leaving through a rear door. He smiled up at her and waved back.

—————— ♦ ——————

"What's up, teach?" The question came from Josh, who had reached the lectern.

"I've got a special project for you five." Max handed them each a red packet, sealed with what looked like the official stamp of the CIA.

"Whoa, cool. What's this?" Jose asked.

"Yes, very cool," Max smiled. "It's not really official CIA stuff, but I want you to pretend it is. You're now CIA operatives. Well, desk jockeys, actually."

"Desk jockeys?" Hank asked.

"Yes, not every CIA gig is an exciting James Bond field-operative scenario. You're familiar with '3-D worlds'?"

"Yeah," Jill said. "My little brother plays them all the time. There's a bunch out there."

"Take the most sophisticated 3-D world you've seen and multiply the complexity by a million. The result is the world you're going to enter into."

Max grabbed a long packing roll, popped off the cap, and pulled out a blueprint.

"What's the drawing?" Jose asked.

"Pull the desk over here." Max pointed to an empty desk near the wall. While Josh and Hank did so, Max took the lectern off the desk in the center, and they pushed the two desks together. Then he laid down and smoothed out the blueprint.

"Looks like a topographical map of the world, but in 3-D." Hank exclaimed.

"It's much more complex," Max said. "If we lift the edge up slightly, and layer this clear plastic cover down, you'll also see a geopolitical map. But here comes my second favorite part of this masterpiece." Max flipped over another clear plastic cover.

"What are those?" Jill pointed at mock thumbtacks appearing over the map, invisible before the plastic layer was applied.

"Those are your hotspots. Here, here, and here," Max pointed to locations on the map, "are examples of concentrations of intelligence operations. They're marked as red. Your objective is to stay clear of the red zones. Here and here are examples of banks offering anonymity for a price. They're marked as blue."

"What are those black ones?" Ashley asked.

"Those are black-market contacts. Those are your friends because you'll be playing the role of terrorists who need to launder your money. Now, Hank, I believe this will get you reading your material, because you need to learn how to do this properly, without getting caught."

"You said this was your second favorite part of this project. Is there another part to it?" Jill asked.

"I'm glad you asked." Max flashed a mischievous smile, rolled up the blueprint and slid the roll back into the packaging sheath. "Any of you got a vehicle?"

Less than a ten-minute drive away, Max, Jose, and Ashley in Max's vintage Mustang, followed by Hank, Josh, and Jill in Hank's Mini Cooper pulled up at a converted warehouse.

"Hey, teach, what's in here?" Josh asked, stepping out of the Mini Cooper.

"Dude," Hank said, "the teach drives a V8 Mustang and we're in a Mini. I'm feeling a bit emasculated."

"Actually, I've restored her with a V12." Max grinned. "More importantly, the fourth floor of this renovated warehouse is going to be your new home-away-from-home." He pointed up to the top floor. "Let's go, and I'll show you."

They opened a small contraption similar to a freight elevator, slid aside the iron grate, and Max pressed the fourth-floor button.

"Is this yours?" Jill asked.

"It's rented, courtesy of the dean, though he doesn't know it yet."

Hank slid open the iron grate when they reached the fourth floor. A short dark hallway was lit with one bulb hanging limply from a thin wire. An iron door stood beneath the bulb. Max grabbed his keys, unlocked and pushed the door open. When he did, lights came on around a large room. A large semicircular table in the center was covered with monitors and a laptop. The desk and five chairs were hard steel.

"Welcome to Operation Mongoose," Max said.

"Mongoose?" Josh repeated, stepping into the room.

"Yup. Wait. You kids haven't even opened up your dossiers yet?" Max said.

They looked down at their red files, slid their fingers through the round seals holding them shut, and opened them up.

"Whoa, what's this?" Hank asked.

"The details of your operation," Max said. "But I'm too excited to go over those now. Let's look at the pièce de résistance."

He flipped open a laptop and powered it on.

"Why so hot in here, man?" Jose asked.

"It's not only hot in here, but you'll notice there are small devices taped to the windows. This is a mock secure facility," Max said. "Those devices give off small vibrations, meaning no one can use subsonic listening devices here."

"Subsonic what?" Ashley asked.

"Your vocal chords create vibrations which your eardrums interpret into sounds, those sounds into words. Miraculous, really, considering how much I simplified the process. Those same vibrations also bounce off other objects in your vicinity. Windows, for example, and windows can carry sound through them, allowing listening devices to pick up on the vibrations. The subsonic devices mask the vibration of your voices. And the heat?" Max looked at Jose. "It's the same as your outer-body temperature. No one can pick up thermal readings to see when the room is occupied or when it's not."

"The only things kept cool in here are the computers," Max tapped the laptop lovingly.

"Isn't this a little over the top, Mr. Braxton?" Jill asked.

"I believe in not doing anything if you're not going to do the best," he replied.

"And the dean is picking up the tab? Dude, the bill's gotta be like, what, ten grand?" Hank asked.

"Let's just say nothing's too good for my students, shall we?" The laptop had loaded and Max flipped a switch on the metal desk, flooding the monitors with light, all interconnected with the laptop.

"Hey, I'm no computer genius," Josh said. "I'm not so sure I can operate this thing."

"Piece of cake, man," Jose jibed. "I can handle the tech side of this Mongoosey operational thingamajiggy." He sat down and clicked on the sole icon on the desktop.

Max had stepped back to watch their initial reaction and track how well they would work together. This was by far the most sophisticated project he had established for the semester.

"Well, Jose, if you get stumped and need a blonde with brains behind the keyboard, let me know." Ashley smiled.

The application filled each monitor.

"Did you build this, prof?" Jose asked.

"No, a friend of mine from, well, from a government branch built it for me. The monitors have varying data, as you can see. This one up here," Max pointed to the top left, "has your contact list. The next one holds streaming data. These are bank accounts filtered through all the international banks across the globe. The center screen is the largest because it's the electronic version of the blueprint you saw earlier. You can layer the topographical map, geopolitical map, and hotspots all together or separately."

"This is amazing. Is all this data real?" Ashley inquired.

"Some, yes. The monitor to the right of the center screen folds in mock feeds from international intelligence agencies. That data is most definitely not real. The last monitor to the right is our three-degrees screen."

"Three-degrees screen?" Jill repeated.

"Yup, you've heard of the six-degrees game?"

"You mean, like the six degrees to Kevin Bacon game?" Hank posed.

"Exactly. Pick any movie or any actor and within six turns you can find how they relate to Kevin Bacon. Well, we're a bit more sophisticated than a cheesy campfire game. We've got three degrees. Essentially, it's a social networking map of all intelligentsia. Jose, type in the name Jackal."

Jose fingered some keys and a profile photo of the infamous international assassin known as Jackal popped up in the middle of the screen, with a web of lines coming out from him and pointing to several names, scattered all over the screen.

"Cool." Jose exclaimed.

"It's confusing to me, though," Jill said.

"Jose, click on the white box in the legend at the top of the monitor there," Max instructed. "As you can see, this filters the list. Now you can only see those members of the intelligence agencies affiliated with the Jackal. Most likely, these are all members involved in the hunt."

"Most likely?" Josh asked. "What else could it mean?"

"Well, this program isn't maintained manually. We don't have agents keying in connections. The software pulls in bank data, phone records, and ties, within three degrees, all related parties."

Jose crossed his arms. "So, hypothetically speaking, one of those filtered out through the white box there could be a rogue member of law enforcement? Like dirty cops or something?"

"Yes," Max answered. "Hypothetically speaking, you're correct. If you filter through the black box there, all the black-market members show up. If you click on the blue box, then all those who are filtered are not recognized as law enforcement and have no criminal records. These are just innocent society members somehow involved."

"How so?" Jose asked.

"Well, even villains need lairs." Max smiled."

"I'm, like, so lost, man," Hank said, putting both hands on his head.

"The long and short of it is this, folks," Max said. "You're CIA desk jockeys pretending to be bad guys who need to launder money. You need to find out how the real bad guys would do it. What would be their route?"

"And you're saying we'll succeed in finding a way to do it?" Josh asked.

"What I'm saying is, you'll find several ways. This is your own virtual world. You can zoom in on the map in the center and even create your own mock characters to walk from shop to shop. It's static satellite imagery, fed and refreshed once every two hours."

"No way," Hank said. "I've watched enough movies to know this can't be true. Satellites orbit the earth and cost billions of dollars just to re-task."

"Mostly true, but you're missing the obvious. Several satellites orbit the earth, feeding us constant imagery. We're not re-tasking anything, we're just downloading the imagery every few hours."

"Yeah, dude, seriously. I'm sure they're a bit more sophisticated than Google Earth." Josh cracked.

"Listen, guys, read through your red folders. Understand most of what you'll see is dummy data, aside from the satellite imagery. Do not share your key to this door with anyone else and do not let anyone else up here. Not to impress any girls or any guys. I'll not only flunk you immediately, I'll get you expelled. Understood?"

"Yes, Mr. Braxton," Jill said. They all nodded in agreement.

"Here's your key. Just this one. The five of you should come in together, not alone, so you shouldn't need more than one key. Jill, I'll entrust it to you. Any questions, the door to my office is always open and my cell number's in the red folder."

———•◆———

The Atlanta Financial Center is a stunning structure—a black-aluminum- and glass-frame design with elegant granite and marble lobbies. Two thirteen-story towers interconnect with one another, and a nineteen-story centerpiece looms above the landscape like a scary stealth bomber.

The gateway to Atlanta's Buckhead financial district, the upper floors loom out over the six-lane Peachtree Road and the GA 400 beyond as if to subdue the peons around and about the building.

The myriad tenants include a bank, a communications giant, and several high-profile businesses as well as the City Club of Buckhead and the Athletic Club and Spa.

Avi Navon belonged to the athletic club and spa where he kept his sixty-three-year-old body in shape on treadmills and various workout hardware, stretched his muscles in the pool, and received what were—outside of a certain Dead Sea spa—the best massages on earth.

But today was a work day and "work" this day meant untangling every fiber of his being, every nuance of his support, and every contraption of his business having been connected in any way with Ridley Jones. He intended to do so using the acumen he had employed in building those same ties.

Avi sat behind his desk in his corner office on the fourteenth floor of the Financial Center's East Tower. His assistant, Jonas Mandrell, sat in a chair to the right of his desk. Chief Financial Officer Dan Ogilvy was seated next to Jonas, and Lana stood at Avi's side.

Avi's eyes and mind were focused on Dan, who returned his gaze with apologetic eyes. "They won't give the money back, Avi. Not a dime of it," Dan said.

Avi had no reason to question him. He was his oldest friend in America, like a brother to Avi and an uncle to Lana, and an important cog in the import-export company crucial to launching him into the stratosphere of successful entrepreneurs.

"How much?"

"Four-point-two million."

"Do we go public to ask for the money back and see if they back down to pressure?"

"Perhaps."

Lana interjected: "We could use the issue to embarrass Ridley and tell how he has reneged on his promises."

Avi steepled his fingers. He thought he liked the suggestion. "Let's chew on the idea. Remember what Chinese philosopher Lao Tse wrote."

Lana chuckled. "No disaster is greater than underestimating the enemy."

"You've learned well, dear," Avi said.

"But, as John Adams said, 'Facts are stubborn things,'" Dan said. He reached over, placed a hand on Lana's hand and added with a wink, "And we have Ridley's promises on videotape in his speeches as well as in emails and letters to Avi and others."

"Egregious and brazen promise-breaking," Avi agreed.

The next hour was spent spinning a whirlwind of ideas.

Dismantling the Jones for President website Avi's team had created was easy, but taking down the site wouldn't affect Jones now he was in office.

Disassembling the Move Forward for Jones election team was already basically completed since the election last November, so the impact of its removal was nil as well.

However, the court of public opinion is the soft underbelly of any politician and could be targeted, most notably among many of the major financial contributors Avi had recruited to support this young upstart from Atlanta.

True, he was now "leader of the free world." But Avi had played a key role in catapulting him into his presidency, and Avi figured he could de-rotate the torque that powered Ridley's catapult. Jones's supposed undying support of Israel was the common cornerstone for many of these donors. Pulling the plug on their bankroll could be like a run on a bank.

Financially, all of them would be in the same boat as Avi. They had given their money. They would never get their contributions back. But they could expose the president's character.

Chapter Six

Friday, January 24

Ned Zapper, President Jones's chief of staff, stood in the doorway of the western entrance to the Oval Office. He felt like a guardian. Behind him was the president's private study where Jones's secret personal phone could ring at any moment. Before him, Jones sat at his desk listening to reports from two men just as secretive as that telephone.

This room inspired awe, and he didn't know if he would ever overcome the sensation. From where he stood, the distance was twenty-nine feet to a set of doors leading out to the Rose Garden to the east. The room was a full thirty-five feet from the fireplace on the northern wall on his left to the three tall, south-facing windows behind the president's desk. The domed ceiling was eighteen feet high at its peak.

Maintenance had not yet installed Jones's new oval carpet, but Zaps was eager to see the huge rendition of the eagle and the dove he had helped Tamika Jones design. The rug would be the perfect complement to this room, from whose walls history seeped. Before Zaps was born, a young JFK broke the news of the Cuban missile crisis to the country from this room. When Zaps was a youngster,

President Reagan addressed the nation from this room about the Challenger space shuttle disaster. Bush 43 addressed his fellow Americans about the World Trade Center attack on 9/11 from this room when Zaps was teaching theology and government at Georgetown University, and just before he had converted to Islam.

Here, presidents and their trusted colleagues had planned policy changes transforming the financial mechanisms of the country, political campaigns turning ne'er-do-wells into Speakers of the House and Presidents of the Senate. From this same room, opponents' reputations had been destroyed, wars moving nation-state boundaries were executed—leading to the deaths of millions and creating heroes and traitors.

And here, just four days into office, Zaps stood in wonder. Zaps had never been modest about his capabilities, but now as the highest-ranking member of the Executive Office of the President, he realized he was the second most powerful person in Washington. As Chief of Staff, he was gatekeeper to the president. If someone wanted in—no matter how rich or famous—they went through Zaps.

He could not aspire to the presidency; such ascendancy had never happened before for anyone in his position and wouldn't for him, either. So, personally, this was most likely the apex of his potential for changing the culture of this country, and he was darn well going to take advantage.

Zaps and Ridley had been as close as brothers in college. He had taken the younger Jones under his wing, guided him through freshman orientation, helped him plan his course schedule, and led him as a pledge to join his fraternity. They had disconnected for a while after college—until Ridley decided to run for the presidency. But now they were together, and Zaps intended to make the most of the renewed association.

So here he stood, attentive to the goings-on in front of him, apprehensive about the red telephone. "If it rings," Ridley had said, "let me know, no matter what."

President Jones and his two confidants were gathered to plot methods to devastate the fortune and reputation of a former associate of the president. And not just an associate, but an ally who, until three days ago, had been devoted to and enthusiastic about Jones's ascendancy to this very office.

Zaps shook his head at the thought. Now was too late for a preemptive strike because Navon had already gone public with his negativism. He considered how Jones's predecessors had delved into this dark world of vengeance. Every president compiled an enemies' list and pity the poor fool whose name occupied space there. They could expect surreptitious calls to the Internal Revenue Service, break-ins into psychiatrists' offices to dig up dirt, and character assassinations.

Nothing was beneath some people. A half-century ago, LBJ's Daisy Girl ad sealed the fate of Barry Goldwater's presidential campaign. Even earlier in the nation's history, Thomas Jefferson's opponents circulated a red-devil-eye drawing of the candidate.

Today's victim? Avi Navon.

"Why take Navon out? What's the worst he can do?" asked White House Communications Director Paxton Twill.

"His power exceeds finances," said Trevor Madden, a senior aide who was as short and obese as Twill was tall and skeletal. "Even his influence on the Jewish vote is minor compared to his pull among the major financiers of the world. He can shake stock markets."

"Then we need to distance the president from him before discrediting him to the world," said Twill, "but we must do both—distance and discredit."

"I announced my candidacy in his home," Jones said, his chin on his chest.

"Obama was successful in deflecting the fact he announced in the home of a domestic terrorist, William Ayers," said Madden. "It can be done."

"It's a tricky business, concerning how close he's been to the campaign from its inception," said Twill. "But we've got the playbook from Clinton and Obama. You're right, Trev. It can be done."

"I don't want to know how," Jones said.

"You shouldn't and you won't." Twill stood, straightening his bowtie and the lapels of his designer suit coat. He ran a hand over a close-cropped, nearly bald head. "Leave it to me, Mr. President."

"We'll leave you be, sir," Madden said, lifting his bulk out of his chair.

Just then the telephone rang in the president's private den. A moment later, Zaps stepped into the room. "Mr. President, it's your call—"

"Okay, Zaps. I'm coming." Jones rose as well. "Good luck, gentlemen. Do not, I repeat, do not underestimate Avi Navon."

———— • ————

As Jones disappeared past him, Madden whispered to Twill, "Sometimes the *quickest* answer to a problem is also the best solution."

Twill's face twisted into a question mark.

"Accidents happen, Paxey. Accidents happen," Madden said.

Twill put a hand on Madden's chubby arm. "You don't mean—"

"I do mean."

"You're courting danger, Trev. Hell, you're courting jail." Twill's voice rose and he caught himself, looking over his shoulder toward Jones's private office. The door was closed and both Jones and Zapper were on the other side. He turned back to Madden and murmured, "Besides, how would you find somebody with the wherewithal to accomplish such a thing?"

"This discussion has to happen elsewhere," Madden said. "Far away."

"The Reflecting Pool," Twill said.

"The Reflecting Pool," Madden agreed and the two men left.

———◆———

Max hadn't heard the inaugural speech, but what he was hearing secondhand was disturbing. Radio talk shows, Fox News and commentary broadcasts, Twitter and conservative blogs were still buzzing three days after the inaugural address with complaints, counter-complaints, derision, approval, acquiescence, ambivalence—every emotion.

Although the major news outlets and newspapers across the country avoided deep analysis, the airways and social media were filled with blurbs and sound bites. Israel's ambassador to the United States was in a dither and unable to schedule an audience with the president. Israel's prime minister was "waiting for clarification."

Max decided to read the entire original text. When done, his face was red. What could have brought this about? He felt a prodding—a familiar, unrelenting poking.

In the early afternoon, Max walked to Sterling Memorial Library, a tall stone structure resembling a Catholic church that stood just a block away from the Beinecke. Once he found the periodicals section, he sat down for an afternoon read-and-search. *This college teaching is cool—a one-hour class twice a week. What do these professors do with their time? And no wonder they want to preserve the rule of tenure.*

Three hours later, he checked his notes. The fact President Jones's father, Reginald, was a US diplomat and had been stationed several places around Southeast Asia and the Middle East was well publicized. Ridley, in fact, had been born in Indonesia and had grown up living with his parents in Malaysia, Saudi Arabia, Uzbekistan, United Arab Emirates, and Bahrain. There was a brief debate whether he could legally be president because he was born abroad, but his parents' citizenship status negated such an idea.

Jones had employed his background as a positive, declaring himself "a citizen of the world," familiar with other cultures—something to which every American should be exposed or aspire.

When a photo emerged of a teenaged Jones dressed in Muslim attire, political opponents pounced on the impression this picture portrayed. Jones countered he had, in fact, attended a Muslim school while his father was stationed in Saudi Arabia, but his father declared his schooling was because he wanted Ridley to understand "other world views" than the West's.

Then there was a Nile TV interview given the previous year with the Egyptian foreign affairs minister who disclosed "the American Democrat nominee for president told me in confidence he is a Muslim." This, Jones said, was a misinterpretation by the Egyptian.

Nevertheless, like Barak Obama before him, Jones appeared ready to bend over backward to accommodate one deeply problematic organization, the Muslim Brotherhood (or *Ikhwan*), who purported to wage "a kind of grand *jihad* eliminating and destroying Western civilization from within and 'sabotaging' its miserable house by their hands and the hands of the believers so Allah's religion is made victorious over all other religions."

Stretching his knotted neck and shoulder muscles, Max found a vacant couch to relax on and think this through.

Could it be? No, the president had declared in no uncertain terms he was a "committed Christian." He wouldn't say such a thing if he were not. Muslims killed people who converted from Islam to Christianity.

Was Jones being blackmailed by terrorists? Max could even hear the words out of their lips: "Give in or we will continue to blow up your country."

They had proven they could do so in the most egregious ways and populated places.

President after president had declared America does not negotiate with terrorists. Yet George W. Bush had met with Yasser Arafat, a terrorist's terrorist, and the little weasel was even awarded the Nobel Peace Prize. Palestinian Authority President Mahmoud Abbas had been Arafat's right-hand man with the paramilitary Hezbollah, yet he was welcomed to the White House again and again by multiple presidents.

So much for the proclamation we do not negotiate with terrorists. So, was Jones giving in to jihadists in an even more substantial way?

Max signed out an autobiography Jones had penned, *Dreams to Fulfill*, the center of which contained numerous photographs.

A minute later, Max stepped out of the library. A cold wintry blast met him. He turned to huddle in a crevice of the building, pulled his cellular phone from a pocket and dialed. He had no numbers stored in his cell—in case the phone got into the wrong hands. He kept his contact list in his head.

The call was picked up on the first ring. "Yes."

"It's Max."

"Ah-h. Semper fi, my friend. Your book? A great read."

"Semper fi and thanks."

"The guys all love how you tell it straight."

"No other way."

"What's up?"

"I need your help."

When Max put away his cell moments later, he turned and scanned the snow-covered lawn fronting Sterling Memorial Library. Students were coming and going, but the movement catching his attention came from a tiny stone outbuilding to his left about fifty feet away. Was the motion a man scurrying behind the building or a trick of the eye? If so, was the person the same one he spotted in the mirror at the café the other day?

Max hurried down steps to ground level in the direction of the building, but two coeds stepped in front of him. "Mr. Braxton!" one of them enthused. "I'm so glad to run into you."

"Excuse—" he started to say as he attempted to sidestep them, but a third student joined the group. "Sir," he said, "can I have a word, too?"

Max shook his head in resignation and spoke to the students while looking over their shoulders to spot if anyone came out from behind the building. No such luck.

When the students went on their way, Max rushed to the little building. Along the way, he patted the Glock 23 in his IWB holster at his right hip. Simple security. Once there he discovered a single set of footprints with a unique swirling tread—man's size ten, he guessed. What good reason would someone have to be standing in this spot? He followed the footprints around the back and side of the building to the footpath, where they joined in with dozens of others.

———————— ♦ ————————

An hour later, walking from a campus parking lot to the nearby Wooster Square area of New Haven en route to Kat's address, Max familiarized himself with the surroundings. Winter's early darkness had set in.

The square sat east of downtown across State Street. A statue of Christopher Columbus, standing high atop a base of large rocks, watched over Wooster Square Park. The cherry blossom trees looked naked and cold against the chill. Across one street stood St. Michael's Catholic Church, snow-white trimmed in gold.

People strolled along the sidewalks, no hustle, no bustle. *What a contrast to Manhattan.* Max pushed aside his months of covert work at the United Nations.

Along the streets, small flags in the red, green, and white colors of Italy hung from the top of streetlights, telling visitors they were in Little Italy. The title was even emblazoned on signs and store awnings. Frank Pepe's Pizzaria, the home of the American pizza, nearly shouted out "old-time landmark here." In stark contrast, the elegant Tre Scalini Restauranté reflected wintry surrounds off shiny black granite and glass.

Max checked the reflection to see if his friend from outside the library was tailing him. No sign.

He crossed the street at a light and a few yards along the sidewalk retraced his steps and re-crossed at the same light. No sign.

Then he rushed across the street and quickly covered the three blocks to the street number Kat had given him. Again, he checked—still no tail.

An interesting building. He sized up the converted warehouse that reminded him of the bat cave, his home for Operation Mongoose. He pressed the buzzer to Kat's apartment. A moment later, she buzzed him in.

One flight up wide stairs, a heavy door opened. Kat's broad smile greeted him. Beside her, Tuck's tail wiggled like an airplane propeller.

Behind her, a wide room with huge floor-to-ceiling windows. Kat stood before him, exquisite, even in casual clothes.

"Love your place, love your dog." He crouched down and scratched Tuck's chin.

"Thank you."

Kat waved him inside. Looking about him at rich but comfortable furnishings, Max figured the apartment could have been grandiose. *The lady has taste.*

Kat gave him a tour, which consisted of the enormous great room containing a kitchen, dining and living room area. Max guessed the room covered eight hundred square feet. From a large bedroom with sliding doors onto a small deck, they could see the Quinnipiac River lit up in the darkness not far away. The large bathroom had two sinks and a grand walk-in tub.

"Have a tub." He laughed.

"I do," she responded with a smile.

A thick butcher-block table stood like an anchor in the kitchen area. A small, round bistro table was nearby.

After a delicious meal, they sat in a lush, brown leather love seat.

"I can't match your espresso con anything, so here's my neighborhood's version of fine coffee," Kat said as she set down two mugs of steaming coffee and a plate with three pastries. "I admit the cannolis are from Libby's Pastry Shop and the coffee is from Fuel— the best brew you'll ever taste in this wee village if not Connecticut, by the way, Mr. Braxton. But the entertainment will be mine."

Max raised his eyebrow.

She laughed and slapped his shoulder. "Don't misinterpret."

He raised his hands, palms-up. "I plead innocent. How do you know I wasn't hankering after the coffee and cannolis?"

She shrugged.

"We'll see how yours compare to Mike's in Boston's North End."

"Game on," she scoffed and shook her head playfully.

"Here's what I meant by 'entertainment.'" Picking up a remote control, she pushed a button and a large flat-screen television came to life on the opposite wall.

"Voilà! Me—the entertainment." Kat exclaimed. A professional video began to play. "A little documentary being shown on Discovery Channel next month. This is its local premiere."

"Truly?" Max's interest was piqued, and he sat forward. "A premier for the two of us?"

Kat nodded.

"I wish I'd brought a red carpet for you to stroll down," he said.

"There's a carpeting store up the street. I'll wait." She smiled.

Max began to stand, then she pulled him back down to the sofa. "Sit." she said. The word was firm, the tone lighthearted.

They both settled in to watch the documentary.

On the screen, Kat stood atop a hill.

Looking keenly at Kat and the small city spread across a valley behind and below her, Max turned to her. "Stop right there, will you?"

Kat did as he asked, and he stood and walked to the screen, pointing. "So, this isn't about the dig on Dragot or your discovering the music?"

She shook her head no.

"This is a different story?"

She nodded.

"I think I've been there," he said.

"When?"

"Five, six years ago." Max hesitated and scratched his chin while scrutinizing the landscape. "Is it the Golan Heights?"

Kat hesitated, then nodded.

"Near Kiryat Shmona?"

"You amaze me, Maximus Braxton."

Max turned to look at her and shrugged. "I've been around is all."

"Well, you're looking at the biblical city of Dan in the valley behind me. It's just a mile or so from Kiryat Shmona where there've been some interesting digs. In fact, that's where I was working when you saved my bacon in Tiberias."

"You never mentioned."

"Well, we had the greatest find of the millennia on our minds, didn't we?"

He figured his smile made him look silly. But Kat didn't seem to think so.

"Okay, so you were standing in a dangerous place even before jihadists came after the two of us. When I was there," he pointed again to the television, "Hezbollah was bombing Kiryat Shmona mercilessly."

"Yep. No different than thousands of years ago, ever since the Jews took over, long before Hezbollah, long before Islam." Kat straightened in the loveseat. "In Judges 18, men from the Hebrew tribe of Dan spied out that territory and reported *We have seen the land and indeed it is very good.* Then the prophet Micah told the Danites they would find a secure people and large land but God would give the region into their hands. He said the site was *a place where there is no lack of anything that is on the earth.*

"Well, the land may not lack anything," Max said. "I remember a nature preserve filled with eucalyptus, pistachio, oak trees, the Dan River—"

"And the history is fascinating," Kat said. "There, in the mid-ninth century BCE, King Hazael of Damascus invaded and conquered the Israelite territory. Digs have found the oldest known gated archway in the world, King Jeroboam's temple he built to house a golden calf, early Bronze Age stone fortifications—all sorts of treasure."

Max returned to sit beside her. "Which of those digs is this film about?"

Kat smiled broadly. "None of them."

He looked at her questioningly.

"Do you know what a stele is? S-t-e-l-e?" she spelled.

Max shook his head.

"A stone slab or pillar, usually engraved and set upright. There's one in Dan, describing Hazael's victory. The pillar was smashed by Jehoash, king of Israel, who fought the Aramaeans three times and recovered the territory around the city of Dan. That broken stele is one of the most important finds in Israel and the first nonbiblical text mentioning the House of David by name."

Impressed, Max nodded.

"Until then, there were a lot of naysayers claiming King David never existed."

"Really?"

"It's all in 2 Kings 13:25," Kat said. "What is *not* in the Bible is what this documentary is all about."

Kat had aroused Max's interest. He had turned to face her and was locked in on her green eyes, captivated by her exuberance.

"Well?" he said.

"Watch," she answered and turned back toward the monitor, pressing the Play button.

The story unfolded of an archaeological dig Kat led in the hills to the south of the city of Dan.

As an aerial video showed the general topography of the land, a man's rich baritone declared in a voice-over: "Lying along the main trade route between Damascus and the Galilee, and with the Dan River being one of the three main sources of the Jordan River, Dan was an important strategic outpost. Indeed, the city was the most important in the northern part of the Kingdom of Israel.

"Archaeologists in the past have discovered evidence of settlement dating to the Neolithic and Chalcolithic communities of the sixth to fourth millennia BCE. Israelites, Aramaeans and Assyrians fought throughout the Iron Age to control the city."

Suddenly, the monitor showed a symbol of two equal-sized overlapping squares, one turned on an angle. The result was an octagon. A small circle occupied its center.

"This is the Rub El Hizb," the moderator said. "For many decades, the symbol was thought to have originated as Islamic, designating the Qur'an was divided into sixty groups of roughly equal lengths. In Arabic, 'Rub' means one-fourth while 'Hizb' means a group or party.

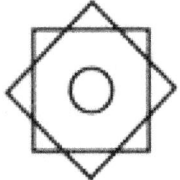

"The ancient civilization of Tartessos, based in Andalusia (a map flashed on the screen, indicating Andalusia's location as a large autonomous community in southern Spain on the Mediterranean) used an eight-pointed star as its symbol. This has suggested the origin of Rub el Hizb, in truth, lay with the Tartessos because Islamic dynasties conquered and ruled Andalusia for eight hundred years.

"For centuries, Muslims have used the Rub El Hizb in a variety of ways—from the coats of arms of both Turkmenistan and Uzbekistan to the official flag of Azerbaijan and the octagonal ground plan of the Umayyad Dome of the Rock shrine."

Max had seen this symbol before but never conferred any significance on it.

The moderator continued, "As I say, until now experts thought it an original Islamic symbol or at least one co-opted from Tartessos. But a recent dig, led by Dr. Kathrine Cardova of Yale University's Department of Archaeology, disproves the notion. Dr. Cardova is a world-renowned expert in semiology, the study of signs and symbols.

"She and her colleagues have, indeed, unearthed proof the Rub el Hizb originated with King Hazael, the ruthless Syrian who became king by suffocating his sovereign leader and seizing his throne. Dr. Cardova has discovered evidence proving Hazael created the Rub el Hizb to signify 'Terror for victory's sake' and the symbol was meant to terrorize Hazael's countrymen."

Max harrumphed. "How fitting," he said.

Kat appeared on screen from her waist up. Several people—picks, trowels and tiny brushes in hand—knelt in small quadrants behind her, carefully removing dirt from the site. Kat raised her hand, showing a small coin about the size of a halfpence.

"We discovered this and similar coins in the remnants of an ancient home from the early 1800s BC," she said. "The symbol is the Rub el Hizb and says in Aramaic, 'Terror for victory's sake.'"

"King Hazael, the Aramaean who ascended to his throne through murder, fought with terror, conquered with terror, and ruled by terror for thirty-seven years until 805 BC. Terror was in his DNA. He wanted his subjects to be reminded every time they paid for or were paid for something, terror awaited them if they strayed from his control.

"Hazael died, and with him, the coins went out of favor. But the symbol reappeared more than a millennium later with the advent of Islam."

A close-up of the coin replaced Kat on the screen. The image of the Rub el Hizb on the coin was then superimposed onto the Turkmenistan coat of arms, the Azerbaijan flag, the Kazakhstan customs flag, an old Moroccan flag, and finally, the octagonal ground plan of the Umayyad Dome of the Rock shrine on the Temple Mount in Jerusalem.

In the voice-over, the moderator said, "Dr. Cardova makes a convincing argument about the origins of the Rub el Hizb."

Again, Kat, her face now framed tightly, spoke to viewers. "In their time, Muslims knew without doubt, the terrorizing message of the Rub el Hizb. Yet a fanatic Muslim society, cloaked in mystery, used the symbol as its own."

The moderator asked, "What is this mysterious group of terrorists?"

"Warriors for Allah," Kat declared. "We've found written materials about the creation of this group in a nearby plot, where artifacts have been dated to the ninth century AD—about two hundred years after Mohammed's death in 632 AD and fourteen hundred years after King Hazael's reign.

"The Warriors emerged to help Allah conquer new lands, terrorizing along the way, forcing people of other religions to convert to Islam or die. While Islamic armies fought other soldiers, this group terrorized the women and children, the elderly and invalid, the preachers and teachers of other religions—not on the battlefield but in the homes, the places of worship, at watering holes, and other public places. Just as King Hazael had done and just as Mohammed did and tells them to do in their holy book: Not just kill, but kill with trauma and shock and severe suffering; behead, disembowel, use the most barbaric attacks possible."

The moderator asked, "As a semiologist, have you discovered what the parts of the Rub el Hizb signify?"

"Yes." Using a pencil, Kat pointed to the symbol on the coin she held. "The Warriors for Allah's internal writings reveal the little circle in the middle signifies Islam's Allah is the beginning and the end. All else emanates from him. This imitates the Judeo-Christian God declaring he is the Alpha and the Omega.

"The eight points of the octagon denote the areas of the human body designated to be cut off because of sins of unbelief: two legs, two hands, the eyes, the ears, the tongue and, finally, the head. Any of these could, in the eyes of the Warriors, lead a person to sin against Allah, so they deserve to be severed from the body. You steal, you lose a hand. You defame Allah, you lose your tongue. In the end, a simple beheading served the purpose of destroying an 'infidel'—an 'infidel' being anyone not a Muslim.

"In its totality," Kat continued, "the Rub el Hizb symbolizes a more virulent declaration than the exclamation 'Allah Akbar' terrorists often yell when blowing themselves and others to pieces. It's worth noting this new proclamation doesn't even evoke the use of the name of the Muslim god. They terrorize simply to terrorize and intimidate their enemy, hoping to frighten them into submission."

"With this knowledge," the moderator said, "Dr. Cardova, and others involved in this historic dig wonder if the Muslim world will renounce the Rub el Hizb and turn to another symbol to denote its religion."

An elderly black man, his clothes dusty from the dig which continued in the background, spoke to the camera, "The good people in my home state of Georgia finally relented and removed the rebel flag from the statehouse. They removed the flag because it symbolized a tyranny against a race of people. In this sense, I see no difference between Georgia's flag and the Rub el Hizb. I would expect a 'good people' to condemn terrorism, unequivocally denounce the slaughter of the innocent and remove the symbol from everything Muslim—temple, Qur'an, clothing, anything. I guess we'll see."

An Indian woman then appeared on camera. "Five hundred people were killed or injured in the Mumbai attack by the Army of the Righteous group in Pakistan in 2008. My sister was one of them."

Her eyes misted over as she continued, "I ask, what is righteous about slaughter? Explain this to my people. Explain to the many people who lost loved ones in the 9/11 attack in America, what was righteous about such a massacre?"

Max reached over and touched Kat's arm to get her attention. "Man, those two people's comments really relate the past to the present, don't they?"

Kat shrugged. "I'm an oddity among most of my colleagues—a creature tied to the past but intent to live in the present. My field assistants, at least some of them, appear to have a similar trait. We learn from history. The old saw is true, "Those who cannot remember the past are condemned to repeat it.""

"I'm impressed," Max said.

"Impressed? Why?"

"Most people misquote Santayana and say, 'Those who ignore history are bound—or doomed—to repeat it.""

Kat's eyes opened wide. "My, you are a widely read man. But …" she punched him playfully on the arm. "I, dear fellow, am the history maven and don't you forget it."

Max rubbed his arm. "Oh, I won't."

"Watch," she said.

They both turned their attention back to the television. On-screen, Kat again flashed her green eyes in a close-up. "The indelible truth of our find leads to this: the high crimes of terror my friends Clarence and Deepika mention are those of 'ordinary' terrorists. So, what are the members of this highly secret, radically terrorist group, Warriors for Allah, up to? A group knowing the full meaning of its symbol?

"Look at the Muslim al-Quds star—al-Quds being their name for Jerusalem." The monitor showed a white octagon inside a thick green octagon. "Does this tell us this group's next target?"

"I hope the answers won't lie in rubble for future generations to discover—or in some dig a thousand years from now."

Kat pointed her remote control at the monitor and clicked off the TV.

Max blew out a breath. "I'm impressed, Dr. Cardova. Very impressed."

She turned to face him and smiled in acknowledgment. "So, Maximus Braxton, the news, historically speaking, is this secret Muslim society is said to be the equivalent of the black-ops units operated by America's most highly trained military forces."

She peered into his eyes, expecting a response.

Max simply responded, "Hmm."

"I expected a bit more of an answer." She acted good-naturedly perturbed.

"You want an answer?" Max asked. "Everyone wants to be a Marine. A chosen few want to be black ops. Their odds of success?"

"Shoot."

"Try winning the lottery instead." He smiled and after a moment added, "I was on a dig of my own this afternoon."

"Oh?" Kat tilted her head. She took his right hand in hers and looked at his palm and fingers. "Looks pretty clean for someone on a dig."

Her touch roused feelings Max hadn't harbored in some time— well, since their time on the mountaintop on the Israel National Trail, a moment tainted with the knowledge a sniper was zeroing in on them. He savored the moment, smiling. Then said, "Mine was a different kind of dig—a bibliotechish dig."

Kat laughed softly and subtly kept hold of his hand. "I think you just invented a word."

"Maybe bibliotech will be a new branch of science. I could be the twenty-first-century Galileo."

"Just what you need—another acronym after your name."

"Look who's talking, Miss World-Famous Semiologist/Archaeologist/Linguist whose name is followed by BS, MS, and PhD times three."

"It's only PhD times two."

"But you're probably working on a third."

"Not enough time in my life."

"Yeah, time." He hesitated. "A commodity I'm afraid we may be low on."

Kat's brow knit in question, but she left her hand comfortably in his. "How so?"

"Your find in the hills outside Dan. And our president's incredible statements about Islam in his first hour in office."

"I've read some of his speech, but I haven't connected the dots. My find and the president?"

"Here," Max said, "is what we're dealing with: men—and women—who are convinced they are right, their religion should rule the world, and who don't mind killing the infidels—and themselves—to get to the end game. Hey, the female bombers don't even have the promise of seventy-two virgins awaiting them in heaven, so what else could be the attraction?"

Max recalled his last stay in Jerusalem when a teenage Muslim girl walked into a market on Ben Yehuda Street and blew herself and a half-dozen others to kingdom come. When the bombing occurred happened, Max was around the corner on Jaffa Street, no more than two hundred yards away and heading to the same market. A girl with her whole life ahead of her and she did this. *Brainwashed. An awful thing.*

And why did those people die and not him?

Kat pointed to his coffee mug. "Refill?"

"Please. Good stuff."

"Fuel," she said. "Remember the name. It could be our next date."

Kat went to the kitchen, returned with a thermos bottle and poured more coffee into both mugs, then pointed to the folder full of papers Max had brought with him. They lay inconspicuously on the end table. "These are the findings from your 'dig'?"

"Yep."

"Want to tell me about it?"

Max opened the folder and laid a stack of papers on the coffee table in front of them.

"Photocopies of news stories and feature articles about our newly installed president," he said. "My working theorem is, unbeknownst to the public, we're being blackmailed."

Kat looked at him quizzically. "Blackmailed?"

"Yes. My thought is either the mullahs of Iran, the imams of Syria, or perhaps simply ISIS or another organized terrorist group like al-Qaeda, or maybe your Warriors for Allah has—behind closed doors—told our president, probably also our secretary of state, if we turn the screws on Israel, pressuring it to give over Jerusalem as a Palestinian capital, if we stop clamping down on and arresting Muslim terrorists, they will reward us by stopping their attacks against Americans."

"Quite a theorem."

"You think me foolish?"

"I don't know. Are there any other reasons why Jones would change his mind about supporting Israel?"

"Well, I haven't found any. Not unless it relates to his being educated for a few years in a Muslim school. Maybe he has friends from his childhood. I don't know. I thought I might find a clue in this stuff."

"*Time Magazine, Newsweek, US News & World Report, World, GQ, Esquire*—" Kat rifled through articles Max had photocopied and stapled together along with Jones's autobiographical book.

They both spent a half hour scanning the articles. Kat broke the silence, saying, "One name keeps coming up. Avner Navon, the billionaire."

"The money guy behind Jones's rise to power," Max said.

"You know what they say about mysteries?" Kat's eyes caught Max's.

"Right," he answered. "Follow the money trail."

Chapter Seven

Saturday Evening, January 25

The 30327 zip code is among the most affluent in America. Avi Navon didn't live there to flaunt his wealth but because he felt the setting necessary in which to host the world's richest, most powerful industrial leaders. Indeed, abundant riches didn't impress him much. What did? Integrity, honor, truthfulness, reliability, ultimately a man or woman who would risk their own life for the lives of others.

As a recipient of the Medal of Valor, the Israeli Defense Forces' highest honor for heroism in the heat of battle, he had nurtured these attributes ever since his father's funeral when Avi was fifteen years old. At the funeral, after the cantor sang psalms and the *Eyl Malei Rahamim*, the traditional memorial prayer, the rabbi gave a eulogy about "this great man, Binyamin Navon."

Between sobs, the rabbi recited the *chesed shel emet*—acts of kindness with no ulterior motive—Avi's father had performed in his life. The rabbi recalled the deceased's intimacy with Elohim, the Lord God of the Jews, who helped him and Israel survive the 1948 battle for life and statehood.

The eulogy was brief but powerful, causing young Avi to spend the seven-day *shivah* mourning period in deep thought and prayer.

Not only did Avi recite the Kaddish every day for a week, but he continued to do so beyond the traditional *shloshim*—the first thirty days—and indeed for a year. And today, this very day, was not only Shabbat but marked the fiftieth *yahrzeit*—anniversary of death. And so, as he did on every *yahrzeit*, Avi had recited Kaddish for his father, whose life, whose love, whose philanthropy continued to inspire him.

With a heavy heart, Avi silently sat beside Lana as their chauffeur, Stan, waved to the guard at the gate, and after the heavy barrier swung open, wove the Lexus limousine up the long winding driveway.

Evening spread over Avi's world like a funeral pall. The tall pine trees shouldering the asphalt drive sometimes reminded him of sentinels on the Golan Heights.

———— ◆ ————

Lana knew better than break the silence. If she had, she might have complained the trees spooked her, and she would prefer a string of streetlights along the darkened way. The mansion sat amid ten acres of woods, a rarity in even this richest of Atlanta West Buckhead suburbs. Despite the twenty-four-hour guards at the front gate and an extensive alarm system, Lana wished they lived shoulder-to-shoulder with neighbors in a row of brownstones.

Her papa could keep his $19-million estate, swimming pool, tennis courts, fitness pavilion, solarium, guest house, and ten-bed, ten-bath Tudor. She'd take the brownstone, thank you very much.

She needed his companionship in the wake of her fiancé's murder, and he needed her presence since her mother died of breast cancer less than a year ago. The two deaths, one almost immediately after the other, had left them devastated, almost codependent, drawing closer in an already tight father-daughter relationship. He was her abba, her daddy, but they were also best friends.

———— ◆ ————

When the limo reached the circular brick area in front of the house, Avi got out, waved good-night to Stan and opened the door for Lana. They walked side-by-side to the front door, which he opened with a key.

"I'm going to the den for a few minutes, dear. I'll see you in the morning.

"Night, Papa." Lana kissed him on the cheek and swept through the foyer and up a double staircase toward her bedroom on the second floor.

Avi stepped over to the security panel at the far-left side of the foyer. A small red light blinked. "Hmm." He flicked a tiny switch and pushed a reset button.

Next to the panel was a telephone link to the front gate. He picked up the phone and asked, "Harvey, did anyone come to the house today?"

"No, sir, Mr. Navon," the guard said.

"The alarm didn't sound?"

"No, sir."

"Nothing unusual?"

"No, sir. Anything the matter?"

Avi hesitated, then answered, "I've got a red blinking light here."

"I'll be right up, sir."

"No, no. I'll check it out."

"But—"

"I've got it, Harvey."

————— ♦ —————

At the gate, Harvey Newman knew enough not to dismiss his boss's orders. Billionaires—especially those who happen to be war heroes—are not used to insubordination. Nevertheless, he clicked on the radio attached to the shoulder strap of his jacket.

"Jack, it's Harvey."

"Ten-four."

"Seen anything out there lately?"

"Not a thing."

"Nothing unusual at all?"

"No, why?"

"Mr. Navon had to reset the alarm 'cause the red light was blinking."

"Probably just a glitch. I'll go in and check."

"Better not. He said not to."

"Well, I'll do a closer walk-around of the main house."

"Roger. Out."

Inside, Avi strode across the large foyer, past the double staircase. Lana had continued her mother's tradition of always having fresh flowers in tall vases between the staircases. Their housekeeper and cook, Esther, fastidiously tended them, but this week of her vacation Lana had done her duties. Lamps on hip-high tables illuminated the grand vestibule and staircase, showing off finely milled wood paneling.

Avi continued through a sitting room and living room with a wide white-stone encased fireplace and leather couches. He passed through a wide hallway leading to double-wide sliding doors to the back.

He looked out onto the swimming pool and lawn behind the house. Dim outdoor lights revealed a rectangular pool, an open-walled stone bathhouse, a semi-circular solarium, fitness pavilion, and a huge octagonal roofed outdoor room, complete with stone fireplace, large barbecue grill. The back acreage featured a par-3 golf hole and, beyond, a small guest house. He waved to his guard Jack Noll as he passed.

The one reminder of his homeland was a beautifully carved four-person bench made from one large piece of white Jerusalem stone that sat next to the golf hole, which Avi used as an evening entertainment for guests. The par-3 was a "betting hole." He had even used golf once during a difficult business negotiation at the mansion.

"Listen," he had said to the corporate president across the table, "neither of us is budging, so let's settle the issue out on my little par-3 hole." The man, considering himself a superior golfer, jumped at the offer, only to see Avi drop in a ten-foot putt for a birdie. Hole won, negotiation complete, a fine profit in his hand, he used part of the profit to have the bench carved and imported.

A smile crossed his face as he remembered. Then he entered his den, the one place he could go to leave the world behind, light a fire in the fireplace, and settle into his favorite, old winged-back chair with a glass of kosher wine grown in his beloved Golan Heights. Tonight's choice: Margalit's 2006 cabernet sauvignon.

He flicked the light switch, and a floor lamp in the far corner came on. The first thing he noticed was the shades for the four outdoor windows were drawn all the way down. Odd.

The next sight sent Avi nearly falling backward. In the shadows, a man was sitting in his winged-back chair, his right arm resting on the chair's arm, a hand-gun settled in his palm.

"Wh-who are you? And how did you get in here?" Avi stammered. The demand was instinctive. The intruder was obviously an Arab terrorist ,and how he'd gained entrance to the highly secure home mattered not an iota. Neither did the question "Why are you here?" need to be asked. The answer was obvious: to take Avi's life.

Good. Take my life so I can go home to heaven with Ruth.

But the next thought finally sent chills of fear through him, and he grabbed the doorframe to steady himself. *Lana.*

"You don't need to know who I am," the intruder deadpanned, "and as for how I got in here? If I were you and serious about protection, I'd go a little further than those two jokers you have protecting this place and install some twenty-first-century security— not something from 1990. I could slip into this place blindfolded and walking backward."

Avi was dumbfounded and stumbled for words. The accent sounded American, not Middle Eastern.

"No need to be afraid," the man said.

Sure, a trespasser with a gun and no reason to be afraid. "Right."

The man offered, "The gun's for my protection. I only want information."

You want information at the point of a gun. Again: "Right."

The intruder slid the gun into a holster on his hip.

Avi resisted the impulse to grab his phone and call the guards. The more Avi focused on him in the dim light, the more English or European he looked, though his accent was American—Texan, maybe? And he apparently didn't want to take Avi's life. But was the information he wanted something with which Avi could part?

"What sort of information?" Avi asked.

"The president," the man said. "I want to know about Jones."

Avi took a step inside the room. "I probably know less than you. I discovered four days ago the man I thought I knew I don't know at all." The words dripped with scorn.

———— ◆ ————

Max noticed Avi retracting his shoulders. He was telling the truth.

"Have a seat," Max commanded, motioning to a chair near him. He knew a rich man like this must be cringing at being ordered to sit in his own home, his own sanctuary. But Navon acquiesced.

"You're the money behind the president," Max charged. "Without you, he'd be sharpening pencils for the next city council meeting in Atlanta, dealing with zoning around Woodruff Park, the number of toilets in restrooms, and twisting small businessmen's arms for campaign contributions for a run at mayor or county commissioner."

Navon shrugged. "True."

"But with you, he finds himself president, leader of the free world and in a position to kowtow to every Muslim whim."

"True again."

"I find myself often baffled by you Jews, who after centuries of being battered, bombed, and beheaded by Muslims, continue to think you can attain peace with them; who, despite hearing Islamists declare they'll drive you into the sea, insist you can be their pals.

"American Jews are apparently unaware of the perils their fellow Jews face in Israel and they somehow view the Jews of Israel as ogres, as prison-keepers of the Arabs there. They're unaware the Arabs in Israel enjoy voting rights, have their own representatives in the Knesset, own businesses—all the things Arabs will never allow Jews or Christians to do in Arab countries."

Navon sat silent.

"What baffles me more," Max said, "is Jews—like you, Mr. Navon—who though born in Israel are so often filled with self-hatred. I don't know what else to call it—a denial of facts, both historical and present, all proving the putrid character of many of your neighbors. The 'patrons of peace' living in Israel who are deaf and dumb, but by no means mute, the silly who border on sinister, those whose tainted righteousness has turned them into traitors, Israelis who hate Israelis.

"Are you one of those Jews, Mr. Navon? And is this why you've bankrolled Ridley Jones right into the presidency?"

Navon's head was bowed. Max noticed a sudden slouch in his posture. His body language was screaming sorrow but at the same time no-no-no.

Navon looked up in obvious anguish. "No, in fact, I am not one of those Israelis who hate Israelis. But, I admit, this is all much to my chagrin." He breathed deeply. "I lived in Israel when we agreed with the PLO, the Palestinian Liberation Organization, to surrender territory for Palestinian promises of moderation."

Max nodded.

"Time and again we surrendered land to the PLO only to have the Arabs escalate their war of terror—not only against our troops but against children in schools, patients in hospitals, families celebrating marriages in hotels and restaurants.

"I joined the IDF and fought an unforgiving enemy full of hate and venom, a nemesis who rarely if ever does what he agrees to, who never even simply recognizes Israel as the Jewish state it is. I lived in Israel in 1993 when the Oslo peace accord was signed, a pact creating a framework for our country to surrender even more land.

"IDF soldiers forced families out of their homes in Gaza, Judea, and Samaria and crammed them into trailers in the Negev

Desert. Our reward from the Arabs? Thousands of Israelis killed and maimed. Every time we move out, they move their fighters into those areas, set up barracks, use women and children as human shields, and lob mortars into our neighborhoods. Yes, I've lived there and seen the relentless, murderous intent of Islam on the Jews. And now I see a similar character here in America. Even after witnessing the transformation in Europe and then England, Americans thought Islamic terrorists would never arrive on these shores.

"Well, they were wrong. And now my adopted country is about to bow to Muslim demands exactly as my homeland has done—" Navon moaned like a boxer reacting to a body blow, "and I helped put in power the man who will lead the charge."

Max sat forward in his chair. "You expect me to believe you, a man who has made a vast fortune reading the character of the top businessmen in the world, was fooled into funding the presidential run of a mid-level political hack who secretly hated you and your people all along?"

The man nodded his head in acceptance of the sorry, inexcusable fact.

"How could I have been so foolish, been so carried away by charisma, and so utterly fooled and used by some man twenty-five years my junior?" Navon said. "The enormity of the deception confounds me and fuels self-contempt—something I've never before felt."

Max read the emotion in the tension of Navon's brow, the tightening and loosening of his left hand. This was a tormented man.

"My beloved sister," Navon said, "died in a Palestinian mortar attack more than thirty years ago. My two brothers died in Israel at the hands of these terrorists for Allah. Less than a year ago, my daughter's husband-to-be perished in New York City at their hands.

The world is their battlefield, and we continue to engage with them in talks of peace. Both in Israel and here in America, we are politically correct and blind."

Max crossed his arms. "Say I believe you. Then explain to me Jones's steadfastness now to implement policies tantamount to calling for Israel's destruction as a nation."

"I, too, am confounded." Navon shrugged and raised his hands palms-up.

"You must have a clue—an iota of a thought?"

"Blackmail." Navon shrugged. "Nothing else makes sense."

"So, what are you going to do?" Said as a demand, as if coming from an IDF general—exactly Max's intent.

Navon looked keenly at Max, eyes hot. "I've pulled all my funding, taken down websites, sent out emails and personal mailings to many, many colleagues in the business world, calling for everyone I know—and those I don't know—to remove all support of any sort for this administration. The biggest donors and my closest friends? I've called most of them, apologized profusely, and will call the rest."

"Really?"

"Really."

"Then why hasn't your change in loyalties made the news?"

"Perhaps because the emails and letters all were sent out just before Shabbat, yesterday at sundown. Perhaps because the media— at least the mainstream media, minus *Fox*, the *Washington Times* and a couple others—are full-fledged behind Jones and driven to support him."

"No surprise," Max said. He shook his head. His contacts had given him the inside dope on Navon and his mansion's security. Max had caught a ride on a navy cargo plane to Dobbins Air Reserve Base outside Atlanta, snuck past Navon's security and into his home, rifled through his desk and whatever other materials he could find, and now this dead end. How else could he view the outcome other than as a cul-de-sac leading him back to where he started? He was no closer now to knowing the motivation for Jones's unexpected anti-Israel pronouncements in his inaugural address than he was when he researched the president at the Yale library. Unless Navon's guess was correct: blackmail.

What now?

"Would you mind telling me who you are?" Avi's question interrupted Max's thoughts.

"Yes."

"You've decided not to shoot?"

Just then Lana called from the other room, "Papa?"

Max jumped to his feet and reached for his holstered handgun. Avi stood and raised his arm toward Max, hand up in a stop position. "My daughter."

Max stood still.

A moment later, Lana stepped into the doorway. Her tall, slim figure was wrapped in a deep-green terrycloth robe, pulled tightly about her. Her long black hair hung loosely over her shoulders. She couldn't prevent a startled look at seeing a stranger in the room. "Hello?" she said tentatively.

"Sweetheart, this is my friend—"

"Jake," Max finished the sentence, nodding a hello in her direction.

"Oh. Hello." A heavy moment drifted slowly by. "Jake—?"

"Jake Longley," Max finished, managing a crooked smile.

"Aha. Nice to meet you, Jake. I didn't hear you come in." She stepped forward and extended her hand. "I'm Lana."

"My pleasure."

"Papa," Lana said, "I was just checking to make sure everything was all right. I saw Jack outside checking the grounds, and it's not his normal schedule."

"If he's got a normal schedule, he's got a bad schedule," Max said. "If there's normality, the bad guys can figure out the routine easily.."

"Oh?"

Navon interrupted. "Lana, Jake here is trying to unravel a mystery—the mystery of our president and his change of heart about Israel, the Palestinians, and Muslim terrorists."

"Aha." Lana inspected Max.

Max remembered an old Yogi Berra quote, "You can observe a lot by watching." He could tell she knew he was lying. Further, he was certain he could trust her father. The nuances, the body language all supported his conclusion. So, suddenly and very much against his training, he decided to come clean.

Looking first at Navon and then Lana, he said, "Actually your guard is probably looking for me. My name is Max. Max Braxton."

Navon locked his eyes on Max's and, after a few moments, extended his hand. "I'd never thought I would extend a handshake to an intruder, but—"

Lana had taken a step backward. "So, you're a trespasser," she protested. "How did you get in?"

"Honey," Navon interrupted, "I think our new friend Max has special talents we know not of. Explains how he got in here." He looked at Max.

Max nodded. "But I wouldn't say my training was much different than your own, Mr. Navon." Max nodded to a mannequin standing in the corner near Lana. The dummy was dressed in the garb of the IDF Special Forces, along with the paratrooper's brigade insignia, a knife, and parachute.

Navon chuckled. "I'm afraid I couldn't do nearly the things I used to."

"I trained with the Yehidat Shaldag and the Sayeret," Max said, referring to the Israeli Air Force Commando unit and its reconnaissance unit. "I'd say any IDF Special Forces vet can pretty much handle himself in any situation."

Navon shrugged.

Silence followed and Max decided the two were waiting for him to expound. He shrugged and said, "You wonder why I'm here? I love America. I also share a love for Israel. The Jewish land is the only solid democracy in the Middle East, the only country in the world whose very existence is constantly under attack. Israelis worship a good and just God, not the evil, conniving god of a certain other religion. And America just took one giant step toward nullifying eighty years of support for Israel, support which started to go south when the first President Bush took office with an anti-Semitic secretary of state. So, when I read Jones's inaugural speech, I—"

Max stopped, the complexity of the politics like a roadblock to his thoughts.

Lana placed her hands on her hips. "What do you want with my father?"

Navon interjected, "He thinks, or thought, I had something to do with Ridley's sudden transformation into an Islamic apologist."

Lana snickered.

"I followed the money," Max said defensively.

"Uh-huh." Lana nodded.

"Usually works," Max said.

"I'm sure."

"Not this time," Max acknowledged.

Lana shook her head.

"What are your plans now?" Navon asked.

"Back to the drawing board."

"How do you start over?"

"Dig deeper. An archaeologist friend would say I need to start using the smaller utensils, the fine brushes, get deep below the surface to discover the full truth—the source of the stream making the waterwheel turn. She says she must get her hands dirty if she's going to unearth enough new knowledge to keep her students properly updated and informed. She'd say, 'Your hands aren't dirty enough, Max.'"

"Sounds like a wise lady," Navon said.

Max smiled crookedly.

"I hope you can accept my apology for the intrusion," he said.

"Break-in, you mean." Lana's face reflected the sharp edge of her words.

Max shrugged. "Break-in." He took a step toward the den door. "I'll be on my way—of course, unless you intend to call the security guards and the police."

"I've a mind to—" Lana began.

But Navon's upheld hand cut her off and he looked intently at Max. "You're going to dig deeper?"

"Yes."

"Then how about doing so on my dime?"

"What do you mean?"

"I'll hire you to ferret out the truth."

"Papa." Lana objected.

But Navon looked intently at her. "I want answers, sweetheart. Perhaps this man can unearth them." He turned to Max. "I'll underwrite any expenses and pay you a hundred grand if you can get to the bottom of this."

Max didn't flinch. "Thanks for the offer, but no thanks. I intend to dig into the core of the apple but the discovery itself will be my pay."

"Well, how can I help then?

"Information is all."

"I'll make some coffee," Lana said. She faced her father. "And I suppose, kindly father, you're even going to offer our—guest—a room for the night. Esther's not here, so I'll prepare a guest room and inform Jack and Harvey a friend has paid a surprise visit so they can step down their alert." She hesitated, then added, "I'll be back with coffee in a few minutes."

Navon winked at her and looked questioningly at Max.

Flabbergasted, Max thought for a moment, then held up a hand in protest. "Thanks, but I have a rule to never spend the night in homes I've—broken into."

Lana's eyes pierced his like daggers. "Then this is a habit of yours?"

"Sorry. I spoke in jest. Thank you for your offer, but no thanks, ma'am."

"Ma'am?"

"Miss."

"Then I'll just bring coffee." Lana turned and left the room. Navon motioned for Max to retake a seat. Max conceded.

"I'll tell you the spin our president shared with me from his new throne on high," Navon said, then retold his conversation with Jones at the inaugural ball in the Air and Space Museum.

———•◆•———

When Lana returned with a tray filled with coffee mugs, cream, sugar, and Danish, Max was walking around the den. Navon watched him attentively.

Two small photographs sat prominently on Navon's mahogany desk, one with him and an attractive gray-haired lady, another with

Lana at their side. Max glanced at Navon's hands. He wore a wedding band on the ring finger of his right hand. Max knew Navon was a single man, but obviously, a widower whose love for his dead wife went beyond this world and worldly possessions.

Interestingly, there was no Wall of Honor, no excess of photographs of Navon with other mighty men of the world. Max thought of the offices he'd visited. Men and women in high places tended to fill walls with photographs flattering their egos, illustrating the heights of their importance. Their arms were around Ronald Reagan or Bill Clinton or Barack Obama or Vladimir Putin or Donald Trump or George Soros. Whoever might inspire admiration from the minions.

"None of you and Jones," Max observed. He took a seat and grabbed a mug of black coffee from the tray Lana had placed on the coffee table. "No photos of your pals in the Senate or Knesset, your colleagues who head up international corporations."

Navon, sipped his coffee and shook his head. "No need." He hesitated, then added, "Oh, I have a few in a drawer over there." He pointed toward drawers at the bottom of a bookcase.

"May I see them?" Max asked.

"Certainly." Navon stood and walked to the bookcase. He pulled out an eight-by-ten-inch photo album and flipped to the back pages. "Here they are," he said, passing the album to Max.

Max held the hefty binder and studied the photographs. One showed Navon and Jones shaking hands.

"The day he announced his run for president," Navon said, gesturing outside, "right out on the veranda here."

"Hmm." Max looked at the two faces smiling back at him. Obviously close friends.

Another photo showed the two men on a yacht, Navon apparently instructing Jones how to reel in a catch with a deep-water fishing rod. Here they were chatting with an aged Andrew Young and Max Cleland. Here Navon was introducing Jones on stage at some sort of meeting. Here the two men were holding up a Jones for President poster.

"The first one printed," Navon explained.

"His office?" Max asked.

"His home."

"Hmm." Max looked more closely, squinting. He turned to Navon. "Do you have a magnifying glass?"

"Sure." Navon walked to his desk.

"Whatever for?" Lana asked, stepping up behind Max and peering over his shoulder.

Max glanced at her and smelled a perfume reminding him of someplace familiar—and sweet. He thought of Kat and ever so slightly shrugged away from this beautiful lady. "Where there's a bookcase, there are books. And, as they say, books—"

"—tell you about a man," Navon finished, handing him a Sherlock Holmes-type magnifier.

Their three heads close together, they looked over the titles of the books in the bookcase.

"This seems to be a section of classics," Lana said, pointing to books in the top left including *Robinson Crusoe* and *Treasure Island*. The top-center section was filled with resources like an Oxford dictionary, Barnes book of quotes and a world atlas. Top right was dedicated to sports—the Atlanta Falcons, the Atlanta Braves dynasty, the Atlanta Hawks, a biography of Red Auerbach of the Boston Celtics. Down the bookcase they searched. Politics ruled one section: James Carville's *40 More Years: How the Democrats Will Rule the Next Generation; Chain of Command: The Road from 9/11 to Abu Ghraib*. Max paused at one title: *Rules for Radicals* by Saul Alinsky.

Max shook his head. He made note of the unsettled groan from

Navon and the "Oh, my" from Lana.

Finally, down in the bottom-right corner, almost out of sight, was a very thin binding. No words adorned its spine, but an interesting symbol: a square within a square, one of them turned a quarter turn. A small circle was in the center.

"It's the Rub El Hizb," Max said.

"The what?" Lana asked.

Max explained the terrorist symbol, then asked, "May I borrow these photos?"

"Of course. If they can be of help." Navon straightened. "I think I'll forego the rest of my coffee, dear," he said to Lana. "Suddenly, I feel very tired."

———— ◆ ————

Avi took Lana's arm, and they walked from the den together. At the door, he said, "Perhaps Max will change his mind about staying the night."

They turned to ask, but Max was gone. Avi walked behind the desk. Nothing. He pulled the curtains. Not there. He looked at Lana, lifted his arms in a question and shrugged.

The photo album lay on the coffee table. Avi picked up the book. The sleeves at the back were missing the photographs of Jones.

"Who in the world was he?" Lana asked.

"I don't know, but I'm finding out." Avi opened the top-center draw of his desk and withdrew a slim gray book. Opening the volume from the back, he ran his finger down a list of names written in Hebrew, right to left, then picked up his phone and pressed twelve digits.

A voice answered after five rings. "Alef."

"Shin," Avi said.

"Ah, my friend. So late. You must be in America."

"Ken." Avi drew a breath and spoke in Hebrew, "I apologize for the late call but I need information immediately on a young man."

Lana turned and left the room. She looked out through the large windows to the patio and pool. She thought she saw a dark shape moving quickly toward the trees beyond the putting green. But she couldn't be sure.

Chapter Eight

Saturday, Late night

Rather ordinary, Max thought as he reconnoitered President Jones's Atlanta residence. The older, two-story white clapboard home sat on a smartly landscaped lot in North Druid Hills.

No lights were on, but nearby streetlights revealed a large, attached garage on the front left, and three small pillars adorning a front porch. The house stood nearly elbow-to-elbow with its neighbors, but tall trees in the backyard waved in a slight breeze. Max guessed the house's size at around twenty-five hundred square feet.

Max had easily avoided the two-man Secret Service detail stationed outside the home. He recalled the layout of the house and the specifics of the security system his old colleague had provided.

"What in the world are you up to?" his friend had asked, with no trace of astonishment. He knew Max well. The two men had partnered in some bold, clandestine operations in the past. Max trusted him with his life. He had certainly saved Max before—more than once.

"You don't want to know," he responded to his friend's question. Enough said.

Max took stock of the situation. *What is it with rich people like Navon and political bigwigs like Jones using such amateurish security systems? Even the Secret Service hadn't upgraded the unit. Where's the challenge?*

He'd normally plan a job like this for a week, but not only could he not afford the time—he figured he didn't need the time.

Twenty minutes later, he was belly-walking along the floor of Jones's den, approaching the mystery book in the bottom shelf of the bookcase in the photograph. The book was still there.

Grabbing his target, Max crawled to a door, reached for the handle and turned. The closet was indeed the one he recalled from the blueprints. Once inside, he could photograph the book without the flash being visible outside through the den windows. He shut the door behind him, sat on his butt, flicked on a penlight. Emblazoned on the first inside page was the Rub el Hizb, and beneath, the Secret Society symbol with the fingernail moon on its back.

"Phew." Max exclaimed. Surprised or not, he had to take a deep breath.

Then, with a miniature camera, he photographed the booklet page by page. Seventeen pages long, written in an odd Arabic-looking type with which he was unfamiliar. He had learned modern Arabic; this was apparently a precursor and he'd need someone else to decipher it. Kat.

Done, he crept to Jones's second-floor bedroom and rifled through the five drawers in his bureau, looking for a clue to the inner man and his secrets.

Holding his penlight in his teeth, he scrambled through the top drawer, careful to put everything back in its place—underwear, socks, handkerchiefs. A small square ceramic dish held tiepins, a Democrat Party lapel pin, three pairs of cufflinks. Nothing unusual. Indeed, everything was usual.

Drawer by drawer he found nothing but clothing. Then, in the bottom drawer, he noticed something odd. It seemed not to be as deep, front to back, as the others. He ran his right hand along the back of the drawer. At the far-left end he felt a button. *A hidden button? Hmmm.* Pushing the button, he heard a snap, like a latch being unlocked, and the back fell forward.

Pointing his penlight into the darkness at the back of the drawer, he saw only empty space. Back and forth, he slowly moved the penlight, then spotted a wooden box the size of a deck of cards in the left-rear corner.

He pulled out the box and opened it. Inside was a pinky-finger-sized flash drive.

May be something interesting here.

He unzipped an inner pocket in his jacket and pulled out a tiny gadget, then plugged the flash drive's USB port into it. A moment later a tiny red bulb lit up for two or three seconds. Max returned the gadget to his pocket and replaced the wooden box with its flash drive in place.

———— ◆ ————

Three hours later, Max sat in the co-pilot's seat behind the pilot in the cockpit of an F-20B Yellow Jacket, flying north out of Dobbins Air Force Base. The plane was a hybrid of the F-18E Super Hornet and the F-16 Fighting Falcon, known as the Viper due to its resemblance to a viper snake and the Colonial Viper Starfighter in the movie *Battlestar Galactica*.

They were cruising at Mach 2.2.

"The guys at McDonnell Douglas did themselves good with this baby." Deon Rivers slanted the plane eastward and angled down toward the ocean at a surprising speed, even for Max who was used to his old pal's maneuvers.

"I'm impressed," Max replied.

"Well, I'm just checking to see if you're awake," Deon said. "I haven't seen you so quiet since the night in the bats' cave in the mountains of Afghanistan."

"Bats." Max spat.

"Afraid of a few little birds?" A good-natured taunt.

"Vermin, you mean. Nightmares from my childhood. My grandmother's attic."

Deon chuckled. "First time you've admitted nightmares to me."

"Those aren't the only ones, my friend."

"Oh?"

Max's voice was serious. He was quiet for a moment, then, "I see dead men's faces."

"Dead al-Qaeda?"

"Terrorists are men."

"Feeling sorry for those swine?"

"I just told a friend killing them didn't bother me an ounce."

Deon was silent, waiting.

"I'm afraid sometimes it does—" Max let three clicks pass, "—for a moment."

"But then you think of the hundreds of innocent people you could be saving for every terrorist you take out."

Max hesitated, then, "Right. That."

A minute later, Deon spoke again. "By the way, Max, the guys I've spoken to about your book—"

"Yeah?"

"They're all right-on about it, man. Thankful, every last one of 'em. About time someone spelled out the situation in black and white, no sugar-coating."

"Thanks," Max said, then fell silent. Before releasing his book for publication, he had checked with friends from the army's Delta Force under Joint Special Operations Command (JSOC) and Rangers, the navy's Dev Group (DevGru) and SEALs, and a couple others. He feared being branded persona non grata for revealing information to outsiders as had happened to others before him. But everyone had given him a green light.

Max looked out the window to the east. Although the rising sun peeked over the horizon, the sky remained oddly dark, even at forty thousand feet. He wondered if the sight portended the future of the country he loved.

He thought of the Rub el Hizb he'd photographed in President Jones's booklet. Today was, indeed, a bleak day. No sugarcoating this opinion, either.

———— ◆ ————

Five hundred miles south, Avi Navon was answering the phone in his expansive second-floor bedroom. Through the window, he saw an entirely different picture than Max and Deon's. The rising sun colored clouds in the winter sky with a golden hue. *Stunning. Beauty is deceiving.*

"Shalom," he said.

"Seated?" the voice at the other end asked in Hebrew.

Avi settled into his plush couch. "Now I am."

"Max Braxton." Said as a complete sentence.

"Yes," Avi said.

"You want to be on his side."

"I do?"

"If you're in a battle. If you're in a war. If you're in any sort of military—or any other kind of—confrontation. Please, Avi, I hope you're on his side."

"But is he on our side?"

"On the side of Israel? He saved three of our Yehidat Shaldag guys in a firefight on the Lebanese border two years ago. Spent close to four months in Mayanei Hayeshua Medical Center. General Weizman bestowed him with the Medal of Valor."

"Whoa. Well, this is good." Avi twirled a pencil in his fingers like a baton and turned to look at his own Medal of Valor. A rarity.

"There's more, but even I can't access the information. Super-secret stuff. But I can tell you this: Max Braxton is welcome in Israel any time. As a matter of fact, he could stay the night in the prime minister's house if he cares to."

"He could probably break in if he didn't have an invitation," Avi murmured wryly.

"What?"

"Oh, nothing. Thanks, Shamir. This is a big help. Shalom." Avi slowly placed the phone in its cradle, set down the pencil and drummed his fingertips on his knee. The cadence of the "United States Marine Corps Hymn."

Odd I would think of this song, he thought as he recognized the beat. He looked again at the clouds as they turned purple in the rising sun. *I wish I were a prophet.*

Chapter Nine

Sunday noon, January 26

Max had slept Sunday morning in a visiting officers' house at the Naval Submarine Base in New London, Connecticut. Under his pillow lay his evidence—information he indeed hoped led somewhere other than where he expected.

Deon's snoring woke him at noon. He got up, showered and dressed, left a note thanking his friend for the "lift," grabbed a sandwich at the galley, then drove west on Route 95 the fifty miles to New Haven and Yale.

As he crossed the Pearl Harbor Memorial "Q" Bridge over the Quinnipiac River from East Haven to New Haven he spoke at his car-phone. "Call Kat." *She's already in my dialing system. Why so, Max?*

On the third ring, she picked up her cell phone, sounding winded. "This is Kat."

"Kat. Where are you?"

"Tuck and I are running in East Rock Park."

"East Rock? You're made of steel."

"What can I say, I've been reborn as a mountain girl. We love this place. We cycle here in the summer, snowshoe in the winter, and today we're running. And park rangers are busy getting ready for the Winterfest. Sounds like you're familiar with the place."

"Yeah. Listen, I'm crossing the 'Q' right now," Max said. "Meet you at the Soldiers and Sailors Monument in fifteen minutes?"

"Sure. What's up?"

"Something important. I need your help."

"We'll be there." Kat slipped the phone into a special pocket of her jogging pants and looked at Tuck who stood attentively at her side, tail wagging. He loved these runs, too. "Well, Tuck, you want to see your buddy?"

The dog cocked his head like he wondered which "buddy."

"Max," she answered. Tuck stood and yipped. Kat laughed and patted him on the head, then set off toward the monument.

———— ♦ ————

Located on the 366-foot summit of East Rock, the Soldiers and Sailors Monument stands another 112-feet-high and is visible for miles. Max caught glimpses of the statuary as he wound through the streets, then suburban roads en route to the park. Built in 1887, and surrounded by an eight-foot-high black metal fence, the monument honors New Haven residents who died in the Revolutionary War, the War of 1812, the Mexican War, and the Civil War.

Kat and Tuck were looking up at the south face when Max strode toward them.

"See any names you know up there?"

Kat chuckled. "You're talking to an archaeologist here, soldier, and the Revolutionary War is as far back as this monument honors. To me, this is modern history."

Max laughed. "So, these heroes aren't old enough for you to know, you say?"

"I know one hero, and one's enough for me." Kat's smile lit him up despite what had been occupying his mind.

Tuck barked and took a half-dozen steps toward Max, wagging his tail all the way.

"Hey, boy." Max knelt, held out a dog treat, then scratched Tuck behind his left ear as he chewed and wiggled in satisfaction.

"You know the way to my dog's heart," Kat said.

"I figure a way into a woman's good graces is through her dog."

Kat laughed as Tuck put his paws on Max's knee and licked his chin.

"What do you need my good graces for?" she asked.

Max stood and reached into an inside jacket pocket. Pulling out an envelope filled with photographs, he said, "These." He pulled a tiny digital camera from another pocket and added, "And the booklet from Jones's bookcase, which is on this memory stick."

Kat gasped.

"Whatever else we find need to know may be on this copy of a flash drive I discovered in his bedroom bureau."

Kat took a step back. "You didn't."

"I did."

"But how?"

"I'll tell you the whole story."

Kat scanned the sky, then looked down the path. "Shouldn't the Secret Service be helicoptering in here or racing up the summit after you right now?"

"Believe me, Kat, they don't know I exist."

She shook her head, hesitated … "Okay, then, I'll look at what you've got."

"My place or yours?"

"Better be mine. Tuck will want his dinner, and I'll put together something for us."

"A girl after my own heart," Max said, lighthearted but sincere.

Kat smiled. "Nice to hear."

"I missed you."

"You've been gone a day." Kat hesitated. "But I missed you too. I wanted to take you to church this morning."

"Next time?"

"Next time." Kat raised up on her toes toward him and they kissed gently. "But the pastor did quote a scripture I've prayed a couple times this afternoon."

"Which one?"

"Jesus was talking about being aware of evil men and he said in Luke 8:17 *Do not be afraid of them. There is nothing concealed that will not be disclosed, nor hidden that will not be made known.*"

"Gotta like such a word," Max said. "I think your prayer might be answered. I can't wait to see what you find out."

———— ◆ ————

Max followed Kat's car to Little Italy and a private parking lot beside her apartment building. He parked in the street and met her at the front door. Tuck took the opportunity to dive headfirst into a two-foot-high snowbank nearby. Once in, he burrowed his head along the bank like a mole for about two feet. Coming up, he snorted and again, Max thought, laughed.

"Tuck, buddy, you're one-of-a-kind," Max said.

"He's my Rin-Tin-Tin, but a little more on the humorous side," Kat said, "although you might consider him the cavalry after the times he's come to my rescue."

"Besides saving President Hall's granddaughter?" Max said and patted Tuck on the head.

They all went up the stairs to Kat's apartment.

Max looked to the right down the hallway. "How's your security in here?"

"What security?"

"Hmm." He frowned. "Why do you think we had bodyguards with you for the last several months?"

"But I'm home in America."

He shook his head. *This is not good.*

They stepped inside, removed their coats, and hung them up.

Brushing aside Max's security concerns, Kat nodded toward the cache he held in his hands and said, "I've got to say, I'm pretty anxious to see what you found in Atlanta."

"So am I. Can I use your printer?"

"Sure."

Max showed her the memory stick containing photos of the pages in the book he had discovered in President Jones's den. "I'll print this out. Only sixteen pages. Shouldn't take but a couple minutes."

When he'd finished printing, Max sat beside Kat on the couch. He set the papers down on the coffee table and, beside them, a small pile of photographs.

"These," he said, tapping the photographs with an index finger, "are from Avi Navon, from his personal photo album."

Kat's eyebrows raised. "You stole these photos from Avnor Navon?"

"No, he gave them to me. Look at this one." Max pointed to the one on top, a picture of Avi Navon and Jones in Jones's den.

"Yes, and?" Kat said.

"Here, use this.' Max pulled a small but high-powered magnifying glass from his pocket. "See the bottom right book in the bookcase?"

Kat grinned and held her hand up, refusing the magnifier. "You're not playing with amateurs here, soldier." She stepped to a roll-top desk and returned with a contraption that looked like a giant cousin to the glasses gemologists use to evaluate precious stones.

"It's like a jewelry loupe on steroids," Kat said. "Next to putting a specimen under a microscope, this will do just fine." Max shook his head in dismay.

Kat held up the photo, peered at the picture through her magnifier, then looked at him. "It's the Rub el Hizb."

"And …" Max leaned back to the end table and picked up the stack of pages he had taken off the printer. "Here are the pages of the president's little book."

Placing her magnifier on the cushion beside her, Kat held the pages in her left hand and flipped slowly through the papers.

Suddenly her breath caught short and Kat went back to the first inside page. She read for a minute, then looked at him in alarm. "Max, this is dangerous."

Suddenly, she swiveled and looked at the large windows on her east wall. She stood, hurried to the window and pulled down a series of Venetian blinds.

"What's the matter?" Max asked.

"I'm scared." She hurried back and slipped down beside him.

Max's brow furrowed and he put his arm around her shoulders. "Scared? Scared of what?"

"What if they find out you have this? And now I have the information?"

"They who?"

"I don't know. They." He could feel her body tense.

"Kat, believe me, I was undiscovered—a ghost. If they don't know about me, they certainly won't know about you—and Deon."

"Deon?"

"My ride down to Atlanta and back."

"Oh, boy."

"Please don't be worried."

"I *am* worried. These jihadis are dangerous. They're killing people in churches and malls and all sorts of places."

"Yes, but suddenly, right now, you're scared?"

Kat's eyes flashed toward the printout.

"It's the book," he guessed.

"Yes."

"Kat, tell me, what do the contents say?"

She flipped through the pages, returned to the blank cover, and then the first page.

"The book is about something called The Three Sixes. And that sounds dangerous—treacherous. Just scanning, I see the words 'infidels,' 'murdering Jews,' 'Allah's hated enemies,' 'worthy to be killed.'" She drew a sharp breath. "This frightens me, Max."

"Then, forget what you've seen, Kat. I don't want you involved and getting scared to death." He grabbed for the photos and she stopped him.

"Forget?" Her voice rose, her look fierce. "I will not forget such horror, Max. Do you think I'll wilt in the face of fear? Just because I'm a woman?"

"I—I—" Max was taken aback. "Kat, I've seen you face death—more than once. Petra, Dublin, Wales. I know you won't wilt. I just don't want to put you in danger again."

"Give me a day, and I'll tell you all about what this is." She poked hard at the small pile of pages. "I don't know if it's a tutorial or what, but I'll find out."

Whoa. Fire in her bones.

"Are you sure?"

"I'll start on this tonight."

Max squeezed her shoulder and asked, "This is the Midwest girl in you, right?"

She pursed her lips. "You haven't met my mom and dad, soldier."

Max leaned over to the end table again and picked up a small cube-shaped apparatus. "While you check out the booklet, I'll take this baby home and see what's on our president's personal flash drive he's hidden away."

The discussion meandered into the idea of the antichrist not being a man but an organization and the eternal battle of good-versus-evil. Eventually, Kat spoke of her archaeological digs and the thrill of unearthing ancient societies.

"Ancient societies," Max said. "Let me ask you this: If in Gaza, they cheer the murder of a three-month-old baby, what do such reactions say about the evolution of their society?"

"When was this?"

"In 2011. I was in Israel when a Palestinian sneaked into a Jewish home in Itamar in the middle of the night, killed both parents, a baby in her father's arms and two other children, and returned to his home to sleep the rest of the night away. The next day, in the wake of his exploits, the town cheered him as a hero."

Kat looked down, shook her head and sat a moment in silence. Finally, she looked at Max and said, "I'm sure there are many, many fine Palestinians who were appalled at those murders."

"But," Max interrupted, "generally speaking, the Palestinian culture is one of hostility, brutality, and death. They cheered the news of 9/11. Yet their neighbors, the Jews—living in the same territory, breathing the same air, coming from the loins of the same ancestor, Abraham, possess a culture of peace and life. They grieved with us on 9/11.

"One Hamas MP declared, 'We desire death like you desire life.' Having fought with Israeli soldiers, I found, to a person, the Israelis thought warfare was regrettable but an absolute, necessary means to an end. Facing Palestinian terrorists is like a policeman facing a man bent on suicide-by-cop. If you don't shoot, you die instead of them."

Kat nodded. "I know. Some people will point to the rare occasion a Jew commits a terrorist act. But those are more an anomaly, and when they occur, the Jews widely condemn them—"

"Whereas," Max said, "Palestinians widely acclaim terrorism. Hey, they even name streets honoring their martyrs."

Kat shivered and stood up. "I've got to change the subject."

"Okay."

"Let me whip up something for us to eat."

"Agreed." Max smiled and relaxed.

———— • ————

A few minutes later, Max stood at the tall window looking east over the river. The waters dimmed in the twilight as Kat stir-fried a concoction whose odors stimulated his taste buds.

"Just me, or does it seem we're always eating with one another?" he asked.

"Just you," Kat chuckled. "Everyone's gotta eat. Usually three times a day. Say, ninety minutes a day, plus prep time which can be more than an hour for dinner. Out of the sixteen hours a day we're awake, we're talking about one-fifth of our waking time. Total it up and—"

"Okay, okay." Max gave in. "Doesn't matter. I like being with you no matter when or doing what."

Kat placed a handful of pasta into a boiling pot and stared at him. "So, you broke into the mansion of one of the richest, best-protected men in the world. Not satisfied, you burgled the home of the President of the United States of America. Did I get your story straight?"

"Are you an informant for the secret district attorney or something?"

She laughed. "No."

"Are you in any way connected to the US Department of Justice?"

"No."

"If I were to designate you my confessor, would you be bound to hold this conversation in confidence?"

"I don't think so."

Max mused, then, after a minute, said, "I trust you, nevertheless. You're right." He held up his index finger. "But I think the results may be worth the felonies."

"Couldn't you be tried for high crimes? Treason or something?"

Max shrugged. "Maybe. I weighed the possibilities before acting. Ended up, getting in and out was a piece of cake—both places. I had good intel."

"Intel on the president's personal residence?"

"The president may have professional quote-unquote people. I've got something better—trusted friends."

—————— ◆ ——————

Kat shook her head and mused. Here she was, a girl who'd played straight her entire life, who'd excelled in school, won scholarships, and studied at the most prestigious universities. She'd been invited on one important dig in the Southwest, which led to another more important one in the Middle East, which led to another, and finally, her own project on the other side of the world. She'd dated a ton of guys of all sorts from high school through college, then more and more sparingly as she forged her way through graduate school and into her teaching profession.

And now here she was falling in love with a fellow who'd made a living blowing things up in covert operations. Max Braxton had taken out bad guys by the droves—permanently—with his own hands. And now, when he was apparently rejoining the world in a legitimate way as a university instructor, he had broken into the house of the leader of the free world.

She recalled being threatened by an armed Muslim terrorist and Max taking the guy down with a knife thrown from about twenty feet away.

She chuckled to herself and stared down at her feet. *Yep, they were her feet, at the ends of her legs. She looked up and across the room. And, yep, there he was—wilder, more handsome and more fun to be around than she could have asked of a genie if she had happened upon a magic lantern.*

The sound of water boiling behind her broke her thoughts, and she turned to tend her angel-hair pasta.

———— ◆ ————

Max wondered at his own alacrity at revealing his break-ins to her. Confiding in her shattered all his personal codes of silence outside his combat comrades-in-arms. But as soon as he considered what he'd done, he set the concern aside. Kat had gained his trust faster than anyone, ever. From the moment he had met her, in torment over her endangered friend, through their treacherous adventure hunting down King David's music, she had proven steadfast and reliable.

He thought of his mother in Dallas. He'd told her all about Kat—stuff not printed in any of the magazine articles or television specials. His mom? She would flat-out adore this girl. He thought of his sister, Maise, the school teacher in Arlington. She would feel right at home with Kat.

Then he wondered if, despite their past, he had scared Kat away by his revelations. Really, how many girls—actually, women besides motorcycle mamas—wanted to date a fellow who dared do what he had done this weekend?

A couple minutes later, they were sipping chardonnay and eating chicken stir fry flavored with ginger and assorted spices along with water chestnuts, snow peas, and green and red bell peppers.

"So, tell me about your, ah, escapade to Atlanta," Kat started. "But, first a question."

"Shoot."

"Is she pretty?"

The question took Max aback, and he simply stared at her, a question mark sketched on his face. After a moment, he knew what she meant.

"Lana Navon?" he asked.

Kat nodded. "Pretty girl?"

Max hesitated, then answered, "I've gotta say, she's stunning."

"Glad you said so," Kat said.

He cocked his head.

"I've seen photos and she is, well, dazzling, elegant," Kat said. "I was just testing you."

"And I passed?"

"You passed."

He leaned in to kiss her. The kiss was like the first, sweet taste of meringue. Yum. He hoped she thought the same. He didn't know how he tasted, but he smelled of Old Spice, which she had revealed was her favorite.

———— ◆ ————

Later, dishes washed and put away, Kat sat beside Max. Looking up at him, she said, "So tell me about Avi Navon, what sort of man he is."

"Avi Navon," Max repeated. "I think he's actually on the right side. But he's a one-issue guy. To him, Israel is tantamount. He just backed the wrong man—and now, too late, realizes his mistake."

"Really?"

"Perhaps the most humble billionaire I'll ever meet."

Kat nodded. "And you meet billionaires quite often?"

Max laughed. "No. He's my first, actually, but wasn't what I expected. For instance, I would expect someone finding an intruder ensconced in his den with Glock in hand would be afraid, intimidated, more surprised than he was."

"You threatened him with a gun?" Kat's jaw dropped.

"No-no. I was just holding one—nonchalantly, just to show him I was armed."

"Oh, that's all." She sounded unconvinced. "And he simply stood there unafraid." She crossed her arms, a sure sign of skepticism.

"Perhaps his response has to do with his military background. He was quite the fearsome soldier in his time."

Kat raised an eyebrow.

Max chuckled. "Or perhaps the players in the world of high finance are more lethal than we know."

"Yeah, right. No longer do they say, 'Show me your portfolio of oil companies, and I'll blow you away with my boat-full of plutonium.' Now the word is 'Show me your Uzi, and I'll show you my rocket-propelled grenade.'"

Max laughed. "Here's our favorite archaeologist talking Uzis and RPGs."

"Warfare was a way of life thousands of years ago too," Kat said. "Catapults, longbows, crossbows, King David's slingshot." Her green eyes lit up. "I'm on top of this subject, mister."

Max shook his head. "I know of your expertise. I've seen it first-hand. I owe my life to you and yet here I am, asking, 'What have I gotten myself into?'"

"A very powerful man's estate, for one thing," Kat replied. "The president's house, for another."

"No-no-no," he said. "I mean you can even talk about ancient combat. You amaze me, Cardova."

"Thank you," she said, her look demure. "I have a book on historic armaments you can borrow if you're interested." She pointed to her bookshelves.

"Thanks, but I've studied the history of arms."

"Of course—at the Citadel."

"No, at the Naval War College. They took weaponry to a whole other level. Now we have weapons capable of blowing up cities, but we don't use them because we're more concerned we not harm the innocents—women and children. So, we're back to doing battle like a hundred years ago, only with higher-powered crossbows. We call them tactical weapons, but they're assault rifles and submachine guns."

"But you're fighting terrorists who have no such qualms about women and children."

"Right."

"You must think this unfair."

"Well," Max said, "the Jews to this day are victimized by descendants of the people they did not kill when they had the chance."

"So, then," Kat eyed him with keen intensity, "are you advocating blowing up neighborhoods with women and children in them?"

Max held up a hand of protest. "No. But the terrorists are getting away with using women and children as human shields. We also have to live with the fact the children of dead terrorists live to follow in their fathers' footsteps. Many follow the same vitriol from the imams their fathers did. Others seek revenge. By letting them live today, we're allowing them to kill us tomorrow."

"Pretty pessimistic."

"Pretty true."

"The fate of an unsaved world, Max. Will you go back there?"

Max saw her furrowed brow and wrapped her hands in his. "A question I'm battling in my mind. I hope I can leave such a life behind. But, the fact remains, if my government calls me to service I may be compelled to acquiesce. And, even if not, if I believe my country to be in danger—" His voice trailed off.

"Then I fear for you as well as myself," she said.

———— ◆ ————

"I wish you hadn't defamed my car, man." Hank slapped at the steering wheel of his Mini Cooper.

Josh chuckled at the hurt look on his friend's face. Their windows were open, the heat blasting full strength, the car idling in park outside the warehouse. "What?"

"You know, picking on my Mini. Didn't you see *Italian Job*? If Mark Wahlberg drives one, this baby can't be *that* girly."

Josh laughed. "Whatever, dude. The teach drives a V12."

Just then a car pulled up beside them on Josh's side, gravel crunching beneath the tires. The passenger window rolled down, revealing Jill sitting behind the wheel. Josh's heart did a flip. *Somebody ought to replicate her face on a doll. Barbie, move over.*

"Did we really have to meet this late?" she asked.

"Afraid you won't get your beauty sleep?" Hank leaned forward to try to look around Josh and Josh bent forward to block his view—just for fun.

"Shut up." Josh hit him in the arm. Then he looked over at Jill. "Don't listen to him. He's just jealous 'cause the ugly fairy hit him too many times."

A Jeep pulled up on Hank's side of the car. Jose was driving and as he parked, he flicked off his lights. Ashley, in the passenger seat, rolled down her window.

"Ready, girls?" Jose smiled, winking at Josh and Hank.

"Yeah, who's got the key?" Josh asked.

"I do," Jill said.

Everyone rolled their windows up and climbed out. The cars beeped in unison as they hit their locks. On their way up the elevator, Hank asked Ashley, "Where's your schoolbag?"

"Just because you have a man-purse doesn't mean I have to carry one," Ashley said with a smile.

"Whoa, look at you," Josh said with a laugh, "breaking out with the wisecracks when the teach isn't around." He raised his hand for a high five which Ashley ignored.

"Whatever," Hank said, "where's your school work?"

"It's all up here." Ashley pointed to her temple. "Photographic memory."

Jill rolled her eyes. "Let's just focus on what we need to do, okay, guys?"

The elevator reached its floor, and Josh pulled open the iron-gated door.

The light bulb in the hallway flickered and swayed.

"It's like there's a ghost or something," Josh said.

He couldn't take his eyes off the bulb as they stepped forward. Jill unlocked the door.

When the door swung into the room, the lights came alive and the computers turned on, the monitors displaying a moving wind across them in one smooth motion, the set screensaver.

———◆———

"This place hasn't gotten any less cool than the first time around," Jose said. Josh winced as Jose cracked his knuckles and sat down at the main keyboard. Josh and the others sat around him, pulling out the dossiers Max had given them.

"Okay, where do we start?" Jill asked.

"Well," Josh offered, subconsciously rubbing his chin and looking at the computer monitors, "Mr. Braxton said we need to launder money, just like terrorists would. We need to find their loopholes."

Hank pulled out his CIA dossier. "This is smack, man. Look at all this."

"Yeah, I looked through the file last night," Ashley replied. "Contains a list of all the FTO groups, their suspected locations, including training grounds and sleeper cells."

"FTO?" Hank asked, looking up from his open folders.

"Yeah, Foreign Terrorist Organizations, remember? From class?"

"Hank was probably sleeping." Jose chuckled.

Ashley pointed at the middle screen. "Can we start by poking around, guys?"

Jose stretched again and smiled. "Alrighty, then, let's take a look-see."

With a few taps of the keyboard, the world map slowly started spinning. Josh's mouth opened in admiration.

"Type in coordinates N34° 31' E70° 31'," Ashley said, poking her finger on the Middle East on the monitor.

Jose tapped away and the map focused on Jalalabad, Afghanistan. "Did you memorize those coordinates?"

"Yup, like I said, photographic memory."

"I thought you were joking," Jose said. "You've suddenly become a lot hotter."

"Pig," Ashley slapped the back of his head. "Focus on the screen, Computer Monkey."

"Okay, okay." Jose laughed, holding up his hands. "Let's try clicking on these icons at the bottom of the monitor. I think they're the layers."

"Try the icon marked 'Topo,'" Josh suggested.

Jose clicked on the icon and a topographical map layered over Jalalabad, making the city three-dimensional.

"Check out the black hats," Josh said.

"Those are boxes," Jose said.

"Yeah, I know, duffus. An expression, you know. Black hat?"

Jose clicked on the black box and several popped up. As he moused over them, a bubble appeared, giving more detailed information.

"What is Sipah-e-Sahaba Pakistan (SSP)?" Hank asked.

"A Pakistani terrorist group," Ashley answered.

"But what are they doing in Afghanistan?" Hank asked.

"I think there's some speculation the SSP is coordinating with the Afghan Sunnis. Could be the rise of a whole new civil war across the borders," Ashley said.

Josh and the others stared slack-jawed.

"What?" he asked. "I'm not really an idiot, I just play one on TV. You didn't think I got into Yale just on my good looks, did you? I got brains. I just choose when to show them off. Don't want to stir up too much jealousy."

Jill pulled her hair back, one hand on the top of Jose's chair, and looked up at Josh. "Can you imagine? Sunni groups coordinating for civil war? So far, they've apparently only been fighting for control in individual countries, but if Pakistani Sunnis and Afghanistan Sunnis coordinated—"

"A scary scenario," Josh finished. A shiver ran down his spine.

Jose clicked on the arrow icon at the bottom of the SSP bubble on the monitor. A box within the screen popped up. "Look at this, guys. Gives the whole history of this group."

Jose read the bubble: "Established in 1985 by Maulana Haq Nawaz Jhangvi, Maulana Zia-ur-Rehman Farooqi, Maulana Eesar-ul-Haq Qasmi, and Maulana Azam Tariq."

"Let's try a more interesting coordinate," Hank offered, his face buried in the dossier.

"Someone take a photo," Josh said. "I've never seen Hank so studious, and if we don't capture this moment, no one will believe us."

"Shut up, man," Hank said, looking up from the dossier. He looked serious, but Josh was undaunted.

"Dude," he said, "your parents would be so proud. I can see them now." Josh had put his arm around Jill, in mock fashion of Hank's parents. "'Our son. We always knew he had excellence in him. Sniff, sniff.'"

"You know," Hank said, "I hope in the first spring practice the offensive line levels you."

Josh laughed. "Not a chance, man. I fly like a butterfly, sting like a bee."

"More like dance like a princess in a tutu," Jose laughed, bumping fists with Hank.

Josh was about to bop Jose on the head when Ashley, frustrated, said, "Boys, can we concentrate on the task at hand? I have better things than school work to do with my evening."

"Right. Task at hand," Hank mimicked. "Like I said, let's try some more interesting coordinates. Type in N38° 53' W77° 02'."

Jose turned around and tapped in the coordinates field. Rubbing his hands together in anticipation, he punched the Enter key.

"Whose group is this?" Jill asked. Her face had turned pale.

"The Fatah. Has an X next to its name," Ashley said.

"Which means," Jose said, squinting up at the X on the monitor, "Fatah is no longer listed as an FTO officially, but is still under watch."

Josh's eyes went wide. "They're right smack in downtown DC."

"Yeah, but they're no longer part of the FTO," Ashley replied.

"But, guys," Jose said, "look at this. Right next to them on the map is another black box. Moused over, the data gives us ISIS. And when moused over again, see what happens?"

As Jose left-clicked on the ISIS bubble, lines formed all over the earth, which started to slowly rotate in 3D mode. Lines formed to South America where TBA lit up in bright red, then across the ocean to several areas in Europe, Africa, the Middle East, and even over some of Russia.

Hank looked up from his folder to the monitor. "What's the TBA stand for?"

"Tri-Border Area," Ashley said.

"To put in terms you would understand, TBA kind of like Mad Max land," Josh replied.

"Ah, right. Argentina, Paraguay, and Brazil," Hank said, still looking in his dossier.

Jose looked back at him. "Hank, you've got to be the smartest dumb person I know."

"Excuse me, but I prefer to be the dumbest smart person you know." Hank chuckled.

Now Josh noticed a strange little icon at the bottom of the main screen. "Hey, guys," he said, pointing to it, "what's this red rocket?"

"It's tiny," Jill said, leaning forward.

"I didn't even notice it until I reset the screen back to the main global 3D view," Jose said.

"Click on it and see what happens," Josh said. Both his hands gripped the back of Jose's chair as he watched the screen.

"Is it safe to, though?" Ashley countered.

"Chill out. The prof put the icon up there, so it must be fine," he said.

A strange feeling of doubt came over Josh, but before he could voice his feelings, Jose had clicked on the icon. A wash of numbers covered the screen and started a slow spin, changing back into a 3D globe— the topographical, geopolitical, and economic layers covering it. Then another layer covered the map on the screen, like an infrared filament. White darts appeared and began moving.

"Whoa, I'm not so sure what we're looking at anymore," Josh said. He stood up straight, his eyes shifting from one monitor to the next.

"It's got to be fake real-time tracking," Jill said. "I wouldn't worry. I'm sure Mr. Braxton just forgot. He covered a lot of ground on this application in a short period of time."

"Yeah, but look at the streaming data over there." Jose pointed to the monitor second to the left. "It all changed. I recognize some of those names."

"So?" Josh asked.

"So?" Jose said. "Don't you know who some of those names are?"

Josh concentrated on the monitor. "Nope. No idea."

"Before, I didn't recognize any of the names, but now, well, look there. Charles Calthrop. Jacobo Arenas. Carlos Castaño Gil. Sabri al-Banna."

"And?" Hank asked.

"And? Dude, those are the leaders of the FARC, the AUC ,and Charles Calthrop is better known as Carlo the Jackal."

"And," Jill added, "Sabri al-Banna is Abu Nidal. He's a Palestinian terrorist. But he's dead."

"Guys, what are you getting freaked out about? This is all fake data, remember?" Ashley said.

"Yeah, well, all I know is everything looked fake before I clicked on the little icon," Jose said. "Now I'm recognizing at least every third name scrolling up the screen."

They all stood for a few moments in awkward silence.

Jill spoke up. "Alright, guys," she offered, "let's just get to work. We can double-check with Mr. Braxton the next class, okay? Quite honestly, the fact they have the Jackal and Abu on the screen makes me feel better anyway because they're both dead. Kind of confirms to me this is dummy data we're seeing."

"Can I take a seat?" Ashley asked.

"Be my guest." Jose stood up and patted the chair.

Ashley sat behind the keyboard and started tapping away in the coordinates box. "I'm just using some DOS on a hunch."

"DOS? What, you mean the ancient computer language? How'd you learn DOS?" Jill asked.

"My computer-geek brother used to hack sites for fun. He taught me a few tricks before getting locked up for inadvertently hacking into the Pentagon mainframe."

They all grew silent again. "Ha—just kidding." Ashley said, looking back. But her smile faded when she turned back to the keyboard. "Oh, man. Those moving darts are all government vehicles."

"What do you mean?"

"The government keeps track of all agents in every branch. This allows headquarters to offer backup when radios break down and to keep tabs on some undercover work."

"How did you know this?" Josh asked.

"And don't say the information was part of the reading," Hank chimed in.

"My dad was in the government. He worked in the satellite imagery offices. I'm not quite sure what they did, but he'd tell me some things when I pried, as long as they weren't classified."

Jill arched her back and stretched. "Okay, guys, let's try to focus a bit here. We need to set some goals and figure out how to get there."

"Right," Josh agreed. "Let me toss out a few ideas I was thinking about on the way over and tell me if any of them grab your interest."

While Ashley continued to click away, the others turned to Josh to listen.

"Ashley?" he asked.

"I'm listening," she said over her shoulder.

"Okay, so we could pretend we're an arms dealer who just unloaded $300 million in weaponry to a group in Beirut. We need to launder the money from there."

"I like that scenario," Hank said.

"Actually," Jill suggested, "I was thinking maybe we could start with something a little larger. You know, surprise Mr. Braxton with a mega bang."

"Like what?" Jose asked.

"Like, maybe we take one of these accounts already in existence—"

"Like this one here?" Ashley asked, cutting her off.

They all looked over at the first monitor. The bank accounts were still streaming in the background, but a box appeared in the forefront, showing an account with holdings topping $3 million.

"Yeah, like that one. Maybe an account with even more holdings. Then we could use those to find another black box up there on the main screen to buy some weapons."

"But we're supposed to launder money," Jose interjected.

"I'm getting there. So, we buy the weapons from a small group over in the Middle East somewhere. Then we smuggle them into the United States."

"Smuggle?" Hank interrupted.

"Right. Into one of the ports." Josh looked back up at the main screen and pointed toward North America's East Coast. "Like through a port up in Boothbay Harbor, Maine, or even down further south, along Cape Cod in Massachusetts."

"And how would you propose we get this done?" Ashley asked, still tapping away in the first monitor with the accounts.

"I didn't think you were still listening." Josh laughed. "Well, we create a diversion."

"A diversion?" Jill asked.

"Yeah, let's say, further south, like Miami."

Hank interrupted, "If we're looking for a diversion, I think we'd do better to bring the action closer to the actual location. We could try to smuggle some weapons along the coast right here in DC." He pointed to the map on the main screen. "Something big enough to warrant most of the FBI and Coast Guard's resources to come in and assist."

"Why closer?" Jose asked.

"Hank's right," Josh said. "I doubt the FBI in the Northeast branches would assist a Miami incident, but they might assist something closer to their states, like DC."

"Good point," Jill said. "Then, a day after the shipment is caught, we bring in the goods farther up the coast where I pointed out."

"Hmm." Jose rubbed his chin., "You've got some guts."

Jill's smile was mischievous.

"I'm still listening, though, Blue Eyes." Josh grinned. "What's next? We haven't gotten to the laundering just yet."

"So, once we're here, we target some of the black boxes inland. Like here." Jill turned and pointed on the map of Arlington, Virginia.

"And then," Hank said, "sell the arms to them for more money than we bought them for because the hard part of getting them into the States has been done."

"Precisely, dear Watson." Jill lit the room with a smile ,and Josh knew he was in love.

Jose broke the moment for Josh. "But I think maybe we should find a black box further north. Maybe up in Massachusetts. If we want the arrest to take place in DC then there'll be too many pigtails to make the sale there."

"Pigtails?" Jill asked.

"Yeah, you know, cops, feds."

"Oh, pigs. I get it." Hank laughed.

"The only pigs I see are right here," Ashley said, looking at Jose.

"Hey, my uncle was a cop," Jose replied. "I was just foolin' around."

"What do you have there?" Jill asked Ashley. Obviously, she was hoping to steer the conversation in a different direction.

"I've pulled up a few more accounts. If we're going to hit Mr. Braxton with a bang, then we need to steal more than a couple million bucks."

"So, what are you thinking?"

"I'm thinking we target a dozen accounts or so. Bring the total up to a few hundred million."

"Shouldn't we start off a little, I don't know, easier or something?" Jose suggested.

"No guts, no glory," Josh said. "They're just fake accounts, remember."

"Yeah, okay. I wonder what happens if the fake feds catch us with the fake weapons or the fake millions," Jose shot back. "Would the prof find out?"

"Well, let's just make sure he doesn't," Ashley said, turning back to the keyboard.

———— ◆ ————

Approximately two hundred eighty-five miles away from Yale, in the bowels of the National Security Agency, a door banged open, and all the board members turned to the sweating intern, shirt half untucked, tie over his shoulder as if he'd run a fifteen-hundred-meter sprint. The board room was located at the far end of the NSA's ten-acre underground establishment, he may have had a much longer run.

"What is the meaning of this?" the fat man at the end of the table asked.

"I'm so sorry, sir," the scrawny young man said, straightening his glasses, "but we have a problem."

"It better be in the sum of North Korea to interrupt our meeting like this," the fat man threatened.

The intern paused, stuttered slightly, "I'm sorry, sir. I'm just, it's just—"

"Well, spit it out."

Sitting next to the fat man, Alan Sturgen intervened. "Easy, Reynolds. Remember our College Champion Program? We take in college students to give them a taste of what working at the agency is like? Philip here's with the program, so let's go a little easier on him."

"You're telling me a college intern interrupted this board meeting?" Reynolds bellowed.

Sturgen smiled as best he could and then addressed the boy, still stammering and attempting to straighten himself out in the doorway. "What is it, Philip?"

"You're needed right away, sir. Secure Room Gateway."

"Under whose request?" Sturgen asked, trying to assess whether he should leave the weekly intelligence briefing.

"M—m—Assistant Director Crowe's," the boy stammered.

Sturgen smiled. Monica Crowe could instill the fear of heaven and hell in anyone, much less an intern. If she had summoned him from the weekly briefing, though, the matter must be urgent.

"Very well. Thank you, Philip. Let her know I'll be there in five minutes."

"Yes, sir." Philip turned, shut the door behind him, and sprinted back through the underground hallways.

———•◆•———

When Sturgen entered Secure Room Gateway, Monica was sitting between two senior mathematicians, staring at a laptop screen, whispering.

"You interrupted the intelligence briefing. I hope this is good."

Monica glanced up. "It's not good. It's bad. It's very bad." She paused, perhaps assessing how best to convey what had happened, and then stood up, flicking on the overhead projector. "Sam, can you please pull up the first few accounts?"

Sturgen stayed on his feet, his back resting against the closed door. Secure Room Gateway was equipped with soundproof walls. Encased underground and secured from any wireless devices. Anything said in the room, stayed in the room.

Sam Flaherty pulled up a row of bank accounts on the screen.

"Aren't those our Cayman accounts?" Sturgen asked.

"Yes, sir," Monica said. "The FirstCaribbean International Bank, to be precise. The Regatta branch. You can see the first four accounts affected—"

"Affected by what?" Sturgen cut her off.

"Well, we're not sure what happened, sir, but someone broke into the account and transferred all assets to a Swiss bank."

"Broke in? As in balaclavas and machine guns?"

"No, sir. Electronically. They hacked into the accounts."

"But, how did they know the account numbers?"

Flaherty nudged his fellow mathematician, Loni, who looked up from the screen. "We're not sure yet, sir, but the chances of someone stumbling upon this are approximately four billion to one. Assuming those four billion have the same IQ as we do."

"Four billion to one is too close, apparently," Sturgen said with a sigh. He pulled a chair out to sit but instead started pacing. "Are you sure they couldn't dump in a Trojan to dig up the numbers? Were we hacked?"

"No, sir," Loni answered, "we weren't hacked. Our servers not only show no signs of someone trying to break in, but the doors weren't even opened by an official key."

"Okay, what accounts were affected? I see four on the screen here. Four is all?"

Sam and Monica exchanged glances.

"I'm losing my patience, Monica," Sturgen said.

"I'm sorry, sir. It's just, well, twenty-seven accounts were affected."

"Twenty-seven?" The stack of papers he had in his hands fell onto the chair he had pulled out.

"Twenty-seven. Yes, sir."

"The good news, sir," Sam said, "is we headed off the hacker. He, or she, was attempting to hit Abu Abdullah Shafae's assets, which we acquired in 2007. We inserted one of our toughest Trojans back through his line to head him off."

"It's good news we stopped them from getting twenty-eight accounts?" Sturgen's voice rose several octaves ,and Loni shrunk further down into her chair.

"Sir, if I may," Monica intervened, "the Trojan Sam is referring to is a highly sophisticated one."

"Sophisticated enough to transfer all funds back into our off-shore accounts?"

"No, but sophisticated enough to settle down into the hacker's host account and ping us their IP address."

"Monica," Sturgen sighed, "I deal with transferring our coders' work to the field agents of our branches. I require the intel to be broken down a little further."

"Sorry, sir. Translated, we will know the hacker's location very soon."

"How very?"

"Very, very."

Chapter Ten

Monday Morning, January 27

Early Monday morning, while most of their fellow students were punching the snooze button on their alarm clocks or yawning themselves awake, the bat cave was alive. After agreeing on Jill's plan the night before, they had decided to meet now, anxious to have something to show before the next antiterrorism class.

Ashley found hiding her self-satisfaction difficult. Having worked all night in the bat cave, she opened the door to the startled faces of Josh, Hank, Jose, and Jill.

She broke her news to them and savored the wide-eyed responses.

"$742 million?" Josh exclaimed.

"Let's say three-quarters of a billion. Sounds more impressive." Ashley stretched nonchalantly, waiting for applause.

"How did you steal so much so quickly?" Jose asked. "Were you here all night?"

"The account access codes were in the dossier," Josh said, looking at Jose.

"Yeah, but even with those codes, this must have taken forever."

"A few hours, yes," Ashley said. "I established our own account, entitled Mongoose Enterprises."

"Which bank?" Jill asked.

"I thought creating the account in the very bank we pilfered would be entertaining," Ashley answered, "although anyone examining the accounts would think the money was transferred to a Swiss bank. A cunning ploy if I say so myself."

She smiled broadly.

"Right there in the Cayman Islands?" Hank asked, surprised.

"Right there in the very same FirstCaribbean International Bank."

"Wait, you're telling me every account you hacked into was in the same bank?"

"Well, no, actually. But I'd say forty or so were."

"Forty?" Josh exclaimed. "How many did you hack?"

"Forty-five."

Jose sighed. "So, what possessed you to hack so many accounts?"

"I'm sorry, I just couldn't help myself. The challenge was fun—like Monopoly combined with Risk and on steroids. You know, to see how much money we could get." Ashley pulled her shoulders back and added, "I don't remember ever having so much fun, and I'm wide awake."

"The adrenaline's speaking," Josh said. "Like game time for you, right?"

Ashley nodded.

"Guys," Hank started, "I know we wanted to hit Teach with a bang on our first assignment, but you do realize the bigger the bang, the harder it will be to pull off?"

———— ◆ ————

Outside, two vans pulled up about fifty yards away. A black Mercedes with heavily tinted windows followed their lead. Alan

Sturgen and Monica Crowe stepped out of the Mercedes and walked to the driver's window of the first van.

"Where are they?" Sturgen asked.

"Right over there, sir," the driver answered, pointing down the street and repeating the exact address, "in the middle one of those three converted warehouses."

Will Shackler stepped out of the other van and joined them.

"What's the plan, Stash?" Sturgen said.

Will smiled. Sturgen had called him Stash for years due to his formidable brown mustache. He and Sturgen had known each other since college and were recruited at the same time—Will to the FBI and Sturgen to the NSA. Sturgen had made a rapid rise on the intelligence ladder, while Will excelled in field operations.

"Sturg, I'd really like to get closer."

"This is too big to blow up," Sturgen replied. "Whoever this is, we need to catch them. I don't want to take a chance our presence might tip them off."

"I'm not a rookie. My men know how to blend in."

"I'm sure your men can blend in, but the microwave has to stay in the van and vans don't blend in. They scream surveillance."

Sturgen was referring to the equipment which reads temperature through walls and was routinely used to determine the number of bodies inside a structure and even give a rough idea of a building's layout.

"We could do the whole ice-cream-truck routine," Will suggested.

"With our luck, kids would come running, even in this warehouse district," Sturgen replied. "Let's just do this, do this right, and be back at headquarters for lunch."

Will hated to create plans last-second and without more intel, but he sighed and pulled out a map of the area. "We'll do this your way, then. The warehouse is four floors and has been renovated for condos. The subjects are on the top floor. We'll do a flag-and-tag."

"Flag-and-tag?" Crowe asked.

"You want them breathing, right? We've loaded our guns with tranqs so we can bring them back home safe and sound and have a chance to question them."

"Good." Sturgen peered down the straight street toward the middle warehouse. "But we're treating this as a terrorist act. No Miranda rights, no lawyers. These guys are going underground in one of your tanks for questioning. Got it?"

"Got it," Will answered. He opened the side door of the van, where seven of his team were waiting. "Okay, guys, here's the plan."

———— ◆ ————

In the bat cave, Ashley reminded the A-Team, "It's just a game."

"It's our grade," Josh shot back.

"Guys, c'mon now," Jill said, putting her arm over Ashley's shoulder. "What happened to 'no guts no glory,' anyway? Don't tell me the women in this room are the only ones with moxie."

They looked around at each other.

Jose broke the silence, "I'm in."

"Me, too," Josh said.

Hank sighed. "Man, I have a bad feeling about this. But, okay, I'm in, too."

Ashley sat down at the keyboard. "Okay, guys, here's the account. Our business is imports and exports, specifically pottery from Johannesburg."

"Shouldn't we discuss the front company?" Josh asked.

"Too late. I had to fill out a form to open the account, and I had to open an account so I had a place to store our funds."

"A form?" Jill asked. "This is so real. I wonder how Mr. Braxton built this."

"His friend did it, remember?" Hank said. "CIA spook stuff."

"Anyway, I figured imports-exports was the route to go. Prices on artwork and pottery are always subjective," Ashley said.

"Very cool," Jose said. "So, our next step is?"

"Well, I did the hacking and got us our funds, so don't look at me. The rest is open for debate." Ashley held up her hands. "Jill, this was your plan, right? What's next?"

———◦◆———

Monica sat beside Sturgen, watching from the comfort of their idling car, the heat blowing. The cold weather worked to their advantage. Will's team hid their guns under their long coats. They were posing as friends coming home from an all-night party.

"Think they can pull the operation off?" she asked.

"I trust Will. He's the best at what he does."

"Yeah, but about the 'off-the-books' thing, sir—" Monica started.

Sturgen cut her off. "Unless you'd like to go before a congressional hearing and explain how funds no one knows exist in off-shore accounts which we aren't supposed to have were hacked and pilfered by people who might pose a terrorist threat, then trust me, you want this off the books, too."

Monica turned to watch Will's team who were ambling up toward the warehouse.

———◦◆———

Will led the way as his team reached the door. Four went around toward the back of the building, one to each side, and two stayed by the front entrance holding wrapped "gifts" in their arms.

There was one button for each floor. Will pushed number three.

"Hello?" A young female answered.

"Hi, we're here for the party." Will said as jovially as he could.

"The party?" the voice said. "At this time of the morning?"

"Yes, well, it kind of started last night and hasn't stopped," he replied. "Wait, you don't sound like Kathy."

"I'm not. I think you have the wrong place."

"This is Mattapan Street, right? Did I push number three?"

"Yes, this is. Maybe you have the wrong address?"

"Shoot, you're probably right. Can I come up real quick and use your phone? I need to call her and I don't have my cell on me."

"Uh, sure, I guess." Her voice was followed by a buzzer sounding. Will and his partner entered.

"We're in," he said into the mike on his wrist.

"No side entrances, boss. We're coming around."

"Okay, I've propped the door open. You four out back, stay put. Let me know if you see them coming out."

They sidled up the stairway, handguns drawn. "Fourth floor," echoed into their mikes. "Repeat, fourth floor. My lead," Will said.

———— ◆ ————

"My plan wasn't with three-quarters of a billion dollars, though," Jill said. An odd excitement stirred her—a feeling she hadn't had before even though this entire operation was pretend. Peculiar, she thought.

"Forget the amount right now," Hank replied. "Let's just focus on the steps. What are the next steps?"

Jill thought for a moment. "Okay, I like the idea of attacking twice. One small-arms shipment in Washington, DC, for a distraction and then one larger one where the larger law enforcement wouldn't be, like the Cape."

Jose, now in the control seat, tapped away on the computer and pulled up a map of the Northeast Coast. "We could have the shipment come into a freight yard in New York and then be delivered by truck down to Washington."

"Looks like your idea would be our best bet," Josh said. He pointed toward the coastline by Virginia. "Doesn't look like there's an optimal port down here."

"There are other reasons too," Hank said. "The more freight boxes, the longer law enforcement will have to take to find the cargo. There's a better chance they'd need to pull in additional help from neighboring FBI and Coast Guard offices."

"I like the plan," Jill said. She stepped back and took a broader look at the map. "Then the much larger shipment can hit the Cape and be shipped to Boston by truck for the arms sale."

"So how are we going to handle this?" Jose asked. "Are we using the $700 million to buy the arms and order the freight shipments?"

"Right," Jill said. "And then we sell the arms. Once we do, Mr. Braxton's assignment of laundering the arms-sale money kicks in."

"My uncle used to work down by one of the shipping yards in New York," Josh said. "Let me give him a call. If we're going to contact one of those fake black boxes now, we might as well get some accurate information beforehand, so we know where to have the shipment sent." He dialed his smart phone.

"There's no signal in here, remember?" Jill said. "Mr. Braxton blocked out signals for the security detail he set up for this little headquarters."

"Oh, right. Forgot."

"I'll go outside with you. We can make the call from there," she said. "Plus, it's way too warm in here."

"While you two make the call, we'll get started finding the right black-market contact for the initial arms purchase," Ashley said. "With any luck, by the time you come back up, we'll even have the ships we want the arms purchases on."

"Alrighty. Be right back," Jill said.

She and Josh left the room and she punched the elevator button.

"Let's just walk it," Josh suggested. "It's only four flights."

"What's the matter?" Jill asked and winked at him, thinking she wouldn't look bad on the arm of a handsome football star. "Afraid to be alone with me in the elevator?"

———◆———

As Will and his team stepped their way up toward the fourth floor, he heard the elevator whir to life. Through the iron grates, he saw the lift make its way up from the first floor past the second.

He pointed at the back two men on the stairwell and motioned for them to return to the ground floor in case their target hit the elevator before they reached the fourth floor. Then he pointed to Jim behind him to follow him the rest of the way. They moved more quickly and kept to the outside of the stairwell.

He didn't see anyone coming down the stairs, but as they reached the third floor, the elevator door shut and started down. Will peered over the railing and lifted his wrist mike to his mouth. "At least one in the shaft," he whispered. "We'll make our way to the fourth. No shots. We want the tango conscious. Don't use the tranq gun unless you have to."

He shifted his bulletproof vest, a bit bulky, raised the Glock in both hands and hurried up the final set of stairs.

Just before the fourth-floor landing, Will held his hand up, stopping Jim behind him. Down below, he heard the elevator shaft open, a woman scream, and then the familiar voice in his earpiece. "Tango down and breathing. And conscious to answer questions."

Will smiled. He checked over his shoulder. Jim gave him a thumbs-up, and they swiftly stepped onto the fourth floor. Double-steel-enforced and hung on in-built hinges like a bank vault, the door was obviously meant to keep people out.

Will raised his ring and index fingers, signaling his partner to blow the lock. Quickly, Jim set a small charge of plastics, they stepped back and he pushed the button on the detonator.

Boom! The locking mechanism blew inward and Will rushed forward and shouldered the door open.

———— ◆ ————

Outside, Sturgen shifted in his seat, anxious. Finally, a voice came over the walkie-talkie.

"Sturg? We have a problem."

———— ◆ ————

Josh slammed the bat cave door open. "Guys, we have a predicament."

"A serious predicament," Jill resounded.

"What is it?" Jose asked.

"Just get your stuff, quickly, and hurry out of there," Josh said. He felt like he was calling defensive signals and none of his teammates were understanding.

"What are you talking about?" Hank asked.

"Just get your stuff," Jill said. She looked over her shoulder at Josh, panic filling her eyes.

"Okay, okay," Jose said as they all stuffed their papers in their bags. "Where are we going?"

"Doesn't matter," Josh answered.

"Just out of here. Let's go. Hurry up." Jill screamed.

Ashley was the first out the door, no bag to carry, and hit the elevator door button.

"No, we take the stairs," Josh said.

Ashley looked back at Josh, alarm in her eyes.

"It's just faster," he answered.

Hank locked the door behind them and they scrambled down the stairs. When they reached the ground floor, Josh turned and stopped them.

"What? What is it?" Jill asked, panicked.

"When we head out, we need to act calm, smiling. We'll all climb into Jose's Jeep."

"Why don't we take our own vehicles?" Ashley asked.

"Right now, we need to stick together."

"I don't understand," Jose replied.

"I'll explain on the way," Josh answered. "Just, right now, let's act unruffled and head to the Safari. Hank parked it over there."

Josh pointed out the glass door toward the right of the parking lot.

———— ◆ ————

"What's the problem?" Sturgen asked into the walkie-talkie.

"Unless our tango is an eighty-year-old woman drinking tea while watching *Good Morning America*, we have the wrong place."

In the background, Sturgen could hear an old lady hollering, "You're darn right you have the wrong place. You ruined my five-star safety door and nearly gave me a heart attack. Are you okay, Mittens?"

"And a cat," Will said.

Sturgen exchanged looks with Monica.

"Get your team back here and tell me what happened."

As Will's team exited the warehouse, a Jeep slowly passed by Sturgen and Monica, with five young adults inside, their attention fixed on the FBI.

———◆———

"And you think those guys were after us?" Hank asked. His hands shook on the wheel.

"A bad feeling is all," Josh answered.

"I hate to say so, but I think Josh is right," Ashley said.

"Explain," Jill said.

"When I was hacking the accounts, I was bouncing my IP address off a neighboring signal. Could well have been that warehouse. The building does contain apartments."

"How did you learn to do this 'bouncing' stuff?" Jose asked, turning to her in surprise.

"Not really an important question right now." Josh was aggravated. "We have a bigger problem. Getting away from here."

———◆———

Max sat on a barstool at his kitchen island and sipped espresso con panna from a demitasse cup. To a stranger looking on, the scene would have seemed unusual—this rugged man, finger and thumb wrapped around the handle of a tiny cup. He might have been playing tea party with a daughter. Only he was all alone, the drink was real, and he was enjoying the familiar taste, remembering his last time in Vienna, the feeling of a job well done, taking down a horrible man, a mass-murderer, and without anyone else getting hurt in the process.

"Here's to you, Herr Müller," he said, raising the cup. He drained the espresso con panna and smacked his lips.

He stood and walked to the bathroom, stopped at the doorway and did twenty chin-ups on a bar across the top of the doorframe, locked the door and stepped into the shower.

When he stepped out fifteen minutes later, the phone was ringing inside the pocket of his robe. He grabbed a bath towel and dried himself as he picked up the phone.

He looked at the screen. "Yoni," he said.

"Call me back on your sat, scrambled." The line went silent.

Yonatan Yishai was on to something—for Max's ears only. Max finished drying, stepped into some khakis and put on a shirt. Inside his bedroom closet, he kneeled, moved aside boots and sneakers, and stuck a finger in a knothole in a floorboard. The board creaked as he pulled upward. Scrambling through his secret stash, he picked up a satellite telephone.

A special-ops phone, "Scramble" was an option, but most of Max's calls on the device were secretive. "Scramble" was its normal setting.

Max had called Yoni Sunday night, after his time with Kat, and asked him to look into the school President Jones attended when his father was stationed in Saudi Arabia.

Just speculating on what Yoni might have discovered sent a charge of adrenaline through Max's body.

He sat on the edge of his bed and speed-dialed a number.

One ring later, "Shalom." Yoni sounded like he was in the room with Max.

"Shalom aleichem, my friend," Max said. "You have something."

"Ken. Indeed."

———————◆———————

Paxton Twill sat in an overstuffed leather chair in his West Wing office, feeling satisfied, sure he had kick-started the mission. "Discredit, disgrace, and defeat" the enemy defined his philosophy, and he was sure the strategy would work well in Operation Demolish Navon.

Amid the frenzied hustle of his surroundings, he felt a sudden calm as he watched Eleanor Monk leave his office and walk down the corridor. The driving force behind Media Tracker, a self-described nonprofit progressive research and information center dedicated to monitoring, analyzing, and correcting "misinformation in the media," Monk was a bulldog and would accomplish the mission.

Some called her a piranha, thinking the term derogatory, but, hey …

Who better than Monk to feed a rumor to the news directors at the television networks and certain cable channels who supported President Jones?

The rumor? Well, something to do with Avi Navon and the possibility of his mishandling his empire's funds. With a little nudge from Twill, Monk easily read between the lines. Jones had discovered Navon's supposed indiscretions and was going to set the Justice Department loose on him. Angered, Navon had fired a preemptive strike disavowing Jones's presidency.

For Twill, as for the president, the crucial goal was to discredit anything and everything about Navon, who had gone so far off the Jones reservation as to require banishment.

Monk and her friends at Media Tracker met frequently with network news directors and a handful of newspapers. Oftentimes the so-called news they shared made the national newscasts and newspapers unedited and unverified.

Twill smiled and leaned back. *A cigarette would go well right now.*

————◆————

Avi Navon climbed out of his pool. Late January in Atlanta might be too cold for the natives to take a morning swim, but Avi found a dip exhilarating.

Lana, dressed in an Israeli-blue fleece and shiny black gym pants, hurried toward him, a cell phone in her hand.

"It's Shamir," she said. She handed him the phone and sat in a wicker chair poolside.

"Yes?" Avi's forehead wrinkled, guessing the reason for the call from his old friend in the Mossad, the Israeli intelligence agency.

"Max Braxton." Like the last time Shamir called, the name was a complete sentence. Like Braxton was a noun and verb rolled into one.

"Again, our topic of the day," Avi said.

"I thought you'd be interested to know he has reached out to us again for information."

"What about?"

"Specifics about the Muslim school the American president attended when a teenager in Saudi Arabia."

"And what was he told?"

"The truth."

"Which is?"

A minute later, seething—with himself more so than anyone or anything else—Avi clicked the phone dead and laid the instrument on a small table between Lana and where he had taken a seat.

Lana leaned toward him, concerned. "What is it, Papa?"

"I've been a fool twice over." Avi shook his head. "What's my first rule in business, my dear."

"To know the people with whom you're to do business—"

"*Before* I do business with them," Avi finished.

"I know, Papa. It's why Boaz is on staff as our private detective."

"But, what did I do before getting into the political bed with Ridley?"

"I thought you had him checked out."

"Yes, but not far enough back."

Their housekeeper Esther stepped onto the patio. "Mr. Navon, the guard house called. There's a reporter here to see you—someone from the *New York Times*."

"Who?" Avi asked.

"A Jonathan Thudd."

"Oh, Jonathan. Have them send him up, then show him on out here, will you, Esther?"

"Yes, sir."

Several minutes later, Thudd appeared. "Thank you for seeing me out of the blue like this, sir. I was in Atlanta on a story and got a call about something I need to speak with you about."

"Sure. Come sit, Jonathan. I haven't seen you in months." Avi waved Thudd to a poolside chair under an umbrella and offered him a drink.

"No, thank you. I have something serious to ask you. Have you heard about the allegations of fiscal wrongdoing?"

"Allegations? Against who?"

"Against you, sir."

Avi was stunned. He looked at Lana. She shook her head.

"They're vague but pertain to you skimming funds from one of your companies, Isra-America."

Avi peered at Thudd. "And why would I do such a thing, Jonathan?"

"I don't know, sir. But expect to be hearing from the press with this question. The rumor started this morning and is spreading."

"Rumor from where?"

"I don't know, sir."

"Jonathan, you certainly know who shared this rumor with you."

Thudd stammered.

"Well?" Lana asked. "Who is this, spreading horrible things about my father, Mr. Thudd?"

"I c-can't s-say," Thudd stuttered.

Avi crossed his arms. "Does this come from Washington?" he asked.

Thudd stared at him and seemed to falter in his resolve.

"Does this come from the White House?" Avi demanded.

"Papa." Lana obviously hadn't thought such a thing could be true.

Avi looked at his daughter. "Well, darling, who would want to discredit me at this time?"

"Ridley?"

"Ridley, Zapper, Trevor Madden—" Avi stopped in mid-sentence, the thought striking him, and he locked his eyes on Thudd. "Paxton."

Thudd looked away.

"Paxton and his little meetings with Media Tracker—meetings starting back when Ridley was running for the nomination. Get the windmill spinning. This time with hot air."

"Jonathan," Avi grabbed the man's attention. "Lana will take you to our offices, right now, and open up our books to you. Whatever you want."

"Papa." Lana protested.

Nonplussed, Avi held up his hand. "I know, sweetheart. No privately owned company ever opens its books like this to the media. But how else to stop such a vicious lie?"

Lana thought a moment, then shrugged. "Okay, Papa. I'll do this."

When Lana and Thudd had left, Avi picked up his phone and hit a number he had thought he'd never call again. Ridley was going to get one last tongue-lashing from his former mentor.

———— ◆ ————

Ned Zapper picked up the red phone in the president's private office. A fierce and angry Avi Navon railed at him, demanding Jones's ear.

"What's this all about?" Zaps asked, trying to remain calm.

"Rumors of my alleged evil," Avi barked. "And I can only conclude they originate with the Oval Office, Zaps."

"No," Zaps said. "I assure you."

"You can assure me nothing, not anymore. I've learned my lesson well, young man. Give me the president—now."

"He's not available. He's meeting this morning with the president of Brazil."

"Tell him when he's finished he'd better meet with me—over the phone. Or the sky will fall on his head." Avi gave the order like he would to an indiscreet servant, then slammed down the phone.

———— ◆ ————

A minute later, Max's cell phone rang. Max picked it up off the coffee table. A Georgia number appeared on the display.

Max hesitated, then picked up the phone. "Yes."

"Mr. Braxton, it's Avi Navon."

Max didn't answer right away, and Avi jumped in. "I understand you've inquired about Ridley's Muslim school."

The less information you give out, the less trouble you can find yourself in. Max had broken the rule once or twice. Once, afterward, he'd discovered he was lucky to still be alive. Mum was a great three-letter word.

Not getting a response, Avi continued: "My sources tell me what yours just, apparently, told you."

Max broke his silence. "Are you on a secure line, sir?"

"No."

"Call me when you get one."

Max hung up.

———————◆———————

Avi gazed at his cell phone in disbelief.

He walked inside the house to his den and went straight to his bottom-right desk drawer.

He tapped the digits of Max's number from a scrap of paper he had placed on the poolside table.

Max picked up the call on the first ring.

"Think you might be overreacting?" Avi asked. "I mean, who's going to tap your phone?"

"Not mine. Yours."

"Are you sure you don't want my help?"

"Sure."

"I apologize, Mr. Braxton."

"It's Max, and why would you apologize?"

"I guess I'm apologizing to the world."

"I'm one man. There are more efficient ways to reach the world."

"Gotta start somewhere." From his voice, Max guessed the man was still in pain.

"You need help of any sort? Any?"

"I think I may have to travel to Saudi Arabia to check out the school," Max said. He reached to the coffee table and picked up the flash drive he'd taken from Jones's home. "If I don't already have what I'm looking for right here."

Avi was bewildered. "What do you have?"

"Better you not know."

"You have my number," Avi said, "and you have my resources if you want them."

"Give my regards to Lana, sir." Max hung up.

Chapter Eleven

11 a.m. Tuesday, January 28

Max stood in the hallway, arms folded, peering through the doorway at the front of the lecture hall. The door was open a crack. He scanned the crowded room, checking, always checking; head cocked, listening, always listening.

The number of students in the class had swelled, and if a handful more came in, they would have to settle for sitting on the floor in the aisles. Certainly, a number were auditing the course or simply visiting out of curiosity.

Among the muffled voices he heard one dark-haired young man complain, "I tried to call Braxton's office to add his class, but there was no voicemail."

"Well," said his female companion, "I went right to the registrar and they said I'd have to get the lecturer's approval, but it might be possible. As long as I do so before add-drop on Thursday."

A tall, redheaded fellow leaned in between them and chimed in, "Not going to happen, though, man. We've all been divided into teams and given assignments we've been working on since last Thursday."

The dark-haired boy cursed.

Undeterred, the girl raised her shoulder and sported a flirting smile. "I've heard excuses before. I'll find a way."

Seeming to read her mind, the dark-haired boy said, "From what I understand about Braxton, what you're thinking won't be the way."

"Really?"

"I went to his office, and he'd posted some rules on his door. One was he wouldn't meet alone with female students. There'll always be someone else in the room." He hesitated, then added, "So there you go, Bright Eyes."

The girl frowned.

Around the room, students found their team partners and put their heads together to compare progress. They shared phone numbers and set additional meetings. Exasperation flashed on some faces, gratitude on others.

———◆———

At eleven o'clock, nearly everyone had found a seat and attentively looked to the front to watch for Max. The second hand clicked past twelve. Feet shuffled. Papers ruffled. Nervous coughs were muffled.

No one seemed to notice a swarthy man in his late twenties slip into the last empty seat, next to the back-right door. His eyes flirted between his wristwatch and the clock on the front wall. Back and forth. Back and forth. One hand drummed on the desktop, the other fidgeted with a cord on his heavy winter jacket. He tugged his dark-blue knit hat down over his ears. Yet, sweat glistened on his forehead. He swiped his brow with the back of his hand. His right heel began a rhythmic thumping.

Two minutes passed. Three minutes.

A blonde girl sitting next to the young man turned and asked, "Suppose he's not showing up?"

He glared at her, then shrugged. But a look of angst betrayed his concern.

———— ◆ ————

Max had walked up the hallway and around to the back door. He silently opened the door beside the young man and lunged forward, grabbed his right arm and twisted his elbow severely behind him, then drove the man's head to the desktop. Just as swiftly, he yanked the man's left arm up and over his head disabling him.

The young man squealed in pain, and the entire class spun in their seats to watch the disturbance.

Max put his knee to the fellow's spine. With his left arm, Max head-locked him, and his right arm constrained the man's right arm. Cries of alarm flooded the room as students realized their teacher must have confronted danger in their midst.

Just then Josh walked through the door beside Max. Behind him were Hank, Jill, Jose, and Ashley.

"See the cord hanging out of his coat?" Max asked Josh.

Josh nodded.

"Be careful not to push the plunger on the end," Max said. "Follow inside his coat and see what the cord is attached to."

Max pulled the man upright to his feet. Josh unzipped the man's coat. Beneath was a full vest of plastic explosives.

"A suicide bomber." one boy nearby called out.

Gasps filled the air. Some students dove for cover, some rushed for the exits, but most stayed to watch the fascinating takedown.

"Filled with nails, screws, ball bearings, and assorted other mischief, no doubt," Max told Josh. "See if you can unbuckle the thing, and—" he looked over Josh's shoulder, "Jill, call campus police and have them contact the FBI and get over here."

After a minute's struggle, Josh removed the vest.

Students around the room started hollering.

"You murdering freak."

"Assassin."

More cries of anger, disgust, and fear filled the air.

Max held up a hand to quiet everyone. With his other arm, he kept the man in an arm-and-headlock and asked, "So you were targeting Yale University students?"

The man grunted something undecipherable.

"Simply my class?"

Another grunt.

"Whose orders are you acting on?"

The man didn't answer.

Max twisted his arm a click counterclockwise. The man yelped.

"I asked, whose orders are you acting on?"

The man remained silent.

"Are you ISIS?

The man shook his head.

"Al-Qaeda?"

The man shook his head.

Max spoke in a language no one around him would recognize. The words were intense, his face threatening.

The man spat at him ,but Max turned aside and the spittle hit the floor.

"Crude," Max said. "You're a guest in this country?"

The man shook his head.

"You live here?"

The man was silent. Max twisted his arm yet another click counterclockwise. The man shrieked and whimpered in pain.

Two uniformed security police appeared at the door at the front of the room, spotted the ruckus, and hurried up the steps to Max.

"We'll take him from here, sir," one of them said.

Max continued his lock on the man. "Show me your badges."

Both men opened their coats revealing badges attached to their belts.

Max held the man's arm in a straight-armed position toward one of the officers, who promptly slapped on one of the handcuffs, then spun the terrorist around to manacle both arms behind him.

Josh stepped forward holding high the dangerous vest. "Here's the bomb, loaded and live," he said and handed the vest to the second officer.

Just then a broad, muscular man Max's height stepped inside the doorway past Jill and Hank. He looked at Max. "I'm Seamus MacMillan, the chief of campus security, you're Colonel Braxton and this man is the bomber in question." Statements, not questions.

Max nodded and reached to shake the man's hand.

MacMillan shook the hand firmly, then turned to the room and ordered, "No one leave until I tell you you can. I need some eyewitness reports."

Two more officers entered by other doors.

"These officers will take your statements and get you all out of here as quickly as possible," MacMillan said.

"Let me speak to my class, will you, chief?" Max asked.

"Sure."

Amid chatter filling the room, Max strode to the front and turned to face the students. Despite the chaos, the students watched his every step and quieted down.

"Obviously nerves are frayed, but try to remember details, folks. Be as helpful as you can. The class will meet again at the same time on Thursday."

A hand shot up in the middle of the room.

"Yes?" Max asked.

"How did you know?"

Max looked at the black-haired girl and cocked his head.

"How did you know he was a terrorist?" she said.

Max shrugged. "He'd recently shaved a full beard. He wore brand-new everything. He wasn't used to these cold temperatures. His coat was a bit too bulky, yet he kept it on. He was too nervous. His eyes betrayed him."

"Nothing to do with him appearing Arabic?" Dean Stewart had just entered the room through the back-left door and made his presence clear.

"Only a contributing factor, Dean," Max replied. "Homegrown, white terrorists are harder to spot, for sure."

Max turned to speak to MacMillan when Josh and Hank rushed forward.

In a hushed whisper, Josh said, "Sir, we have to talk to you."

"Josh—" Max began, about to brush him off.

"In private," Josh murmured.

"We think we're in trouble," Hank interjected.

"What?" Max was mystified.

"The bat cave," Josh said, a bit too loud. He caught himself. "We really need to speak with you, sir."

"Can it wait until I speak with Chief MacMillan?"

"Barely," Hank said.

———————— ◆ ————————

One hour later, Max had finished being interviewed by the police. The FBI would want to question him later.

But before he could call Josh and Hank, a tidy-looking older woman ushered him to Sheffield-Sterling-Strathcona Hall, a building reminding him of a basilica he'd seen somewhere in Europe—tall and majestic. He was seated in a soft leather chair in the Office of the President, Nathaniel Hall.

Five others, who could slip seamlessly into a GQ photo shoot, sat on two couches and a chair.

Hall introduced them to Max counterclockwise.

"You're acquainted with Dean Stewart," Hall said. Max nodded toward Stewart but the dean pretended Max was the Blob or some other creature undeserving of attention. Stewart's chin was raised an extra inch higher than normal, perhaps as a show of superiority, perhaps to distance himself from the stench of such a foul affair at his sacred university.

"Dean for Faculty Development Carl Mussinger," Hall motioned to a gray-haired man who personified "distinction." Handsome and, Max guessed, cultured. "Carl's here because, well, this does involve faculty."

Mussinger reached out a hand to shake Max's. A firm handshake. Cordial.

Next was a middle-aged fellow with very long, wavy hair reminiscent of the ten-dollar-bill version of President Andrew Jackson. "Joseph Wales," Hall said, "our Charles Goodyear Professor of Global Affairs, whose international perspective is crucial in this case."

Wales directed a twisted smile, as if someone were pinching his cheek, toward Max. Max smiled back, he hoped squarely.

To Wales' right, a lady in a pinstriped suit half-smiled as she was introduced. "Linda King is our vice president and general counsel, overseeing all our legal affairs, which might come into play." Hall said. Max nodded at her.

Finally came a nattily dressed younger woman. "Shauna Robison handles our media relations and may have her hands full with this one," Hall said.

"Ladies, gentlemen," Max said, "this incident appears troublesome to you all."

"Tell us what happened," Hall said.

Max retold the story from his viewpoint, how he had a gut feeling someone of ill intent would be in the classroom, had spied out and spotted, then disarmed the terrorist.

"He's in the law's hands now," Max said, "and I hope they can extract information leading them to his cell, or imam, if his mosque is preaching this sort of rubbish."

"If I may," said the lawyer, Linda King. She glanced at President Hall for his consent to speak. Getting permission, she proceeded, "Now that we've experienced this attempt, if there were to be a terrorist attack of any kind on campus—and if any students or faculty were injured—the university could easily be held legally responsible. A lawsuit could cost us many millions of dollars."

Max put his hand to his chin and listened. He didn't have a law degree but what she said seemed to be true.

"And some courts might even hold you to be partly responsible, Mr. Braxton," King added.

Max nodded ever so slightly. *Doubtful, but possibly true.*

"As dean of academic affairs," Stewart interjected, "I've been against this experiment, this class of yours, from the beginning, Mr. Braxton. I've seen your, ahem, teaching procedures, first-hand, and they've done nothing but aggravate any underlying tension in the Muslim community."

Max's eyes hardened as he looked at the man with the ponytail. He simply nodded slightly.

Max chuckled to himself as he recalled the old Don Schlitz song, "The Gambler," that Kenny Rogers made famous. Talk about reading faces. Stewart wore everything on his sleeve, holding back no silent salvos. *He'd be a horrible poker player.*

"Yale University can hardly be placed in the international spotlight as an institution of learning if we question the validity or humanity of one culture or religion." This came from the professor of global affairs, Joseph Wales.

As Wales spoke, Max nodded, indicating he was listening, not necessarily agreeing. But he turned his eyes toward President Hall to gauge his reaction.

Unlike Dean Stewart, Hall was a difficult man to read. *He would be an excellent poker player.*

"Such an event," Robison said in response to Wales, "would be a public-image as well as financial catastrophe."

Sounds like doubling down on a losing hand.

Max turned his attention to this young lady, noting a fire engine-red scarf and eyes accented by red eyeliner—looks that were disconcerting at best.

Well, on balance, Max's days as a Yale visiting fellow apparently were over a week after they'd begun. And he had laid down six months of rent in advance. *Time to fold and walk away or run.*

Just then, Dean for Faculty Development Mussinger leaned forward in his chair. "Turn tail and run, then. Is this what I'm hearing?" he said.

"Frankly, yes," Stewart replied.

"Retreat is not always defeat," said Wales.

"Really?" Mussinger countered.

When Max looked closely at Mussinger, he recalled correspondence he'd had with the dean and how, reading between the lines, he'd recognized a possible comrade in arms. Perhaps in hiding, but in arms. Liberal universities are, after all, a deathbed for anyone independent or conservative. Kat had probably survived because her field of anthropology and archaeology was so far removed from politics and civil affairs.

Mussinger faced Wales. "Joseph, if we run from every issue, we'll stand for nothing. Would our faculty and students, our alumnae and the general public want Yale University to have a backbone or to cave in to threats and every innuendo coming down I-95?"

Stewart, his voice rising, broke in, "Carl, be honest. You'd retain the class—at the danger to our students and faculty—because you're the one who invited Braxton here to teach on terrorism. This is your baby and you don't want anyone to touch it."

Mussinger's baby? And now it's Braxton, not Mr. Braxton. Dean Mussinger's only input Max knew about had been to tell him to show up and teach the students what he knew, pulling no punches. *Yes, his exact words had been "no holds barred."*

"I'm simply speaking from my heart and with a little common sense, Alden," Mussinger said to Stewart.

"May I say, regardless of feelings and common sense, we may put ourselves in serious legal danger if any students are harmed in the future because of this class." Linda King straightened her back like any good lawyer, her voice authoritative, her demeanor forbearing.

"I have to have an official statement to the media within the hour." Robison sounded worried.

This was getting interesting. A quandary. A conundrum. On the one hand, Max wished he could unilaterally make the decision. On the other hand, he was glad the verdict was not within his power. What if another attacker succeeded and his students were hurt? Or even killed? Unacceptable.

"Well," said Stewart, "I vote for extricating the school from this situation before it escalates and more terrorists sneak in here looking for blood."

"Some of our students are Muslim. A few of our biggest donors are Muslim," said Wales, the global affairs expert. "Do we want to anger them? I concur with Dean Stewart."

"I agree," said King, looking more judge than lawyer.

"I can draft a statement in ten minutes and have it back in here for your approval, sir." Robison directed her statement at President Hall.

Sure, walk away, but what were the odds for getting Max's rent money back?

As Robison began to stand, President Hall raised his hand to stop her. His eyes narrowed at Max. "You've said nothing, Colonel Braxton. What are your thoughts?"

Max castled his fingers before him. He thought of the time he was camouflaged under the turf of the Golan Heights within yards of a Hezbollah-manned rocket launcher. Before the mission, the Israeli IDF special forces soldier who laid next to him had said something Max had remembered ever since.

"An inch is a mile," the soldier had declared as they sat together on a tank the night before the mission. "Give in one inch and the enemy spots weakness, he can make you stretch a mile wide and a mile long."

Max locked eyes with every person in the room, individually, then gazed at Hall.

"Hide away your bodies, seal away your voices, and the enemy has won," he said, "*whoever* your enemy is—an Arab Muslim terrorist in this case.

"As the Israelis illustrate every day, continue living your life, or you will have no life as such. Silence from the world of infidels— including you and me, Dean Stewart—is considered, by terrorists of all stripes, as a victory."

Max shrugged and looked at Stewart, and then Wales. "Cancel my class on terrorism and, in the wake of this morning's event, both things make news around the world. They'll dance in the streets of Tehran and Gaza. They might even dance in Xicheng, where there is a government of another evil stripe. But dance they will. And the next attack you face will come more swiftly and with more animosity. Why? Because the world will know you're weak, susceptible, and submissive. In time, you'll be completely under their will."

"Nonsense," Stewart exclaimed.

"Pure speculation," Wales declared.

How meager the counter-arguments had become, Max thought. *When you have no retort, you're out of aces.*

But Attorney King was not finished. "I go back to my point. Can we afford a multimillion-dollar lawsuit if a terrorist is successful on our campus? With deference to my friend, Mussinger, I vote with Dean Stewart and Professor Wales. We should cancel the class."

President Hall stood, walked around to the front of his desk, then sat back on its edge with his arms folded. "Folks, we can take all the votes you want, but ultimately it's my decision here today."

Max sat forward on his seat. He had to admit he felt tense.

"We're not a republic or a democracy—as much as it might seem sometimes. And, Mr. Braxton," he eyed Max, "Colonel, neither are we as yellow-bellied as some might think." Hall looked around the room. "I hear what you all have to say and here's my response."

Hall made eye contact with Stewart and said, "I understand, Alden, your office has been inundated with student requests to have Colonel Braxton teach again next fall because so many could not register for the class this semester. They say you've been noncommittal at best, defiant even."

He looked at Wales. "I understand, Joseph, you're a self-declared citizen of the world. Well, parts of this world silence speech, and I think those parts are the same ones you would say we should befriend—the Arab world, the Chinese, certain African nations. Thankfully, our country—historically, if not always currently—

protects freedom of speech. Perhaps we should choose which philosophy we support."

Max fought to keep his jaw from dropping. This was Yale—the ultimate in liberal academia—normally. *What's going on?*

Hall looked at King. "Most of all, I understand your concerns, Linda. I hope cooler heads will prevail if such a time comes. The damages from the lawsuit filed against Virginia Tech were ultimately tossed by a judge. Nor have lawsuits followed any of the attacks at malls and other institutions around the country."

Hall looked at his watch. "I'll authorize hiring added security around the campus, and especially at the hall where Colonel Braxton's classes are held."

"But President Hall—" the Robison objected.

Hall motioned for silence. "This is my decision, Shauna. You can draft a statement, run it by me and Dean Mussinger and we're good to go."

Max allowed a slight smile but said nothing. He did allow a fantasy of sweeping the winner's pile of chips off the card table. But whatever ground he stood on was fragile. He had once walked across an old lava field and watched as a colleague, not even ten yards away, fell a dozen feet through the ground into an air hole, breaking a leg and a couple ribs. He could envision such a fall happening to him if he considered himself on solid ground here.

He'd take the advice of The Gambler and not count his winnings until the hand was over.

"Thank you, everyone." Hall's sentence was a dismissal. Everyone rose and made their way toward the door. Stewart shuffled dejectedly. Wales shook his head. King pursed her lips while Robison hurried to slide out the door.

Dean Mussinger was moving sprightly as if he were a race driver taking a victory lap.

"Wait up, Colonel," Hall interrupted. With new respect, Max turned to him.

Once the others had exited, Hall said, "Do you want a personal bodyguard? I can arrange for one."

Max shook his head. "Thank you for the offer, sir, but I can take care of myself."

"An understatement, I understand."

Max grinned and turned to leave.

Hall interrupted him. "Just so you know, I'm not completely comfortable with this situation. There are valid points on both sides of whether to continue your course."

Max nodded.

"I hope you will no longer be our first line of defense. I anticipate we'll have security enough to stop another, ah, incident like this should one occur."

"You know, sir, simply adding security isn't enough. Those personnel need to know how to recognize a potential threat. I'd be happy to lead a teaching day on the subject, if you'd like."

"Excellent idea. I'll have Seamus MacMillan, our chief of security, contact you and you two can set one up."

"Thank you, sir." Max turned and left the office.

Carl Mussinger was waiting for Max in the hallway. The others had scattered. He'd finished his victory lap and returned to the site of the skirmish.

"I want you to know, Max, I'll fend off the hounds as best I can," Mussinger said. "But beware. Those hounds have teeth sharper than you might imagine."

"Oh, I believe you," Max said. "I see the froth at the edges of their mouths."

Mussinger chuckled. "Well, good luck then." He offered Max his hand. Max accepted, and they left the building together.

They parted ways outside the building. A cold frost met them, but Max thought ruefully, nothing compared to what he'd faced inside.

Kat and Tuck were waiting for him. "Hey, there. How'd it go?"

Dressed in a fire engine-red, knee-length coat with a long, bright-green scarf around her shoulders accentuating her eyes, she could have been a model strolling down a runway. *Beauty, thy name is …*

Max met her question with a frown.

"I think I can remove my flak jacket now," he said, bending to scratch Tuck behind his ears.

"You're kidding." Kat poked at his chest. "No flak jacket there, mister. You're braver than I thought."

"Well, believe me or not, the result was better than I thought going in, and, in fact, during the Inquisition." Max hesitated, then added, "Hey, did Joan of Arc wear protection at hers?"

Kat simply shook her head.

With Tuck at her side, Max took Kat's arm and walked her toward the coffee shop they'd visited their first hour back together. On the way, he told her about the president's decision and how his stance had irked Stewart and the others, except Mussinger.

"So, you survived Dean Stewart," she said.

Tuck growled. Max looked down at him.

"He growls at Stewart's name now," Kat said.

"Stewart," Max declared, "is a supercilious popinjay."

"A what?"

"Supercilious: full of contempt and arrogance. Popinjay: a vain and conceited person."

Kat shook her head and laughed.

———— ♦ ————

"So, what's next?" Kat asked as she sat in the coffee house, sipping from a hot mug of cocoa.

"It's onward and upward. The students are all excited."

"Well, you're the talk of the town. Headlines tomorrow," she held up her hands, pretending to hold a newspaper, "Green Beret Yale Visiting Fellow Saves Students."

"I'm not a green beret—"

She cocked her head and narrowed her eyes. "You get my drift, soldier. I can see the *New Haven Register* right now. They're probably knocking down the door to your office, trying to beat the *New York Times* and *Washington Post* to the story. The networks are helicoptering people here from the city as we speak."

"Yeah." Max put his head in his hands. "The PR gal mentioned the response, but, really, heightened attention is all we need."

"Hey, the media will get the word out. Everyone in this country should have their heads up, their eyes alert, because you never know when some fanatic will blow up whatever and whoever ticks them off."

"Right, but I need just enough anonymity to be able to chase down my inquiry of the president."

"Wearing a hat and holey jeans will do the trick." Kat smiled.

In a mirror, Max noticed his tail squeezing quietly through the door into the café.

He squinted to get a better look at the man's features. Middle Eastern. Dark-haired. Long, crooked nose. He was taller, broader, older than the young man Max had disarmed in the classroom. Five-foot-nine or ten, a hundred and eighty pounds. Pretty much like one hundred million of his fellow Arabs.

Max looked back at Kat and grinned. "You're loaded with good advice. So, what's been happening with you today?"

Kat's face turned serious.

"I've scrutinized the book you got from Jones's house."

"Serious, right?" Max asked.

Kat dug into her handbag and pulled out a paper. "I'll show you how much." She unfolded the paper—a twelve-by-sixteen-inch map of the world.

Max saw the map and quickly put his hand on the document. "Put the map away, Kat. Now." His voice was urgent, clipped.

Her look was a question.

"Not here," he said. "In private."

He glanced up to the mirror to check on his tail. The man was staring at them, his interest apparently roused.

"You're scaring me, Max."

Noticing his attention was elsewhere, Kat turned to see what he was looking at. Max grabbed her shoulder to prevent her from giving away the fact he knew the tail was there. Tuck jumped to his feet, ready to defend his mistress.

"He's behind me, Kat," he said. "A Middle Eastern man who's been following me."

Kat looked over his shoulder. "Do you mean the man leaving the café?"

Max spun around and saw the man hurrying out the door.

"Stay here. Wait for me," he said, then jumped to his feet and rushed to the door. As he reached the threshold, a group of six students was crowding into the café. Max attempted to squeeze through them but by the time he got outside, his tail had disappeared.

"Darn." He shrugged and reentered the building.

Sitting down again at the table, he apologized.

"How do you know he's been tailing you?"

Max simply took a deep breath.

"You learn these things, right?" she asked.

He nodded.

For a moment, she looked worried. "Has he followed you to my place?"

"No. I'm sure he hasn't," Max said. "I've been very careful and kept an eye out. Doesn't mean you shouldn't be vigilant, though. As a matter of fact, his presence probably means you should steer clear of me."

"No way, mister."

The way she addressed him might be playful but Max knew she was not easily dismissed or dissuaded.

"I'm in this 'til the end." Kat smiled and added, "Can I show you the map now he's gone?"

Max looked around the café, scrutinizing each table, then nodded. "Spread her out, Ms. Archaeologist slash Semiologist."

Kat laid the map before them, placing her mug and his on opposite corners.

"Here's the world," she declared, "and the world, they think, is their future empire."

"They?"

"The Three Sixes."

Kat took a deep breath and exhaled. "The flash drive you found spells out their code, their reason for existence. And their existence is as a terrorist's All-Star team. Masters of horror."

She reached back into her bag and pulled out the photocopy of the booklet Max had given her. She flipped over the top page and pointed to a symbol. "This was drawn on the first inside page."

Central to the symbol was what looked like an upside-down L with a curl on the bottom. To its left was a forward slash, and farther still to its left, a w with an extra curl to its left. Beneath these, almost in a semicircle, lay a fingernail moon on its back.

"In Arabic, the symbol means 'Three Sixes,'" she said.

She moved the booklet aside and pointed to the map. She'd drawn a bold red oval around North, Central, and South America; a green circle around Europe, Greenland, and Africa; and a yellow circle around the Middle East, Asia, Australia, and New Zealand.

"The Three Sixes," she said, "refers to three super-secret death squads, each given these boundaries to work within, each led by one shrouded man whose identity is known by only a handful in the world. I'm not entirely certain, but I think one of the six, six, six cells has been called to duty. The cell in Asia. If so, it would've been a month ago—on Christmas Day. I'm not positive."

"A frightening thought," Max said, "given terror cells are already inflicting mayhem here and around the world."

Kat nodded. "They're very date-driven, but information appears to be in some sort of code, and though I'm no decoder, the numbers twelve and twenty-five were in there."

She folded the map, then locked her eyes on Max's.

"There's more," she said. "In the Book of Revelation, it says the anti-Christ will be known by the numbers six, six, six—"

Max straightened.

"I checked, Max. In Arabic, the verse in Revelation about six, six, six reads, 'In the Name of Allah.'"

"Whoa." An electrical shock of excitement—or agitation, he didn't know which—shot through Max's body. "This Islamic black-ops group could be the anti-Christ of the Bible?"

Kat flinched and hesitated. "I'm just saying—"

Max held up a hand.

"What?" Kat asked.

"I'm just thinking. Remembering something I've seen. A ring—actually two rings soldered together. One ring contained the Rub el Hizb, the other the symbol on that page."

Kat's eyes widened. "Where'd you see it?"

"On a dead man."

"Oh." Kat's eyes went to the floor.

"In a combat situation, Kat. He lost." Max's voice sounded almost conciliatory, then he mustered a hint of victory. "I did say these people would like to be our equivalent."

She looked back up at him like she was trying to read his mind. He was afraid she could.

After a moment, she appeared to have reached a conclusion. "Max," she said as if she had figured out a mathematical equation, "I'm glad we have men like you—willing to put their lives in danger for the rest of us. If bad men must die to protect good people, then someone must be the right hand of justice. I get the fact. No apologies necessary."

She put her right hand on his left. Her hand felt good.

After a moment, she took a sip of hot cocoa, then continued, "So-o, you saw these two rings on a dead man."

"Uh-huh."

"In the Middle East?"

"No. Here in America."

Kat's shoulders stiffened.

"On a pier—in lower Manhattan."

"I never heard the story on the news."

"You wouldn't have."

Kat blinked. "Right here in America as close as New Haven is to Manhattan?"

Max nodded. He figured he knew what thoughts were whizzing through her mind. The existence of terrorist cells in the United States was common knowledge. For years, Muslims had been discovered with bombs and bomb-making apparatus. Plus, the attacks on dams, shopping centers, military bases, and other assaults were obviously "native." But the thought was still frightening. He could read distress in her eyes, the tension in her brow, her body going slightly rigid.

More alarming was knowing these terrorist All-Stars existed and might even be walking the streets of New Haven.

"You know, Max, just because the booklet and flash drive were in the president's house doesn't mean he has any ties to the Three Sixes."

Max cocked his head. "You're right. Could be completely innocent. The booklet could be connected to a secret report he got from the CIA. But why, seeing he just now became president?"

"Presidents-elect, before their inauguration, are given top-secret information privy only to a few," she said.

"True. But the photo showing the booklet in his bookcase was taken at the time he announced he was running for the presidential nomination. Besides, wouldn't he now keep such a document in a highly secure place at the White House?"

"You'd think so," she said. "Perhaps he has the book because of some sort of research on his own."

"Heck, I'm shocked the thing was visible—unprotected in his private home." Max hesitated. "And what of the flash drive hidden away in a secret compartment of his bedroom bureau?"

Kat shrugged.

Leaning forward, Max said, "So, what can you tell me about

their code, their operations?"

"This information I'll share now is all from the flash drive," she said. She pointed to the folded map and added, "There is an *amir*, or commander, for each region. Al-Umara oversees the Middle East-Asia territory. Al-Muminin calls the shots in Europe-Africa—"

"And the Americas?" Max asked.

"Lodestar."

"Makes sense. An amir in an Arabic army is equivalent to a general or admiral in our army or navy."

"Yes," Kat said. "An Amir-i-Nuyan is a commander of five thousand, an Amir-i-Tuman is a commander of ten thousand."

"Impressive." Max grinned. "Your historical military studies come in handy—again."

Kat turned her head in modesty.

"So, Lodestar is the chief kahuna for the Americas," Max said. "Would be appropriate since lodestar means a guide that leads people in the right direction. I've followed a lodestar many times myself—out in the wilderness or the desert."

"Al-Muminin means commander of the faithful," Kat said. "And stresses leadership over all Islam but especially in the military form of jihad.

"And al-Umara is a commander of commanders."

"Probably fitting," Max said, "since al-Umara is in charge of the Middle East, right?"

"Right. And I think we can expect any references to these leaders to be shortened—Muminin, Umara, Lodestar."

As her voice trailed off, Max asked, "Why Lodestar? They have these Arabic names elsewhere and then Lodestar here."

"Perhaps they wanted an English-sounding name because North Americans speak English. Perhaps they thought they would increase the odds of being discovered if they used Arabic names like Muminin or Umara here."

"Then the question of the hour—"

"Who is Lodestar?" Kat finished.

Max shrugged.

"Want to guess?"

Max put his chin in his hand, mulling over the possibilities.

"Probably someone we don't know," Kat said.

"Or someone we do know—all of us."

Just then the café door opened, and Hank's voice was loud and clear. "He's in here," he called out the doorway.

Within seconds, Josh, Jose, Jill, and Ashley were following Hank to Max and Kat's table. Max introduced them to Kat as "my A-Team."

The students all said hellos to Kat, then pulled empty chairs from the tables around them and huddled close to Max and Kat.

"We've been looking for you ever since the campus police held us for questioning," Jill said. "We need to talk about the bat cave."

"The modular you had set up was fake, right?" Ashley asked.

Max sensed something wrong. "Yes—why?"

The students all started talking at once.

"Whoa. Whoa." Max held up a hand. "One at a time."

Josh leaned in close to Max. "We think the modular maybe worked too well."

"*Too* real," Jose corrected.

"Too well, too real," Hank agreed.

"What happened?" Kat asked.

Ashley proceeded to tell the story of how she had pilfered three-quarters of a billion dollars from terrorist accounts and funneled the money into an account she set up.

Max's jaw dropped. "Amazing. Unbelievable." He sat back and frowned. "So, where's the problem?"

"Well," Jill said, "we didn't think there was a problem. In fact, we were elated. We thought the theft was a coup."

"The theft was a coup," Ashley interjected.

"But then we saw a team of FBI types loaded for bear and surrounding the building next door," Josh said. "There were those big black Expeditions they drive and men with guns. Big guns."

"And some weird-looking ones, too," Jose said, "like the tranquilizer rifles you see in those African movies."

"You say they went into the building next door?" Kat said.

"Yeah, well, probably because I was bouncing my signal off the neighbors instead of our own building," Ashley said.

"So—" Hank said, "they thought they were coming after us, but they were in the wrong place—"

"At some point, they'll figure out the right place, though," Jose said. "They're no dummies."

"If they're the FBI, you're right," Max said.

Everyone fell silent for a couple moments.

Max made his decision. "I'll have to talk to them," he said.

"The feds?" Josh asked.

"Whoever came after you. Explain to them you're not at fault. I'm the one who got you into this."

"Your buddy set up the system," Hank protested.

"I approved the modular. I set up Operation Mongoose."

"How are you going to find them, whoever they are?" Jill asked.

"Shouldn't be hard," Max said. "They're probably all over the bat cave right now, figuring out who we are."

Max put his hand on Kat's and started out of his seat. "Looks like my teaching career may, indeed, be the shortest on record."

She managed a weak smile. "I'll pray for you. Let me know what happens as soon as you find out."

"Right. We have to finish our discussion—what we started here."

Max leaned down toward Tuck and the dog raised his paw for a shake. Max shook the paw. "Watch your mistress, bud."

Tuck barked once, twice.

Max turned to leave, then caught himself and turned back to Kat. "The flash drive?"

"Yes," she said.

"I'll get the drive to my decrypting friend."

"Aye-aye, Colonel," she said with a wink.

"It's only sergeant to you, ma'am, you being on Discovery Channel and all." Max flashed a grin. He noticed, before leaving the café, his A Team seemed to breathe more easily as they stayed behind and started chatting with Kat.

———◆———

A light snow began to fall as Max drove his Mustang slowly along the route to the warehouse, thinking through the situation. He couldn't let his students receive any retribution from the authorities—none. He cringed at the thought of them taking heat.

In the short time he'd known them, he'd become attached to these kids. He'd placed them at risk. He slapped the steering wheel in disgust. "Julius." The name of his friend who had created the software spilled out of his mouth. All the 3D imaging, the mapping, the real-time transactions and tracking. The system had all *looked* so good.

Julius was a genius as well as one of the best special-ops comrades with whom he'd ever fought. How could Julius have messed up like this?

Max pulled the car curbside and drew his cell phone from a

pocket and called his friend.

"Max." Julius, all right. Always up. Even when knowing a sniper could be zeroing in on him from an unseen hide.

"Julius, we're in trouble."

"Yeah, they're talking about you on Fox News. Who knew you'd be fighting the global war on terrorism at Yale?" He chuckled. "Man, blowing an IED at Yale is like red on red."

Max shook his head. "We have two or three friends here, Julius, believe me or not. Not why I'm calling, though. Actually, it's nothing compared to what I've got to tell you."

He related the students' story. Julius was speechless.

"I'll fess up, man. The problem's all on me. I don't know how in the world the package went real. I've got to deep-six it until I find out."

"Well, for now, just stand by in case I have to reach you in the next hour or so. I'm going to find the feds right now. They're probably National Security Agency. Where are you, anyway?"

"I'm in Australia, hanging around but on call. Looks like something might be brewing in Morocco of all places."

"Right-o," Max said. "The wealthy are a soft target there for extremists. Later." He hung up and drove back onto the street. *Australia. He would take more than a day to get here.*

He headed down Mattapan Street toward the warehouse. Sure enough, two black Escalades were among the vehicles sitting out front of the bat cave building. Max parked and hustled inside. Ignoring the elevator, he sprang up the stairs. At the top, he was met by a large man wearing a dark-blue suit, white shirt, red-white-and-blue-striped necktie—and a mean expression.

The man showed him a badge identifying him as Agent Alex Franken of NSA. "You can't go in there," he said, pointing at the door to the bat cave.

"I think your boss will want to speak to me," Max said. "The place is mine."

Franken quickly pulled a gun out of its holster. A Glock 22, 40 caliber. Standard issue.

"No need for the handgun, friend," Max said.

"Nevertheless," Franken said, his hand steady while pointing the Glock directly at Max's chest. "Walk on in."

Max preceded Franken inside. The place was steamy and teeming with action. A three-man forensics team was dusting for fingerprints and collecting other evidence. A computer technician was checking out the computer bank. A man, about thirty, and a woman, about forty, appeared to be overseeing the investigation.

"Very impressive," the computer forensics expert was saying. "Why don't *we* have something like this?" He turned to the man and woman, then caught himself short when he noticed Max.

Everyone turned.

"Fella says this is his place," Franken said.

After a moment's hesitation, the man in charge blurted out, "You're the one who wrote the book—"

"Max Braxton," the woman finished.

"Yeah, the one who just disarmed the bomber," said the technician.

Max managed a half-smile and nodded.

"I love your book—" the man began, then stopped himself in mid-gush. "I'm Senior Agent Sturgen, and this is Special Agent Crowe. We're in charge of this operation. But what do you have to do with all this?"

Max spent the next hour explaining his course at Yale, Operation Mongoose, and how everything had apparently gone awry.

He pointed at the wide desk. "As you now know, these monitors all have varying data. The top left has the contact list. The next one holds streaming data. These are bank accounts filtered through all the international banks across the globe. The large monitor in the center can layer the topographical and geopolitical maps and hotspots all together or separately."

He pointed to the monitor to the right of the center screen. "This computer folds in mock feeds from international intelligence agencies. *That* data is most definitely *not* real. The last monitor here to the right is our three-degrees screen, which is basically a social networking map of all intelligentsia—the terrorists—connecting them with their, um, colleagues around the world. The software pulls in bank data and phone records and ties together all related parties—within three degrees."

"This is all so sophisticated," Crowe said. "Did you put it all together?"

Max chuckled. "My capabilities fall so short, Special Agent Crowe. I'm thankful I can even navigate the thing. No, a friend of mine created what you see to exercise his brain cells, basically. When he told me, I jumped at the chance to use the real life prototype at Yale.

"I told my kids," he continued, "they were to be, well, desk jockeys for the CIA, and to pretend to be bad guys who need to launder money. They were supposed to find out how the *real* bad guys would do it."

Max shrugged. "Somehow, I don't know how—a glitch in the program, I guess—they tapped into the real world. In no way did I expect this system would go live and get my students in the middle of anything dangerous. And grabbing three-quarters of a billion dollars? Phew."

"Three-quarters of a billion, did you say?" Special Agent Crowe asked.

"They just told me the figure."

"Well, you got $200 million from accounts we'd confiscated," Sturgen said. "Where was the rest?"

"I can tell you," the computer tech broke in.

All eyes were on him as he explained. "Whoever ran this program actually tapped into the accounts of some *real* bad guys. I guarantee there are some furious terrorists out there this very minute. They're missing a half a billion-with-a-b bucks."

Max and the others took a collective breath. He wanted to say, "Way to go, Ashley." but thought better.

"Man, these kids are good." the computer tech exclaimed.

"So, between our accounts which they pilfered and the terror cells' accounts, they made off with $750 million." Crowe drummed her fingers on the top of the chair in front of her.

"I want to speak to those students ASAP, Colonel Braxton," Sturgen said.

"Can it be here?" Max asked.

"Here's as good as anywhere. It'll be more under the radar than meeting on campus."

Max took his cell phone from his pocket. "I'll call them, but as you may have noticed, cell calls can't come in or get out of this room. I'll step outside if you don't mind."

"Go ahead," Sturgen said. "but just on the other side of the doorway." Sturgen looked at Franken. "Keep our friend company and the door open."

———— ◆ ————

As Max stepped outside, he heard Crowe say to Sturgen, "Can I speak to you alone?"

With Franken keen on watching him, Max dialed Josh and looked over the agent's shoulder at Sturgen and Crowe.

They stepped over to the windows on the far side of the room. Crowe said something to Sturgen. He shook his head.

Animated, Crowe spoke again. Sturgen shook his head.

With no hidden agitation, Crowe rose on her toes, apparently trying to stretch herself to his height or to raise her argument to a higher plateau. After several seconds of monologue, she ended with the simple question, "Well?"

"Well." The one word Max could discern as he finished his own conversation with Josh, who'd agreed to bring the entire A-Team to the bat cave.

Max body-read the slump of Sturgen's shoulders and lip-read his reply: "Okay. You win."

A broad smile crossed Special Agent Crowe's face, and she turned to walk back toward Max. Sturgen, obviously the superior in rank, had been won over or badgered into submission, agreeing to whatever plan Crowe had envisioned.

———— ◆ ————

Within a half hour, the five students came up the elevator. Agent Franken escorted them into the bat cave. Anticipating their fear, Max met them at the door.

He looked them each in the eye and said, "Don't worry. It's all been worked out. This is an NSA team and they want to meet with you."

They released a collective sigh of relief.

He waved them into the room and introduced them to Sturgen and Crowe, who introduced them to their tech expert, David George.

"Hey, another double," Jose said and reached forward to shake George's hand."

"Double?" George said.

"Yeah, like me, Jose Frederick—two first names."

"Ah."

"Agent George here tells us this software is extremely complicated," Sturgen said.

"He's amazed someone could grasp the complexity in the four days you've been working with the equipment," Crowe added.

"Well, actually, a weekend," Jose said.

"One night," Ashley corrected with a coy smile.

"Well, I've got a PhD in computer science and haven't figured this setup out. There are icons here I've never seen before, like this one." He turned to the computer and began to move the mouse over the tiny symbol for a map legend at the bottom of the screen.

"Whoa." Jose blurted. "Don't touch that one."

Startled, George turned to him. "Why not?"

"Well, Ashley and I haven't discussed this yet, but I think the tiny map might be the culprit. Once I clicked on that icon, the world was covered with an infrared filament, the white and black dots began moving, and the monitors lit up with all sorts of information."

"Right," Ashley said. "We thought the real-time tracking of all those terrorists' names in the far monitor was fake. But the tracking is the real deal."

Sturgen looked at Max and said, "Call your friend who created this, this, marvel and ask him to explain."

Max left the room and did so. Julius answered on the first ring. "Yo, Max."

"The tiny map-legend icon."

"Tiny icon?"

"Yeah, the one at the bottom of the monitor, not the larger one at the top."

"Omigod." There was silence at the other end of the call. Seconds clicked by, then Julius spoke. "You're saying the tiny legend is visible?"

"Yes, Julius, it's visible. What does the little bugger do?"

"Max, I'm so sorry. I can't believe this happened. I gave you the wrong disc. My software can go real-time live—and the tiny legend is the key instigating everything."

"Excuse me, Julius, but are you telling me whatever we've done since clicking on the icon has activated real-life scenarios—hacking into bank accounts and such things?"

Julius hesitated. "Max, I'm just messing around here on my own, having a little fun, killing time. You know I don't sleep. And this is my baby, but I didn't mean to give her to you full-birthed, so to speak."

"The answer, Julius."

"The answer is, yes. If you have a little map-legend icon at the bottom of your screen—which I did not think you did—when you click on the image, you immediately leave virtual behind and go real."

Max's throat constricted. He took a deep breath, stepped into the room and relayed the information.

"Tell your friend we need to see him. Now," Sturgen said. "Where is he?"

Max stepped back into the hall and spoke into the phone, "How soon can you get to New Haven?"

"I'll check the JOSAC flights, or hitch a ride otherwise, and get there ASAP," Julius said, referring to the Joint Operational Support Airlift Center. "My TOA will be at least a day, even if I can catch a flight right now."

"Let me know soon as."

"Right. 'Til then. Semper fi."

"Semper fi."

Max reentered the bat cave. Sturgen's face had hardened. He

looked at the students and said, "We need you to tell us who you stole the money from."

"Let's steer away from 'stole' and other incriminating words, shall we?" Max said.

Sturgen gave him a look of consternation and said grudgingly, "Roger." He turned to Ashley, "Which terrorists did you, ah, relieve of their funds, young lady? Can you fill us in?"

"Tamper might be a better characterization," she said. "Of course, we can help."

"Anything to stay out of jail," Josh added.

"We're taking from the bad guys, man," Hank said. "Maybe we should expect a medal, not jail time."

Max shook his head. These kids were so bright and yet so naïve.

With a flourish, Ashley pulled a notepad from a satchel hanging over her shoulder. "The list. Here are the bad guys, their accounts and how much we, ah, maneuvered from their account to ours."

Crowe snapped the notebook from her hand. "Your list includes money from our own accounts which were, in turn, pilfered from the bad guys, as you call them."

Ashley stepped back. "I didn't know."

"You wouldn't," Crowe replied.

This woman is cold as a tomb, Max thought.

"Agents," Max said, "we're on the same page, aren't we? I'm referring to the fact any legal problems we might have here are on me, not my students."

"Colonel," Sturgen said, "we don't care to bring this to a court of any type. We simply want to get our arms around what's happened. I think we're actually thrilled your friend has created such a—what can I say—mega system as we see here."

"Well, his genius is off the charts," Max said.

"Is he in the book you wrote?"

"He's in there."

"But not his name?"

"Not his name."

Sturgen nodded. "Then I certainly want him on our side."

Chapter Twelve

5 p.m. Tuesday, January 28

Max and the students caught the elevator down from the bat cave, glad to be out of the over-heated room and the clutches of federal agents. The light snow had stopped. Darkness was setting in. Most of the combat team had left three hours earlier, the forensics team two hours ago. Only Sturgen, Crowe, George, and two armed agents remained. Sturgen had scheduled round-the-clock guards at the bat cave in case any of the terror groups whose funds had been pinched by the A-Team were able to discover the location.

The students were not only relieved, they were euphoric. They were not just off the hook with the law, but they were also able to help NSA empty the coffers of terrorists, including a cell based somewhere nearby in New York State.

Max got every student's cell number and had them all create special ring tones so they would know when he called them. He did the same from each of their phones. He bid them all goodbye and climbed into his Mustang. Just then his cell phone rang. He checked the LED and answered, "Mr. Navon."

"Avi."

"Avi. I'm honored."

"I'm the one who's honored. You saved my countrymen's lives on the battlefield of Israel."

"Well, they'd have saved my life if they were in my shoes. Great soldiers." Max thought a moment and added, "So, you've checked up on me."

"Yes, indeed. Enough to know you and my friend the prime minister are on good terms and you're looking into Ridley's school."

"You have contacts. I'm impressed."

"It's my country. The prime minister, the president, many in the Memshelet Yisrael as well as the IDF are my old comrades as well as businessmen and scientists. We share friends—"

"And allegiances," Max said. He looked in the side-view mirror and noticed a black sedan that hadn't been there before. The driver made no attempt to exit.

"True. And allegiances." Avi hesitated. "I see you're on the news. You can't fly under the radar anymore."

"'Fraid not."

"Do you still not need my help?"

"I might have to get to Riyadh Air Base, but I should be able to catch a military flight there."

"Riyadh," Avi repeated. Max could imagine Avi mulling over this tidbit. "Our president's old Muslim school."

"Right."

The sedan was still there, the driver still seated, exhaust in the air showing the vehicle was running.

"May I ask what you're looking for?"

"A list of their students and whatever else I can discover. Listen, Avi, we can't be having this conversation over an insecure line."

"Understood." There was silence on the other end of the line, then Avi spoke up. "Well, the Saudis won't let my plane into the country, but my invitation stands to anywhere I can fly: my plane is yours. Just let me know when you're ready. I can get my plane into Tweed-New Haven Airport wheels-down in an hour and a half, and from there the world's yours.

"Meanwhile, remember, the terrorist groups in Saudi Arabia are kidnapping Westerners at a rate of two or three a week, especially in Riyadh and Al-Qasim."

"They won't even see me." *But this guy in the sedan certainly can.* "I believe it."

"Please give my regards to Lana."

Avi chuckled. "You like sharp-edged swords?"

"My love's elsewhere, I'd say. But I'd like to gain your daughter's friendship at least." The sedan sat idling, the driver pretending to read something.

"Well, you've got her respect. All things in due time, son. All things in due time."

Max couldn't help but laugh.

———— ◆ ————

Five minutes later, Max was driving down Orange Street to his Ninth Square apartment. Orange was a narrow street with restored brick, flat-roofed buildings, close to the Coliseum, but with the perception of an enclosed community. The area felt comfortable to him. Except, as he looked down the street, comfort gave way to concern. Not only was the fellow in the sedan tailing him—badly but nevertheless he was still there—but two vans were parked on his side of the street in front of his apartment building and a third sat across the street. All were equipped with satellite dishes. *TV reporters. They've found out where I live.*

The thought struck Max he had been too busy with the NSA and the kids to tune into the Yale press conference about the terrorist.

He had no idea what had been reported, what eyewitnesses had been interviewed, what perceptions had been given by talking heads.

He grabbed his cell phone and pushed a button.

Two rings later, Kat's voice came on.

"Can we meet?" he asked.

"Sure. When and where?"

"Pepe's Pizzaria."

"In ten minutes, then?"

"Well, give me twenty. I have to lose a tail."

"A tail?"

"The guy who's following me."

Silence. Max could only imagine the expression on Kat's face. "Okay."

Then he had a better idea. He pushed open his glove compartment and pulled out a device about the circumference of a quarter but three times thicker, and placed it in his shirt pocket. Gauging how the dusting of snow would affect his Mustang's rear-wheel-drive performance, he turned out into the street and stepped on the gas. He sped down the street about thirty yards, laid rubber for another twenty, then slammed on the brakes and spun the steering wheel counterclockwise. The Mustang responded like Jeff Gordon was behind the wheel, swirling into a hundred-eighty-degree turn.

At the corner of Orange and Crown streets, Max turned west onto Crown. He looked in the rearview mirror. His tail had apparently made a three-point turn in the street and had fallen badly behind. *Not a pro, for sure.* Max slowed down to let him get closer. Three blocks up the street, he turned onto College Street and a few seconds later drove into the Shubert Theater parking lot.

The tail followed him into the lot and Max doubled down on his previous one-eighty by pulling another, speeding back past the tail, slamming on the brakes again, and turning the Mustang sideways to block the entryway.

The tail tried to duplicate Max's maneuver, but with mediocre skill. The results were the car sat idling like a wounded duck in front of the Mustang. Max sprang out of his car, and before the tail could react, slammed his Glock, butt-first, into the driver-side window. Splinters of glass sprayed into the vehicle.

The man ducked, then, eyes wide in fear, looked up at Max. Max glared at him. He wasn't the same man Max had spotted in the café, though he, too, was Middle Eastern. His full beard tried poorly to cover a pock-marked face and a panic-stricken countenance.

Max grabbed him by the collar and drew back a fist to punch him, but the man stepped on the accelerator and turned to the left heading behind the theater in search of the rear exit.

Max allowed himself a self-satisfied grin. As the car spun away, he'd been able to pull the little GPS locator out of his shirt pocket and place it into the rear wheel hub.

He walked back to his car, reached into the glove compartment again and pulled out a GPS tracking device the size of the palm of his hand. Powering on the device caused a map to flash on the monitor. His tail was escaping along York Street, heading south.

This should make Sturgen and Crowe happy.

He settled into his seat and revved up the Mustang. He called Kat. When she answered he said, "I'm going to be a few minutes late."

"Everything okay?"

"Yes. Just got to go back to the bat cave first."

"I'll be waiting at Pepe's."

Max drove back to the bat cave and ran up the stairs. Again, he was met by an agent with a gun, but Sturgen and Crowe were still inside.

Max handed Sturgen the GPS tracker.

"What's this?" he asked.

"See the little blip?" Max pointed to the map showing his tail's location on Route 34 heading west out of New Haven. "You're going to want to get someone following this vehicle. A late-model black Honda Civic. I'll guarantee the driver's with a terrorist cell, probably the same one as our friend who wanted to bomb my classroom this morning."

"We've been working with the FBI team checking out your would-be terrorist," Crowe said. "These people don't like you, do they?"

Max shrugged, then told them what had just transpired.

"We'll get on this guy," Sturgen promised. "A brilliant move," he added, pointing to the GPS tracker.

"I *would* like the tracker back at some point," Max said.

"Yes, and a new locator," Sturgen said with a smile. "Thanks, Colonel."

"Max."

"Max."

Soon Max was seated at Pepe's, savoring a white spinach, mushroom, and gorgonzola pie. Across from him, Kat forked her Pepe's salad, loaded with greens, grape tomatoes, cucumber, shredded red cabbage, kalamata olives, and Romano cheese.

"Here are the facts," he said. "Islamic terrorists have been wreaking havoc in the United States for months now. The Mall of America, Liberty University, a Christian school in St. Louis, the courthouse in Houston. They've exploded bombs here, there, and everywhere, not to mention infiltrated gunmen into our own military ranks. The president, a man who has said he wants to reach out to our enemies, takes over the government.

"This is my theory—the American component of The Three Sixes lets the president know they're willing to stop the carnage if—" he raised his index finger, "and only if, the US government withdraws support from Israel."

"That," Kat said, "would explain Jones's inaugural address."

"There's just one thing gnawing at me."

"What?"

"If this ultimatum is true, did Jones just throw up his hands and give in, entirely?"

"You think there's something more."

Max shrugged. "A gut thing."

"Then how about this?" Kat reached into her coat pocket and withdrew a paper. "Recognize this?"

The paper was blank except for four letters in lower case, followed by four periods, at the lower right-hand edge of the page: lode....

He looked up at Kat. Her eyes sparkled. "Is this—?"

"Yes," she said. The final page in the booklet you photocopied from the president's den."

"Could this be—"

"Lodestar's copy? Yes. Or just a coincidence."

"I have a problem with coincidences," Max said.

"As a scientist, so do I. But coincidences make you take a closer look at the possibilities—like the spokes of a wagon wheel emanating from the hub. Which one needs your attention?

"You settled it. I *do* have to get to Riyadh."

Kat looked puzzled.

"I want to get a peek at a list of Jones's classmates."

"I thought you got all you needed from your Israeli contact."

"Everything but Jones's buddies in the student body, plus other information on the school itself. Who runs the place? Where does the funding come from? Who are the faculty and students?"

"Are you thinking what I'm thinking?"

"Yes. But I'm not sure even with a list of students we could figure out if any one of them is a leader in The Three Sixes.

"I'll look deeper into the flash drive while you're off to the other side of the world."

Max hesitated a moment. "My class is in two days."

"You've given your students enough work for a month. Be at one with the rest of the faculty. Cancel the class."

Max laughed. "I can?"

"I have a colleague at Rutgers University, a full professor, and he only teaches twice a week. He thinks he's overtaxed."

Max chuckled. "You're in a whole other world."

"You bet, soldier, and now you are, too."

"For a moment, at least."

"Just make sure Dean Mussinger is aware. His secretary will alert all the students in your class."

"Got to love emails and text messages, huh?"

Kat smiled. "Sadly, it's the way of the world, but immensely helpful in cases like this."

———— ◆ ————

Avi and Lana Navon stepped into the elevator from their offices atop the Atlanta Financial Center. With them were Avi's assistant, Jonas Mandrell, and Chief Financial Officer Dan Ogilvy.

Avi squeezed his daughter's hand and asked Dan, "Where do things stand with detaching from the president?"

"Except for the two or three dozen you and Lana wanted to handle yourselves, I've personally spoken with the entire list, Avi."

"How'd they sound?"

"In a word? Upset."

"I've angered many friends." Avi hung his head. A week since the inaugural address, and he still couldn't forgive himself.

"Papa," Lana objected.

"No," Dan cut in. "Not upset with you. The president. To a person, they would strangle the guy if they could."

"Even Nathan Levinsky?"

"Well, less so with Nathan. He dislikes the prime minister and the minister of defense. But even he is disturbed by Ridley's about-face."

"Well, Ridley is now 'Riddles' to me," Avi said, "and I shall call him 'Riddles' if I ever lay eyes on him again."

"Riddles Jones," Dan repeated.

They all chuckled.

They stepped out into the front foyer and headed out the door. Jonas had phoned Stan to be waiting at the front entrance in Avi's limousine.

As they reached the limousine, Avi put up a hand. "Well, then. Much bridge-mending still lies ahead, but let's have dinner and celebrate this task being finished. Where do you say, Lana? Fogo de Chao? Nava? Tavern at Phipps? How about Au Pied de Cochon?"

Lana laughed. "You just like to say *'Au Pied de Cochon'*."

"Plus, he likes their logo," Dan said.

"No-no," Avi objected. "Washington, Montreal, here, you can depend on them. I'd have something like Plogue à Champlain."

Lana laughed. "Again, something you like to pronounce. Your Israeli accent adds a foreign flavor to a foreign meal. Papa, you know you simply like their peg-legged pig with the eye patch."

Avi shook his head as if he were giving up the fight. Yes, he did like the peg-legged pig. His daughter knew him well. Interesting how a simple thing like a logo could attract business. He had even used the phenomenon himself in several of his endeavors.

"Let's just go back upstairs to the club and eat here," Lana said. "I feel like baked salmon tonight."

Avi motioned to Jonas, "Tell Stan we're going up to Buckhead ,and he can leave without us. We'll buzz him in a couple hours."

Avi took Lana's hand and spun around, heading back into the Center. Dan was a step behind as they entered the building.

Just then, an explosion behind them rocked the air, shook the ground, and shattered the glass in the windows and doors. Avi, Lana, and Dan were blown off their feet. The windows and doors shattered ,and shards of glass sprayed through the lobby, covering the three of them and a dozen others.

Avi hadn't felt a concussion since a battle years ago in the Golan Heights. The memory flashed back to him as he lay face down on the floor. His ears throbbed and he recalled the fear battling his mind. Suddenly he realized Lana must be in full fright at this moment. He turned on his side to check on her. She was on her knees, mumbling something.

Avi scrambled to put an arm around her shoulders.

"Sweetheart, are you all right?"

She looked at him, dazed, her eyes unfocused.

He engulfed her in his arms.

"You're bleeding, Papa." she blurted and put a hand to the back of his head.

"Ouch!" he responded to her touch.

She pulled her hand away. There was blood on her palm.

"It's nothing," Avi said and looked around for Dan.

Dan was sitting up. He ran his fingers through his thick hair, scattering bits of glass onto the floor.

"You okay, Dan?" Avi asked.

"Sure. You?"

Avi nodded.

As his head began to clear, Avi pushed himself upright. Looking out the front door, he gasped. His limousine was upside down, a heap of metal and smoldering ruin. A smear of blood on the sidewalk became a trail to the side of the building where the remains of Jonas Mandrell lay.

Inside the limousine? Avi had no doubt: Stan, too, must be dead.

Avi quickly turned to Lana and stood to block her view of the carnage.

"Don't look, my darling," he said hoarsely. "Don't look."

———— • ◆ • ————

Max sped down the highway to New London. If he hurried he might catch a navy flight to ComUSNavCent in Riyadh.

He turned on the radio and found a news report.

And in downtown Atlanta shortly after six o'clock today, a bomb took the lives of two men—limousine driver Stanley Woods and Jonas Mandrell, the personal assistant to Israeli-American billionaire Avner Navon. Navon was central to the election of President Ridley Jones, but has been vocally angry with the president over the last week.

Navon and his daughter, Lana, were nearby the limousine when the bomb exploded. They sustained only minor injuries.

Police investigators and an FBI detail are on site. So far, all we've been told is the bomb was an IED—an improvised explosive device—set off by radio control. It appears the target might have been Navon, but that is unsubstantiated, and so far, nobody has taken credit for the attack.

Max flinched at the news. He pulled out his phone to call Avi but thought better. The man had more important things to be concerned with right now than talking with him. But he made a mental note to call later.

Chapter Thirteen

1 a.m., Wednesday Morning, January 29

In an apartment in a rundown section of Albany, New York, Ahmed, unaccustomed to being shackled to a chair and beaten, was not handling himself well.

"Maybe we're going about this the wrong way." The words were spoken in Arabic. Ahmed's aggressor massaged his bloody knuckles and slowly paced back and forth behind the chair. Ahmed flinched at the thought of what damage the man might do from behind him.

The room was about twice the size of a walk-in closet and almost twice as dark, the forty-watt bulb straining the last bit of life out of itself on the broken table in the corner.

Ahmed had decided to stop crying for help. At first, he had hoped the padding along the walls was thin and his voice would find a helpful Samaritan, but after the first two hours had passed, he knew his pleas were fruitless. Besides, his tongue was swollen from the gasoline he was forced to swallow and his lungs had no desire to burn with his screams.

"I tell you, I don't know what happened to the money."

Sharuk lifted his hand to strike again. Ahmed flinched.

"Ah, you've got a very thick skull, Ahmed." Sharuk smiled in scorn. "Let's reassess your situation, shall we?"

"Please, Sharuk."

"Don't beg, Ahmed. Pleading only makes you appear weak and makes me want to strike you harder." Sharuk walked over to the broken table and played with the brass knuckles leaning against the small lamp.

"Please, Sharuk, no, no more, please."

Sharuk picked up the brass knuckles and slid them onto his right hand. "Your situation, as I was saying, Ahmed, is dire. One hundred and thirteen million have gone missing from our funds. Both accounts drained. And who, my dear friend, had access to these accounts besides you?"

"But, Sharuk," Ahmed began, but stopped in mid-cry when Sharuk's brass-knuckled fist crushed down onto his knee. The padded walls stifled his shriek.

"Who?" Sharuk bellowed.

"Just you and me, Sharuk." And then, as quickly as he could blurt out, tears streaming down his face in pain, he hollered, "But I did not take the money."

"Well," Sharuk said lightly, as though discussing second-grade mathematics, "if I did not take it and you did not take it, then, hmm—who do you suppose could have taken it?"

Ahmed's mind, though clouded, came up with a possibility. "Perhaps a hacker?"

Sharuk turned to him. "Two and one-half hours of this beating, and just now you come up with the possibility of a hacker?"

"Yes, Sharuk, just now."

"You told me the firewall of our account was impenetrable. Nothing could touch the accounts we hold. You swore."

"The feds, Sharuk. The feds couldn't touch them because, on the surface, our business is legitimate. But maybe someone else."

Sharuk pulled off the knuckles and flipped them between his fingertips. "Such as?"

"I don't know, but maybe I can find out if you let me get to my desk."

"Maybe you can find out?"

"Definitely. Definitely, Sharuk, I can find out."

Sharuk sighed and looked at his watch. His night out at the club with his women was already ruined. Though the party didn't start until one in the morning, midnight had already passed, and he'd have to get cleaned up before going out. Besides, now he was tired. His energy always drained quickest when torturing someone.

He looked over at his chubby colleague and felt a bit bad for him. One eye was swollen shut, his knee was shattered, and he'd thrown up a half-dozen times from the gasoline Sharuk force-fed him.

"Okay, Ahmed. You have one hour."

"One hour? But, Sharuk—"

"Okay, then. One day." Sharuk hollered, holding up the brass knuckles. "Or we will see how well you can scream with no teeth in your mouth. Perhaps, even, no head on your shoulders."

— ◆ —

Six o'clock always comes early in the West Wing of the White House. Sometimes the action is constant, twenty-four hours. This was a morning to stay clear of the Oval Office.

Inside, standing behind his desk, President Jones was livid. He glared at Ned Zapper, Trevor Madden, and Paxton Twill.

He threw a National Security Urgent Report onto his desktop. In bold letters near the top it read: "IED explodes in Atlanta, kills two. The target: Avner Navon."

"What do you know about this?" Jones demanded.

Zapper crossed his arms and turned a keen eye on Madden. Madden shrugged and shook his head.

Twill threw up his hands. "What you know is what I know, Mr. President."

"Does the FBI know who carried this out?"

"Not yet and no one is taking credit," Twill said, "as far as the networks are reporting. But Fox News is making the point Navon and you have had a severe falling out. And since a plurality of the country listens to Fox, we've got to squelch any idea the Oval Office is connected."

"No one would believe I'd call for the assassination of an American," Jones scoffed.

"With all due respect, Mr. President, that's a bet you really don't want to take," Twill said. "The fifty-six percent who voted for the other two candidates might well believe you would."

Zapper stepped in. "I agree, Mr. President. We have to get out in front on this, decry the attack on your longtime good friend and declare you will go after the bomber with the full force of America's intelligence forces."

"I'll call a press conference," Twill said, "and declare how appalled you are at this attack on one of your close friends. If a reporter mentions Navon's actions this last week, I'll point out every friendship faces difficulties. The best of pals don't see eye-to-eye on every single issue. You admire Navon for his contributions to the country, and, in part, you even owe your election to him."

Jones rubbed his chin. "Okay, Pax. Do so, but leave out the last bit about him being a big part of my election."

"Sure."

———————◆———————

As they left the Oval Office, Twill turned to Madden. "Trev—"

"Don't say what you're thinking." Madden put a finger in Twill's face. "I swear this was not me. I was actually planning something less, shall we say, explosive."

"Not your cronies, either?"

"Nor my cronies."

"Then who?"

Madden shook his head. "I honestly don't know."

Chapter Fourteen

Wednesday, 3:00 p.m. Saudi time

Thursdays and Fridays are a normal day off in Saudi Arabia, so Max was glad he could fly in today and not have to wait three days.

Riyadh was familiar to him. The city was large and sprawling but short, reminding him of Dallas-Ft. Worth but boasting more modern, and by far, more impressive architecture than the Metroplex. Some might call Riyadh's wealth decadent, but he'd seen worse—in Dubai before the economic collapse.

He drove down a wide boulevard, the norm of three lanes on each side, separated by tall, broad palm trees. Many signs on the Western-friendly highway were written in both Arabic and English.

On the flight from New London, he'd contacted Yoni in Israel for details of the school layout and security. But before doing anything clandestine, he thought he'd employ a straightforward approach. He'd go to the school office and innocently ask for the information he wanted.

He found the Diriyah Islamic School for Boys in the Al Wurud district, not far from the Four Seasons Hotel Riyadh, a spectacular place where he could only dream of staying. He recalled chasing a suspect in an attack on the US ambassador through the hotel's kitchens and almost stopping to admire the impressive cookware.

He parked outside. *Diriyah Islamic School for Boys must be to schools as the Sheraton Riyadh Hotel and Towers is to hotels.* Not a dime—or in this case riyal—was spared in its construction. After all, young minds were being molded here. What they were being molded into was what he intended to discover.

Officially, the Saudi Royal Family wanted no part of extremist Islamic efforts, but they did little to deter them, especially in academia. And they'd had nothing to fear from American reprisals going back to President Carter—Reagan being the lone exception.

Students had gone home, but the place was open, and Max walked straight to the reception area in front of the office of the headmaster, an imam.

A short, thin man wearing a long, flowing, gold-trimmed, white dishdasha, and on his head, a red-and-white shemagh, welcomed him formally. Sporting a heavy mustache and thick goatee, he looked a miniature version of King Abdullah.

"I hope you can help me," Max said in Arabic.

"Perhaps I may," the man replied in his native tongue.

"I met a Saudi man a couple weeks ago on a flight to France. We had a wonderful discussion and exchanged business cards, intending to remain in contact. However, I lost his card and want desperately to reach him. But I do recall he mentioned attending your school about twenty-five years ago."

The man nodded.

"I'm sure I would know his name if I were to see it again. My hope is by looking at your student enrollments from those years, I will notice my acquaintance."

The man nodded.

Max waited for a response but the man simply gazed at him. If revealing students' names was not allowed, the man need only deny him using policy as his excuse. His delay indicated he could indeed share the enrollments. Max smiled dolefully, hoping to win him over.

Finally, the man shook his head. "I am so sorry, sir. Only our imam could approve this and he is out of the country for a month, raising funds in America for scholarships. I certainly wish I could help, but—"

Max shrugged. "Well, worth a try."

"Perhaps your friend will contact you," the man offered.

"Perhaps," Max said. "Thank you for your valuable time, sir."

The man bowed.

Max returned the bow and left. He had eight hours to kill before returning to this very office. As he walked to the entrance, he surveyed the place. Indeed, there were surveillance cameras, just as Yoni had reported, but there were blind spots.

———◆———

Avi had sequestered himself at his estate and sat in his den, his chair turned to look out the window at the rear terrace. He checked his watch. *Ten a.m. Time is standing still. When would Jonas's parents arrive? Jonas. A good boy, a bright young man, and now he was dead.*

Avi blamed himself. Why hadn't he thought to heighten security in the face of all the anti-Semitic attacks around the country, the denigration of synagogues and cemeteries, the verbal assault by Muslims and even some Jews compliant to demands they put up or get out? He surely should have had his vehicles under protective scrutiny.

He groaned in mourning.

My airplane. The thought struck him if an enemy would bomb his car to kill him and others, they certainly would do the same with his jet., which provided an even better target. No one survives falling from the sky.

He called for Lana. She must have been outside his door waiting for him to call, for she entered immediately.

"Lana, call Jerry, will you," he asked, referring to his head of security, "and make sure he has our plane totally checked out and locked down so no one can blow it, or us, up?"

"Certainly, Papa."

"Then we need to talk."

"Talk?"

"Yes, about your being here. Perhaps this isn't the safest place for you. Perhaps you should live somewhere at a distance from me."

"Papa." Her intense look startled him. "You can't be serious."

He was bewildered.

"Papa, my place is at your side. It always will be."

"Lana, I want you by my side, too. But I'd rest easier if I knew you were safe. For a Jew, Israel is safer than America right now."

"If I were at a distance, I wouldn't be able to think of anything or anyone but you, Papa." She rushed to him and bent down to hug him. "Please don't make me go elsewhere."

Avi returned the embrace. His little girl was now a woman, and she still carried his heart in her hands. "Okay, dear heart," he acquiesced, "then with me you will stay."

———◆———

Max had spent the time from mid-afternoon until eight o'clock observing the Islamic school. He drove around and spotted the small, attached room housing the security surveillance equipment. Security was certainly off-site. No reason for school officials to fear intruders.

He walked the boulevards across the streets surrounding the school, watching, ever watching. He sat at a maqha—coffee shop—and kept track of the few comings and goings.

Kingdom Centre, a ninety-nine-floor, thousand-foot-high marvel costing two billion Saudi riyals, lorded over the city and loomed in the nearby business district of Al-Olaya. Even in the dark of night, its brilliant white exterior was difficult to miss.

Between sips of Turkish coffee, savoring the hint of cardamom—and saffron?—he wrote down the times. At five o'clock, the first-floor lights came on, one room at a time. He surmised a janitorial crew—perhaps one person, maybe two—was making its rounds. At a few minutes past six, the second-floor rooms were lit up one at a time. Certainly janitorial. At 7:17, the first third-floor light flicked on. These folks were certainly consistent.

There were only three floors. Max figured at 8:34, the custodians would be finished and go home. He'd let the place get nice and sleepy—wait until ten o'clock before he went in. He checked his watch. He had two hours to prepare. He ordered another cup of Turkish coffee. A half-hour later, his plan of action mapped out in his head, he paid his bill, then ambled to his car.

His next task was easy—drive to the dark parking lot a half mile away and prepare. He had all he needed in the trunk of his vehicle. Black clothes. Black nylon pullover hat. Black lipstick. He only had camouflage face paint, but the paint would have to suffice. Should be a walk in the park.

————— ◆ —————

Dark permeated the atmosphere as Max stole silently along the corridor, staying low and close to the wall, his soft-soled shoes silent on the tile floor. Soft lights in the ceiling dimly lit the hall and other areas. Black marble was everywhere.

The front office was dead ahead thirty feet.

He vaulted himself over the countertop of the long reception area and landed on his feet on the other side.

Squatting on his haunches, he hurried to the next room, another outer office area with photocopiers, a printer on steroids, a paper shredder also on steroids, three desks, a coffee maker, and assorted other equipment.

He looked around. There were two doors, one rectangular and unmarked, the other rounded across the top and sporting a rich-looking gold nameplate: Imam Abdul Baqi Meshaal. *The headmaster. Perfect.*

He hurried to the door and reached to turn the doorknob. Locked. This was unique, locking an inner-office door.

No problem. Max reached into the left thigh pocket of his cargo pants and withdrew a small metal ring holding several sizes of picks. He separated two from the others and worked on the lock. *If only this were as quick as in the movies.*

A good half-minute elapsed before he felt a click. Holding the tumbler in place with one pick, he worked a second pick around. Seconds ticked by. He was out of practice. A minute. This task was certainly not in his wheelhouse.

Finally, the lock clicked. *Phew!*

Max opened the door just wide enough to squeeze inside, then shut himself in.

He turned on a thumb-sized flashlight that lit up a large office. A rich, predominately red Persian rug centered the cherry-wood floor. Large woven wall hangings—one depicting Mecca, the other the Dome of the Rock—graced the two side walls.

The desk, a gleaming cherry wood with nothing but a computer and a gold pen set on top, was straight ahead. Max walked around the desk and turned on the imam's computer. The oversized monitor lit up, a window asked in Arabic for the password. Again, Max slipped his hand into a jacket pocket and came out with a small square box with one cord sticking out the side. The device would run through hundreds of thousands of possible passwords in Arabic.

As he reached to plug the cord into the computer's USB port, he chuckled to himself. *I think I'll play a hunch.* He typed Allah Akbar. The 9/11 hijackers screamed "Allah Akbar." before crashing their planes. Army Major Nidal Malik Hasan hollered "Allah Akbar." before massacring thirteen fellow soldiers at Fort Hood. Egyptian Muslims cheered "Allah Akbar." while trampling the remains of dozens of Christians eviscerated in a suicide bombing at a church in Alexandria. The phrase was emblazoned in their hearts and bore witness on their tongues.

The monitor made a noise like a muezzin's call to worship from a minaret and whirred into start-up mode. In a few moments, the computer was up and running, displaying only a hard-drive symbol called "Imam Meshaal's Drive" in Arabic.

Max slipped a flash drive out of his right thigh cargo pocket and stuck the drive into a USB port. When the flash-drive icon appeared, he dragged the icon to the flash drive. He could hear the computer whirring, copying. A one-terabyte flash drive should be able to copy the entire hard drive, he thought. He checked his watch: 10:23. No problem. He had an hour before the plane he intended to catch would leave the tarmac.

Suddenly sounds echoed from the entryway. Men's voices. And heavy footsteps. They were coming his way. He turned off his flashlight and hunkered down low behind the desk. *Hurry up, flash drive.*

One of the voices rose above the others, carrying a weight of authority. *The imam. Gone for a month? Sure. Hurry up.*

The footsteps sounded like they had reached the reception area.

"The words I speak come from the throne room of Allah," the imam said.

"Yes, Imam Meshaal."

"When I speak you should be more intent, Aaban."

"Yes, Imam Meshaal."

Hurry. Max urged the flash drive.

Max heard the clicking sound of the half-door built into the far side of the reception desk. They were coming in. *Please, God.* Max prayed.

Now they were all walking at a steady pace into the inner office area.

"I want my monthly reports from each region, and I want them as soon as they arrive, not an hour later, Masum."

"Absolutely, Imam."

Max checked the monitor. A bar showed the hard drive was nearly transferred.

"And you, Tariq?"

"Yes, Imam."

"The financial funnel must continue unabated. Some of our greatest work, praise Allah, is about to come to pass. You must keep a firm grip on all our sources."

"Of course, Imam Meshaal."

Hurry. Tick-tock.

They had reached the door to the imam's office. A hand turned the doorknob.

"What's this?" Meshaal asked. "My office is unlocked?"

"The janitor must not have locked it on his way out," one of the others said.

———— ◆ ————

At the moment the imam and his men stepped into the room, Max slipped the closet door shut behind him. He patted the flash drive in his thigh pocket and zipped it closed, then snapped the flashlight back on. The closet was about six feet square, the back wall with wide floor-to-ceiling shelving containing old records and copies of several books—all written by Imam Meshaal.

"About the finances, Imam—" It must be the finance guy, Tariq.

"Yes?"

"Sharuk called—in a panic."

"Sharuk AbdelMassih?"

"AbdelMassih, yes."

"Why the panic?"

"Our bank account in CaribbeanFirst Bank has been emptied."

"Emptied?"

"One hundred and thirteen million American dollars, gone."

The imam used a word Max didn't know, but uttered like a curse. "How did this happen?"

"A hacker."

"May he become a decaying corpse." The imam paused. "One hundred and thirteen million. Any idea where the money went?"

"Ahmed, Sharuk's right-hand man, the fellow who handles the finances, is a computer guru. He has spent days on this and has tracked the hacker to a place not far from them—America—Connecticut—New Haven."

"New Haven? The place our man got caught before he could blow up the infidel guerilla fighter Braxton."

"Yes."

"I'd kill him myself if I could get my hands on him," the imam said.

"Slit his throat." Another voice.

"From ear to ear." Yet another.

Max's back went up. *Maybe I'd be better off ending this now.* His hand went to the handle of his Glock 23. The gun held ten semi-jacketed rounds, enough to send these four or five guys to their share of virgins in Paradise.

He played the scene out in his mind. *Swing the closet door open. Tap-tap. Tap-tap. Tap-tap. Tap-tap. Four down with two bullets remaining in the magazine. Retrace my steps. Get away clean.*

"The swine needs decapitation," one man spat out. "On camera, for the world to see."

What a nasty comment. Max swallowed hard. In your dreams, pal.

He reached for the closet doorknob, then a thought struck him. Probably the imam—and the others, too—had armed bodyguards waiting for them outside the front of the building, perhaps even inside in the corridor. His escape route was to the side of the building.

Max gulped a deep breath. He despised the idea of having Islamic hit men out to kill him, and here he could take out the head of the viper.

Though he preferred to thoroughly plan a mission, he was trained to freelance. He felt confident. He felt fear. The mix had served him well. *Somewhere there's a John Wayne quote.*

Here he stood, able to put a big dent in what appeared to be a Saudi terror group. They certainly weren't discussing food for the hungry. Heck, if he took them out, the Saudi Royal Prince would probably shake his hand. But Max no longer worked for his government. He had no orders to do so. If he were killed—or worse, captured—it would be an international story.

If alive, he would be tried for murder. The American government would be accused of an assassination of a popular imam, a paragon of peace. Forget the fact Kat would be affected—perhaps even heartbroken. His mother and sister would suffer public scorn—perhaps even retribution. This wouldn't be the first time Islamic militants had targeted family members. Just last month, terrorists had killed not just the judge who had imprisoned one of their own for life, but his wife and three children as well.

In fact, hearing the imam call him by name urged Max to remember to contact his mother and have her take a protracted vacation incognito somewhere. He'd make the call tonight.

Another deep breath.

Max reached for the doorknob with his left hand, his right palm loaded with the Glock.

"Shhh." one of the men said. Max could sense them look toward him.

"You hear something?" the imam asked.

Rifles were slipped from shoulders and cocked. A pistol was drawn from a shoulder holster. The sounds were distinct and all too familiar to Max. He could envision the men. He'd waited too long.

———◆———

Imam Meshaal eyed his closet door, listening intently. What lurked there, if anything? Probably nothing at all. This was, after all, a school. Benign. Unthreatening. On the face of it, the school held nothing valuable to be stolen.

This assumption made him glance down at his computer monitor. A tiny white light told him the machine was in sleep mode. Oy, this only happened when the computer had been on. But he'd been away for three days and no one—absolutely no one—was allowed on his computer.

He reached down and tapped the Return key. The monitor flashed on. The only icon was "Imam's Hard Drive."

Had someone copied the drive or part of the information? And, if so, which part?

Imam Meshaal pointed to the closet. "Open the door."

Tariq, the smallest of the men, stood by the imam, his pistol drawn. Aaban, toting a Russian AN-94 Abakan assault rifle, and Masum, with a firm grip on a Type 56 rifle, rushed the closet. Their rifles were aimed ahead of them.

Aaban, at the door, pulled. The closet was empty.

———— ✦ ————

Putting one foot onto a waist-high shelf, Max had been able to pull himself to the ceiling and push open two eighteen-by-eighteen-inch squares, then pull himself through.

He had to turn on his flashlight. Dark as a tomb in here. Wooden beams traversed the overhead every eighteen inches, but there was only about three feet of head space.

Ha. More like waist space.

He bent his six-foot-two frame in half and squat-stepped his way in the direction of the side door he'd entered. The cramped quarters slowed him, but greater still was the difficulty of seeing where he was going. He put the flashlight in his mouth and clamped down on the handle, "walking" his hands along with his feet across the beams.

In the closet, Aaban looked around closely.

"Nothing," he reported and stepped out into the office.

Masum shifted his rifle to his back, went inside and peered around. Everything seemed in order. He bent his head and peered at the ceiling. "Hmm."

He flicked a switch and a light on the wall beside him lit up the small space. He then squinted up to the ceiling.

"Something's amiss," he said.

"Have a look," Aaman said and offered his hands as a stirrup.

Max saw the outside wall ahead and bent down on a beam on one knee. He pulled up a ceiling square and shined his flashlight into the space below. A classroom, like any American classroom, with a whiteboard, flat-screened monitor, about twenty student desks, and a larger desk in the front.

He lifted two squares out of the way and swung into the opening, holding himself there with one arm while moving the squares back into place with his free hand. Then he dropped to the floor.

He hurried to the exit, cracked open the door and peeked outside. No one was in the corridor, so he hustled the ten feet to the outside door.

Masum set down his rifle and stepped up, then reached for the ceiling.

"One of these tiles is askew," he said.

"Maybe someone was in here—"Aaman said.

"—and escaped through here," Masum finished.

Imam Meshaal had walked to the doorway. He growled, "Get up there and find out. If someone indeed got information from my computer, they could harm the whole network."

"I'm not tall enough," Masum said to Aaban. "Can you lift my foot higher?"

Aaban grunted with the effort and lifted his hands to shoulder height. Masum pushed the ceiling square up and out of the way, then the neighboring square. He grabbed a beam and pulled himself through.

"Dark as a dead infidel's soul up here," he said.

Aaban found a flashlight on a lower shelf and tossed the instrument up to Masum.

"Go." Imam Meshaal ordered.

"I'll need your pistol, Aaban. There's not enough room to maneuver with my rifle up here."

Imam Meshaal turned to Tariq, who stood behind the imam's desk. "Run, Tariq. Tell the guards to circle the building. If there's an intruder, I want him alive. If not possible, kill him."

———— ◆ ————

Max had lifted the outside door latch as quietly as possible, opened the door narrowly, and slipped outside. Parking-lot lamps shed dim light. No armed guards were in sight. A small quadrant of darkness lay ahead, a patch of bushes he had scouted out earlier. He scrambled toward the thicket. His car was parked not far from there. In his camouflage, he was a shadow himself.

Thirty steps later, he leaped and rolled into the darkness and came up with dirt in his mouth. He spat out dust and turned to look toward the door he'd exited. Just then, two men rushed around the front corner of the building, fifty feet from the side door, rifles at the ready.

Max sat quietly and watched. He reached down and pulled out his Glock 23.

One of the gunmen pulled on the school door. When he discovered the exit was locked, he swore loud enough for Max to hear. The other slowly scanned the area, looking for any movement. Max wondered how trigger-happy he was. More than once he'd watched Muslims fire weapons into the air willy-nilly, usually in celebration but sometimes as a show of machismo, apparently never concerned with the fact that what goes up must come down.

Max reached into a rear pocket and pulled out small night-vision binoculars. He locked his eyes on the gunman.

The door swung open and out came a man with a rifle, and behind him, obviously from his garb, the imam.

The imam was waving his hands furiously. Max leaned forward, straining to hear any words. This could be interesting.

"... deadly information ... enemy hands ... him or else...."

Talking about me, are you, pal?

Two other men stepped out of the door.

"Fan the area," said one holding a rifle.

Max eyed the imam. From his bearing, a most important man. Too important to simply be the headmaster of a boys' school. He got a good look at the imam's face and locked it into his memory. Taller and broader than the others. An imposing figure. A large nose, a larger mouth, the normal full beard. A fierce look in his eyes.

This might mean it's worth taking a chance on targeting the imam.

Max felt the heft of the Glock. A familiar feel. A comfortable feel. A confident feel. He guessed the distance to the imam at thirty yards, the outer edge of accuracy for most people with a G23, but he recalled a bet with a couple buddies, both Rangers. They all had G23s shooting from fifty yards. One of his friends hit center mass of the target with two of five shots; the other hit it three of five. Four of Max's five rounds found center mass, winning him the bet and dinner at his favorite steak restaurant in the northern section of North Dallas. But in this circumstance, with no government behind him, no tactical support and with gunmen all around, he didn't like the odds of a miss.

Suddenly another gunman came around the back corner of the building, ten degrees to Max's right. Without a word to the imam or the others, he walked directly at Max, almost as if he could see him.

Max thought of taking him down with a bullet but decided to instead hunker down and stay still. The gunman's determined walk slowed as he drew closer. A few feet away the pace became step, pause, step, pause. He stopped two or three feet from Max and peered into the darkness, pointing the rifle in front of him. No surprise there—even in the darkness, Max recognized the Russian AN-94 Abakan assault rifle.

Max wished he had either his favorite, the Israeli Tavor, or one of the short-barrel POFs, in his hands. But here he was, squatting in a patch of bushes packing a G23 with an assault rifle pointed at him. The question was if the guy even saw him? Max's guess—no. In his camouflage, Max blended perfectly into the bushes.

But in a flash, he decided not to take the chance. With trained swiftness, he slipped to his left, reached forward, grabbed the rifle barrel and pulled the weapon roughly past his right side. The gunman, a little man, was yanked along with the rifle. Max put one hand flush against the man's mouth while grappling him into a choke hold. No more than ten seconds, and Max had stopped the air flow enough to render the gunman unconscious.

Max glanced up to see if the others had noticed his mini tussle. Yes, two of the men near the imam were looking his way, one of them picking up his feet to run.

Max laid the man to the ground and slipped out the back of the bushes. The streets all around were dark and there was no traffic—the only light a soft glow from the Al Wahu Palace Hotel a couple blocks away. Max kept low to the ground and raced across the street.

Behind him, he heard the shout. "Imam, over here. One of our men."

Max angled between two buildings. This was a low, sprawling city, topped out by four- and five-story buildings. In this neighborhood, the buildings were mostly businesses, hours ago shut down for the night.

No traffic, no police, and, he hoped, no problem. But he was never one to count his chickens. He'd seen one mission go terribly wrong when a member of his team slacked off, thinking the job was done and the enemy far away. All it takes is one bullet from one gun at just the right time and …

Max had to tell his dead friend's widow her husband had died a hero. If he himself caught a bullet tonight, who would tell his mother? His sister? Kat? Would his body be delivered to America for burial? And, if so, with his head intact?

Max sprinted between two more buildings, along their rear walls, and then down an alleyway past two others. As he reached the corner of a two-story structure, he stopped, pulled a tiny mirror from a pocket, held it at eye height to the corner and checked for people or traffic.

All quiet there. With speed and stealth, he scrambled across the street to a parking lot filled with vehicles. Straight to his Crown Victoria sedan, a remote-control click to open his door and in he slipped. Wasting no time, Max turned on the engine. Lights out, he flipped the gear shift into first.

In a minute, he was putting distance between himself and the school and any possible pursuers. He felt compelled to turn his headlights on or risk getting pulled over by Riyadh police. He'd planned out his route. He'd drive several blocks to Route 65, turn east a half-dozen blocks to Eastern Ring Branch Road, drive south several blocks to a street returning in this direction. There, he could catch King Abdul Aziz Road, which would take him back southeastward to the US air base. No harm, no foul.

The only exception to his plan was he had to pull over to the side of the road and wipe camouflage paint off his face and hands. The post guard might think it odd for him to return to the base in this state of concealment. His reputation would only carry him so far, he figured.

Max pulled over, wiped off the camouflage, then angled back onto the highway. There was no traffic, no sign of life. Riyadh was asleep. He resisted the temptation to smile.

He drove along at a reasonable speed. To his left was a high chain-link fence, on the other side was the quiet US military air base, only slightly lit up. He checked his watch. The cargo plane would be leaving soon and he had to drop off the car at base ops. Time was tight.

Later, he'd have to call his friend Monty, the chief of the United States Military Training Mission (USMTM) to the Kingdom of Saudi Arabia. A major general, Monty served as the Department of Defense's representative for Saudi Arabia and had cleared the way for

Max's entry and exit. Between the two old friends, approval was just a wink and a nod.

Besides a "thank-you," Max would tell Monty whatever he found out about the school if indeed he found anything.

Suddenly, lights flashed in his peripheral vision. A car's headlights were racing at him. *Oh-oh.*

Gauging the vehicle's speed, Max knew the driver was not about to brake at the stop sign at King Abdul Aziz Road. He figured he had a better chance of avoiding a collision by speeding up rather than hitting the brakes.

He slammed his left foot down on the clutch, slipped the gear shift from fourth to third gear and rammed the accelerator to the floor. The Crown Vic's rpm meter whizzed upward, tires hurtled forward, and Max, jaw tightened, clutched the steering wheel.

In a moment, the approaching vehicle swerved right at him and crashed into Max's right rear fender. The Crown Vic spun around a hundred eighty degrees, Max's head cracked into his side window, and he looked up to see he was driving in the opposite direction.

He looked over at the other vehicle. The rear wheels were off the road in a ditch a couple of feet deep—probably not deep enough to hold the vehicle for long. The vehicle was an Expedition, a high-powered, four-wheel drive.

As Max thumped his foot down on the accelerator, the passenger window and then his own window exploded in almost instant succession, spraying him with small chunks of glass. He quickly shifted from first to third gears, then pulled off his U-turn move. *Interesting, twice in the last couple of days after years without the need.*

Again, racing through the gears, Max pulled out his Glock. Roaring back past the Expedition, he aimed out his broken window and unloaded two bullets into the front left tire and two more into the radiator of the vehicle.

A crack-crack of automatic rifle fire responded. He ducked. Bullets may have hit the side of his car but he couldn't be sure. He simply slammed down on the gas pedal and barreled down King Abdul Aziz Road. As he did, he patted the pocket holding the flash drive with the imam's information. *What in the world have we here?*

Three minutes later, he approached the guardhouse to the air base. He had no window to roll down.

"Have a little trouble, did you, sir?" a young corporal asked.

"You might say it was a spirited time," Max answered with a chuckle he hoped would end the conversation.

"After reading your book, Colonel, I can understand how a visit to this part of the world might result in, eh, some broken glass." He waved his hand. "You'd better hurry on in, sir."

Max smiled and drove on. He'd have to pay for the repairs to the car, but the money might be the best he'd spent in years.

Chapter Fifteen

Early Thursday, Germany time

Several hours later, Max was catching some sleep on a cot in a hangar at Nordholz Naval Airbase in Germany. After years in the military, he could sleep anywhere—on the hard desert floor in the shadow of a tank, on board a rolling ship at sea during a storm, underground in the Golan Heights, even in a tree once in the mountains of Colombia.

After escaping from the Islamic school, he'd caught the late-night flight out of Riyadh. And here he was, waiting for an early-morning flight to New London, arriving at mid-afternoon.

When the first ray of sunlight skipped off a small window into his room, he awoke. Sliding his feet over the edge of the cot, he rubbed his eyes and checked his watch. 6:12 a.m. He'd gotten ninety-three minutes of sleep. The flight was leaving in thirty-eight minutes.

Should he check in with Kat? No, it was midnight in Connecticut. But he was too excited and anxious not to call her. But, then, he didn't want to wake her. He absolutely should have called when he'd arrived at 4:39 a.m.—10:39 p.m. in New Haven.

This wavering was so unlike him. Normally, he simply went with his gut instincts, but since he'd met Kat he sometimes felt he was like a wave in the ocean, a double-minded man. He was sure of his feelings for her, but he didn't want to get too close and put her in more danger.

At the same time, if he didn't remain close, the relationship might go no further. Could he, should he, would he? He slapped himself on the forehead. *Shape up.*

———— • ◆ • ————

Kat stood at her bank of windows, looking at the lights reflecting off the Quinnipiac River in the distance. She couldn't sleep. Tuck, sitting at her side, whimpered like he was wondering what was troubling her. Or perhaps he was simply upset—when she couldn't sleep, neither could he. He was a border collie. Border collies needed jobs. And his unique job was protecting her.

She reached down and scratched the back of his head. "I'm sorry, boy."

The white tip of his tail wagged ever so slightly.

After classes, she had spent the evening scrutinizing The Three Sixes booklet more closely and one name leaped out at her—Abdul Baqi Meshaal.

The name sounded so familiar as if she'd heard or read about him somewhere in her Middle East wanderings. She mulled over the name. Abdul Baqi meant "slave of the Eternal," while Meshaal meant "torch or beacon." His parents must have dreamed of a son who'd be dedicated to Allah and be a light guiding other Islamic followers.

Apparently, their aspirations were fulfilled. He was the imam who wrote the pamphlet.

If only Max were here for her to share this with. She wished he'd call. Why hadn't he called?

She shivered at the thought he'd met with trouble. She knew Muslim justice was sometimes a serious form of masochism. This was true not only currently, but from historical and ancient archaeological evidence, dating to the seventh century. And if the criminal in question offended Islam, either deliberately or accidentally, there were dire and deadly consequences—few or no questions asked.

Just then, Tuck turned his head toward the apartment door and growled. He flashed her a look, then turned and trotted to the door, his hackles up, a rumble deep in his throat.

A flitter of fear ran down Kat's neck. She'd done her best to hide where she lived. No listing in the phone book or the faculty directory.

When he was with her, Max had spotted someone tailing him, and when he came to visit her at her apartment, he'd taken extra precautions to lose the tail. But had someone followed her?

Kat looked around the great room for something to use as protection. She had no guns. She didn't even have a fireplace poker. She almost laughed at the thought of nunchucks, which she had used in a self-defense class when she was in high school.

Tuck stood and stared at the doorknob. He growled, turned to look at her, looked back at the door and started yapping. While he didn't have sheep to herd or cows to bully, Tuck did indeed take this job seriously. Max and President Hall were the exceptions when it came to allowing men within touching distance of her.

Kat had faced danger during the entire chase for David's music. She had faced threats on her recent tour of universities. But she'd had Max at her side during the chase and bodyguards protecting her on her tour.

Being alone with only Tuck somehow felt more vulnerable. She scanned the room. Her eyes stopped at the kitchen island. *My knives.*

She hurried to the wooden knife holder and yanked out the biggest one—so big she had never used it before. *This one must be for killing cattle.*

"Tuck, hush." she said and strode to the door. Her heart pounded.

Tuck obeyed and dropped to his belly on the floor. It appeared he was trying to peer underneath the door. *Smart.*

Kat looked through the peephole and saw no one, so she mimicked Tuck, laying with her head beside Tuck's. She saw no shadow, no movement.

She stood and leaned over Tuck, her ear to the edge of the door, listening. No sound.

No sight, no sound. Good.

"Okay, Tuck," she said. "Up."

He stood. With the knife in her left hand, in one swift motion, she unlocked and swung the door open. No one there. She looked down the hallway in both directions. To her left, the heavy door at the end of the hall leading down the side stairway swung shut. She heard the shallow click of the latch.

Grabbing her keys from a peg next to the door, she looked at Tuck, pointed in the direction of the closed door, and said, "Run, boy!"

Tuck tore off down the hallway barking, Kat racing behind him. Tuck reached the door, stood on his hind legs and tried to turn the door handle with his front paws. He managed to turn the knob a quarter-turn, but not quite enough to open the heavy door.

Kat reached him and pulled the door open. A stairwell led to the first floor. In front of her, a huge window gave a view of the side street. She looked out. A shadowy figure was turning the corner at a full run.

Kat considered mounting chase with her knife and her dog, then glanced down. She was dressed in her robe and slippers, in ten-degree temperatures. What on earth would she do if she ever even caught up to the culprit? Blowing out a long breath, she called after Tuck, who'd run down the stairway and was waiting at the first-floor exit. "Come on, boy. Let's go home."

Tuck whined, looking from her to the door to her and back. Boy, did he want to give chase.

She sighed. "Not tonight, Tuck."

She leaned down and scratched behind his ears—his favorite spot. His tail metronomed a contented beat. *This is some pooch.*

———— ◆ ————

As Kat and Tuck stepped back into her apartment, the telephone rang. Kat almost jumped out of her slippers. *Boy.*

She didn't know whether to feel relieved or angered.

She closed and locked the door, picked up the phone.

"Kat Cardova," she answered, her voice shaky.

"Kat." Max sounded apologetic. "I'm sorry for calling so late, but is something the matter?"

She hesitated. "No, just a little fearful. I think we had an intruder."

She could sense Max react on the other end of the call.

"What happened?" His voice was sharp with alarm.

She told him, then added, "Please don't worry. We're all right."

"I wish I were there."

"So do I." Kat sat on her couch and pulled her robe tight around her. She patted the cushion next to her, inviting Tuck to her side. He hesitated, she patted again, and he hopped up and lay down against her leg. "Where are you, and how did you do?" she asked.

"I've got the list of students—and faculty—since the school began in 1971," Max said. "I've also got all sorts of information they don't care to hide—stuff like their history, their mission statement, board of directors. But also, some stuff they absolutely do not want the public to know."

"Yes?"

"Yes, like all their financial backers."

"Whoa." A thought struck Kat and she asked, "Does the name Abdul Baqi Meshaal ring a bell?"

"Meshaal? Yeah. He founded the school."

"Max, he wrote the Three Sixes booklet."

A moment of silence, then, "Honest?"

"Honest. In 1992."

More silence, then, "Jones was a student there in 1991 and 1992, leaving halfway through his senior year."

Kat blew out a breath. This was getting interesting. "So, Jones would have known Meshaal."

"Maybe the book is a keepsake from his time at the school."

Kat rubbed her neck. "Maybe."

"Maybe it's more than a keepsake."

"Maybe."

"Our conversation is full of 'maybes,'" Max said. "How about we end with an absolute?"

"Which is what?" Kat asked.

"I see you when I get back."

"When?"

"We're air-bound in a half hour. We'll arrive around three o'clock this afternoon."

"You travel halfway around the world and back, and in the meantime, break into an Islamic school, getting away with secret records—and you do it all in one day?"

"Yeah, I guess."

"So, you ought to get to Yale around five-ish?" Kat asked.

"Thereabouts."

"Call when you arrive."

"Deal."

Kat patted Tuck on the head. "Thanks for your protection, my prince."

Tuck luxuriated in her attention, leaning his head back so she could scratch his chin. He was worth every bit of her love.

Kat thought of Max. A man on a mission. She realized while neither he nor she fully comprehended precisely the mission, the task seemed to be taking on more importance.

The last mission—the music—was hers and Max had stuck with her every dangerous step of the way. This mission was his, and she was darn well going to stick with him, too, "even if the creek rises," as her dad would say.

One question nagged at her—did the near-attack in the classroom and the person tailing Max have anything to do with what he was investigating overseas? Were they simply retaliation for his book and outspokenness about militant Islam, or was something else driving them? And who was at her door a few minutes ago?

She shivered, pulled a throw around her shoulders and snuggled up to Tuck.

Chapter Sixteen

Thursday morning

Clair Braxton scrutinized her partner across the table. She and Nancy had played cards together for twenty-three years. They weren't twins. They weren't even related, but they might as well have been. One's thoughts were often the other's. And in playing bridge, closeness came in handy.

They had even won a vacation on a cruise ship a couple years back. Clair was proud of the accomplishment, but not as much as she was for their three Dallas Metroplex Contract Bridge Championships the last four years.

Advancing beyond Dallas Metro had so far eluded the two friends, but a victory today would be a true thrill—the Southern Regional title, leading to the North American Bridge League Championships. A win here and she and Nancy were off to Seattle next month.

She looked at her hand again and announced, with firm conviction, "Three spades."

Just then her cell phone vibrated. The sound was ever-so-dull, but the man to her right also heard the noise.

"Against regulations, madam," he declared. "Cells must be off."

"But the ring is off," Clair protested. "It's only on vibrate because I haven't been able to contact my son."

"And your son is—" he asked, indignant and scornful. "Who? The governor? The president?"

"Colonel Max Braxton," she said. The cell continued to vibrate.

"And a terrorist tried to kill him and his students," Nancy offered. "At Yale University. The national news covered the incident."

"On Tuesday," Clair said, "and I haven't been able to reach him."

The cell vibrated again. Clair pulled the phone out of her purse and glared at the man for permission.

"Well," said the woman to Clair's left, "those are extenuating circumstances, Bob. I saw the report on CNN last night."

Clair checked the monitor. "It is my son," she said. "May I?"

The man scowled but nodded assent.

Clair put the phone to her ear. "Maximus."

"Yes, Mom, it's me."

"You all right?"

"I'm fine. Sorry I haven't called you. I've been—tied up—first with the FBI and NSA, then I had to take a trip nine time zones away. I apologize."

"I just want to know if you're okay. If you were hurt."

"No-no. I'm great. But, Mom—"

"Yes?"

"I'm concerned for you."

"Me?"

"Yes, for your safety."

"Why me?"

"Because I think these people may stop at nothing to get at me, including harming you."

"Oh, Max, you can't be serious."

"Dreadfully serious, Mother."

Alarmed, Clair looked at Nancy and imagined men wearing keffiyehs wrapped around their heads and faces surrounding the home they shared. She felt her heart flutter and stifled a stutter. "Well, what do you want me to do?"

"Take a prolonged vacation. A cruise. Something. I'll pay the bill—all of it. An early birthday present."

———◆———

Max ended the call and peered out the window at the clouds. He was aboard a US Army C-143, a descendant of the C-141 Starlifter cargo craft, heading from Germany to the States. This fear for his mother, the would-be attack on his classroom, he had not envisioned any of this when he wrote his book about the perils of war without strong political leadership or followed up on advice to teach at Yale University.

He had spent many years away from home. He'd fought in desert trenches on New Year's, in Afghan mountains on Christmases, and in the stink of Bosnia on his parents' fiftieth anniversary. He'd been fortunate to be able to come home between black-op missions for his Dad's funeral.

This was one time he wished he could hold his mother in his arms and promise her all would be right with the world. Even if he could, he knew he would be lying. All was not right, and this time he didn't know if he could make the world even a tad better.

America was disdained, if not disliked, on all sides. Even longtime allies like Canada and Great Britain sometimes looked askance at the once-great republic. Past presidents had made mockeries of old friendships. He recalled Obama declaring Israel should revert to its indefensible 1967 borders, his sending back to England the bronze bust of Sir Winston Churchill that had stood in the White House for decades, and giving as a present to the Queen of England an iPod loaded with his speeches.

Past presidents had flown into battles with enemies when they should not have like Iraq and Libya, and not gone to battle when they should have like Iran, twice.

No, as positive an attitude as Max normally maintained, there were times when he felt like one of the king's men looking at a shattered Humpty Dumpty. Could this great nation be put back together again?

He shook his head and hoped his mother would take a luxurious vacation at a beautiful, sun-drenched spot where she could lay in the sun, play tennis, and read her books without fear. A Caribbean cruise would be perfect. He'd even offered to pay for Nancy to join her. He hoped Nancy accepted.

He checked his phone for other messages he hadn't answered and dialed his sister, Maise. He got her voice mail and said, "Hey, sis. I'm doing fine. Don't worry. But please ask Mom about our conversation today and make sure she takes a holiday—until things simmer down. I'm counting on you. I love you. Give my best to Dan and hugs to the kids from their Uncle Max."

Another message was from Julius, his genius guerilla-fighting computer whiz of a pal. Julius said simply, "Call me."

Max dialed Julius' number. On the fourth ring, a voice mail announced: "I'm off grid. Leave a message." *Darn.*

———— ◆ ————

Josh stared at the pepperoni pizza in front of him. What was wrong with him, anyway? He usually inhaled a ten-incher in short order and here he was, half of the pie uneaten.

"What's the matter, 59?" Hank had taken to calling Josh by his football jersey number. "Want me to finish for you?"

Josh pushed the plate across the table. "Yeah, go ahead."

Stunned, Hank reached for his iPhone. "I've gotta write this down to remember the moment." He started keying in the letters, repeating: "The first time since I've known him—what eighth grade?—Josh Andrews did not finish a pizza—" he hesitated, "in ten minutes."

"I'm worried's all," Josh said.

"You're the consummate worrywart. Never stopped you from eating before. Remember the night before the Nebraska State Championship?" Hank laughed.

"Well, I've never had to face the feds before." Josh was dead sober, morose even.

"What, this afternoon?" Hank waved a dismissive motion with his right hand. "They're on our side, man. Or we're on their side. Whatever. They love us."

"Well, they love Ashley and Jose anyway," Josh conceded. "They're the computer geeks who can steal truckloads of money from the bad guys."

Hank grabbed a slice of pizza and chomped down.

"Well, after we helped Teach when he took down the terrorist in class, I think we don't have to worry about the campus police or feds from here on out. Did you see Chief MacMillan's face when he came in to interview us? Whoa."

Josh lightened up. "Yeah, and when he introduced us to the FBI guys, he was proud of us—pleased we were Yalies."

"Right. And they were a different group than the NSA team at the bat cave." Hank bit down on another piece of pizza. "Yum, man, this is good."

"Hey, I'll take back one of those pieces," Josh said and grabbed one.

"Feeling better, eh, 59?" Hank smiled.

"Yo." Jose called and walked toward their table. "Hey, guys, look who I brought with me."

He waved his arm behind him, and Ashley and Jill stepped around him.

"We thought we'd have a little huddle before heading over to meet with the feds," Jill asked.

"Huddle? So, some of us is rubbing off on you, eh?" Hank joked.

"Hopefully not too much," she replied. "I shower daily."

"Ouch." Josh said, placing his right hand over his heart.

———◆———

Lana Navon stepped into the rear seat of the Escalade, followed by Avi. They were second in line in the contingent of vehicles leaving the funeral services for Jonas Mandrell and heading to the Tikvah V'Shalom Section of Greenlawn Cemetery.

The service, interment, processional, burial, and graveside prayers had been spiritually, emotionally, and physically draining. Now they would head home. *But life was changed forever for Jonas's family.*

She and others at the grave site had formed two rows, creating a path for the family's exit and reciting the ancient words of consolation: "Ha-Makom yenahem etkhem b'tokh sha ar aveilei Tzion v Yerushalayim," which meant "May the Omnipresent comfort you among all the mourners of Zion and Jerusalem."

Lana knew everyone there would need every ounce of comfort God would provide, far beyond family.

Lana had known Jonas was a wildly admired young man since her father had hired him four years before, but now his popularity was clear. Friends and family had flown from all over the country to Jonas' hometown, Columbus, Ohio. Classmates from high school in Columbus, Clemson University in South Carolina and Wharton Business School in Philadelphia, had attended. A contingent from Atlanta had flown there aboard Avi's jet.

Dan Ogilvy, Avi's chief financial officer, was driving the vehicle and private detective Boaz Erdan sat in the front passenger seat.

"May Adonai bless Jonas's family," Avi said. "What a loss for us all, but especially for his father and mother and his young sister. She obviously loved him so."

"Tragic." Lana wiped tears from her eyes with a tissue. "What a sweetheart he was."

"And brilliant," Dan added. "He wasn't long for a promotion, was he, Avi?"

"No, no, he wasn't." Avi pulled a handkerchief from his pocket and blew his nose. "And to think, they meant their bomb for me— me, who's lived a full life. And what happened? A young man with a lifetime ahead of him was taken from this world. The world will be a poorer place without him. If only—"

"Papa," Lana interrupted, "we've been through this before. You can't continue to blame yourself. The bomb was an act of terror. We all would have died—you, Dan and me as well as Jonas and Stan—if the bomber had been successful."

Lana put her hand on her father's. She'd become adept at soothing her father—a tactic she'd developed as a child watching her mother minister to his grief when he lost siblings to Palestinian terrorists in Israel. Her Dad was a people lover, even more so when those people were family. She knew he felt the pain of Jonas's family at this moment.

She had inherited her father's compassion. She hoped she had also inherited some of his resolve, for when the great Avner Navon set his sights on something, he felt like he did back in the IDF setting the sights of his rifle on a target.

Avi breathed out loud, raised his shoulders and declared, "All right, then. Let's get the mamzer who did this. How's your investigation going, Boaz?"

Boaz turned his broad shoulders and looked at Avi and Lana.

"The FBI isn't releasing this yet, but my sources tell me the bomb was an IED, much like any other IED you'd find from Afghanistan and Iraq to Paris, London, and now, here in America, but with one distinct difference—"

"The difference being?" Dan asked.

"While the bomb's projectiles were the normal nails, screws, and ball bearings, the coroner also discovered a surprise: a very sharp knife with the halal marking from an imam."

"A kosher knife?" Lana was astonished.

"Yes," Boaz said. "Halal, or haraam, is the Islamic version of kosher. And these knives are approved to make a swift, deep incision at the front of the throat, the carotid artery."

Lana flinched.

"So," Avi said, "you're saying the bomb maker determined to send a message—we were their meat to be carved up, slaughtered?"

"I don't know. No one knows," Boaz said. "But a knife of this kind was found in one other bombing."

"Where?" Lana asked.

"In the Philippines last month."

"The assassination of President Aviles?" Dan guessed.

"Correct."

"A Christian," Avi said.

"Yes. On Christmas Day."

"The Sulaiman Islamiyah, one of the lesser-known Islamic terrorist groups, took credit in The Philippines," Boaz said. "And, get this, in their chest-thumping they declared they were the strong arm of something called Warriors for Allah."

"Never heard of them," Avi said.

"This I did not get from the FBI," Boaz said, "but from a friend of yours in the Mossad, Avi. He told me Warriors for Allah is an ancient clandestine Islamic group only a handful of the most elite Islamic leaders have even heard of—very secretive, very vicious, and now, apparently very powerful, pulling the puppet strings of terror worldwide at the highest levels."

"And in the Philippines, they used a knife like the one in the bombing meant for my father?" Lana asked.

"Yes," Boaz said.

"So how do we find the meshuggeners who did this to us and ours?" Dan asked.

"We may be closer than you'd think," Boaz said. "There's evidence the bomber placed the IED under the limo while parked in your space beneath the financial center, Avi. Could have been any time after you arrived at six thirty in the morning. They're checking tape from surveillance cameras stationed at the entrance and at the elevator near your space—the lift you take up to your office suite."

Lana brightened. "Could be definitive."

"Right, Miss Navon," Boaz said. He ran his fingers through a thick head of hair. "And one other thing—"

"Yes?" she asked.

"The container holding the detonator, trigger, charge, ball bearings, nails, screws, and the knife—all the innards of the bomb—was an oil pan from a Honda Civic. They found a little serial number to the oil pan in the debris and are tracing the number to a car built at the assembly line in Greensburg, Indiana. From there, they can trace the car to the dealership who sold the car and then to the buyer. Maybe the information will tell us, directly, who put the bomb together."

"More than likely the car was in a junkyard somewhere," Avi said.

"Perhaps. Perhaps not," Boaz said.

"Why haven't we heard of this group before?" Lana asked.

Boaz shrugged. "We're like most of the rest of the world. The Mossad knows little of the group. I do know this—they do not go the way of other Islamic terrorists, proudly and boldly proclaiming their killings. For some reason, they want to hide in the shadows."

Chapter Seventeen

Thursday afternoon, January 30

The A-Team arrived outside the bat cave in Hank's Mini Cooper and Jose's Jeep and piled out, Josh leading the way to the steps.

He turned and looked at the others. A handful of college kids. Yalies, yes, but college kids.

"I really can't imagine we can give these guys much help," he said. "I'm sure the NSA's got brilliant IT guys."

"Remember, the feds couldn't hack the terrorist's Apple phone back in 2016?" Hank said.

Josh nodded. "Oh, yeah."

"Besides, you underestimate my skills," Ashley said, her lips curling into a smile.

"And mine," Jose said, pulling a hood over his head and batting his gloved hands together against the cold. "Let's get inside."

"Jose," Josh said, "you should have stayed in Florida or somewhere else in the South, where the temps don't get below fifty degrees."

"Make that sixty, which is plenty cold enough for me," Jose replied. "In Miami, in January? Right now, I'd be in shorts, sandals, and nothing else.

"Oh-oh," Jill said, "perish the thought." She laughed and the others joined in.

"Have your laugh," Jose said, "but my dreams of lying on the beach down the street from mom and dad's house keep me warm at night."

"Yeah, yeah, yeah," Josh said. "Let's get up to the bat cave and see what's up."

They crowded into the elevator and slowly ascended the four floors. Agent Alex Franken greeted them when they spilled out onto the landing.

"They're waiting for you inside," he said and opened the heavy door.

Josh was first in and spotted Sturgen and Crowe backs to them, sans coats in the warm room, huddling over the Operation Mongoose monitors. Two men were sitting at the controls.

Crowe heard them enter and turned. "Hey, the Yale gang is here."

Sturgen turned then, and, behind him, a lanky man who appeared in his late thirties or early forties. He was taller than Josh and looked like he could play alongside him at linebacker, or perhaps as a tight end or fullback.

Sturgen broke the silence. "Kids, I want to introduce you to Colonel Julius Pérez Rodríguez."

Josh was first to shake his hand. "So you're—"

"The troublemaker," Julius said. "When I gave this system to Colonel Braxton to use, I never meant for the thing to go live and get him and you kids in trouble."

"No trouble," Hank said.

"Yeah, a lot of fun," Jill piped up.

"All your 3D imaging, the mapping, the real-time transactions," Jose said, "pretty cool stuff."

"Scary stuff," Ashley said. "I'm a city girl, New York City, but this even scares me."

"Stealing $750 million didn't scare you?" Crowe asked.

Ashley smiled coyly, "Well—"

"My fault," Julius said, "all my fault. I left the rascally little window-to-reality in the program, one little trick which happens to make the whole thing go live and in your face."

The man Josh figured was the NSA computer forensics expert spun around in his chair. "But at the same time, what you created, Colonel, is genius. We could tear apart terrorist bankrolls with this."

"Thanks, Johnson," Sturgen said, "and break all sorts of US and international laws. We could land in jail, not to mention Congressional hearings, being fired from NSA, losing our pensions—"

"Sending our families into poverty—" Crowe added.

"Hold on," Julius said. "Do you think a terrorist cell is going to call the cops and tell them someone has stolen their blood money? People, people, you've got lawyers coming out of your ears over there at the NSA and FBI. There must be a way to legally sell this as part of the war on terrorism."

"Remember, President Obama, years ago, commanded no one to use the phrase war on terrorism," Crowe said. "Islamic extremists, war on terror, anything someone might see as denigrating Islam was expunged from government documents—"

"And from our very tongues," Sturgen said.

"Well, we all know the order was just plain silly, don't we?" Julius asked.

Johnson snickered. Sturgen and Crowe shot him withering looks.

"Well," Johnson objected, "even if we used the other parts of this software apart from the banking capabilities, it would be a great tool. Besides, doesn't the colonel have a good point? What terrorist cell is going to call the authorities about any money we pinched?"

Sturgen and Crowe looked at each other and both shrugged. "Dunno," Sturgen said. "I think you may be right."

Josh exchanged looks with his friends. They all agreed, too. But at this point, obviously, they weren't a part of the discussion.

Josh didn't have a clue why they'd been summoned to the bat cave, and he knew his friends didn't, either. They'd relinquished the bat cave's use to the feds. And Hank was right. Now it appeared they and the Teach were all out of trouble.

"Excuse me," Josh said. "What do you want us here for?"

Sturgen answered. "First, we simply wanted you to be able to meet the colonel, the Wizard of Oz behind this invention—since you mastered the programs so quickly. Second, we've received word the Department of Justice agrees with our recommendation and will not be leveling any charges of any sort against you, Colonel Braxton, or Colonel Rodríguez here."

———◆———

Maybe years of experience with extraordinary sleep deprivation and battle fatigue were the explanation. Maybe the feeling was supernatural, but Max was astonishingly energized.

Yesterday he had traveled all the way to Saudi Arabia and spent the day in Riyadh. Last night he had traveled from Saudi Arabia to Germany, and today he flew from Germany to America. Now he was on his last leg, driving to New Haven. He'd slept a couple hours on the cot in Germany and a couple more on the plane, and yet he felt like he'd stepped out of a refreshing shower.

He recalled a Scripture, something about the Lord being your strength, or giving strength to your bones—and smiled. *This is evidence.*

On the outskirts of the city, he had received a call from the Yale PR lady—the, as-he-recalled, nattily dressed Shauna Robison.

"Colonel Braxton," she said, "the press won't let us alone until they speak with you."

"I think it best if I remain faceless, Miss Robison," Max said.

"Have you seen the news at all the last two days?" The girl sounded astonished.

"Actually, no."

There was silence.

"I've been out of town," he said.

Silence.

"Out of the country."

Silence.

Max decided to meet silence with silence. His military training had taught him to be tight-lipped except with those you absolutely trust. Here, his trust was in Kat and, well, Kat.

"Well, you're no longer faceless," she said. "All the major news outlets and cable channels have been showing your face and talking about your book and your class on terrorism. You'd call it a deluge. They're hunting down and interviewing your students, scouring the campus to find professors to interview. Dean Mussinger got buttonholed by three or four of them. Chief MacMillan, too. But, bottom line is they all want you."

Max was silent, mulling over the information and trying to avoid an aggressive tow-truck driver cutting in front of him.

"Sir," Robison said, "can I schedule you for a press conference this afternoon?"

Max hesitated. "Oh, no—"

She cut him off. "All you have to do is tell what happened in the classroom and answer a few of their questions. President Hall has given his approval."

Max didn't know he needed anyone's approval, but he thought about it. This was exactly the discussion he had had with his publisher in their initial interview a year ago, before his escapade with Kat. His publisher would have been ecstatic about the publicity surrounding the music of the Psalms, but Max had made Kat promise to keep his name out of the press. And, in this case, his publisher would probably start another press run in anticipation of an avalanche of calls for the book.

But Max's mind was elsewhere. On the one hand, he was apprehensive about personal publicity. He had always shied from it even when told he had to give a salutatorian speech and when starring on his high school and Citadel football teams.

But on the other hand, he wanted the world to hear his message—"When politics gets tangled up with war, soldiers die. Yet the people who send those soldiers to die are the very ones deeply involved in politics. Too often they make decisions based on their self-interests, not those of the soldiers, or sometimes, the country."

This message was, after all, why he had decided to lecture at Yale.

"Okay," he finally answered. "But I have to do something first."

"How soon can I schedule the press conference?"

Max looked at his watch. Sixteen minutes past four o'clock. "Six o'clock."

"Six, it is," she said. "In the entry to Sheffield-Sterling-Strathcona Hall."

"See you then," he said and clicked off the phone. *Hmm, a press conference.* As he thought about the conference, he felt like he was in a weird sort of reverse Jeopardy, the game show. He felt he'd know the answers, but would he know the questions?

———— ◆ ————

Max drove to his apartment house, but a jumble of television trucks was still out in front. He drove to Rosenkrantz Hall to get into his office, but reporters were still hanging around outside there as well. *Boy, these folks are relentless.* So, he had called Kat to meet him at her office.

By the time he backed his Mustang into an on-street parking space outside the tree-canopied Department of Archaeology on Sachem Street, dusk had settled. His face lit up when he saw Kat walking briskly toward him. Tuck, his tail wagging as fast as a fan, pranced along beside her. Again, Max could swear the dog was smiling, just like his mistress.

He met her where the narrow walkway in front of the building converged with the sidewalk.

"Boy, are you a welcome sight," he said.

Kat lit up. "Why, thank you. So are you."

They hugged. Tuck yipped. And they both bent down to scratch him behind an ear.

"I have a press conference at Triple-S Hall at six," he said. "But I wanted to see you first."

"Six, huh? Hitting the ground running, aren't you?"

"Can't help it. Even President Hall wants this to happen, and he'll be there with me, along with the chief."

"Sure," Kat said. "By the looks of news crews hustling around campus, you're their red meat."

Max shrugged and shook his head.

"There's no incognito for you anymore, soldier," Kat said.

"Guess not."

"Well, then, do you want to hide away in my office for a bit? You can tell me what's up, and I can do the same."

"Lead the way."

As if reading their minds, Tuck pranced back to the building on the narrow walkway, barely wide enough for two people to walk side-by-side. Tuck leaped twice up the half-dozen stairs and stood looking back at them.

The house reminded Max of his grandfather's home in Charleston, complete with the porch and small, second-story balcony and an overhang between the second and third floors. Max would have suggested they paint the house a light green, or maybe the colonial blue he'd seen in the famous old city.

They caught up to Tuck, and Max opened the door for them. Kat led the way up two flights of stairs and down a corridor. Along the way, several students and faculty turned their heads to look at them. He felt self-conscious, an odd feeling since he was so at ease in front of hundreds of students. A confused gurgle came out of one student's mouth—as if she wanted to say something but wasn't sure exactly what, so no words formed.

Kat unlocked the door to her corner office, flicked on an overhead light, and asked Max to hang his coat behind the door with hers. Then she pointed to a wide, well-worn chair in front of a wall of ancient-looking books.

Max took a seat and she joined him in a chair opposite.

Max condensed his trip into about fifteen minutes. Kat's eyes sparkled in amusement when he told about walking into the school and straight out asking for information. Her eyebrows went up in fear when he told about his close escape from the building and the SUV crashing into his car's rear end. She breathed a sigh of relief when he told of flattening the SUV's tire and destroying its radiator as he sped off to the airbase.

And then her eyes widened and her jaw dropped when he showed her the flash drive containing the imam's computer.

"Treasure trove," he said.

"You looked at it yet?" she asked.

"Briefly, on a secure military laptop at the base in Germany."

"And?"

"Well, I need more time. Can you transfer it onto a flash drive of your own, so you'll have a copy, too?"

Kat took the flash drive, stepped to her desk and turned on her computer. Then she dug into a desk drawer and pulled out a flash drive.

"What we're looking for is names—Jones's classmates, financial backers, anything connected with Warriors for Allah, In the Name of Allah, or any other terror group," Max said.

"I'll dig. I'm good at poking about."

"And, I must say, you do dig very well."

Kat flashed a smile and held up her two hands. "My evidence—no fingernails."

He laughed. They were beautiful hands. She could be a musician—a pianist or guitarist with those long, thin fingers.

Kat plugged in Max's flash drive. "Whoa. How many gigs is this thing?"

"Twenty-four."

"This will take a couple minutes." She looked at her watch. "Before you go, let me tell you what I unearthed."

Max leaned forward, intent on her every word.

"Imam Meshaal did indeed write the booklet you found in the president's den. The publication was not printed by a publisher but was privately hand-bound. There is no mark of ownership, no copyright, no address to connect with. Clearly meant for very few eyes."

Max nodded. "Any idea whose eyes?"

"I believe those of maybe a half-dozen or so men, although they can share the information with members of their teams."

"Teams?"

"Max," Kat's face matched the seriousness of her voice, "the three regions of the world I showed you—?

"Yes?"

"The ruler of each region was to get a copy of this booklet."

"So, whose copy does Jones have?"

Kat didn't say a word.

"Do you mean—?"

Kat cocked her head and squeezed her lips together. A sign, Max knew, of dread at the thought circulating in her mind.

Chapter Eighteen

5:56 p.m., Thursday, January 30

Max decided he would forever think of the entryway to Sheffield-Sterling-Strathcona Hall as a basilica. He'd been to the Vatican and those structures had nothing over this place. Word had spread about the press conference. Or perhaps a student rally was going on. Blue uniforms were everywhere. The university must have hired off-duty police to augment its own security force.

He and Kat nodded at a police officer who stood guard at a quiet side door, and they entered a building connected to the mainframe of the superstructure. As they neared the front foyer, a scattering of people turned into a bunch, then a gathering, then a crowd.

"What's all this?" Max asked Kat.

"Max Mania," she said. "I tried to warn you."

Holding Kat's hand, Max put his head down and walked forward, squeezing the two of them through clusters of three, four, and more people. Tuck stayed on Kat's heels.

En route Max heard snippets of conversations.

"The guy's a hero, man—"

"I heard he's a scary freak—"

"Disgusting. Pretending to have gunfire and bombs in his classroom—"

"Got our attention, though. I was there."

"Think of the poor good Muslims—"

"They never apologize—"

"He's so ruggedly handsome—"

"The world's watching—"

"Yeah, a Bozo like this trained killer—"

Suddenly, Max felt a firm hand on his elbow. He stopped and turned. He was face-to-face with a seething Dean Stewart.

"Braxton," he breathed between clenched teeth, "I am going to do everything within my powers to see you do not keep this job."

"You, Dean Stewart, are the least of my concerns," Max retorted. "And this is less a job to me than a mission to inform the misinformed, to shed some light on the very real peril of political correctness as PC blinds us to those among us who not only wish us dead but take action to kill us."

Max turned away, Kat on his other elbow, and walked on.

As they approached the eight-by-eight-foot makeshift platform, Max looked up. Camera crews were focused tight up on a temporary riser.

A lectern sporting more than a dozen microphones stood in the middle of the platform.

Max felt a hand on his shoulder. President Hall smiled at him. Standing beside Hall were Linda King, the general counsel, and Robison.

Hall nodded at Kat, then at Max, and said, "Well, son, are you ready for this?"

Max shrugged. "As I'll ever be, I guess. This is a first for me."

"I'll make a quick statement, then introduce you. Just tell everyone what happened and then open it up to questions. Stay true to yourself ,and I'll stay true to you," Hall said. He smiled at Kat and gave her a hug, then stooped to pet Tuck on the head.

Then he stood and spoke to Max, "But please remember, Yale is a multicultural institution and a global one as well. I don't want you to flinch from the truth of what happened, but if you can avoid pejorative or confrontational statements, please do."

Max smiled crookedly. He turned to look at Kat.

"Go get 'em, soldier," she said.

"Sir," Shauna Robison broke in. "It's six o'clock."

"Then let's get it going," Hall said and led the three of them onto the platform.

Hall stepped to the lectern and grabbed its edges. "The campus has been in a hubbub since Tuesday morning when one of our visiting fellows, Colonel Max Braxton, disarmed a would-be bomber in his classroom. Yale has since then increased security campus wide, with the safety of our students, staff, and teachers utmost in our minds. But members of the media have been scouring the university for details of the incident. So, we felt it best to bring the man at the center of the controversy before you. Colonel Braxton will, I believe, answer all your questions so we can return to normal around here."

Hall motioned Max to the lectern.

Max stepped forward. Bright lights shone on him. Cameras flashed.

He pondered what to say. He'd thought about his statement driving to the hall—the only chance he'd had. He now wished he'd taken a few minutes to pray and talk with Kat.

He looked over the crowd. There was Kat close-up on the left. A frown playing the edges of her mouth revealed concern, but her eyes sparkled, lightening his spirit. To his right and halfway back in the room stood his A-Team, shoulder to shoulder. Ashley teetered on her toes to see over a man wearing a mammoth stocking hat shaped like a moose's head.

He noticed other faces. There was Joseph Wales, the politically correct Charles Goodyear Professor of Global Affairs, who probably came to gloat over the destruction of a nemesis.

There was Dean Mussinger. Max liked his face.

There seemed to be more Yalies than there were media, and there were plenty of media. He dropped his eyes to the bank of microphones before him. Major networks, local outlets, acronyms he did not recognize.

He looked up at the crowd. "First, I'd like to thank President Hall for his support and leadership, and for his courage to continue my course on terrorism despite challenges from certain segments of the university, and obviously, outside the campus. I also want to thank Yale Security Chief Seamus MacMillan and his men and women for their professionalism."

Max took a deep breath. "Winston Churchill once said, 'There's nothing more exhilarating than being shot at without result.'"

A cheer arose from the students. Max was floored and offered a hint of a smile. Then he squared his shoulders and went on, "An old Marine friend once said to me when he returned from Vietnam he was asked if, lying in a foxhole over there, he'd been afraid to catch a bullet with his name on it. 'No,' he replied, 'I was scared to death of all the bullets named Anonymous.'"

The students howled.

"Foxholes. They're so confining—and frightening. And today, wherever we are, is like being in a foxhole. We're in danger, apparently, anywhere—not just on our military bases, but in our malls and our cathedrals. And as far as anonymous is concerned, our enemies don't care about our names, just that we're us.

"The Qur'an, Surah 4:56 tells Muslims: 'As for those who disbelieve our communications, we shall make them enter fire; so oft as their skins are thoroughly burned, we will change them for other skins, so they may taste the chastisement; surely Allah is mighty, wise.'"

"No." screamed a man to Max's right.

"Sorry. But yes," Max replied. "Furthermore, the Qur'an, in Surah 9:5, tells Muslims to 'fight and kill the disbelievers wherever you find them, take them captive, confine them, lie in wait and ambush them using every stratagem of war.'

"And an ambush is exactly what awaited us in the classroom on Tuesday. My students were the latest, but sad to say, probably not the last American kids to face this type of threat. If you can't see this observation, then you, sir, are blind."

He looked down at Kat. She stood in rapt attention which strengthened him.

"I haven't known my students long. Don't yet know most of them, really, there are so many. But my students are my charges, my responsibility to protect. And, like protecting this country, I take my responsibility soberly."

A cheer reverberated off the high ceiling. The response inspired him.

"I had an odd feeling—perhaps a premonition—before Tuesday's class. I'd been followed around campus by a shadowy person, and I had an inward warning."

"Colonel Braxton," a reporter shouted, "was the person a terrorist?"

Max held up his right hand. "Let me tell you what happened, then you can ask your questions."

He breathed deeply and continued, "In the battlefield, you cultivate a sense of danger, of events before they transpire. A sixth sense. Foreboding. That's the feeling I had. So, I stood outside the classroom looking in. Looking for the source of uneasiness.

"Reading people is something I've learned through the years. Some are difficult"—he looked back at President Hall. "Some are easy"—he looked over at Linda King. "This man, this would-be bomber, was an open book. Actually, he could have been a primer for first graders."

Laughs greeted this remark.

"Some of my football-playing students are familiar with playbooks. Well, Islamic terrorists have expanded their playbooks. The O's are the offense, the X's are the defense. In their playbook, anyone and everyone not an O is a target for attack.

"In fact, a couple of my students, Josh Andrews and Hank Clauson, helped disarm the bomb strapped around our intruder—"

Cheers broke out so loud Max had to stop. He waited for the noise to subside, then looked around the room. "Are there any questions?"

"It sounds like you're anti-Arabic," said a woman near the podium holding a tape recorder. "Are you sure you don't simply just hate them?"

"Two of my closest friends are Arabic—and heroes," Max replied. "Not all Arabs are Muslims and not all Muslims are terrorists. But have you heard of any terrorism from the Welsh lately? Or the Spanish? Or the Aussies, or Mexicans, or Canadians, or Icelandians?"

The woman stared back at him, shaking her head.

"No," Max said, "eighty-five percent of the terror attacks around the world are carried out by Muslims. Muslim organizations argue they're involved in only six percent, but those figures include the thousands of drug cartel-related incidents in the total mix—a bogus argument. Draw your own conclusion, but I suggest not burying your head in the sand, or you may end up one of the ones being buried in the sand by their tactics."

Shouts of objection rolled through the crowd, then were overwhelmed by a roar of approval.

"Many are saying you're a hero—" a male reporter hollered over the din.

Max cut the man off. "In my book, any man or woman who climbs into fatigues or any combat uniform is a hero. That includes our police officers, several of Yale's own, who responded to the call Tuesday. Next question?"

"What do you think can be done about the terror problem?" The question came from a blonde middle-aged woman three people back from the podium.

"The world has one major problem and it will not, cannot, be resolved," Max said.

"What's the problem?" she asked.

"The world's too small."

A spattering of laughter greeted his answer.

"The—world—is—too small," he repeated slowly, "to accommodate multiple cultures and religions when one of them is intent on destroying all the others who will not conform to their way, or when one of them feels the infidels are not worthy to draw breath. Indeed, when one of them commands followers to drive a particular country into the sea. With the exception of Jordan and sometimes Egypt, I'm speaking of the Muslim countries and their aggression toward little Israel."

A man raised his hand and asked, "You don't believe the West is partially to blame for terror attacks?"

"No."

"Not one bit?"

"No."

"You're, in effect, damning an entire religion," said another reporter.

"No, their own religion is doing the damning all by itself. Needs no help from me."

Wails of protest were overmatched by cheers of agreement.

Then a man with an accent Max guessed was Pakistani, called out, "Many of these people you call terrorists consider themselves freedom fighters."

"We have freedom in America and all our citizens are welcome to this liberty, including Muslims. In fact, they now enjoy greater freedoms in our country than many of our own citizens?"

"How so?" someone called out.

Max thought for a moment. There were so many examples. How should he begin?

He breathed deeply and said, "Christianity and the Bible are now banned in schools, but our children are being taught Islam, made to recite Islamic prayers while kneeling on prayer rugs. Those prayer rugs are now a prerequisite in schools, businesses, and airports. Suddenly, we can't serve pork in prisons. Muslims are suing employers or refusing to do their jobs because they feel they conflict with Sharia law. A president declared it's NASA's mission to reach out to Muslims. NASA? Really? One former attorney general even vowed to prosecute anyone who engaged in anti-Muslim speech, while her president was comparing what's happening today to the Crusades a thousand years ago."

A stirring by the entryway drew Max's attention. A police officer was standing face-to-face with a young man wearing a hooded coat and carrying a backpack. Calm voices became more heated. The officer pointed to the backpack. The fellow lifted a shoulder and removed it. The officer bent and riffled through it. A moment later, the officer pointed to the young man's mouth, then motioned for him to move along. Everything was all right.

Max looked back down and found the man who had asked the question about freedom fighters.

"But," Max said, "free as they may be here, like everyone else, they may have a nasty attitude with a law enforcement officer and get away with it, but they're not welcome to commit crimes, especially murder."

He pointed at the man. "Let me tell you about your so-called freedom fighters, specifically, the ones living in Israel, a country which, by the way, allows them to vote and to sit in the Knesset. Have you heard of the Abu Jihad Center for Political Prisoners' Affairs at al-Quds University in Israel?"

"No," the man said.

"Well, it's Palestinian and its museum contains a reenactment of the Sbarro pizza restaurant suicide bombing in Jerusalem, complete with body parts and pizza slices strewn around the room. The suicide bombing killed fifteen Israelis and the bomber. Palestinian students are taken to this exhibit on August 19 each year to mark the date of the murders.

"This, my friend, is the mind-set of your freedom fighters."

A reporter directly in front of Max took a step forward. "Getting back to the question of fault," he said, "you don't believe the West is at fault, in any way, for these attacks."

"Correct," Max said.

"But the president does believe so."

"If so, he's naïve and needs some historical perspective. Perhaps new advisors."

"Or your book." Josh yelled out.

Cheers erupted from many students.

"About your book, Mr. Braxton," a tall, lanky lady called out. "Beyond your experiences as told in the manuscript, what can you tell us about your, ah, missions?"

"Nothing."

"Why not?"

"Beyond what I wrote, there are two possibilities," Max said. "First, the information is top secret and out of bounds for public consumption. Or secondly, simply isn't interesting."

"What about you—your background?" she asked.

"Most of what can be told is on the book cover. Either there or the information is top secret." Max chuckled and added, "Or the bio is merely … not interesting."

People laughed at the casual delivery.

———————◆———————

In Dallas, Clair Braxton was ironing clothes for her Caribbean cruise. Her friend Nancy was packing her own things in her bedroom.

Clair flicked on the television remote and the news flashed on with the words "Special Report" across the screen.

Looking directly at her was—

"Max." shot out of her mouth.

"What?" Nancy called from the other room.

"My son," Clair said. "He's on television."

She read the subject on the screen: "Live press conference from Yale University with Col. Max Braxton."

A short, overweight woman in a pantsuit was speaking. "Some say you and your comrades are no more than trained killers."

"Are you trained in self-defense, ma'am?" Max asked.

"Why, no."

"Then there may be a time when you need my comrades' training, or you may die at the hand of a terrorist."

"You tell her, son." Clair exclaimed.

The female reporter stammered.

"You're paid to kill," said a young man with a pen and writing pad.

"I've been paid to protect my country—perhaps even defend you. I see a difference between killing and protecting."

Nancy, now at Clair's side, pumped a fist in the air.

"I haven't seen you so excited since we beat the Watsons in bridge," Clair said.

They both chuckled.

———— ◆ ————

Laughter exploded from many in the hall.

Hank smacked Josh's arm.

"Teach rocks," Jose said.

A student nearby overheard and called out, "Teach rocks."

Jose picked up the chant. "Teach rocks."

Hank shrugged, looked at Josh and they both joined in.

Hank looked at Ashley and Jill, who both appeared embarrassed but a moment later called out, "Teach rocks."

More voices joined the cheer. "Teach rocks."

Jose changed the words. "Teach rules."

"Teach rules. Teach rules." rang out around the hall, and the roar became a cacophony. "Teach rules."

———— ◆ ————

Max looked out at the throng, sure his face was turning red, and shook his head. This was not what he'd expected. He glanced down at Kat. Her face shone and she locked her eyes on his. He could detect a twinkle in those beautiful green eyes and allowed a smile to play at the corners of his mouth.

He motioned for the students to stop the chant, but they continued for a half a minute.

Finally, the clamor calmed enough for a reporter to be heard. "How exactly did you spot the bomber in such a large classroom?"

Max listed the factors. "First, the coat he was wearing was far too bulky for his frame, yet he kept the garment on although he was sweating heavily—from anxiety, I assume. Second, he'd recently shaven a full beard. Third, he was too nervous. I'm not *that* scary—"

The students roared.

Max smiled and continued, "Also, he didn't have the aura of the Yalies we all know and love."

Another cheer.

"And, yes, he was Arabic, though his race was not a major point in this case."

"What if you'd been wrong," the reporter asked.

"I would have looked foolish, been embarrassed and had to apologize profusely," Max said. "Would the mistake have been worth the risk? Yes. I think this all points to political correctness and loss of common sense."

"What do you mean?" a female reporter asked.

"Political correctness has hampered this country's every move in several arenas, not least of which are homeland security and our military battles overseas. If someone is offended at one of our actions, do we defend what we did, or do we promise never to do so again? We promise never to do so again. Witness, for instance, airport security—the epitome of political correctness and foolishness.

"Listen, the Israelis know what to look for at their airports and they haven't had an airplane hijacked or bombed in memory. Yet they don't put people through all the rigmarole we do in the United States. Why not? They don't care about political correctness. They care about protecting their citizens from destruction.

"But here in America, since we need to pat down potential terrorists, we must, in a show of fairness, frisk grandmothers and four-year-olds, and have everyone remove their shoes. This is absurd and stupid. And why? So we don't offend the possible terrorists."

Wails of agreement.

———— ◆ ————

Kat stood still, looking up at Max. With so many people, the big hall had gotten warm. She had removed her scarf and just now noticed she held the material tight in her fists, twisted like a pretzel. The animosity of some in the audience concerned her, but she was thrilled at the response of the students—some of them her own. She was proud and anxious to get this over with.

A media person standing next to her spoke up, "I just finished reading your book, Colonel—"

Max turned his gaze to the man. "Glad to hear *someone's* reading it," he said.

Scattered laughter, then "Teach rules." chants again filled the hall.

A half minute later the cheers died, and the reporter continued, "Evidence appears to show the planned attack was in protest of your course on terrorism. Do you think your book also had anything to do with the man's motives?"

"Did The *Eye of Evil* instigate the attack?" Max said. Kat noticed he was making strong eye contact with the reporter. "Hatred and fear are dangerous companions, and I think you'll find my book elicits both reactions from some—most particularly terrorists and politicians."

Max ran his fingers through his hair and let a few seconds elapse. Then he continued, "Fear follows the feckless. I've witnessed this—people who believe a thing, or think they do, are afraid of anyone who contests their belief. They may be certain grandma's molasses cookies are the best in the world, their car's better than their neighbor's, or their religion is the only true faith.

"If something or someone challenges their belief, the feckless— meaning the incompetent, the weak, and the spineless—retaliate so they don't even have to consider any truth to the challenge, let alone counter the argument. If you blow up your opponent, your challenger, then you dispel the unpleasant possibility of your belief being proven wrong."

Max was silent for a moment. Kat was just absorbing this statement when he continued, "Sad, but most people today do not want to challenge anyone on anything whatever. Truth, for them, is a matter of convenience. Truth's flexible, open for discussion like sitting around a boardroom table determining office decorations.

"And, as my book says, in our foreign policy, truth has become a bargaining chip. Do all the Arab nations want to destroy Israel? If we're keen on buying their oil, then regardless of historical and current fact, the State Department's truth is, 'The Arab countries are fine neighbors to the Jews and would never harm them.'

"Are there certain Islamists who want to kill Americans? If we do not want to anger them further, our presidents and other leaders acquiesce to a truth asserting we somehow provoked their anger and we should watch our tongues.

"Regrettably, the human condition in today's world has deteriorated in many ways. What are ethics anymore? Moral principles? Values?"

A woman behind Kat and to her left spoke up. "Your book, Colonel, appears to blame politics for some of our more notable military failings."

Max replied, "Not politics but politicians, ma'am. Listen, our military leaders know how to fight a battle, win, and then get out. When we fail, the reason nearly always is the fault of some politician, who simply because he has the title of commander-in-chief, fancies himself knowledgeable in the art and science of war. If you were going into major surgery, would you hand over the instruments of the operation to the hospital's chief executive officer?"

Kat heard no reply so she looked in the direction of the female reporter. Everyone around her was looking at her, waiting for a response. She seemed tongue-tied, simply staring back.

"Well, would you?" Max asked.

She stammered.

"I actually believe having a nonmilitary person in charge of the military is important in any country, even a republic like ours," Max said. "But at the same time, this person must realize his or her limitations in the arena of warfare. I've too often seen a military decision made by a politician with his eye on the all-important election cycle. The calendar's the thing for them. This, friends, is a recipe for disaster, a tragedy Americans have tasted all too often in the last two decades."

Max smiled ruefully and added, "We should all remember what Benjamin Franklin said about democracy and liberty: 'Democracy is two wolves and a lamb voting on what to have for lunch. Liberty is a well-armed lamb contesting the vote.'"

The hall exploded in laughter.

"Amen!" someone hollered, and the sentiment was echoed.

Kat couldn't help but smile herself. *What a card. A walking Bartlett's.*

Max apparently knew what she was thinking because he was looking straight at her with a grin. Then he continued, "Toss the complications of politics and war into Ben Franklin's observation and you can extrapolate his opinion out into some seriously frightening conclusions."

Kat slowly shook her head and smiled to herself. Not since their last time together in Israel months ago had she and Max touched on any of this. And here she was, reminded about the depth of this man.

———◆———

Max hesitated, weighing whether he should say what was next on his mind. He looked out at his A-Team and saw expectation on their faces. Hank appeared about to jump out of his shoes and was only waiting to hear, "Hike."

Then, Max noticed his buddy Julius Rodríguez standing a few feet behind Josh and Hank. Julius. His spirit soared. Julius recognized Max had spotted him and gave the thumbs-up. So, Julius had taken Max seriously and come. What had happened with Julius since Max left for Saudi Arabia he wondered. Had he been to the bat cave? Had he been in touch with Sturgen and Crowe?

Max shook his head and realized he was gripping the edge of the lectern so hard his knuckles were white.

Then he let fly his feelings.

"Politics is a selfish beast," he said. "Once upon a time, Western societies lived, fought, and died to protect their beliefs or spiritual convictions. An abundance of evidence tells us such a time is largely behind us. Today, the more appropriate description of our nation's standard operating procedure is 'protect your political hide at all costs, even the cost of Americans' lives.'"

A sudden, heavy hush fell like a cloak on the crowd.

Max turned to President Hall and said, "I think I've said enough, President Hall."

Hall nodded.

Max turned back to the lectern. "Thank you, everyone. Please, you in the media, let this be the end of your coverage here. The professors need to be able to get back to teaching without tripping over camera crews. And our students deserve some peace."

As Max turned to leave the platform, the chant began again. "Teach rules. Teach rules."

Hall spoke into Max's ear: "You and Kat can escape out the door directly behind the platform if you'd like. Chief MacMillan has one of his men guarding the door and will let you through, then secure it. I'll take a couple questions, then bring this to an end. Thank you, Max. Well done." He patted Max on the shoulder.

"Thanks." Max shook Hall's hand, then motioned Kat to follow him, which she did, with Tuck along beside her.

———— ♦ ————

As Max and Kat left, Josh turned to Hank. Speaking loud enough to be heard above the cheers, he said, "Not only do you not tug on Superman's cape, pull off Batman's mask, or spit into the wind, you don't mess around with *our Teach*."

———— ♦ ————

Max and Kat, with Tuck running beside them, hustled down a corridor. A right turn out a door off the hall fed them onto a pathway leading in the direction of Max's Mustang.

Max's cell phone rang the first two bars of "Halls of Montezuma."

"Julius," Max said to Kat, then brought the phone to his mouth and answered, "Semper fi."

"Semper fi. Where are you?"

"Go out the front entry and hang a left. My car's in the parking lot straight ahead."

"McQ?"

"McQ."

"McQ?" Kat asked.

"My Mustang's name." Max smiled.

"I've got your A-Team with me," Julius said.

Max stopped in his tracks and held Kat's hand tightly to keep her at his side. "You do?"

"Yes. I checked in at your—

As Julius hesitated, Max could hear a chorus of voices, "Bat cave."

"Right," Julius said, "your bat cave. The NSA team there introduced us. Bright kids."

"Yeah, for sure."

"The DOJ's letting them off the hook—no charges—since I'm the one who ought to be dangling there."

Max sighed in relief.

"What about you?"

"Me, too."

Two minutes later, Max and Julius were exchanging handshakes, and Max introduced Kat.

"This fella saved my life," Julius said, pointing to Max.

"I'd say it was tit for tat, Bud," Max said.

"Yeah and only the angels are counting, right?" Julius said.

"Only them." Max looked at the students and Julius. "How about meeting us back at my apartment? It should be clear of the media now this press conference is over."

Chapter Nineteen

7:13 p.m., Thursday, January 30

Kat watched Max fiddle with his espresso machine while she assembled sandwiches for everyone. Tuck had managed to climb onto a bar stool beside the cooking island and had figured out how to swivel the chair. He sat upright watching over the entire affair while the students took turns loving on him.

"I noticed you no longer have your Ayn Rand books in the bookcase," Kat said.

"You said she hated religion."

"Yeah?" A question needing a response.

"Then I don't want her in my bookcase."

Kat's eyes narrowed in thought. A minute later, she asked, "Do you want to tell Julius about what we're investigating?"

"I think he might help us in walking through the maze."

"But it's best not to involve the kids."

"Right."

"Then we'll keep this get-together about the more mundane things."

"Right, mundane like them snitching three-quarters of a *billion* dollars from terror cells."

Kat rolled her eyes and replied, "Right, that."

She flipped open the lid on the bread box, looked in, and said, "You're out of bread. I'm two slices short."

"I'll just roll up a few slices of salami for myself. No bread necessary," he said. He flicked a switch and announced, "We're good to go, Mademoiselle Chef."

A smile crossed Kat's mouth and she asked, "You've got olives and pickles in the fridge?"

"I'll get them and bring some chips over, too."

Kat delivered the sandwiches stacked on a tray with paper napkins and placed the food on the coffee table where everyone was gathered.

"Cool pad," Hank said, looking around.

"Yeah, you oughta see Hank's room in the frat," Josh said with a chuckle. "Not fit for man nor beast."

"Hey, everything's in my own place of order, 59."

"Then why couldn't you find a pen last time I was there?"

"I don't write with pens," Hank said. "Bad luck."

"Bad luck?" Ashley said.

"Yeah, like writing on stone. If you're wrong, you have to start over. Or if someone messes up, you've got to do it again—like Moses and the tablets with the Ten Commandments. Right, Dr. Cardova?"

Kat just laughed.

"Well," Josh said, "all I know is I needed a pen and you couldn't find one. Ask any of the ladies here for a pen, and they'd pull one out of their purse in an instant."

"I'd guess most ladies' purses are as messy as Hank's room," Kat said with a chuckle.

"A discussion we men will do well to steer clear of," Julius said. "My girlfriend has muscles in places where most women don't even have places, and I think the reason is her carrying around a monstrous purse. I think she's got a howitzer in there."

Max laughed and said, "Julius, I know Pat, and she does not carry around a howitzer. If she did, she'd have used the thing on you."

Julius grinned. "Sad to say, but you're right."

Max and Kat pulled chairs over to the coffee table. Tuck scrambled off the stool and scooted over to sit between them, then rubbed his head against Max's thigh. Max passed him a piece of his salami.

"Dig in, everyone," Kat said.

"Espresso's on the way in a minute," Max said. He looked around the A-Team and said, "So, you've got a clean slate from our friends at the Department of Justice. I'm so sorry this has happened."

"Are you kidding?" Jose said. "Makes my years at Yale worth the pain."

"Yeah," Jill said, "this whole experience has Sociology 101 beat by a light-year."

"In Sociology 101 terms, 'by a head case,'" Hank cracked.

"Certainly one-ups my Semiology 101 class," Kat said.

"I think I want to work for the NSA," Ashley said. "Imagine doing this for a living? Special Agent Crowe is one cool woman."

"You do the computer subterfuge," Josh said, "and I'll do the hand-to-hand combat." He cut a ninja pose and they all laughed.

As everyone munched on sandwiches and chips, Jill said, "There were a lot of disappointed kids last night and this morning, Mr. Braxton, when we found out there was no class."

"Sorry," Max said. "I was … traveling." He stole a look at Julius.

His eyes narrowing and his right eyebrow rising, Julius said, "We also missed you at the bat cave, Batman."

Max knew Julius' look well. His friend had figured out something was afoot. Max shot his friend a look and whispered, "Later," then said more loudly, "Sorry. I was in another hemisphere. But I'm glad you could get here and we didn't all get run into jail. Agents Sturgen and Crowe are pretty straight arrows, I think."

"Well," Josh said, "they and the NSA love Colonel Rodriguez." He twitched his thumb toward Julius. "I think they'd like to recruit you, sir."

"They might," Julius said, "but I've got an employer: the United States Marine Corps."

"They've taken over the bat cave, Mr. Braxton," Jill said, "which takes us out of the loop for our assignment. So, what do we do now?"

"I'll find something else to fill out your semester, but I'd say you finished your initial assignment and will all get As," Max said. "My first grades—all As. I must be a pushover instructor."

"The class is abuzz all over campus," Josh said. "Even in the weight room where the athletes train, there are guys in the class who are in different fivesomes and they're talking about ISIS, the Shining Path in Peru, about Hamas, Abu Nidal, Al-Aqsa Martyrs Brigade—"

"Yeah, someone's even got something called GRAPO in Europe," Hank said.

"I was with the chess team yesterday," Ashley said, "and we all got talking about creating a board game based on this whole underworld of terrorist and guerrilla groups."

"Kinda like the game Risk?" Jill said.

"Similar."

"They should see your software program in action," Max said to Julius. "Doing so might scare them away from such an idea."

Julius chuckled. "Actually, I'm consulting for a game company on something called Code Cell-Hunter, which is about an American black-ops unit charged with taking out various terror groups."

"Wow." Kat said. "Sounds like real life."

"Without the nightmares," Max added.

All went quiet for a few moments as people ate, then Max looked at the students and asked, "Would you like another assignment right now?"

"Sure," came the unanimous response.

"All right. Without duplicating any of the previous attacks on our country, tell me what is the Achilles' heel of the United States? What would be the most devastating, yet most easily accomplished attack? Then figure the best way for our government to prevent the assault from happening."

The students looked at each other.

"Water supply," Josh said.

"Already done—in upstate New York," Julius said. "They got caught."

"Didn't hear about New York," Ashley said.

"No, I suppose you didn't," Julius said.

"Flying an airplane into a nuclear plant," Jose said.

"No duplication," Max said. "No, they haven't attacked a nuclear plant yet, but they did use airplanes on 9/11."

"We obviously have some brainstorming to do," Josh said.

"Let's leave the adults alone," Jill said, then glanced at her wristwatch. "Besides, I've got a date."

"Who dates on Thursday nights?" Jose asked.

"Me and—well, wouldn't you like to know?" Jill grinned.

Avi sat in his favorite chair in his den, disregarding a pile of merger notes in his lap. He was lost in thought, peering at his mannequin clothed in his old military garb. He was proud of his service to Israel, saddened by the absolute necessity of all Israeli young men and women to serve.

One by one, he recalled the deaths of his family members in bombing attacks by the Palestinians and gunfights on the West Bank. He shuddered remembering the heinous murders of his nephew, his wife, and their three young children—their throats slit by Hamas in a home break-in.

He had seen it all, hated war and yet knew conflict was sometimes essential—if only to prevent the extinction of his people—a threat made often enough by enemies of all sorts.

He longed to safely walk the hills above the Sea of Galilee, ride a horse along his favorite trails to the northwest of the sea, stroll the tight, familiar streets of the Old City, even hike the steep hillside trail and visit Megiddo.

In his left hand, he held a Hebrew copy of the Tanakh.

Pray for the peace of Jerusalem, Psalm 122:6 read.

"Lord, may we be safe," Avi surprised himself at speaking aloud and in his native tongue.

"Safe, Papa?"

Lana entered the room, a notepad in her hand.

"May there be real peace in Jerusalem. May our people be secure."

"Psalm 122," Lana said.

Avi nodded.

"Someday," she said.

"Perhaps." He felt so heavy, even depressed, but managed, "In your lifetime, not mine, I fear. And especially not since Ridley made clear his true feelings."

"Maybe another Anwar Sadat will arise."

"Out of the Muslim Brotherhood? Or the ayatollahs?" Avi sneered. "The chances are the same as those you could catch a fish in the Dead Sea."

Lana laughed despite the sad truth.

The telephone on Avi's desk sounded an alto gong. He stood, papers spilling out of his lap onto the floor, and hurried to answer, "Shalom."

"Shalom aleichem, Avi. This is Boaz."

Avi could picture Boaz Erdan on the other end of the phone. Broad-shouldered, bearded, strong as a bear. Like himself, born in the Judean hills but twenty years later.

"Do you have news, Boaz?"

"Yes."

"Let me put you on speaker. Lana's here with me."

Avi pushed the button and sat down, opening the top drawer of his desk to grab a pen and notepad.

"The oil pan containing the bomb was taken from a Toyota Corolla bought new in Jersey City, New Jersey, sold to a mosque in Newark, then eight years later donated to a group called Salam Palestine here in Atlanta. At the time of the transfer, three years ago, the car registered a couple hundred thousand miles, so Salam Palestine must have decided to put the parts to good use—like killing you."

"But, instead, Jonas and Stan." Avi looked morosely at Lana.

"These people think they can bring peace to Israel by killing their detractors in the Philippines and here in the States," Boaz said.

"Detractors? I've never heard of them," Avi said. "Have you, Lana?"

Lana shook her head.

"So, is the FBI going to move on this Salam Palestine group and arrest them?"

"They need more evidence—and may actually have it," Boaz said. "The security-camera video from the underground parking garage below your offices shows a shadowy, hooded figure suspiciously approaching your car and then disappearing beneath it. A minute later, she reappears and hustles out of the picture."

"Did you say 'she'?" Lana asked.

"Yes. They were able to pick up the person leaving the garage on a street camera and followed her for three blocks on other cameras until she got into an unmarked white utility van. Before she stepped into the van, she pushed back the hood. And, voilà, a young woman, obviously of Middle Eastern descent. They're running her through a facial database as we speak."

————◆————

When the students had left the apartment with Tuck at their heels, herding them to the door, Max turned to Julius. "Kat and I have some things to share with you. Things we'd like your opinion on."

Max's cell phone started playing the first notes of "Hava Nagila."

Max turned to Kat, "It's Avi Navon."

He pulled out the phone and answered, "How are you doing, Avi?"

"You'd think I'd get used to death—even death of those close to me," Avi said.

"I know what you mean."

"I'm sure you do," Avi said. "But I'm calling because I have news for you."

"Mind if I put you on speaker?" Max asked.

"Why? Who's there."

"My archaeologist friend I spoke to you about and an old military colleague."

"Is this the archaeologist who suggested you dig deeper?"

"Yes." Max turned and grinned at Kat. She cocked her head and returned her own smile.

"Then go ahead. Put me on speaker. I'll do the same. Lana's here with me."

Avi shared all he knew about the bombing. The tiny knife amid the shrapnel, the oil pan holding the bomb coming from a car owned by Salam Palestine, and the video of the woman bomber.

"Can you send me the video?" Max asked.

"I'll see if my man can get hold of a copy."

Max could hear Lana in the background, saying, "I'll call Boaz now, Papa."

"I can send you a photo of the knife right now, though," Avi said.

"Thanks for filling me in, sir," Max said.

"Not at all. We'll see what a little further digging can discover, eh?"

They said their good-byes and hung up.

"The caller was Avi Navon?" Julius asked, disbelief spiking the pitch of his voice.

Max nodded. "We've made an acquaintance."

"That's what you call it," Kat said with a shake of the head.

Julius' eyebrows rose as he looked at Max.

"I kind of snuck into his home and confronted him—"

"At gunpoint," Kat finished.

Julius stepped back. "Gunpoint?"

"He funded Jones's presidential run and I had to know why," Max said defensively. "He's now a friend." He looked at Julius and motioned to the couch. "Have a seat. We have some catching up to do."

Max and Kat proceeded to fill Julius in on the ten days since the president's inaugural speech.

When they had finished their story, Max's phone again rang with the opening notes from "Hava Nagila."

He snapped open the phone and the LED showed a close-up photo of a tiny knife laying beside a No. 2 pencil to show perspective.

Avi's voice came over the phone, "What you see is it ... the knife."

Looking around Max's shoulder, Kat exclaimed, "That's in The Three Sixes booklet."

"What?" Max turned a questioning look at Kat.

She pointed to his phone. "This little knife, blessed by an imam, is supposed to be used as a sign and symbol in every bombing once The Three Sixes is unleashed."

"What is she saying?" Avi asked.

Max answered, "Avi, a lot has happened since we met in your house. Do you recall the photo you gave me of you and Jones in his den?"

"Yes."

"I photocopied a copy of the little booklet you and Lana and I wondered about."

"How'd you get—"

"I can't say," Max interrupted, "but it's a playbook for a final intifada led by a group called The Three Sixes. This group has divided the world into three sections, each one controlled by a single man. Lodestar appears to be the code name for the leader of the part of the world encompassing the Americas and Canada. And the copy in the president's den has the letters l-o-d-e imprinted at the bottom-right of every page."

There was a gasp at the other end of the line.

Kat broke in. "This does not mean the president is Lodestar, sir. I mean, why would he have such a document in plain view?"

"Perhaps he was sure no one would be checking his bookcase. Hardly anyone ever gets into his den," Avi said. "Except for our photo op, the room has been sacred space for him. The photo session was the one and only time I was ever in there, and we've had dozens of meetings, both social and political."

"Well," Kat said, "he could simply have his hands on a copy of the booklet given him by the CIA or FBI or NSA. We don't know."

"But the photo was taken before Ridley's election," Avi said.

"Enlightening," Max said. After a few moments of silence, he continued, "One more thing we do know is the booklet was written by the same imam who runs the Islamic boys school Jones attended when his family was living in Riyadh from 1988 to 1992."

Again, there was silence on the line, then Lana's voice—"Our detective said an identical little knife was found at the scene of the assassination of President Aviles in the Philippines on Christmas Day."

"An Islamic terrorist group, Sulaiman Islamiyah, took credit," Avi said.

"I remember reading the news," Max said. "I'd never heard of them."

"I had," Julius said. "They take 'wicked' to a whole new level. I'd prefer ISIS behead me with a bread knife than what they do."

Max winced at the thought and wished his friend hadn't been so explicit.

"If what you say is true," Kat said, "according to The Three Sixes booklet, the last intifada began on Christmas Day."

"If so, why wait so long—a month—before attacking again?" Julius asked.

"Perhaps the Filipino group jumped the gun," Max said.

"Maybe they wanted to wait until after the American president's inauguration," Avi said. "Or maybe Ridley was a target and the assassin or assassins were caught and their capture was never made public."

"But why attack you, a civilian businessman?" Kat asked.

"Papa's a Jew and a war hero. Maybe they need no better reason," Lana said.

"Maybe they wanted to make a point on American soil," Max offered.

"Yeah, but they've been making points relatively routinely in the last year or so," Kat said.

"So maybe the bomb to kill Mr. Navon had nothing to do with The Three Sixes," Julius said.

"Remember the knife was in the bomb," Max said. "And Avi *has* been outspoken about America supporting Israel."

"You're saying the attack was retribution for supporting Israel?" Julius said. "Seems such a minor thing if they are, indeed, planning attacks in a global theater."

"Personal revenge can be twice as sweet as impersonal, group payback," Max said. Looking at Julius, he added, "Remember Taloqan?"

Julius nodded at the thought of the Afghan operation. "Right."

"So perhaps the attack on you was especially personal, Avi," Max said.

"What I hear," Avi said, "is a lot of ifs, maybes, and perhaps. I'm more concerned for Lana and the others around me than I am for myself. But, obviously, we require more information."

"I might have just what you need," Max said. "I paid a visit to Riyadh yesterday and came away with an entire hard drive of information from the computer of Imam Meshaal, who wrote The Three Sixes booklet and who runs the Islamic school Jones attended.

314

We have student and faculty names, small to major donors, their mission statement, their call to arms, the whole bit. We just have to look the pamphlet over closely."

"You've got all that?" The response came from two places—Julius standing next to Max and Avi in Atlanta.

Max nodded. Looking at Kat, he replied, "Yep, and the information's in the hands of the smartest semiologist I've ever met."

"Semi-what?" Lana asked.

"Never mind," Max said. "Just know we're *all* looking into the matter up here."

"Can you send me a copy of the flash drive?" Avi asked. "Maybe my man can find something there."

"Sure."

"Okay, Max. Please stay in touch," Avi said. "And if I can, I'll send the video footage of the bomber to you immediately."

Both sides hung up. Max stepped to his computer to email the copy of the imam's hard drive to Avi.

"You said 'we all are looking into it up here,'" Julius said. "Sounds like you're including more than you and Kat."

Max locked his eyes on Julius's. "You did say you were between assignments, and I'm sure Agents Sturgen and Crowe would love to keep you around. So where, and how better, to spend your time?"

Julius shrugged. "Can I bed down here?"

"Of course. Just do something about your snoring, all right?"

"Breathe Rites."

"Huh?"

"Never mind. I've got a solution and I'll handle it."

"And you can't have a nightlight, either."

"Wha—"

"Boys, boys," Kat said. "Sounds like you two've spent too many nights together."

"Right, but this will be the most comfortable one—ever," Julius said. "For one thing, we're not loaded down with full battle rattle."

"Full what?"

"Full battle rattle," Julius said. "It's about fifty pounds of gear, including flak jacket, Kevlar helmet, gas mask, ammo, the works."

"We used to call the gear play clothes," Max said.

"Or momma's comforts," Julius added. "Only the weight is not too comfortable."

"I'll make sure you're comfortable, bud. Don't you worry," Max said with a chuckle. "Comfortable like the bed of pine needles in Pakistan."

"India, you mean, and, okay, then this will be the second-most comfortable one," Julius said with a laugh.

"Changing subjects," Kat said, "we've got to examine the imam's hard drive. What exactly are we looking for?"

"Whatever can be tied to The Three Sixes. Who's connected to the group and to each other? Are they in contact with Imam Meshaal? Where are they? What timetable do they have? What students was Jones connected with in his classes, in the student body, his extracurricular stuff?"

"What about the school's possible connections to terror training camps?" Julius asked.

"Great question," Max said. "I wonder if our friends in the Mossad know."

"Can't hurt to ask."

"You fellas check all those things," Kat said. "I'll scrutinize the booklet more closely for clues to their plans."

She looked at her watch. "I've got a seminar at ten o'clock in the morning. I've got to get some sleep. And ... Max?"

"Yeah."

"You look awful."

Max smiled. "Why, thank you."

"You do—and you should get some sleep, too."

"Aye-aye, General." He saluted her.

"Disdain for higher rank could easily mean the brig for you, Colonel." Kat's green eyes sparkled and her lips turned into a grin.

"No," Max said, "I'm serious. Aye-aye. I'll catch some z's in a bit."

Tuck barked sharply at Max as if to underline his mistress's command, then put himself in position to herd Max toward the bedroom.

Max backed off with a chuckle. "I promise, Tuck. Not right away, but soon."

———◆———

When Kat and Tuck left the apartment, Julius stared at Max and said, "You know as military, the president is my commander-in-chief."

"Mine too.

"Max, you and I've been in some tense situations, scary times, bullets blazing, saying foxhole prayers. But, man, burgling the president's house?"

Max chuckled. "Curiosity, Julius. I just had to see what the little booklet with the Islamic markings on the binding was all about. And I'm glad I did."

"You know, when you told me you were going to teach at Yale, after a laughing spell I thought to myself, 'Good. Max needs to quiet down, take a siesta, back off the adrenaline rushes of combat missions—heck, do some book signings and relish in his newfound fame. It'll do him good, the biggest challenge being to keep his mouth yapping.'" He smiled and shook his head. "But, brother, you couldn't just sit and rest, could you?"

Max shook his head and was silent a moment, then grinned. "Julius, you should've been with me in Riyadh. This guy sticks a rifle in my face outside the school. Thank God, he didn't even see me in the darkness, but the moment was a rush, I must admit. And then flattening the tires of the car that rammed me. Reminded me of the mission with you and Retti in that little village outside Istanbul."

"Oh, yeah. Close call."

"Close?" Max touched a scar on his neck. "Another inch and a bullet hits my carotid artery and bye-bye."

The two friends were quiet for a few moments, then Julius piped up, "We've had some talks about what happens after the bye-bye. Have you had any change of mind?"

"You'll be thrilled to hear this, partner. Yes. The Lord and I got reacquainted in Israel."

Julius let out a whoop and bear hugged Max. "My brother in battle is now my brother in the Lord?"

"You bet," Max said, grinning widely.

"Like David and Jonathan?"

"Like David and Jonathan," Max agreed.

"I'm David the handsome one, and you're Jonathan." Julius laughed.

"Who's to say Jonathan wasn't handsome, too?"

Julius shrugged. "Yeah, I guess. But David was the all-around cooler dude."

"Yeah, cool's you, for sure."

After a moment, Julius said, "So who are David and Jonathan going into battle against?"

"You ask the big question. ISIS? The Three Sixes? Warriors for

Allah? In the Name of Allah?"

Julius held up a hand. "What did you say?

"ISIS—"

"No, the last one?"

"In the Name of Allah. We think they're connected to The Three Sixes—The Three Sixes being the Islamic groups set up to control three regions of the world. Why?"

"Can we get into the bat cave?"

Max pointed and said, "Still my rental and my key's in my coat."

"Then I've got to show you something."

The two men hurried out of the apartment. Ten minutes later they were stepping off the elevator and facing a Marine guarding the bat cave.

"Marine," Max announced, surprised. "Does the NSA use Marines as guards nowadays?"

The Marine, as tall as Max but not as brawny, nodded. "Tonight they do, sir."

"May we get inside?"

"No, sir."

"This is my place."

"Your name, sir?"

"Colonel Max Braxton."

The Marine stood to attention and saluted. "Sir."

Max saluted and motioned toward Julius. "And this is Colonel Rodriguez."

"You're the only two people I've been told can access this room," he said.

"Good," Max said. "I've got the key." He dangled the key in his fingers.

"Thank you, Corporal," Max opened the door and walked in,

Julius directly behind him.

The bat cave hadn't changed. Same over-warm room, same layout, nothing missing.

"The NSA seems to like this place just the way I arranged everything," he said.

"Well, the room is exactly as I imagined when I shipped all the paraphernalia to you," Julius said.

Julius stepped to the computer consoles and sat in the center chair, then pushed a button. All the monitors lit up.

"I have something to show you I saw this afternoon when cruising through the program with the NSA's IT guy and Sturgen."

Julius clicked on the tiny rotating icon that had caused the program to go live. Several seconds later, he clicked on another icon and the world turned into a three-dimensional wonder, with linear and circular lines connecting different spots around the world.

"Here." Julius pointed to a spot in Egypt, just west of the Red Sea, halfway between El Tur Nebq and Qena. His finger landed on a black dot within a thin red circle.

"Yes?" Max questioned.

"Let me zoom in," Julius said. Two keystrokes later the map tripled in size.

Max looked again and clearly read aloud, "Takbīr Qaeda."

"Takbīr meaning 'God Is Great.' This is the God Is Great Training Base," Julius interpreted. He placed the cursor on a tiny curl icon next to the dot and the following words appeared in parentheses: "Training base for In the Name of Allah."

"In the Name of Allah," Max whispered.

"Setting up the program, I was simply plugging in latitude and longitude coordinates," Julius said. "Today, working with the NSA, was the first time I'd really taken notice of this place. And then when you mentioned this group, the name clicked."

"What I'm thinking," Max said, "is The Three Sixes have certain highly secret groups doing the dirty work—at least at this point. The Asian regional leader had Sulaiman Islamiyah assassinate the Filipino president. Then the American regional leader had Salam Palestine kill Avi Navon—or at least try to—"

"And In the Name of Allah will be called on to wreak havoc in the Middle East," Julius said.

"But who exactly is calling the shots?" Max said. "The three leaders of The Three Sixes? Imam Meshaal? Or someone else?"

"Maybe a combination," Julius said.

"As Avi said, we've got too many ifs, ands, and buts."

"Let's shut her down and get some shut-eye," Julius said. "I just couldn't wait to show you the training base. You must be whipped. To the other side of the world and back in less than two days. Pretending you're back with SEAL Team 6?"

"I can't swim with those guys."

"And they can't climb with you."

Waving good-bye to the Marine outside the bat cave, the two descended to the ground on the elevator.

———— ◆ ————

Sharuk pulled the old Cadillac they had stolen into a parking space. Converted warehouses lined the street. One couple strolled along the otherwise deserted sidewalk.

He turned to Ahmed, seated in the backseat, and pointed to the next building up the street. He asked in Arabic, "Are you certain this is the building."

Ahmed looked down at the computer sitting on his lap. "Yes,

indeed. They bounced the signal all over the earth and to the building beside us, but the answer is yes."

Sharuk leveled his gaze on the man beside him in the front passenger seat. "Masum, arm your hand for Allah."

Masum smiled broadly and looked down his long, crooked nose to the Turkish Zigana automatic pistol he fondled. His favorite weapon. "Yes, Sharuk."

Sharuk swiveled to look at the man directly behind him. "Taseen, we are going in. Ready your hand for battle."

Young and wiry, Taseen scratched a would-be beard and leveled his shoulders. He already held a Russian Pistolet Kakarova semi-automatic pistol.

"Yes, Sharuk," Taseen said. "Allah Akbah."

"Allah Akbah."

"Allah Akbah," Masum and Ahmed repeated. They all reached for door handles.

Just then, Max and Julius opened the door and stepped down the stairs and onto the sidewalk.

Sharuk held up a hand to stop his comrades.

"The cursed American who speaks against us and against Allah." Sharuk said.

Ahmed and the others leaned forward in their seats. The car's heater had finally won the battle of the foggy window and they could see clearly.

"I think so," Ahmed said tentatively.

"Undeniable," Masum declared.

"Then we take him down now," Sharuk growled, "then come back for the computer and our money."

As he spoke, Max and Julius slid into the Mustang.

———◆———

When Max pulled out into the street, headlights flashed on in his rearview mirror. Julius noticed, too, and turned to look.

"Coincidental timing?" he asked.

"Let's find out," Max said.

At the next intersection, Max turned right. The car behind them turned right. He turned right again. The car turned right. He turned left. The car turned left.

"Fasten your seatbelt, Julius. We're going for a joy ride."

Max tapped the gear shift, "Let's show Uncle Julius what you're made of, McQ."

Julius looked into the side-view mirror and grinned. *This is more like it.* "Why, Detective Bullitt, I never thought I'd have the pleasure."

Max glanced over as he shifted gears. "How many machs are you cleared for, old fella?"

"Mach 2 at forty-nine thousand feet—and I'm not old."

"We'll see what this tail behind us is made of. Hold onto your dentures."

"Funny," Julius said. "I lose one tooth in hand-to-hand combat, protecting your back by the way, and you mention dentures."

Max laughed and rammed the accelerator to the floor, snapping both their heads back.

As he did, a bullet shattered the back window of the Mustang and did a through-and-through out the front windshield, directly below the rear-view mirror.

"Whoa. These guys are serious," Julius said. "You packing?"

"Of course. Got my G23." He pulled the handgun from beneath his winter coat and stretched the handle toward Julius.

"Naw," Julius motioned him away. "Got my own, thank you."

Julius opened his coat and withdrew a Glock 30 from a shoulder holster.

"Beg your pardon." Max's chuckle was cut short as a second bullet glanced off the top of the car.

"Man, these guys gotta improve their aim," Julius said. Suddenly he had an idea. "Pop the trunk, Max."

"Great idea." Max reached to the left of the wheel and pushed a button. The trunk rose, creating a shield.

Julius tilted his bucket seat as far back as the gear would go and slid out and into the back seat. He hunkered down and peered behind them. Street lights flashed light and shadows, followed by darkness, making vision difficult. Max downshifted around a corner, then double-shifted as he pushed the gas pedal to the floor.

"There's an inch or two beneath the hinge of the trunk I can see through," Julius said. "It's an old Caddy and looks, by the silhouettes, like there's a driver and a passenger, and maybe one or two more in the back seat."

———— ♦ ————

Max checked the rearview and noticed Julius was steadying his two-handed grip on the pistol. Suddenly a wide pothole came into view directly ahead. "Hold on, Julius."

He veered to miss the hole. Coming out of the swerve, Max straightened the wheel.

"I'll slow down," he said. "Shoot straight and true, partner."

The Caddy was about forty yards behind them.

"A little slower," Julius said.

Max slowed further. Where are the police when you need them? Max thought, then considered results might be better without their help.

They were approaching I-91 north- and southbound and he didn't want to chance a pile-up, no matter how few cars would be out this time of the night.

———◆———

Like Max, Julius had been trained for myriad situations black-ops military might encounter. As he tried to get range on the Caddy, he had to admit this circumstance was a first. Good thing Max was a top-tier tactics driver—the best in their old unit.

"Brace yourself," Max said, suddenly gunning the engine. "I'm slamming a forty-five left, then slowing to a crawl."

"Ten-four."

Max pulled off the maneuver precisely.

The Caddy fishtailed, trying to keep up, then straightened.

Julius squeezed off three quick rounds. The first shattered the Caddy's windshield, the second ripped through the front-seat passenger's right shoulder, the third might have hit the rear-seat passenger, but Julius wasn't sure.

Abruptly the Caddy swerved off the road, skimmed past a large box-shaped delivery truck, flew through a closed chain-link gate, and slammed into an oil-delivery truck in a parking lot.

The explosion shook the ground, sending flames in all directions. The blaze shot high into the air and completely engulfed the Cadillac.

Julius turned his eyes from the intense light. He could feel the heat, smell the burning oil.

———◆———

Max pulled the Mustang to the side of the street and looked around. The area was filled with trucking-type businesses. He was sure the explosion had woken up whoever did live nearby.

He looked at Julius. "Haven't lost your touch, have you?"

Julius shook his head. "Been awhile since I've even fired this G30." He kissed the barrel. "But I love her like a daughter."

Max took a deep breath, then lifted himself out of the Mustang, pulled out his cell phone and dialed 911.

The girl who answered sounded harried.

"I'm reporting an accident and explosion," Max said.

"Are you near Bradley Street?"

"I don't know," he said. "I'm a five-iron from I-91."

"We've got fire, police, and ambulance units on the way."

Max looked at the soaring flames from the Caddy and oil truck. Black smoke billowed in a slight easterly breeze.

"I think you can cancel the ambulance," he said. "A coroner's van would be a better call. My name's Max Braxton and you can reach me at this number. I'll stay right here."

Julius had gotten out of the car and stood next to him, his arms crossed as they watched the fire. "Compadré," he said, "I'm trying to count the dull moments I've had with you. I'm up to—hmm—none."

Max laughed and shook his head.

"Yep," Julius added, "you're still making friends wherever you go, aren't ya'?"

"I actually think those might have been your friends," Max said. "They picked us up outside the bat cave, and let's see, what's been going on in there?"

Julius thought for a moment. "Those guys might have been from a cell whose money the kids stole."

"You think?" One eyebrow rose with the question.

A minute later sirens wailed in the distance.

"I think I'd better call Sturgen and Crowe," Max said. He looked at his cell phone and scrolled through his contact list.

"Here," Julius said, handing him his cell phone. "Just dial nine and you'll get one of them."

———— ◆ ————

Sturgen and Crowe climbed into their Escalade. Sturgen turned the engine on and rubbed his eyes. "I don't know about you, but I need some Joe to wake me up for this."

"Count me in. Midnight comes early, doesn't it?" Crowe looked over at him and added, "So what do you know?"

"Max and Julius were at the bat cave for some reason, and when they left they were followed. Whoever was the tail fired shots at Max's car, blowing out the rear window. Max led the tail to a nonresidential area where Julius returned fire, possibly hitting the driver, and the pursuers went off the road and straight into an oil truck. Kaboom."

"No survivors, then."

"No survivors. Max said there apparently were four men in the vehicle. Now they're four pieces of toast. I only hope we can get some DNA."

"Who's there now?"

"Fire department, police, FBI. Max told the police and FBI he'd called us."

Sturgen pulled the vehicle into a Dunkin' Donuts drive-through and ordered two large coffees.

"And a plain doughnut," Crowe whispered into his ear.

"And two plain doughnuts," Sturgen said into the speaker.

A minute later they were heading to the scene. No lights. No siren. Just time to contemplate what they were facing.

"Why were Max and Julius at the bat cave?"

"We'll have to ask."

"Why did people follow them?"

"Perhaps they were staking out the building."

Crowe took a bite out of her doughnut. "Who would be doing such a thing?"

After a few seconds of silence and more than one gulp of coffee, Sturgen said, "Do you suppose they were from one of the groups the kids ripped off?"

A bite, a sip, then Crowe said, "And there were four of them, so they came in force to confront the kids."

"Of course, they didn't know the thieves were a bunch of college students—"

"So, when two grown men left the place, they figured they were the culprits."

"Or they even recognized Max—"

"In the dark at eleven o'clock?"

In the dark of the car, Sturgen didn't have to see the doubt on Crowe's face, but they passed by a lit-up intersection and light shone into the SUV.

"There's a street light directly across from the bat cave," Sturgen blurted out.

"Right. There *is*." Crowe finished her doughnut, wiped her lips and turned to her partner. "So, this is how it went—or we think it might have gone. The terrorist group has been hell-bent on finding their disappearing millions since they discovered their surprising poverty. We've been on the scene, but they don't know."

"And when they do arrive," Sturgen said, "what they see is this guy who's just been on TV for catching one of their own—"

"Possibly."

"Right, possibly. And they figure, rightly so, he's the culprit."

"But if they kill him, how do they get their money back?" Crowe asked.

Sturgen slowed the vehicle and looked at her, mulling the question. Finally, he said, "Jihad. Hatred is a terrible thing and, apparently, overrode the money issue for them."

"Hatred makes you think irrationally," Crowe said.

"And *do* irrationally." Sturgen could see the lights from fire trucks and police ahead and around a corner. There must have been a dozen emergency vehicles of one sort or another. He pulled over to the side of the street, stopped the Escalade, and turned to Crowe.

"Anger took over, Monica. They wanted vengeance, perhaps thinking they could get to the source of the computer theft after settling their score with the villain Braxton."

"In fact, killing Max would get one big annoyance out of their way," Crowe said.

Sturgen nodded.

"What they did not count on," he said, "was the expert gunfighting skills of our military. Ha."

He slapped the steering wheel, then turned back and pulled the SUV out into the street. The accident scene was about a hundred yards away. He asked, "So, did you read his book?"

"I'm halfway through it," Crowe said. "I'm impressed."

"Wait 'til you finish it."

"Yeah?"

"Yeah. You'll have a new hero."

Crowe laughed. "No one can replace Lassie."

Chapter Twenty

6:30 a.m., Friday, January 31

Over her morning breakfast of bran cereal, honey-topped English muffin, and black cherry juice, Kat turned on her television and found a news report on a Hartford station.

A reporter, decked out in a heavy winter coat with a Storm Center 3 logo on the chest, stood in front of smoldering wreckage. It was a nighttime shot, so this was a delayed broadcast.

"… local police say this flaming debris is the result of a gunfight between unknown attackers and two men identified as Colonel Max Braxton and Colonel Julius Rodríguez."

Kat gasped, then stood.

"You'll recall Braxton is the subject of reports the last few days out of Yale University, where he saved the lives of more than a hundred students attending a class he's teaching.

"Police believe four men died when the car they were riding in crashed into an unmanned oil truck and exploded. As you can see behind me."

Kat's eyes widened in horror.

"Police say the incident remains under investigation, and they will release more information later."

The monitor switched to a female news anchor in a newsroom. A closeup photograph of Max appeared in a small box behind her.

"Just yesterday," she said, "Colonel Braxton, teaching this semester at Yale University, appeared in a press conference defending his outspoken criticism of militant Islam. In the hours since Julie Zacko logged the report we just broadcast, teams from the FBI and National Security Agency have arrived on the scene. They too are remaining mum, pending further investigation."

Kat was dumbfounded. Was this man she now was almost certain she loved a changed man, a man of peace who had asked God for forgiveness of sins past? Or was he a purveyor of mayhem? She shook her head as the photo of Max faded into a picture of a winter storm in Illinois.

She bent down to pat Tuck. "What do you think, boy? Do we have a good Max *and* a bad Max?"

The movie *Mad Max* came to mind and she shivered.

At the sound of Max's name, Tuck stood up and wagged his tail. He looked at the door as if expecting him to walk in, then back at her and barked twice.

"Okay, I know your vote."

She reached for her cell phone to call Max, then thought, "Naw, it's six thirty in the morning, after all. And apparently, he had not gone right to sleep when she left, as she had thought he would. He and Julius were probably up all night with police, FBI, NSA, whatever alphabet soup of acronyms now filled the nation's world of security.

Kat wondered how Yale President Hall and the other university leaders would react to this latest event. She could sense another media feeding frenzy coming on.

———— • ◆ • ————

Nine o'clock came surprisingly early. Max slid out of bed, shaking his head at the wasted time. The fact he'd only slept five hours didn't brighten his outlook. He stepped into the shower, turned on the water to sizzle, and soaked.

Muddled thoughts filled his mind. More death. Was this worth it all? He thought back to the bad guys he had helped exit the world. He thought of the fires of hell and wondered if those men had learned their lesson yet.

He recalled his spontaneous remark to the female reporter yesterday: "I've been paid to protect my country—perhaps even you. I see a difference between killing and protecting."

This sentiment now buoyed his spirit.

He turned the water to chilly, let out a whoop and hardened himself against his body's reaction. He counted thirty seconds, then turned off the spigot.

A few minutes later, shaven and wide awake, he stepped out of the bathroom to a distinct aroma.

"Espresso." He quickened his pace into the kitchen.

Julius stood holding a lemon. "Found this in the fridge. Do you want a twist of this to make it café Romano?"

Max shook his head. "No lemon shall pass these lips this early in the day."

"Then I'll double up instead," Julius said. "Happy morning."

He handed Max a demi cup with the double espresso.

"Happy morning." Max took the cup. "We're alive—thanks to you."

"Thanks to my girl, my Glock—and probably a lot of help from God. The shots were like lining up a putt on a heavily shaded green. I hate those putts."

Max chuckled at the thought of his athletic friend and golf—the sport Max loved, but like most people, couldn't seem to conquer. His cell phone rang, an unfamiliar number filled the display.

He hesitated, then answered and heard a strained voice.

"Colonel Braxton, it's President Hall."

Max straightened his shoulders. "Yes, sir."

"I'm just hearing the news—well, from a lot of quarters."

"Yes, sir." Max remembered a friend of his who was an NFL head coach. The friend told him how trying and tense the conversation was when telling a player he was cut from the team. Max envisioned the hammer coming down over the airwaves.

"Remember our dialogue Tuesday?"

"Yes, sir."

"Remember how the conversation ended?"

"Yes, I do, sir, and I understand if you want to reverse your dec—"

"Max," Hall interrupted him, "I'm calling to assure you I feel the same. My decision stands. You're a brave man. I wish there were more of you—certainly on this campus."

"You're saying you want me to continue teaching?" Max stammered.

"I am."

"Th—thank you, President Hall. I certainly will. I—I hope there's no more fallout from all of this."

Hall laughed. "I'm on the same page with you there, young man. I am." After a moment, he continued, "If ever you need an ear, please know my door will remain open to you—either here at the office or at my home. Anytime."

"Thank you, sir. I may take you up on your offer."

"I hope you do."

"Well, good day, then."

After hanging up, Max turned to Julius. "I can't seem to lose this job, even after last night."

Julius smiled. "Vonnegut said, 'History is merely a list of surprises.' Count this as a good one. I mean, if you want to continue to mold young minds."

"There's a lot of mush out there," Max said, taking a sip of espresso, "but my A-Team? They're solid kids."

"Agreed. Impressed me."

"Ashley? Brilliant. Jose? Bright. Josh? My main man. Hank? Our brawn. Jill? She's the equalizer, the counterbalance to anyone about to go off-track."

"Looks like you've got them well-catalogued,—five good choices."

"Happenstance. Completely. I take no credit."

"One thing I've learned, Max."

"Yeah?"

"There is no happenstance. God-cidence, yes. Coincidence, no."

"Well, then, we'll credit him for the A-Team."

"You might want to also consider this young generation is made up of better stock than you've thought. Cheers for you at the press conference—the scene was stupendous."

Max smiled. "Yeah."

"Impressive."

"Warmed my heart," Max said, touching his chest.

"Make light of the applause, if you will," Julius said, "but their response to you spoke volumes—to me and everyone there. Including the president of the university, obviously."

———— ◆ ————

Imam Meshaal's face turned dark. He swore in Arabic and his hand ground the writing paper in his grip to a tiny ball.

He hung up his telephone and looked up at his lieutenant, the assistant headmaster of the Diriyah Islamic School for Boys.

His voice low but seething, Meshaal said in Arabic, "Sharuk and his team who went to confront the thieves of our money are all dead. And the cursed Braxton is the murderer."

"Sharuk?" Aaban bristled, his face turning white. "Then my little cousin Taseen was with him?"

Meshaal nodded.

"Braxton?" Aaban spit out the name, his fists clenched and turning as white as his face. "What must we do to annihilate him? Contact Lodestar?"

"No." Meshaal's response was quick. "We do not simply contact Lodestar. Plus, he needs to stay focused."

Meshaal sat in thought, then peered up at Aaban. "Get Tariq in here. We need to talk money. And I've got a call to make to rid us of this infidel Braxton."

As Aaban left the office, Meshaal picked up his phone again.

———— ◆ ————

Stetson reclined poolside at his favorite West Palm Beach resort. He was the only one there at this early hour. A black coffee laced with Irish whiskey sat in the glass-holder of his lounge.

When his cell phone rang, he thought of not answering. He let it ring once, twice, three times. With an exasperated sigh, he snapped it up. "Yes?"

"Stetson?"

The thick Saudi accent revealed the caller.

"Yes."

"I have a job for which you are uniquely qualified."

"Go on."

When he heard the assignment, a smile spread across his face.

———— ◆ ————

Max looked over his bowl of oatmeal. "Julius, how do you deal with taking life?"

Julius peered at his friend. "The question's kind of out of the blue."

"When I was in the bushes outside the school in Riyadh," Max said, "this guy put his rifle in my face and I pulled him to the ground. I was about to snap his neck and decided instead to employ a sleeper hold. I had what might have been a come-to-Jesus moment."

Julius stepped over to the coffee table, picked up a Bible, and leafed through the pages, finding the Scripture he was searching for. Looking at Max and then back at the page, he said: "This is God speaking to the prophet Ezekiel in chapter 33: *But if the watchman sees the sword coming and does not blow the trumpet to warn the people and the sword comes and takes the life of one of them, that man will be taken away because of his sin, but I will hold the watchman accountable because of his blood.*"

Julius set down the Bible and returned to the table. "This is how I look at the quandary," he said. "Black-ops groups are the perfect ones to belong to. We're not dropping bombs on weapons arsenals or targets where innocents are more likely to die. We're taking out the terrorist leader, the single assassin, the kidnapper, the hostage taker, the bin Laden.

"We're as neat and clean as you can get when you're talking about war, about fighting a group of fanatical gunmen who want to slaughter our women and children and destroy our country.

"This is one reason so many of the guys love your book, man. Have you read your own words lately?"

Max couldn't suppress a smile and shrug. "Actually, no. Not since I wrote the manuscript, and I finished more than a year ago."

"I've got a copy in my suitcase. I'll get the book for you." Julius pretended to rise out of his seat.

"Oh, sit down. I hear you."

"Simple, my friend," Julius said. "If you've sinned, ask for forgiveness from God. He'll grant your request. If you keep beating yourself up over a sin for which you've asked forgiveness, then you're usurping God's place. I don't think you want to sit on his throne."

Max bit his lip as he considered Julius' words. "No, I don't."

A minute later, Max plugged the imam's flash drive into his computer and he and Julius began a tedious search looking for names, clues, whatever might trigger a recollection, feel odd, or simply be conspicuous.

The list of financial donors was tempting, but even more compelling was the list of students who were at the school at the same time as Ridley Jones.

After an hour, Max went back to the kitchen and concocted another coffee. He stretched, thought of Kat, looked at his watch, and figured she was out of her class by now. But he decided to search further before calling her.

Back at the computer, he said, "Somewhere in this list of names are the leaders of The Three Sixes. They have to be. Was it mere coincidence the imam wrote the treatise for The Three Sixes when Jones was there?"

He caught himself short at the mention of coincidence. He looked at Julius and asked, "If there is such a thing as God-cidence, is there also Satan-incidence?"

Julius thought for a moment, then responded, "Perhaps, if people were put together for evil intent."

———— ◆ ————

The sun shone brightly through the floor-to-ceiling windows of Avi's office. The sun even tried to pry off the pall still hanging over him from the deaths of Jonas and Stan.

Dan Ogilvy sat across from Avi, a notepad in his hands. "I've just heard from Guillaume Pauwels in Belgium," he said. "He's anxious to finish up his paperwork on the new GPS module from Internicon. Here are the final figures we worked out."

Dan passed the notepad to Avi, who ran his eyes over the legalese and looked up at his CFO. "You know, Dan, over the years this mumbo-jumbo has taken a decade from my life."

Dan chuckled. "Well, it might be shallow comfort, but this deal will ensure Internicon remains in the black for the next ten years."

"Then I guess we should do it."

Avi reached for his intercom to have his secretary call Pauwels when something stopped him. An odd sensation came out of nowhere. Avi had learned as a child—when "something" stopped him from going out to the chicken house moments before a PLO-launched rocket blew it to smithereens—not to quickly dismiss such "somethings."

He pulled his hand back and looked at Dan. "Pauwels," he said, "we've never had any problems with him, have we?"

Dan shook his head. "No. Everything's always run smoothly."

"Several years ago, before we struck our first deal with him, Boaz checked him out, right?"

Dan shrugged. "I imagine so."

"But you don't know for sure."

"Avi, why the question? We've made millions together with Pauwels."

"I don't know." Avi felt a shiver across his shoulders. "Something."

"Then I'll check it out. I'll be back in five minutes."

Dan left the office, leaving Avi standing and looking out over the city, his arms wrapped around himself.

Shortly, Dan returned. "It appears Boaz was out of commission in the hospital with kidney stones when we made our first contact with Pauwels. We never did a check. He fell through the cracks."

"Get it done now," Avi said, "and quickly."

———— • ————

An hour later, Boaz rushed into Avi's office, eyes wide, face flushed, teeth gritted. The sight of him made Avi rise from his chair.

"What is it?"

"Guillaume Pauwels," he said.

"Yes?"

"The copy of the flash drive you gave me this morning, the one Braxton sent you from the imam at the Islamic school in Riyadh?"

"Yes?"

"It contains a list of students. Along with Ridley Jones is—" he hesitated, "Guillaume Pauwels."

Avi froze, his mind sorting through the implications.

"Pauwels. *That's* not an Arabic name," Avi said.

"In Belgium it is," Boaz replied.

Avi sat back down and pushed a button on his telephone console.

"Yes, Papa." Lana's voice sang through the intercom.

His voice fractured, he said, "My dear, I need you here."

"Be right there."

Mere seconds went by before Lana hurried into the room.

"Tell Lana what you found on the imam's hard drive, Boaz," Avi said.

Boaz shared his discovery and Lana's jaw dropped. "When Ridley introduced you two, did he tell you they were classmates in an Islamic school?" she asked.

Avi shook his head, deep in thought.

"Maybe it's nothing," Lana said, "just a friendly connection, one schoolmate helping another get ahead in the world."

"Or maybe—" Boaz began.

"There we go again with ifs, ands, and maybes," Avi said. "But I'll tell you this, I'm holding off on the Internicon deal until we investigate further." He looked at Boaz. "Go as deep as you can, my friend. If Pauwels and Ridley were pals at the Islamic school, maybe their connection goes deeper still. Maybe there's a connection to the group Max and his archaeology friend were telling us about—The Three Sixes."

Boaz nodded. "As you say." He rose and left the office.

Avi lifted his telephone to his ear.

"What are you doing now, Papa?" Lana asked.

"Contacting our friend Mr. Braxton."

Lana crossed her arms and shook her head. Avi knew she didn't approve, stubbornly accepting his connection with Max as a necessity, not an option. But he liked the guy—a lot.

———— ◆ ————

Max was rustling his fingers through his hair, thinking he and Julius were wasting time doing nothing more than reading a list of names with zero meaning to him. Besides Jones, every name but a handful were Arabic, including a bunch of Mohammeds and a boatload of boys with the surnames Al Bashir, Al Harbi, Al Kahtani, Al Zahrani, Abdullah, Farooqi, Khan, and Said.

"These names are like Smith and Jones in America," Julius said.

Max nodded. "Sorry to say, but you're right."

Hearing a knock, Max opened the door to find Kat and Tuck. His face lit up, he kissed Kat lightly and bent to scratch Tuck behind the ear. Tuck ran into the room and greeted Julius with a high-five and a lick to his hand. Julius laughed.

Just then Max's phone rang. He answered and sat on the couch. "Max?"

"Avi." Max caught Kat's eye and motioned for her to sit beside him.

"I have some information to share and I have a feeling—" Avi began.

Max put the phone on speaker so Kat and Julius could hear.

You have a feeling?" Max said.

"A bad feeling. An ominous feeling. Like you had a friend, a business partner you trusted, and then—"

"Go on, sir."

"Check the names."

After they hung up, a notion struck Max.

He looked at Kat. "Did you notice if the flash drive from Imam Meshaal contains information about clubs or organizations the students were involved in?"

"Sure does," Kat said.

"Then I have an idea. Let's check to see what, if any, groups attracted both Jones and Pauwels. If we find one, perhaps there is a third student close to them. And—"

"And perhaps the third one now lives in the Asian region?" Kat asked.

"And perhaps—" Max left the rest unsaid.

For the next hour, they pored over club memberships. The clubs were listed alphabetically. Arts. No. Chess. Pauwels, but not Jones. Journalism. Jones, but not Pauwels. Soccer. Both Pauwels and Jones.

"Well," Julius shrugged, "you do share a lot in the locker room."

"Yeah, like *you* sharing *my* antiperspirant," Max said and slapped Julius on the shoulder.

Kat interrupted with, "Young Islam."

"Really?" Julius said. Kat nodded and pointed to the monitor.

"Let's see their mission statement," Max said.

Kat scrolled down the screen. "Right here."

She began reading: "We encourage our members to anchor their hearts and souls in the moral framework of an Allah-centered life. We exist to train our students to build more just societies based on Islamic values. Ultimately, we declare the call for any Muslim is to spread the glory of Allah and the victory of sharia to the entire world."

Julius interjected, "And reading between the lines, they could add, 'For those infidels who refuse to accept our benevolent outreaches to them, death is the better end, and sometimes, the cause of a warrior for Islam is to bring their end swiftly.'"

Max and Kat nodded.

"Likewise," Max said, "martyr operations as sanctioned by the Qur'an, in a world of evil and treachery, bring glory not only to Allah but to the martyr."

Max and Kat stared at one another.

"Phew." she said. "Scary."

"It goes pretty far beyond my Catholic friends in school saying their priests believed Protestants weren't saved," Max said.

Kat shrugged. "At least the priests weren't calling for death to the infidels like the Qur'an declares in Surah 3:28.

"What I don't understand," she added, "is, considering their scripture, how a true Muslim believer can befriend a nonbeliever."

Kat reached for her purse and pulled out a tiny booklet with several sticky notes pasted inside, turned to one of them. "This is from Surah 5:51" she said, reading: "'O you who believe. Do not take the Jews and the Christians for friends; they are friends of each other; and whoever amongst you takes them for a friend, then surely, he is one of them; surely Allah does not guide the unjust people.'"

"The doctrine is called the Hadith Qudsi, the al-Takeyya," Max said, "the right to lie for the cause of Islam, or to save yourself from physical or mental injury. Anyway, all the commands regarding non-Muslims are a far cry from Jesus saying, 'Love your enemies and pray for those who persecute you.'"

"You've been reading." Kat said.

"Yes, he has," Julius said.

Max cocked his head. "Some. I know this—one is the truth and the other is a lie. And if the Western world doesn't wake up, we may all soon be awakened at five each morning by some mullah in a minaret calling us to prayer. You don't go? Kaput." He cut his hand across his throat.

Julius nodded in agreement, and Kat winced at the thought. "Let's get back to the members of this distinguished Young Islam Club," she said.

They turned back to look at the computer.

"Scroll down to the year 1992," Max said. "Jones was a senior then."

As Kat scrolled down, the men stopped her three times.

"Hey, there's Majdi Abdullah," Max said. "He's the guy who drove a boat loaded with munitions into the USS *Martin* off the coast of Kuwait."

"There's Shahin Khan, one of the men who masterminded blowing up a convoy I was riding in in Afghanistan," Julius said.

"And there's Bahij Mahdavi, a cruel beast of a rapist and murderer," Max said.

"You've got *that* straight," Julius said.

Kat grimaced and turned to face them. "You know these men?"

"They inhabit my dreams sometimes," Max said.

"They and others like them," Julius added.

Kat shook her head, then turned back and continued scrolling down to 1992.

"Here we are," she announced, pointing. "Let's see. Club Officers. President: *Fariq* El-Hashem."

"Appropriate," Max said, "since fariq means lieutenant general—"

"And *hashim* means 'the crusher,'" Kat added.

Julius, who had been looking over Kat's shoulder, straightened up, his eyes wide.

"What?" Max asked.

"Fariq El-Hashem," he said. "He's the guy we hunted just a few days following the assassination of the Filipino president."

"We?" Max asked.

"Well, you weren't there." Julius shook his head in mock sorrow "But the rest of Sam Bravo 2 was. You were off preparing for your Yale job."

"This was around New Year's, just three weeks ago?" Kat asked.

Julius nodded. "We had intel El-Hashem had put the hit on the Filipino president. He was supposedly headquartered near Sibu, on the island part of Malaysia. We took little time to prepare—nothing like our old days with the Israelis, who train like nobody's business, eh, partner?"

He shot a look at Max, who nodded.

"But when we got to his hideout, nobody was there. No El-Hashem. Empty. Like someone had tipped them off."

"Who knew about the operation?" Max asked.

"General Howard, the president, and us."

"You're talking President Humphrey, not Jones," Kat said.

"Correct."

"Hold on," Max said. "Once a person is elected president but before they're sworn in, they're made privy to all the national security information—worldwide. Right?"

"Right," Kat and Julius said. "The president-elect and, maybe, their immediate circle such as Ned Zapper, Jones's Chief of Staff."

"So, besides Sam Bravo 2, Howard and Humphrey, our president-elect also could have known."

"Could have," Julius agreed.

Kat listened in disbelief, then said, "If he did know and informed El-Hashem, his action would be treason."

The men agreed and took a collective breath.

"Another and-but-if," Max finally said.

"Right," Kat agreed. "Let's go on to the rest of the officers of the Young Islam Club."

They all turned to look back at the computer monitor.

"Vice President: Guillaume Pauwels," Max read, then looked at the others. "Avi's man. Avi will be so glad to hear he's been doing business with this guy."

"And here are the members," Kat said.

They all intently watched as she scrolled down.

———— ◆ ————

Finally, Max's eyes settled on one name. "Ridley Jones." His shoulders lowered. He couldn't believe what he read, but he could, really. He didn't want to accept Jones being on the list as true, but that had been the direction his instincts had taken from the beginning. Otherwise, why even break into the president's home? So, was he surprised? Well, no.

Max looked up. "At least he wasn't an officer," he exhaled. "And I remember one magazine article saying Ridley's father wanted him to immerse himself in the culture."

"Well, he could have gotten the ultimate immersion, eh?" Julius said.

"Hey." Kat exclaimed. "That's three guys, together, in the Young Islam Club. Do you suppose—"

"There's a connection to The Three Sixes?" Max finished.

"And, if so," Julius declared, "this would also be treasonous."

Julius snapped his fingers. "The Holy Land Foundation conspiracy." he exclaimed.

Max put his index and middle fingers to his forehead, trying to conjure the facts, and finally, "Yes."

"What is the Holy Land Foundation conspiracy?" Kat asked.

"There was a memo," Julius said, "found in a concealed archive in Annandale, Virginia, in 2004, introduced into evidence about four years later in the prosecution of the first group of defendants in the Holy Land Foundation conspiracy."

"The largest terrorism-financing prosecution ever in the United States," Max said. "The memo said the strategic plan in America for Hamas and its parent organization, the Muslim Brotherhood, was a kind of grand jihad. They intended to destroy Western civilization from within—"

"So Allah would reign victorious," Julius said.

"The trial also made public a Muslim Brotherhood document our presidents, political leaders, and State Department remarkably forgot rather quickly," Max said. "The document was called, 'Phases of the World Underground Movement Plan' and the Muslims in charge were sentenced anywhere from fifteen to sixty-five years in prison."

"Yeah," Julius said. "The document was pretty precise about how the Brotherhood was carrying out its mission. Do you remember phase one?"

Max shook his head. "I don't have your photographic memory, bud."

Julius cleared his throat. "'The first phase,' the statement declared, 'is discreet and secret establishment of leadership.'"

Kat gasped.

———— ◆ ————

Julius's cell phone vibrated in his pocket. He looked at the screen and said, "I've got to take this privately."

"Use my bedroom," Max said.

Julius left the room, then reemerged a few moments later.

"Well, my brother and Kat, I've got to go."

"Yeah?"

"The orders I was waiting for when you reached me a week ago."

"Where are you off to?"

"The other hemisphere. I can't say more. This is incredible stuff you're looking into, but I really do have to leave immediately. There's a plane waiting for me in New Haven as soon as I can get there. I'll call Sturgen and let him know."

"Darn." Max blew out a harsh breath. "Well, Semper fi, then, Julius."

"Semper fi."

The two men hugged.

"Godspeed," Kat said and hugged him.

"Thanks, young lady. Wonderful meeting you regardless of the circumstances." He nodded toward the computer.

Julius picked up his duffel bag which was packed and ready and tossed the satchel over his shoulder. Tuck followed him to the door, where Julius bent to shake his hand.

Before leaving, he looked back and said, "Psalm 91, Max. Psalm 91. Watch your back, but pray for him to do the same." He waved good-bye and in a second he was gone.

Max scrambled to his Bible on the coffee table and read the passage before he forgot. After a few seconds, he read aloud: *For He shall give His angels charge over you, To keep you in all your ways.* He turned to Kat, "Verse eleven."

She smiled. "Quite a guy."

After a moment, she asked, "So what do we do with all this intelligence?"

"I'll call Avi and tell him what we discovered."

"Then what?"

Max shrugged and mulled the options for a minute. Finally, he said, "I do trust Sturgen and Crowe."

He looked at his watch: 12:20 p.m. "We can tell them. They should be able to spur an investigation. An internal one, probably, but at least the information would get out to people who can do something about it."

"What about the media?" Kat asked, eyebrows raised.

"I trust them as far as I can throw this coffee table."

"Even Fox?" she asked.

"Well—" Max considered the thought. Finally, "No. Maybe if the information goes nowhere with the NSA. But I'd rather not whistle-blow publicly. Not yet."

"Well then, I suggest you tell Sturgen and Crowe, and the sooner the better."

"Okay, but Avi first."

———— ♦ ————

Avi was skipping lunch. He didn't feel much like eating nowadays. Disquieting events unsettled his stomach now that he'd reached his sixties.

The phone call from Max disturbed him even more than before. And now here was Lana with more bad news. He'd call the information distasteful but repugnant would be a better description.

"Papa, this is too coincidental. An hour ago, we're told the tradesmen's union at our Teftile plant in Milwaukee is threatening a strike. And a few minutes ago, Dan gets a call saying the electricians and pipefitters unions in San Diego and all of the unions at Startsol in Chicago are doing the same."

Avi turned and looked out over the vast city of Atlanta. Yes, this was too much of a coincidence. What an interesting day this had turned out to be. First, hearing the news from Max, now spontaneous strikes.

"Of course." These events were clear to him now. "Ridley, you nasty boy."

Avi turned to Lana. "It's all Ridley's doing. Discredit the messenger—me—by first, calling into question his integrity, then siccing Zapper and his hounds on him."

"But you've always treated all the unions well. Higher wages, better benefits, and retirement, the whole works."

"Doesn't matter, Lana. If your biggest asset, who in this case is the president, asks you to jump, well—"

Avi was interrupted by Dan knocking at the door and entering the office.

By the look on Dan's face, he bore more ignoble news.

Chapter Twenty-One

Friday, One Hour Later

Max and Kat, with Tuck to Kat's right, were bundled against a cold wind, walking along a wide gravel path toward the Memorial Monument Flagstaff centering New Haven Green. Sturgen and Crowe were to meet them there.

Expansive, old-age elm trees, naked for the winter, loomed over them. Park benches dotted the entire green which was crisscrossed with walkways. College, Chapel, Church and Elm streets bordered the sixteen-acre park, while Temple Street bisected the Green into upper and lower halves.

"The Puritans established this spot as a marketplace for the New Haven Colony back in the 1640s," Kat said.

"I love hanging with a walking history lesson," Max cracked. "I'll bet you have a knickknack sold here in 1643."

Kat elbowed him. "Seriously, we're walking on historic ground. George Washington spoke here during the American Revolution. Abraham Lincoln made a stump speech right over there," she pointed to a spot, "when he was running for president. The Amistad captives were exercised on this green."

"Ha," Max exclaimed. "I'll bet this is where Benedict Arnold and the New Haven militia convened before rushing to Massachusetts and the Battle of Bunker Hill."

Kat shook her head. "All things military, aren't you?"

"You're getting the idea." Max squeezed her gloved hand. He pulled his coat collar closer around his neck to ward off the cold.

Though the park was just off the Yale campus to the east, the green appeared to be busy for a late-January day. People were scurrying about. Some appeared to take notice of Max and Kat. A few waved to Kat, others nodded to the pair. A few did double takes of Max as though they recognized him but couldn't place him.

They left the tree-lined walkway and moved into an open space, angling toward a white monument about fifty yards away looming skinny and tall.

———◆———

A tall broad-shouldered man leaned against the base of the monument, his eyes fixed on Max. Stuffing his hands deeper into his coat pockets, he shrugged his shoulders and kicked off the monument. Calm. Cool. Casual.

The chill of winter blew through his jacket, but the cold was a small price to pay to be able to more easily draw his handgun without the weight of a heavy winter coat. He watched Braxton laugh with the woman. They were walking straight toward him.

I'll wipe the smile off your face, you prig. Revenge. It's a sweet thing.

———◆———

"What's the matter?" Kat asked.

"What do you mean?"

"I see that look. I just gave you my best joke of the day and your laughter was gone two seconds later. I must be losing my touch."

"I don't know. Maybe nothing." Max wanted to reassure her but was studying the man, about forty yards away, ambling toward them. The man's stride seemed a conscious or subconscious saunter, like he was trying to appear nonchalant but truly walked with purpose.

Max guessed he was military, by his gait, but something else looked familiar. An athletic build beneath the spring coat. Why would someone be wearing such a light-weight coat in this weather? A familiar low jolt of electricity began to flow along his nerve ends. Usually a precursor.

The man was closing in on them, twenty yards away.

Tuck suddenly stopped and growled. Confirmation?

"Tuck, be good," Kat scolded.

But Max angled right to nudge Kat in a new direction, putting himself between this man and her. "Kat—"

Just then, voices rang out, "Mr. Braxton. Professor Cardova."

Max glanced to his left and saw the entire A-Team, quickening their steps to reach them, perhaps forty yards distant.

Kat screeched. Out of the corner of his eye, Max saw a Beretta in the man's hand just six to eight feet away. Tuck sprang at the man. The gun flashed and Tuck fell to the ground, whimpering in pain, blood gushing. Kat screamed again as did the students and others in the area.

Max took one long, quick stride, and as the man turned his aim at him, kicked the Beretta out of his hand. The gun flew into the snowbank along the path.

The man glanced toward the gun. Max used the distraction to smack a quick open-palm, uppercut to the man's chin. His neck snapped back and he fell back limply to the walkway.

Kat fell to the ground, shouting, "Help. Help." She wrapped her arms around Tuck and held him close to her. His blood, warm and sticky, covered her hands.

She looked up, frantic. Max turned back toward her.

"It's Tuck." Tears blurred her vision but she could make out two or three people videotaping the brawl on their cell phones.

She looked fiercely at one of them and cried, "Really? Call 911."

Just then, she looked over Max's shoulder. "Max." she warned.

———————◆———————

Max turned to see the man crouching, drawing a KA-BAR knife from an ankle sheath. Not just any KA-BAR. A D2 Extreme. *This guy's a veteran killer.*

Max focused again on his opponent's face. Finally, recognition struck him like a slap in the face.

"Stetson?"

"About time you recognized me. You're gettin' old, Braxton."

"If I'm getting so old, how'd I knock you on your butt, you foul piece of trash?"

"Oh, I'm going to enjoy this," Stetson seethed through gritted teeth. He circled the knife and sidestepped to Max's left. Max stood still, gauging his moves, aware Stetson was going to Max's weaker side.

Unable to reach his Glock because of his heavy coat, Max decided to work on Stetson's major weakness—his mental state—the fact he'd been caught and imprisoned. "If not for the scar, I might not have recognized you at all, Melvin. *Stetson hated his name.*

"The last time I saw you, Melvin, you were in shackles in Qicheng Prison. Your hair was past your shoulders."

Stetson lunged at him and Max sidestepped. They circled again. Kat screamed in the background.

"Mr. Braxton." Josh shouted.

Max glanced back, distracted, and Stetson took advantage, jabbing at him through the coat. Freakish pain shot through his left shoulder. He fell back on his right knee but grabbed Stetson's knife-wielding wrist with his right hand. He twisted the joint between his forearm and wrist and squeezed like a vise. The knife dropped. Stetson groaned in agony.

Through gritted teeth, Max glanced at Josh and yelled, "Stay—back."

Max had leverage, despite his lower position. He calculated five pounds would break Stetson's wrist. He pulled down hard, then snapped the wrist back, but didn't lean hard enough. Stetson yelped and yanked his hand away.

Blood was oozing from Max's shoulder, and he struggled to shrug off his coat with his right hand.

"When I heard you were my target, Braxton, I almost said I'd do the job for free. The great Max Braxton." Stetson spit on the ground. A hideous grin consumed his face.

"I'm calling the police." Josh hollered from behind Stetson.

Max noticed hesitation in Stetson's face. Yeah, he'd run and come back to strike later—and maybe not just at Max but Kat as well. Max had to prevent an escape. Stetson glanced toward the snowbank where the Beretta lay, but the gun had fallen beneath the snow somewhere.

Max needed to distract him.

"How'd you escape prison, Melvin?"

"Not with your help, pal. You were nowhere in sight with a rescue team."

He continued circling his knife. Max knew he was waiting for an angle, a tell, an advantage of some sort.

"Rescue? You deserved to be there, Melvin. You broke protocol and you went far, far beyond our mission."

"Protocol." Derision oozed from Stetson's mouth.

"Black Ops 101. Overboard, wanton killing? Leaving your team and assignment to carry out a personal vendetta? What were you thinking?"

"You didn't stick around to find out," Stetson said continuing to circle.

"We actually did stick around, waiting for extraction orders, but command ordered a pullout."

Stetson hesitated, thought for a moment, then barked, "You say."

"You'll never take responsibility, will you, Melvin? Never would, never will." Max shook his head. *So sad. Were some people beyond redemption?*

"I was a good teammate," Stetson objected.

"You were the odd man out. The assignment was to be your last. Even before the mission, the order was prepared. You were going to be shipped back to regular army. But after what you did, if you'd come back, you'd have faced a court martial."

"No."

"Yes."

"So superior aren't you, Braxton. You think."

Max clutched at his aching shoulder and took a breath. He had to figure how to disarm Stetson. He had to end this. Forget himself. Kat was bawling nearby, Tuck in her arms. They had to get him to a vet.

"Some men shouldn't go bald, Melvin," he said. "If it's possible for you to have gotten any uglier, you did."

Max's heavy coat was hanging from his left shoulder and he ripped at the sleeve, pulling it off altogether.

Without warning, Stetson lunged the knife directly at Max's stomach. Max turned sideways, the knife barely missing. He chopped down with fearsome force on Stetson's arm with his right hand. The blow bent Stetson forward and Max kneed him in the head, sending him sprawling several feet away. Again, he scrambled to his feet.

Max reached behind to draw out his Glock from his belt, but Stetson came at him, swinging the knife at his face. Max ducked, muffled a cry of pain, then rose sharply and wrapped his arms underneath Stetson's and around him. His momentum drove Stetson to the ground with Max on top.

Adrenaline screaming through his veins, Max pummeled Stetson across the face one-handed. Once, twice, three times, four times, five.

Fighting the urge to batter the evil man under him into oblivion, Max leaped to his feet and raced to Kat's side. He looked back at the crowd and spotted Josh. "They sending an ambulance?"

"Ambulance?"

"For the dog, not that murdering—" Max began.

As the words spilled out of his mouth, a co-ed screamed.

Stetson, on his knees, had uncovered his Beretta and was lifting the gun toward Max.

In a blur, two men flew at Stetson and crushed him back into the ground. The gun cracked. Max felt a sting like a bumblebee along his waist. The strike spun him around in pain.

"Max." Kat cried out.

Wincing, Max smiled ruefully to himself. Not like this hasn't happened before—and because of Stetson. He owed the guy four wounds. Thank God, the lead missed bone.

Kat scrambled to him, leaving Tuck.

He held up his right arm. "I'll be all right. See to Tuck."

He looked over at Stetson. Josh and Hank were grinding him, like so much pork, into the pathway, while Jose pointed Stetson's own handgun at him. Jill and Ashley stood nearby, cheering them on.

"Clock him one, Jose," Jill said. "He tried to kill Mr. Braxton."

"Tie him up." Ashley said.

Max gave them the thumbs-up. "Just don't let him budge, guys."

The sound of sirens split the chatter of the gathering crowd.

Max joined Kat, who was already on her knees, holding Tuck.

Max looked into the dog's eyes. "He's in shock," he said. "We've got to get him help fast."

Campus and New Haven police were scrambling down the pathways toward them. Behind the police, EMTs rushed along from two directions.

"What's going on here?" one policeman called.

A large African-American woman stepped forward. "Officer, this man," she pointed to Stetson, "tried to kill this man," she pointed to Max, "and those boys," she pointed to Josh, Hank, and Jose, "saved his life."

"But my dog, officer," Kat cried, "may die."

"He's in shock, and bleeding badly," Max said. "Can you do anything for him?"

"Looks like you're not doing so well yourself," the officer said.

"Not as badly as Tuck here," Max replied.

Two EMTs rushed up, one to Tuck, the other to Max. The one with Tuck said, "We'll do what we can. There's an animal hospital two blocks away and we'll get him there immediately."

The other EMT said, "Let me see your wound."

Max waved him off. "You can wait on me, but not on Tuck. I'll carry him. Just run."

Max curled Tuck into his chest with his right arm. His left shoulder was throbbing hard. He gritted his teeth, drew on the adrenaline flow, and with Kat at his side, fled up one pathway following the EMTs. As they ran, Max spotted Sturgen and Crowe twenty yards ahead and hurrying in their direction.

"You're a little late." Max called.

"What's happening?" Sturgen asked.

"Follow us and we'll tell you."

———◆———

As Kat drove, Max sat in the back seat holding Tuck. "The first time I was with Stetson he caused me to get wounded, too—a gunshot nicked my shoulder and another above the hip. Same places. Prophetic?

Kat mustered a half-laugh, half-cough, and shook her head.

———◆———

When they arrived at the animal hospital, Chief MacMillan, Sturgen, Crowe, two officers from the city, and the entire A-Team joined them in the waiting room.

MacMillan peered at Max, a twinkle in his eyes, and said, "This campus has been nothing but exciting since you arrived, Colonel."

Shirtless, Max laughed, then winced at the pain as an EMT, a skinny young man, tended his gunshot wounds, his shoulder first, then his hip.

"You're going to be fine," the kid said.

"I know," Max said. "Unfortunately, I've been through this before. By now, I've got lead in my DNA. Thanks for your help."

"And for helping my dog," Kat said.

The EMT and his partner left and MacMillan said, "We're here to take your statements."

"We're here to listen in," Sturgen cracked. "Pretend we're not here—for now."

"Chief, everyone, have a seat," Max waved to chairs around the room. "We're happy to oblige."

As Max wound down his story of the attack, a harried veterinarian stepped into the room. "The bullet miraculously missed all Tuck's vital organs. He's in shock. We've got IVs in him to restore fluids. He lost a lot of blood, but he'll be fine. He's a strong dog. He'll have to spend a few days here recuperating, but he'll be fine."

Crying, Kat leaped from her chair and gave the veterinarian a hug. "Thank you so much."

There were shoulder slaps all around, then the A-Team dismissed themselves, alluding to classes they had to make. The vet returned to the recovery room.

Then Max and Kat finished their story. The policemen left, promising to keep them apprised of the case. Chief MacMillan winked at Max, shook his hand and said, "A pleasure, young man."

Max returned the handshake. "Pleasure's mine, Chief."

As MacMillan walked out the door, Max turned to Sturgen and Crowe. "But do we have a story for you."

Kat reached into her bag and passed an envelope to the NSA agents. "Our documentation is in here to back up what we're about to tell you," she said.

"Will this be hard to believe?" Crowe asked.

"Probably so," Max replied and Kat gave an exaggerated nod.

Chapter Twenty-Two

Sunday afternoon, February 2

Avi smiled at the couple to his right at the dining room table. Max Braxton and Kat Cardova were a striking pair—both had movie-star good looks—and they were obviously attracted to one another, though they weren't being outward about their affections. They were engaging, amusing, and comfortable to be around. Despite his and Max's first moments together, Avi felt extraordinarily secure with him around.

He glanced to his left, to Lana and Dan Ogilvy. He had introduced Lana as "the finest daughter a man could have" and Dan as "my most trusted friend, adviser, and colleague."

Dinner had been delicious. Over coffee, they compared notes on the events of the last two weeks.

"So, let me start the summing-up process," Avi said. "There's this Islamic terror group called The Three Sixes. And, oddly enough, Ridley has a copy of The Three Sixes handbook with l-o-d-e— probably shorthand for Lodestar—on the bottom of the pages and a flash drive about the Islamic school hidden away in his bedroom bureau. Under this group, the world is divided into three regions, with one man in control of each region.

"We think Fariq El-Hashem, Guillaume Pauwels, and our own Ridley Jones are those three regional leaders. And we further believe Imam Meshaal, the founder and head of the Islamic school those three men attended, is the Oz behind the curtain."

Max nodded. "Correct. In fact, I think this guy Stetson, who attacked us at Yale, wants his fifteen minutes of fame. He and I have a history I won't bore you with, but this fits his MO. Yesterday, he gave up and told authorities Meshaal hired him to kill me. But much more important, Meshaal had hired him to assassinate President Jones."

"Then Ridley's *not* part of the plot." Lana exclaimed.

"Sounds that way at first blush, Lana. But no," Max said, holding her eyes with his. "What I understand is Meshaal wasn't absolutely secure Ridley would disclaim any loyalty to Israel. Yes, apparently Jones had signed on. Yes, he appeared to be going ahead with all his demands on Israel. And, yes, he had astonishingly risen to the presidency of the Great Satan. But Meshaal would only be certain of Jones's trustworthiness if, in his inaugural address, he refuted any support for Israel and spelled out all the bargains the United States would demand of the Jews. If Jones did not do this, Stetson was positioned at the top of the Washington Monument to take him out.

"And if there is one thing I know about Stetson," Max added, "he was one of the best snipers in the military."

Kat stepped in. "The Three Sixes were geared to particular dates. Yesterday, on the flash drive Max got from Imam Meshaal's office, I figured out The Three Sixes were to kick-start their global intifada once Jones was elected."

Kat looked at Avi. "Mr. Navon, you must stop kicking yourself over Jones's election. With or without you, the Muslims have the political and financial firepower to have gotten a follower—Jones or someone else—into the White House, sooner or later. Once their man was elected, they were to make a small splash the following Christmas."

"Which they did," Avi said, "when they assassinated President Aviles in the Philippines."

"Right," Kat said. "The plan was for a slow buildup, making sure their engines were firing on all cylinders. Fariq El-Hashem in the Middle East/Asian region had the terrorist group Sulaiman Islamiyah as his hit team. The leader of the American region—whether Jones or whoever—has Salam Palestine as his hit team. And Guillaume Pauwels in his European region has a group called God Is Great out of a terrorist training camp in Africa.

"And," she added, "In the Book of Revelation, where Scripture mentions six, six, six being the anti-Christ, the Arabic reads 'In the Name of Allah.'"

"Fascinating." Avi exclaimed. "Your New Testament prophesies this?"

Kat nodded.

"Worth considering," Avi said, rubbing his chin.

Dan added, "Appears to me they got off their fixation on dates. They tried to kill Max and then Avi on days that seem to have no significance."

Kat shook her head. "Not following script may be their great undoing."

"They let feelings interfere," Max said. "They decided to hate Avi and couldn't wait to put him away. They didn't know me from a candied apple, but when I spoke against them, I was an easy target."

"Or so they thought," Kat said with a smile. "And the attempt on you might have been coincidental. They might have been staking out the bat cave and out you came."

"But at this point, we have no smoking gun on Ridley, Max said. "I doubt the other two of The Three Sixes will give him up.

———◆———

At that moment Max's phone broke into the "Halls of Montezuma." He looked down at the screen before turning it off, but noticed the message: "URGENT."

"It appears I must take this," he said. "Please excuse me.

"Of course," Avi said.

Max left the dining room and stepped into the foyer. "Semper fi, Julius."

"Max." Julius sounded out of breath.

"Yes?"

"We just took out Fariq El-Hashem."

"You what?"

"I couldn't tell you before. But he was our mission. And guess what?"

"What?"

"We've got intel to put The Three Sixes, and everyone connected, in prison or so deep underground they won't show their faces for years."

Max leaned back against the wall.

"Go on," he said.

"Max, El-Hashem was in contact with Imam Meshaal, Pauwels and—are you sitting down?"

"No, Julius. Who?"

"Well, I'll tell you this—the calls went to a special phone off the Oval Office. Max, there are times, dates, the whole works."

Max slipped to the floor, set the cell phone down, and put his head in his hands. *We were right. The president.*

"Max. Max." The voice came over his cell. Max picked up the phone. "Yeah, Julius?"

"We've got to finish up here. It'll take a few days for sure. Then I'll be back to work with the NSA at the bat cave."

"When was the last time you saw Nancy, Julius?"

"Well, I've got news there, too. I called her on my flight out here and proposed."

"Over the phone?"

"And she accepted. What a gal, huh?"

"She is," Max said. "Call me when your flight's coming in."

"Will do. Semper fi."

"Semper fi."

———— ◆ ————

Max returned to the dining room with his stunning news. No hoorahs. No whoops. Instead, people gasped, jaws dropped. Air left the room with a dull thud. Silence stole in, consuming attention as if quiet were a living being. Yes, they'd speculated on this very fact, but now the theory was more than conjecture—

At last, Kat spoke, her voice muffled by sadness. "Not surprised, but this is astonishing."

"So now we have proof positive," Avi said.

"Well, OJ got off with all the proof against him," Lana said.

"You want proof?" The unmistakable voice of Boaz Erdan boomed into the high-ceiled room. "Don't know if this is proof, but the evidence sure is damning."

He walked straight to Avi.

Avi introduced him to Max and Kat.

"Max is like a gentile sabra," Avi said. "Full of power, might—"

"And humility," Lana said with a giggle.

Max shot her a twisted smile.

"I'm so glad we're on friendly terms, Lana," he said.

"I've heard a lot about you, Max," Boaz said, shaking his hand, "and you, too, Ms. Cardova."

"We understand you're the master PI," Kat said.

"I don't know about such a claim, but I do come bearing extraordinary news."

"We're all ears," Avi said.

"The female who planted the bomb under your limo, Avi," Boaz said. "We now know who she is and getting there was quite the trip."

Boaz explained images from the security cameras in the parking garage were too dark and fuzzy to clearly show the woman. But the FBI used cameras outside the Atlanta Financial Center to follow her.

Three blocks away from the building, she climbed into the passenger seat of a black Chevrolet Equinox.

"Now, the license plates were smudged with mud, so the FBI couldn't run them," Boaz said. "But did you notice when she walked past the last light stanchion, she placed her hand firmly on the post? When she did, she left three perfect fingerprints."

"And?" Avi asked.

"She is Alima Haddad. She lives in the West End of Atlanta and worked in Jones's Atlanta campaign headquarters."

"But how do we make the jump from her to the president?" Max asked.

Boaz smiled and continued, "Cameras show the SUV drove to a parking spot near the Financial Center and waited. Five seconds after your limo blew up, Avi, we can see the woman dialing her cell phone. At that precise moment, three calls bounced off the nearest satellite. One went directly to a certain phone in a certain private room off the Oval Office. The call lasted three seconds."

Avi's shoulders dropped, and he blew out a deep breath.

Alarmed, Lana asked, "You all right, Papa?"

Avi waved her off. "I'm okay, sweetheart. As okay as a man can be whose alleged friend tried to have him murdered, and indeed, killed two beloved employees and friends."

Kat turned to Max. "What happens now?"

Max looked around the dining table and shrugged. "If all this information is confirmed, we could see an impeachment and maybe a charge of treason. But—" He paused, raised a hand, then added, "But a famous archaeologist once said to me, 'Dig deeper.' I recall another piece of the puzzle—a certain flash drive has yet to be mined, Dr. Cardova."

"No one has looked at the Islamic school's donors," she said.

"Right." Max dug into a pants pocket and pulled out the thumb drive. "But we could take a look right here tonight."

Minutes later, everyone had abandoned their coffee cups and was standing behind Avi's desk eyeing his computer as Kat loaded the drive and opened the donor file.

"Look for everything over ten thousand dollars," Dan suggested.

"Make it one thousand," Avi said. "Ridley's never earned a big paycheck."

"And from the United States," Max added.

"Make that Washington, DC," Lana said.

"And Georgia," Avi said.

Kat nodded agreement at every suggestion. "Give me a sec. Give me a sec."

"You know, if we find something here, jail's a no-brainer for Jones," Boaz said.

"Oh, my." Kat exclaimed. She pointed to a column of figures. One stood out.

—— ◆ ——

At eleven o'clock Tuesday morning, Josh, Hank, Ashley, Jill, and Jose walked through the front door into Max's classroom. As soon as Josh stepped foot inside the room, a chant began: "A-Team. A-Team."

Shocked, Josh looked up into the seats and saw Yale quarterback Tommy Jacobs standing, leading the cheer. "A-Team. A-Team."

The room rumbled with applause. Josh looked at his friends. They were beaming. He recalled the conversation in Mr. Braxton's office.

"You love your country?" Max had asked.

"Yes."

"You love liberty?"

"Yes."

"You want to protect that way of life for yours and future generations?"

"Yes."

"Well, there's a start. Perhaps you should think through your motives and desires and then decide your next move."

At this moment, Josh realized his next step. He would serve his country in the NSA. A broad smile crossed his face.

—— ◆ ——

Seconds later, Max entered the classroom and motioned for everyone to take a seat and quiet down. Once they had, he began, "When we first met, I mentioned we should all beware. Men and women of evil intent are not only roaming the jungles of South America, the forests of Malaysia, or the deserts of the Middle East but are all around us. We can bury our heads in the sand and hope for the best, that things will somehow miraculously sort themselves out, and we should not simply believe terrorists will somehow suddenly see the light, recognize the evil of their ways, and repent.

"Indeed, I have seen all this happen in a handful of cases. Walid Shoenbrod, a former Islamic terrorist, comes to mind. But, sadly, he is one in a million.

"We must leave their souls and whether they repent in God's hands, but for us, our country, our friends, and family, we should all be alert...."

———————◆———————

Forty minutes later Sturgen, with Crowe at his side, entered Max's classroom through the left-rear door and stood, watching and listening as he wound up the session.

Afterward, a dozen or so students swarmed to the front to speak with Max. Sturgen spotted the A-Team in the center of the room. They were chatting among themselves when Josh saw the NSA agents and waved, followed by the others.

Josh, Hank, Jill, Ashley, and Jose all scrambled from their aisles and up the steps to Sturgen and Crowe.

"You here to see Colonel Braxton?" Josh asked.

"Yes," Sturgen said, trying to hide the excitement he felt at the information he had to share with Max.

"Is there a breakthrough in your investigation?" Hank asked.

"You might say so," Sturgen said, a smile beginning to form.

Crowe opened a briefcase and pulled out four headshots. Fanning them out in one hand, she asked, "Do you kids recognize any of these guys?"

They all leaned forward, scrutinizing the Middle Eastern-looking men.

"An ugly group, for sure," Ashley said.

"The chubby one's kinda cute," Jill said with a giggle.

"He's Ahmed Fayyad," Crowe said, "and he, for sure, was very upset with you all. He controlled the finances of the cell you stole the two hundred million from."

Ashley and Jill high-fived each other.

Josh bent deeply at the waist toward Ashley. "We all bow to her Excellency, Ashley Carr." Hank and Jose followed suit.

Sturgen shook his head. *Kids. The next generation of leaders.*

"Have you actually seen any of these men?" he asked.

All but Josh either shrugged or shook their heads.

"I don't know for sure," Josh said, "but I might have seen the guy with the hooked nose in the coffee shop once or twice."

"Thanks," Sturgen said. "We'll keep in touch."

"Yeah," Crowe added with a smile, "and stay out of trouble, will you?"

Sturgen tipped an imaginative cap and stepped down to the front of the classroom, making eye contact with Max. Max excused himself from the students encircling him and went straight to the NSA partners, extending his hand.

"We come bearing news," Sturgen said.

"Good news by the looks on your faces," Max said.

"Yes, and we need to speak in private."

Max led them down a corridor and into an empty faculty room. Once inside, Crowe again fanned out the four photographs. "Do you recognize any of these men?" she asked.

"Passport photos," Max determined. He peered at the shots, then pointed at a rugged-looking man with a long, crooked nose and dark hair. "I spotted him, let's say, observing me a couple of times—at the café and possibly outside the library."

He paused, pointed at two of the photos and said, "Don't look familiar," then firmly placed his finger on the fourth photo, "but he sure does. The GPS tracker I gave you two? He was driving the car."

Sturgen gleamed. "You win the prize, Colonel."

Max searched his expression.

"The tracker took us to a tenement building in Albany, and an apartment there contained a mother lode of information."

"*The* mother lode," Crowe said, putting the photos back in her briefcase.

"The apartment was the headquarters for The Three Sixes group you and Professor Cardova uncovered," Sturgen said. "We think these are the four men who followed you and Colonel Rodríguez.

"They all had multiple false IDs and passports. There were names and contacts for all three regions of the world. Financial backers. The whole works."

"Obviously they expected to return home the night they died," Crowe said.

Sturgen looked squarely at Max. "Without the tracker you placed, we may never have found their hideout," he said.

"And who knows what havoc the network would have rained down on the civilized world," Crowe added.

Max shook and lowered his head in thanksgiving to God.

Chapter Twenty-Three

Four Days Later
Thursday Morning, February 6

Clouds descended over Washington, DC. A particularly black one hovered over the White House, just three weeks and two days after Ridley Jones had taken office.

The president huddled behind his oversized desk in the Oval Office with Zap, his closest adviser. Both wore worry on their brows and apprehension in their eyes. No Tamika. She was with some interior designers talking about the Blue Room. No Paxton. He was overseeing the writing of the weekly Saturday-morning President's Message. No Trevor. He was off strong-arming some Senate leaders about gun-control legislation.

Just the two college friends-turned-cultural-warriors sat in the big open space. Usually the Zaps' presence calmed Ridley. Zaps had been his mentor and pal for twenty-four years and remained a powerful influence on his life, even agreeing to leave his plush tenured-professor life to join his campaign and then his administration.

But on this day, nothing and no one apparently could break this feeling of dread, this foreboding. Ridley knew about the investigation. The unknown was what scared him. And no one at the FBI or DOJ would reveal anything to him. He hadn't been in office long enough for his nomination for Attorney General to be confirmed, so he had no inside track on this thing.

Would he face shame, disgrace, and dishonor? Would Tamika and the rest of his family be humiliated?

His intercom buzzed, startling him. He asked his secretary to contact his personal attorney and send in his visitors.

Moments later, the head of the National Security Agency stepped through the doorway. Behind him were two agents. Well-dressed, clean-cut, professional-looking men in suits and ties. Very conspicuous. Jones was sure people throughout the West Wing had taken notice of this little entourage, probably were even taking bets about their mission. Of course, no one would win. No one had any idea.

Jones's shoulders slumped and he shared a look at Zaps from their college Texas Hold-'em days which meant "I'm tapped out." Zaps' head touched his chest. No encouragement there.

Silence enveloped the room.

———— ◆ ————

NSA Director Norman LePage wasn't new to this business. He'd worked his way up through the agency, served in every region, commanded allegiance at whatever post he'd assumed, and took over as head of the NSA under the previous president.

This was the most difficult assignment he'd ever undertaken, probably ever would carry out.

He sighed deeply, nodded to Jones, and said, "Mr. President. This is a sad day."

Jones nodded and felt horror to the bottom of his spine.

LePage turned his gaze on Zapper. "Mr. Zapper," he said, "I'm arresting you on charges of conspiracy, treason, and murder."

Epilogue

LaGuardia Airport was bustling this Thursday afternoon, exactly one week after President Ridley Jones's Chief of Staff Ned Zapper had been arrested. As Max and Kat checked into a flight to Dallas to visit his mother, they passed by a news stand prominently displaying national magazines.

On the cover of Time was an extreme close-up photo of Zapper with the headline: "Zapped." And in smaller type: "Treasonous Behavior."

On the cover of Newsweek was a photo of Sturgen and Crowe with the headline: "No Sleepers, These. The subhead read: "Deep 666ing Major Terror Cell."

The Washington Post carried a front-page grabber: "Saudi Imam Jailed as 666 Network Shredded."

"Look what you started," Kat said, pointing to the newsstand.

"We," Max objected. "What we started."

"You and your intuition," Kat said.

"But you were instrumental."

"Well, I'm glad you were able to deflect the credit to Sturgen and Crowe. Otherwise, we couldn't be standing here unhindered, without microphones shoved into our faces." She stopped and looked into his eyes. "Are you glad the sleeper wasn't the president?"

Max shrugged. "Yes, but Jones was implicit enough. He did agree to Zapper's point of view and acquiesced to a foreign policy dictating the demise of our only true friend in the Middle East."

The man and woman stood side-by-side at the newsstand, scrutinizing a copy of Time. The woman asked her companion, "So, what do you think happens to America now?"

"I don't know. Do you think the president can survive the fallout?" he answered.

"The president? What about the country?" she retorted.

Max looked at Kat and asked, "What say you, Doctor?"

"I say the verdict all depends," she said.

"Depends on what?"

"On how we stand in light of Genesis 12:3."

"What's it say?" Max asked.

"The Lord said to Abraham and the nation he would create through him, I will bless those who bless My people, but those who curse them, I will curse."

The End

Note from the authors: Dear reader, we would love for you to take a minute and write a brief review of *The Three Sixes* on www. Amazon.com.

Read the first chapter of Mark Alan Leslie's upcoming action/thriller.

The Last Aliyah

Chapter 1

The call that changed Nobel laureate Omri Zohn's life came at the hour when the most distasteful acts are perpetrated in Washington, DC—when Congressmen can board flights home before the news hits the airwaves.

Omri forced one eye open and squinted to see the phone's caller ID. 202 area code. His friend, US Senator Joseph Frank. His heart fluttered or maybe even skipped a beat. He tried to calm a shaking hand as he reached for the phone.

"Omri. It's Joseph." The voice boiled with tension, urgency. Zohn sat up in bed and struggled to open the other eye. He looked at his clock—2:58 a.m.

"They've done it, Omri." Frank's hoarse utterance quaked between a rasp and a gasp. "The Senate just approved enforcing the United Nations Resolution."

A crushing weight settled on his chest. "Oh, my Lord," rushed in a hushed tone through his lips—more a moan than a statement.

"We Jews are now essentially prisoners in our own countries,"

Frank said. "Not allowed to go to Israel or any country that defies the UN Resolution outlawing emigration to the Holy Land. Get your escape plan in motion, now, as I will mine."

"You said 'we,' Joseph. Even you can't leave?"

The three-term senator from Florida grunted. "Even I. Beware of men in dark suits at your door. They'll hold you here."

Omri shook his head, then said, "My brother, Ariel, just called me yesterday. He's got stage-four cancer."

Joseph groaned.

"Are there no exceptions, Joseph? Any chance at all I can get permission to visit him?"

"'Fraid not."

Omri gritted his teeth. "Joseph. You know my son and his wife and child moved to Israel a year ago. You're saying I can't see them again, either?"

"Not a chance," Joseph said, "unless Benjamin and his family come back to America. But if they did, then, of course, they couldn't be allowed back out of the country. Not unless they've obtained their Israeli citizenship already,"

"Not yet."

Omri flicked on the light of his nightstand and swung his legs off the bed. If the sky was falling, he had to move, get his plans in motion.

"Homeland Security had representatives in the chambers, sitting on the edge of their seats, waiting to give the signal for action to headquarters," Frank said. "Making it more repulsive is today is August second, the last day before the six-week summer recess. So, my colleagues—the brave sort they are—are about to vanish into the countryside and avoid any nasty questions."

Omri chuckled ruefully. "No surprise there."

A pause, then Frank added, "You realize this begins the curse on America."

Omri knew the Scripture: *I will bless those who bless My people, but those who curse them I shall curse.*

"Godspeed, my friend." Joseph said. "I hope we'll meet again in Israel. Shalom."

The line clicked off.

Omri settled the landline phone in its cradle, like it was a grenade. He peered at his bedside clock. 3:01. Appropriate, he thought, recalling the words of Psalm 3 verse 1: *O, Lord, how many are my foes. How many rise up against me!*

He spoke softly the seventh and eighth verses: *Arise, O Lord! Deliver me, O my God! Strike all my enemies on the jaw; break the teeth of the wicked. From the Lord comes deliverance. May Your blessing be on Your people.*

He took a moment to reassure himself the plan he had in place was truly what he wanted. His wife and daughter were buried in Israel, killed by a terrorist bomb at a bar mitzvah celebration for their nephew a dozen years ago. His boyhood home was there. Besides Benjamin and his new family, Ariel and his family, and many cousins and friends lived there. This ban would prevent him from ever seeing them again, ever paying respects to Adina and Devorah, ever setting his feet in the Old City, ever praying at the Western Wall. On top of all that, Israel was the only country in which the Jews could defend themselves.

Omri stiffened his back, swung his feet out of the bed and onto the small sheepskin on the wooden floor. The time has come, he thought. *This will be the last aliyah, the final return of Your people to their homeland, Lord. If we can get there.*

———— ◆ ————

Vice President Daniel Fireside walked to his office, a Secret Service man at each shoulder. The hall filled with the hum of phone calls, the tapping of fingers tweeting as senators hurried to get out of Washington even though daybreak was still three hours away.

The chills of triumph gave him a buzz, but Fireside fought to contain his elation. He'd proven he could indeed push measures through a stubborn Congress—and this legislation was the most contentious in his twenty-two years in this combative Congress in this quarrelsome town, the hub of what was more and more a belligerent country. While he'd needed to merely cajole many colleagues into his and the President's way of thinking, he had to bludgeon others with substantial threats before they succumbed. The eighty Congressmen who'd flipped their votes on Obamatrade overnight years ago paled to this victory.

Most people would be astonished how much you could accomplish by threatening the loss of a coveted committee chairmanship, or removal of a major naval contract from a person's district. Perhaps even more revealing were the senators who would succumb to your will if you merely dangled the idea of slapping their name on a bridge or airport or federal building. *Pride, thou art my velvet glove.*

People were all so—well—self-absorbed, self-centered, and parochial. Politics possessed powerful tools, even when you were voting to outlaw an entire race within your country from traveling to their people's homeland. Served the blasted Jews right. They'd been too powerful for too long and felt far too pleased with themselves and their accomplishments. Fill their champagne glasses with tar pitch for a change.

The atmosphere outside the Senate chambers crackled with electricity. Obviously, he wasn't the only one grinding his teeth.

Senator Halsey leaned on one leg, then another, like she had to pee. Senator Franceour was maybe one decibel below shouting at an aide.

Standing in a wide hallway with gleaming floors and walls soaked with two centuries of rich history, Fireside thought of the consequences. The party had surely alienated the Jewish vote, but the Muslims' high birth rate had already overtaken the Jews in numbers—just like they would in Israel with this ban—so it was a net win at the polls.

Chuck Claiborne, Fireside's chief of staff, refereed a scramble of senators pushing each other aside to get the vice president's ear. One step removed from a Macy's Bargain Basement free-for-all.

"Fireside, you'll pay dearly for this. Your career's over." yelled Senator Bill Bloom.

Fireside winked, smiled and—the trifecta—shot him a thumbs-up. *Billy-boy, dream on. I just jumped aboard a rocket ship, pal.*

Fireside tapped one of his Secret Service protectors on the shoulder. "Wait here by the door. Nobody comes in."

The agent nodded and the two men took up their posts as Fireside escaped to his office. He closed the door—and the hubbub—behind him. He had to place a most important phone call.

Taking a seat behind the historic double-pedestal, mahogany Wilson desk, he wondered how many of his predecessors could have pulled off this coup. John Breckinridge? "Cactus Jack" Garner? No and no. Not even the brilliant John C. Calhoun.

None, except perhaps LBJ, who, like Fireside, had used this office as an elegant and convenient setting for informal party caucuses, press briefings, ceremonial functions and—ahem, this was the bend-your-arm-'til-it-breaks part—private meetings. LBJ might have been considered the master, but Fireside had just one-upped the big Texan's Gulf of Tonkin Resolution with this Jewish emigration ban. *Check and mate.*

Placing his hands on the desktop, he took a deep breath, picked up the red telephone, and punched in a number he knew well.

————•◆•————

When the phone rang beside him, President Herald Smith switched on a low-wattage bedside lamp. He hadn't been able to sleep, but had fidgeted under the sheets for hours awaiting this call. He'd spent his last drop of political capital on this UN Resolution; declaring failure was not an option. Though no one else knew it besides his wife, his future beyond the presidency hung on its success.

His neck hairs prickled in anticipation. Was it good news, bad news, or some dire gray-area result? Smith despised gray areas.

Picking up the phone, he murmured, "Yes?"

"It's done, Mister President. We're a 'go.'" He could imagine Fireside glowing on the other end like a schoolboy after his first frolic.

Smith's eyes opened wide, and he released a breath. "Fallout?"

"Some outrage, plenty of grumble. Good thing Lieberman and Shumer retired. A few almost stalked out of the chambers. Well, Frank and Weiss did—as we predicted. Frank leaving was okay because I thought I'd shoot him, he was so distraught, so righteous, so— Jewish. Broke an arm here, a leg there, but we avoided insurrection and got the law passed without a real bullet being fired. I am glad Armstrong and Bloom weren't armed, though.

"Great work, Dan. Glad you're at my side. Nice to have a majority in both the House and Senate, eh?"

Hanging up, the president turned to his wife.

"The vault door's slammed shut on the Jews," he said with cold certainty.

In the faint shadows of the room, Theresa Smith smiled back and whispered hoarsely, "Well done, my love. You can say you're actually protecting the Jews. Besides, what Jew in their right mind would want to go to Israel, what with the Arabs firing rockets at them day and night?"

Smith nodded, then asked, "Like a drink in celebration?"

"In the middle of the night?" Theresa reached for her nightgown hanging on a nearby chair. "Good idea."

Smith swung his feet over the side of the bed and said, "You know when I first saw this could happen?"

"When?" The first lady was now on her feet and slipping into slippers.

"Back in August 2014 when the UN Human Rights Commission came down on Israel for not sharing its Iron Dome technology with Hamas. The fallout about said everything. Imagine sharing life-saving technology with the terrorists trying to kill you.

"Then, in 2015, when we made the deal with Iran which, everyone knew, paved the way for them to go nuclear."

"M-hm. Shows how much the UN hates the Jews."

"They're not alone," Smith said. "Gin and tonic?"

His wife nodded. "You know me so well, Mr. President."

———— ◆ ————

Fidgety. Agitated. Whatever's bothering my spirit, I hate it, Bunyan "Jacko" Jackson thought, forcing himself from his bed, through the sliding doors to the patio. He stood—all six-foot-four inches and two hundred and thirty-four pounds of him. He pressed his hands against the waist-high railing and peered out onto the dark Atlantic Ocean beyond his expansive lawn.

He tightened the sash of his flimsy cotton robe over his pajamas. It was a warm summer night on the outskirts of Portland, Maine. The nightglow of the city to the north turned the sky a pale fluorescent green. A faint scent of salt drifted in the air. *Tide's out.*

The first couple bars of Louis Armstrong's "What a Wonderful World" on his cell phone wafted through an open window in his bedroom. He hustled back to his room. Who was in the hospital, or who died? What would cause a call at this hour?

He answered, "Jackson."

"My friend, it's me." The distinctive Israeli accent of Omri Zohn made Jackson stand straight in anticipation. "*Aliyah* is on. Plan B."

Click.

Jackson's mouth went wide. He scowled at the phone as if it were a Yankee pitcher, or an implement able to answer the stark questions: How could we? How could the United States do this to its own people? Have we not learned from what we did to the Japanese Americans during the Second World War? Have we not learned from slavery? Have we finally succumbed to an Islamic-driven United Nations gone rogue?

In dismay, he murmured, "Well, Satchmo, today's it's not such a 'wonderful world.'"

He laid the phone down on the bedside table and sat on the king-size bed. He inhaled deeply and peered at a shelf below the tabletop. Reaching down, he pulled out a leather-bound copy of *The Pilgrim's Progress* handed down by his great-great-great-great-grandfather Tice, who had escaped slavery in 1860. The book was an allegory of a man's journey from the City of Destruction, the world, through all sorts of obstacles and diversions to the Celestial City, heaven. It was the book from which Tice had learned to read and taken to heart deep things of God.

Jackson thought of the book's story, then recalled the passage in the ninth chapter of the Book of Amos: *I will bring back My exiled people Israel…*

This was it: the last aliyah. And here he was—retired Major League baseball player, Hall of Famer and descendant of a slave—positioned to pay forward what so many good-minded people had done for Tice. Jackson brought the little book to his lips for a light kiss. "We'll get them to Jerusalem, Grampa Tice. I promise."

He set the book down, picked up a thick, well-worn manuscript in a homemade binder—Tice's hand-written account of his own escape from the South. With a deep love of an ancestor he'd never met, Bunyan frowned at the thought the world had come to this. He stood and walked to a two-shelf glass bookcase and pulled out a world atlas. Opening it revealed a PGP mobile phone hidden in a hollow. He grabbed the phone and texted an encrypted message. When deciphered the note read: "Aliyah is on. Plan B."

———— ◆ ————

Giant red eyes hovered above and behind Ethan Rosenbaum. He hunched his shoulders in the moonless night. Adrenaline pumped energy through his veins, but it seemed as if he was running through deep sand. He could feel sweat behind his ears, an aching right calf—and raw terror.

He crested a hill, heaved himself forward, and landed on the ground. A hissing sound, a snarl slashed the silence. Breaths crowded his ears. Breaths and the death threat.

Ethan pushed himself off the ground and raced down the back side of the hill. He turned to look. Giant eyes rose over the peak only twenty feet behind and ten feet high. His remaining moments in this world were numbered unless … unless a miracle.

A sudden high-pitched jangle shattered the night sky—and the dream.

Ethan shuddered, half relieved it was a dream and half afraid it was a portent. The jingle came from his bedside telephone.

He jerked awake and pushed himself to a sitting position, opened an eye to look at his oversized clock, groaned. Trying not to awaken his wife, Naomi, Ethan reluctantly picked up the phone.

"Aliyah is on," said the Israeli-tinted voice. "Plan B, ASAP."

Click. At those words, heaviness cloaked Ethan, as if the darkness in the room had become a physical mantle. The giant red eyes of oppression.

Suddenly, he was wide awake, but he sat motionless, as if his body had been shot with Novocain, trying to absorb the impact of the news. He remembered as a fullback being flattened by a huge defensive tackle in a high school football game. This time no broken bones, just a shattered spirit.

Since the United Nations had voted for the extraordinary resolution stopping all Jewish immigration to Israel, he had entertained thoughts of what would happen if, God forbid, Congress were to vote in agreement. Once, this possibility had been unimaginable. Over the years the Palestinian-friendly United Nations had passed so many anti-Israel Resolutions coming to naught, they were normally thought of as simple bluster. The United States had usually used its veto power against any measures threatening to harm Israel. But not this State Department. Not this president.

The State Department's anti-Semitism and anti-Zionism, even withholding recognition of Jerusalem as Israel's capital, was common knowledge for several decades. But few had actually believed America and other countries around the world would acquiesce when the time came to enforce this type of resolution. Had they?

Yet, America's government seemed like the antithesis of an elephant. The political powers remembered nothing, learned no lessons. Arab intransigence? Forgotten. Muslim cries of "Death to America"? Forgotten.

Instead of voting no to the UN Resolution, the United States had abstained. Since then the country had been abuzz, but not inflamed. A bad omen.

And now, in the wake of the vote, the Jewish and Christian outrage obviously paled to the "hoorahs" of the anti-Semites and anti-Zionists and failed to dissuade Congress.

How could America, "home of the free because of the brave," abide by such a decision? Surely there would be rebellion in the streets. Right?

Nevertheless, though he and Naomi lived in Charleston, South Carolina, and Omri lived outside Boston, they had devised various plans for aliyah—just in case. *That's what we scientists do: devise tests, plans, and contingencies for various scenarios. Another thing we do: harden ourselves to trust provable facts, no matter the substance or depth of beliefs indicating the contrary.*

The men had a Plan A for Monday through Thursday and a Plan B for midnight Thursday through Sunday.

At his side, Naomi stirred awake. "Who called, Ethan?"

"Congress." His voice cracked. "Lost their collective mind."

She shot up out of the sheets. "No."

"That was Omri," he said. "They did the deed. Congress sold us out."

"So, we're going ahead with our decision and leaving friends, synagogue, jobs." A statement, not a question.

Ethan locked his eyes on hers. "I'll take the visiting fellowship Dr. Ibram offered at Technion—Israel Institute of Technology."

"The MIT of Israel," Naomi nodded with a half-smile. "My brilliant husband."

Ethan laid his hand on her neck and pulled her softly to his embrace. They stayed like that for a minute or so, absorbing how earth-shattering was the moment.

"I'm so sorry, Naomi," he said. "I know you love your job too. Something awaits you there."

She pulled away just enough to look into his eyes. "Leaving our friends and neighbors is worse, darling." She sighed. "But I know the Lord will help and console me in this. Leaving is going to be emotional, but he'll strengthen me—us."

Ethan couldn't muster a response. Naomi had the faith for both of them. She believed; he hoped.

"When do we leave?" she asked.

"Omri said, 'ASAP.' Normally the plan would mean this moment, but today's Friday, so Plan B's different. After Congress's vote, if I don't show up for work this morning, someone will figure out we're on the move. Someone will finger us to Homeland Security. No, we've got to pretend everything's copacetic. You go to work, I'll go to work. We'll come home—and then scuttle out of here on the first train."

Ethan again glanced at the illuminated clock. 3:16.

"I'll get the coffee brewing," Naomi said, "then start packing, but only as much as we can carry in duffel bags. No curling iron, no hair dryer."

"And no board games."

"Spoil sport."

Somewhere in the distance a fog horn croaked hoarsely, and as if in response, a boat's stack bellowed. One "fog," Ethan thought, was causing nautical confusion just as another kind of fog had clouded the thinking of Congress.

To be continued ...

Other Books

by Mark Alan Leslie

The Crossing, published by Elk Lake Publishing Inc., Plymouth, Mass., 2017

Chasing the Music, published by Elk Lake Publishing Inc., Plymouth, Mass., 2016

True North: Tice's Story (a Publishers Weekly Featured Book), available through Amazon.com and Barnesandnoble.com, 2015

Midnight Rider for the Morning Star, published by the Francis Asbury Society Press, Wilmore, Ky., 2007

Putting a Little Spin on It: The Grooming's the Thing!, published as an e-book and available on Amazon.com and Barnesandnoble. com, 2014

Putting a Little Spin on It: The Design's the Thing!, published as an e-book and available on Amazon.com and Barnesandnoble.com, 2013

Walks with God: A Devotional, published as an e-book and available on Amazon.com and Barnesandnoble.com, 2010

Fired? Get Fired Up!, published as an e-book and available on Amazon.com and Barnesandnoble.com, 2009

About the Authors

Mark Alan Leslie

The winner of six national magazine writing awards and several book awards, Mark Alan Leslie has written nine books, including three historical novels, two modern-day mystery/thrillers, two golf books, a devotional and a Christian self-help book. His books include: *Midnight Rider for the Morning Star, True North: Tice's Story, The Crossing, Chasing the Music*—book one in the *Thrill of the Hunt* series. He has two books in the works: *Jeremiah's Jar* (book three) and *The Last Aliyah*, an action/thriller.

Leslie's career as a newspaper and magazine editor and writer spanned 30 years before he began writing books full-time—all from a Christian worldview. He was the founding editor of Golf Course News (now Golf Industry) His two golf books are filled with quotes and stories from his interviews with icons like Arnold Palmer, Jack Nicklaus, and others—*Putting a Little Spin on It: The Design's the Thing!* and *Putting a Little Spin on It: The Grooming's the Thing!*

Darek Leslie

Darek Leslie has assisted with security for the Prime Minister of Israel, studied Terrorism and International Conflict at Hebrew University, and written a Masters thesis on terrorism in Latin America. He has survived a terrorist attack on Ben Yehuda Street in Jerusalem, studied Russian Literature with the Assistant Administrator for the Bureau for Europe and Eurasia at USAID and fostered friendships from Singapore to Romania.

Darek has intertwined these life experiences into his two fiction novels: *Cure for a Kill* and *Splinter.* His favorite written scenes are those he wrote with his father—his inspiration for writing—in *The Three Sixes.*

www.ingramcontent.com/pod-product-compliance
Lightning Source LLC
Chambersburg PA
CBHW060810030726
47503CB00002B/427